CYPRESS POINT

DIANE
CHAMBERLAIN

CYPRESS POINT

MIRA®

ISBN 1-55166-882-3

CYPRESS POINT

Visit us at www.mirabooks.com

Printed in U.S.A.

First Printing: February 2002
10 9 8 7 6 5 4 3 2 1

To my extraordinary sibs,
Tom, Joann and Rob.
What a year, eh?

What fun it's been to research a book
filled with the natural beauty of the California coastline,
the struggles and hopes of compassionate people...
and a little bit of magic. Michael Reynolds helped me understand
what life is like on the Monterey Peninsula.
Mike Woodbury and Karen (KK) Sears gave me virtual sailing lessons.
Suzanne Schmidt, one of my dearest friends and an OB/GYN nurse
practitioner, guided me through the medical aspects of my story.
Fellow author Emilie Richards provided feedback
on my story line with talent and wisdom.

I am also indebted to Richard Bingler, Liz Gardner, Tom Jackson,
Craig MacBean, Patricia McLinn and Katherine Rutkowski
for their various contributions to the story.

As always, I'm grateful to my agent, Ginger Barber,
for her confidence in me, and to my editor, Amy Moore-Benson,
who has a gift for helping me make a good book great.

PROLOGUE

Big Sur, California, 1967

The fog was as thick and white as cotton batting, and it hugged the coastline and moved slowly, lazily, in the breeze. Anyone unfamiliar with the Cabrial Commune in Big Sur would never know there were twelve small cabins dotting the cliffs above the ocean. Fog was nothing unusual here, but for the past seven days, it had not cleared once. Like living inside a cloud, the children said. The twenty adults and twelve children of the commune had to feel their way from cabin to cabin, and they could never be sure they'd found their own home until they were inside. Parents warned their children not to play too close to the edge of the cliff, and the more nervous mothers kept their little ones inside in the morning, when the fog was thickest. Those who worked in the garden had to bend low to be sure they were pulling weeds and not the young shoots of brussels sprouts or lettuce, and more than one man used the dense fog as an excuse for finding his way into the wrong bed at night—not that an excuse was ever needed on the commune, where love was free and jealousy was denied. Yes, this third week of summer, everyone in the commune had a little taste of what it was like to be blind.

The fog muffled sound, too. The residents of the commune could still hear the foghorns, but the sound was little more than a low moan, wrapping around them so that they had no idea from which direction it came. No idea whether the sea was in front of them or behind.

But one sound managed to pierce the fog. The cries came intermittently from one of the cabins, and the children, many of them naked, would stop their game of hide-and-seek to stare through the fog in the direction of the sound. A couple of them, who were by nature either more sensitive or more anxious than the others, shuddered. They knew what was happening. No secrets were ever kept from children here. They knew that inside cabin number four, Rainbow Cabin, Ellen Liszt was having a baby.

In the small clearing at one side of the cabin, nineteen-year-old Johnny Angel split firewood. The day was warm despite the fog, and he'd taken off his Big Brother and the Holding Company sweatshirt and hung it over the railing of the cabin's rickety porch. Felicia, the midwife, was inside with Ellen, boiling string and scissors on the small woodstove, and he told himself they needed more firewood, even though he'd already chopped enough to last a week. Still, he lifted the ax and let it fall, over and over again, mesmerized by the *thwack* as it hit the logs. Every minute or so, he stopped chopping to take a drag from his cigarette, which rested on the cabin railing, and he could feel his heart beating in his bare chest. The hand holding the cigarette trembled—from the strain of chopping wood, he told himself, but he knew that was not the complete truth. He winced every time a fresh shriek of pain came from the cabin's rear bedroom, and he was quick to pick up the ax again, hoping that the chopping would mask the sound.

When would it be over? The labor pains had started in earnest in the middle of the night, and as he and Ellen had planned, he'd run—stumbling in the darkness and the fog—to the Moonglow Cabin to awaken Felicia. Felicia had grabbed her bag of birthing paraphernalia and returned with him to Rainbow, and she'd held Ellen's hand, speaking to her in a calming voice. It had shocked him to see Ellen in the glow of the lantern. She looked terribly young, younger than eighteen. She looked like a frightened little girl, and he felt unable to go near her, unsure of what to say or how to touch her. How to help. Her face was sweaty and she was gulping air. Johnny was afraid she might throw up. He hated seeing anyone throw up. It always made him feel sick himself.

He'd left the two women together and walked outside to the woodpile. But he hadn't known it would take so long. How many hours had passed? All he knew was that he was on his second pack of Kools, and the menthol was beginning to make his throat ache.

Felicia had asked him if he wanted to be in the room with Ellen, and he'd stared at her, wild-eyed with surprise at the question. Hell, no, he didn't want to be in that room. So he'd left. Now he felt like a coward for declining the offer. He knew that some men were fighting for the right to be in the delivery room these days, and that two of the men here at Cabrial had stayed with their women while they delivered. But he was not like those men. He couldn't imagine being any closer to Ellen's pain and fear than he was right now. Besides, that was no delivery room Ellen was in. She was lying on the old double mattress on the bare floor in the tiny bedroom they had shared for the past six months, her butt resting on newspapers, which Felicia claimed were made sterile by the printing process. Felicia was no obstetrician. She was not even a real midwife, merely the mother of four kids who were, right now, playing hide-and-seek in the fog.

When he and Ellen had first talked about it, the idea of Felicia delivering their baby had sounded fine, even appealing; after all, women used to help other women deliver babies all the time. But now that it was happening, now that Ellen's screams made the hair on the back of his neck stand up, many things about the commune that had previously sounded appealing seemed ludicrous. His parents had rolled their eyes in disgusted resignation when he told them that he and Ellen were moving into a Big Sur commune. He told them about the large stone cabin that housed a common kitchen and huge dining room, where the commune residents took turns cooking and cleaning up and doing all the other tasks that were part of living together in a group, and his mother had asked him why he never bothered to help *her* cook and clean up. His parents scoffed at the names of the cabins—Rainbow, Sunshine, Stardust—and they showed real alarm when he told them there was no phone on the commune. Then they threatened him: If he dropped out of Berkeley and moved into the commune, he could expect no more money from them for school or for anything else, ever. That was fine, he said. There was little need for money in the commune. They would live off the land. They would take care of each other.

Right now, he would give just about anything to have his mother with him. She had no idea he was about to become a father. Wouldn't she be mortified to know that her first grandchild was being born this way, far from medical care, not to mention out of wedlock? Johnny could only imagine what she would say about the ritual that would follow the birth, when Felicia would take the placenta and bury it somewhere on the commune grounds, planting a tree, a Monterey cypress, above it, tying the baby's spirit to this beautiful place. Johnny loved the idea, despite the fact that he had not even known what a placenta was before moving here.

The thirteenth child. He was adding freshly split wood to the pile by the cabin porch when it suddenly occurred to him that his son or daughter would be the thirteenth child on the commune, and although he was not ordinarily superstitious, that thought filled him with fear. He didn't want his kid to start out with the deck stacked against him. Lighting another cigarette, he wondered if he and Ellen had treated this whole pregnancy as too much of a lark. They'd talked about how the baby would look. They would never cut his hair. They would let him run around naked, if that's what he wanted. He'd never be ashamed of his body. He—or she—would grow up here in the Cabrial Commune, free of the stifling rules and restraints of the rigid world outside, being taught by other adults who shared their values. They'd discussed names: Shanti Joy, if the baby was a girl, and Sky Blue for a boy. He'd imagined his son or daughter one day going to school in the northernmost cabin, where two of the women and one of the men spent most weekdays teaching the commune's children. It had sounded like the perfect way to live. Now he feared they were playing with fire.

Arms aching, he lit another cigarette and sat down on the porch step just as Ellen began to wail, and he squeezed his eyes shut against the sound. Did he love Ellen? She'd looked like a stranger to him when he'd brought Felicia back to the cabin earlier. A young girl, glistening with perspiration, strands of dark hair stringy around her face, her body taking up far more than her share of the mattress. God, she'd put on a lot of weight. She was going to end up looking like Felicia, like a big earth mother type with long, frizzy graying hair. Ellen already had the bones for it. He growled at himself. *Shouldn't matter.* Looks shouldn't matter at all. He'd probably look like hell himself if he were in her position right now. He was a son of a bitch for even thinking about it.

Crushing the butt of his cigarette beneath his sandaled foot, Johnny stood up. He ran his hand over his dark, sparse beard, the beard of a boy, not a man, and stared into the fog. If the day had been clear, he would have been able to see the ocean from here, beyond a few of the other cabins, beyond where the cliffs plummeted down to the sea. Today, though, his gaze rested on nothing more than drifting clouds of cotton.

He became aware of the silence almost instantly. The wailing and moaning had stopped, and he turned toward the cabin door. Was it finally over? Shouldn't the baby cry or something?

He heard the rapid pounding of footsteps across the splintery living-room floor of the cabin, and Felicia pushed open the screen door. Her face was flushed, and she looked like a wild woman.

"Get help, Johnny!" she said. "The baby's not breathing. Get that woman who came last night. Penny's friend. Carlynn. She's a doctor."

He turned and ran in the direction of Cornflower, Penny's cabin, hoping he'd be able to find it quickly in the fog. He'd managed to find her cabin in the middle of the night several times during the past couple of months, when Ellen had encouraged him to go to the older woman for sex, since she had not felt up to it, and sure enough, his feet seemed to know the way.

He remembered seeing the new woman in the dining room the night before, but he hadn't known her name. She was an old friend of Penny's, someone had told him, just here for a visit. He'd found himself staring at her. She was a small and slender woman with large blue eyes and shoulder-length blond hair that framed her face in an uncombed, unkempt and utterly appealing way. She was probably in her mid-thirties, nearly his mother's age. But she didn't look like anyone's mother. Nor did she look like a doctor.

He burst into the living room of the cabin to find Penny and Carlynn sitting on opposite ends of the old sofa, sewing. They looked up at the sudden intrusion, hands and threaded needles frozen in midair.

"The baby's not breathing!" he said.

In an instant, Carlynn dropped her sewing and ran toward the door. He and Penny followed close behind.

"Which way?" Carlynn called as she stepped into the fog.

Johnny grabbed her arm and ran with her toward Rainbow, but he stopped short at the front step of the cabin.

"In there," he said, pointing.

Carlynn wrapped her hand around his wrist and nearly dragged him up the steps with her. "Your girlfriend will need you," she said, and he knew she was giving him no choice.

The inside of the cabin was hot from the woodstove, the steaming air hitting him in the face as he ran with Carlynn through the living room and into the bedroom. Ellen was crying, shivering as if she were cold, and she reached a hand toward him. A strange scent, a mixture of seawater and copper, filled his head and made him feel dizzy, but he sat down on the bed next to Ellen. Holding her hand, leaning over to kiss her damp forehead, he felt a tenderness inside him that was so sudden it made his chest ache and his eyes burn. He kissed her fingers, rubbed her arms. He was a weak and stupid idiot for making her endure this alone, he thought as he bent over to hug her. He should have been with her throughout the whole ordeal.

Her legs were still spread, her feet flat on the mattress. From where he sat, Johnny had a clear view between her knees of Felicia and Carlynn hovering over something. His child. The thirteenth child.

"The cord was wrapped around her neck," Felicia said to Carlynn.

Carlynn nodded. She leaned over the infant and puffed into the baby's nose and mouth. Johnny waited for the cry, but it was only the sound of Ellen's weeping that filled the room.

Carlynn puffed some more, and then Felicia sat back on her thick haunches, tears in her eyes.

"She's gone," she said, touching Carlynn's shoulder. "She's gone."

"No!" Ellen wailed, and Johnny leaned over to press his wet cheek to hers. "No, please."

"Shh," he said.

Carlynn lifted the baby, and for the first time Johnny could see the infant, her tiny arms flopping lifelessly at her sides, her skin a pale, grayish blue. Carlynn held the baby in a strange embrace, her hands flat against the infant's chest and back, her lips pressed against the bluish temple. The woman's eyes were closed, her lashes fluttering slightly against her cheeks, her breathing slow and deep, and the room grew still. Ellen stopped crying. She lifted herself on her elbows to be able to see better, and for a moment, Johnny wondered if Carlynn were mentally ill. What was she doing?

Carlynn drew in a long, deep breath, then let it out in a slow wash of warmth against the baby's temple. Within seconds, the infant let out a muted whimper. Johnny listened hard, praying for another sound from his child. Carlynn breathed again against the baby's temple, and suddenly a cry filled the room. Then another. The baby grew pink between the woman's hands, and in the hushed room, she wrapped a piece of an old flannel blanket around the infant and handed her to Ellen.

Johnny leaned over to nuzzle his woman and his child, a wrenching ache of love and gratitude in his chest, while outside the cabin, the fog rose into the sky, and for the first time in a week, Big Sur was bathed in sunlight.

CHAPTER ONE

Monterey Peninsula, California, 2001

There were nights when Joelle thought she could actually *feel* the fog rolling in outside her window, cutting her off from the rest of the world. She had trouble sleeping on those nights, and they were frequent during the summer months. She would awaken each morning in the dim interior of her condominium, every window coated in white. She'd moved from Carmel Valley to the seaside village of Carmel two years before, when she was thirty-two and newly divorced, and although she loved the beauty and quaintness of the storybook town, she thought she would never adjust to the closed-in feeling she had in the mornings.

It was more than the fog keeping her awake on this early-June night, however. Joelle turned from side to side in the bed, bunching her pillows up beneath her head, then flattening them again, wondering, as she had for the past couple of weeks, if every twinge low in her belly might be the start of her period.

She had never been regular. Sometimes she could go months without a period; other times she would be surprised by two periods only a week or two apart. The capricious nature of her cycle had made getting pregnant problematic, if not impossible, during the eight years of her marriage to Rusty. The absence of a period would give them hope, which would be dashed when the pregnancy test came up negative. Her failure to conceive eventually led to the end of their marriage. Two years ago, after medical tests had revealed no clear reason for either of them to be unable to procreate, Rusty had told her he'd met someone else and wanted a divorce. Joelle supposed she should have been angry, but in a way it had been a relief. Their marriage had been reduced to one focus, and she was tired of the temperature taking, the urinating on test sticks, the probing of impersonal doctors. The mechanical and regimented nature of their marriage had eaten away at their love for one another.

All the speculation about which of them was the cause of their infertility was answered when Rusty's new wife had gotten pregnant. He now was the proud father of a little boy, and Joelle knew that she, herself, would never have a child.

Laughter rose up from the street outside. Her bed was in the center of a turret, windows on all sides, and the laughter and chatter surrounded her as though the revelers were beneath her bed. Although her condo was a fair distance from Ocean Avenue, the main street in Carmel, tourists sometimes had to park this far from the heart of the village, and she knew that was what she was hearing—people on vacation, who didn't have to get up and go to work in the morning, and who had spent the evening exploring the little shops and art galleries and eating in cozy restaurants. She pressed one of her pillows over her head and squeezed her eyes shut.

Her condo was one of two in a charming old white stucco house, which had, at one time, been a one-family residence. It was only three blocks from the ocean and Carmel's white sand beach, and from the windows of her second-story bedroom and living room, she could watch the sun sink into the Pacific in the evening, when the fog was not too thick. Her neighbors, Tony and Gary, lived in the condo downstairs. Her relationship with the gay couple was affable and neighborly, and she occasionally ate dinner with them or watched a movie on their big-screen TV, but they were in their twenties, and they had each other. Sometimes she could hear their laughter rising up through her floorboards, and she felt her aloneness even more keenly.

The tourists were getting into their cars now, and the sound of slamming doors rose through her windows and slipped beneath her pillow, which she clutched over her head.

It was no use. She was not going to sleep.

Throwing off the covers, she got out of bed and walked into the bathroom. From the cupboard beneath the sink, she pulled out an aging plastic grocery bag and carried it back to the bed, dumping the contents onto the lemon-colored matellasse. Here were the basal thermometer, the ovulation-predictor kits and the home pregnancy tests, items she hadn't looked at since leaving the house she'd shared with Rusty. She was not even certain what had possessed her to bring these things along with her. She stared at one of the pregnancy kits for a moment, then picked up the box and opened it, slowly and deliberately. She tossed the instructions in the trash can; she hardly needed them after having performed this test dozens of times in the past. Removing the test stick from the box as she walked into the bathroom, she tugged the cap from the absorbent tip and sat down on the toilet, holding the stick in the stream of urine, counting to ten. She feigned indifference as she put the cap back on the stick and rested it on the counter. Smoothing her long, dark, bed-mussed hair in the mirror, she waited out the three minutes, then looked down at the strip. Two pink lines, one in each window. She stared at them. For eight years, she had longed for that second line to appear and it never had. Now, the color was nearly vibrant. And now was the wrong time for a miracle.

Fighting to stay calm, she checked the expiration date on the box. Still good for a year. She opened one of the other boxes, a different brand, because she used to try them all, just in case one test might find her pregnant while another did not. Just to give herself that little modicum of hope. She read the directions this time, following them carefully. The results were the same, though, only this test stick displayed a blue line.

Methodically, she wrapped the two test sticks in toilet paper, dropped them into the trash can, then washed her hands. The reality of her pregnancy had only reached her head, not her heart, and she was determined to keep it there.

"Stay rational," she whispered to herself as she left the bathroom. "Stay calm and logical and..." Tears burned her eyes, but she kept them at bay until reaching her bedroom. Lying down on the bed, she rested her hands lightly on her flat belly and stared at the dark ceiling.

This can't be happening, she thought. *A bad joke. Wrong timing. Wrong man.*

She was fairly early. Early enough for an abortion, at any rate. She knew the exact date of conception: eight weeks ago. Quickly, she blocked the memory of that night from her mind before it could haunt her any more than it already did. She didn't need a pregnancy to remind her of what she'd done.

Rolling onto her side, she thought of going to an out-of-town women's clinic for an abortion. She knew many local obstetricians on a professional basis, since she was the social worker in the maternity unit at Silas Memorial Hospital in Monterey, but she didn't dare go to anyone who knew her. Only eight weeks. It would be easy. Over in a snap. But how could she possibly have an abortion? How could she part with a longed-for child?

Getting out of bed, she walked over to the window and stared into the gray night fog, thinking through her options. Each of them was fraught with complications, some with the potential to hurt other people even more than herself. *Eight weeks pregnant.* She leaned her forehead against the cool glass of the window. There would be no sleep for her tonight. Only more staring into the fog, more tossing and turning in bed, as she struggled with the alternatives.

But beneath her worry and fear and uncertainty was a vague, yet alluring, hint of joy.

The maternity unit looked entirely different to Joelle when she stepped inside the Women's Wing of Silas Memorial Hospital the following day.

As she did every morning, she walked toward the nurses' station, past the open doors of the patients' rooms. This morning, though, the sight of the women walking slowly through the corridor as they healed and the cries of babies from the rooms held a different meaning for her. In mere months, she could be one of these women. One of the crying, hungry, beautiful babies could be hers.

She found Serena Marquez at the nurses' station and held out her arms to the head nurse.

"You're back!" Joelle said, giving her a hug. "Do you have pictures?"

"Does she have pictures," one of the other nurses said, wearing a grin. "I think she spent her entire maternity leave with a camera glued to her face. Hope you have all morning, Joelle."

Joelle leaned on the counter, her hands outstretched. "Let's see them," she said to Serena.

"We should talk about your referrals first." Serena was beaming, clearly anxious to hand pictures of her little boy over to an apt audience, but motioning instead toward the forms in Joelle's hands.

Joelle took a seat on one of the stools, then read aloud the names on the forms, and Serena pulled the plastic binders containing each patient's medical record from the turntable on the desk. Joelle studied the referrals: two requests for help at home for a couple of single mothers, one case of questionable bonding between mother and baby, one baby born to a cocaine addict, one father denying paternity, one stillbirth. It was a typical batch of referrals for the maternity unit, including the stillbirth. In Joelle's line of work, where she was invited to see only the problems and rarely the joy, dealing with the family of a still-born infant was all in a day's work. It was never easy, though, and today in particular, when the pink and blue lines were still very much in her mind, she winced as she read through the woman's chart. This was the woman's second stillborn baby. She looked at Serena.

"How is she doing?" Joelle asked.

"Not too well," Serena said. "Nice lady. Thirty-five. They lost the first baby and had been trying hard for this one, apparently."

Thirty-five. If she were to have this baby, she, too, would be thirty-five when it was born.

"Why is she losing them?" Joelle asked.

Serena shook her head. "Unknown cause."

"Poor thing," Joelle said. "To go through this twice, with no answers..." She asked Serena a few more questions about the woman and her family, then reached once again for the pictures of the head nurse's baby. She glanced from the pictures to Serena, as she sorted through them. Serena's cheeks were pink, and although she had not lost all the weight she'd gained during her pregnancy, there was a radiance about her that Joelle envied. The nurse was twenty-eight, and this had been her first child. Joelle wondered if, while Serena was pregnant, she, too, had experienced the maternity unit in a different way. She didn't dare ask.

She made the mother of the stillborn infant her first stop, noticing as soon as she walked into the patient's room that the woman looked a little like her. She had long, thick dark hair with deep bangs and was more cute than pretty. She looked more like thirty than thirty-five. Her husband sat at his wife's bedside, holding her hand, and her mother sat in a chair at the foot of the bed, her hand resting on her daughter's leg through the bed-clothes. There was love in the room, an almost palpable sense of caring between the husband and his wife. That was the difference between herself and this patient, she thought. *This* woman was married, with a husband who obviously loved her.

"How could this happen again?" the woman's mother asked, a question Joelle could not answer. She rarely had answers in these situations. All she had was the training and experience to anticipate what the family was feeling, and the skill to provide comfort or support. She spoke with them for quite a while, letting them talk and cry over their loss, then asked them if they wanted to see their baby.

"No," the woman said emphatically. "We saw our last baby. We held her and..." She began to cry. "I can't go through it again. I don't want to see this one."

Joelle nodded. Ordinarily, she might try to persuade the parents to see their infant, but in this case, she was willing to accept their decision. They knew what they were turning down. She didn't blame them, yet she would stop back later, in case they changed their minds.

She left the room after half an hour, knowing that this particular woman, who looked like her and who had tried hard to get pregnant, would stay with her. Two babies, loved and lost. Joelle thought of the tiny life growing inside her and admitted to herself what she had known since seeing the pink line in the middle of the night: she could not abort her baby.

The hospital cafeteria had been remodeled the previous year with mauve walls and huge windows that looked out on Silas Memorial's parklike courtyard. Joelle stood in the entrance to the dining area, holding her tray, trying to convince herself that the scent of the liver and onions on her plate was tantalizing rather than revolting. She'd selected the liver, along with spinach and a glass of milk, for her lunch. She was eating for her baby, the baby she was going to have, no matter what the cost. Searching the tables for her two fellow social workers, she spotted the men near the windows and walked toward them.

"Hi, guys," she said, setting her tray on the table and taking a seat adjacent to Paul and across the table from Liam. The three of them ate together nearly every day, whenever their schedules would allow it.

"What's with the liver?" Paul grimaced in the direction of her tray.

"I don't know," she said. "Just felt like a change."

Paul Garland handled the pediatric and AIDS units. He'd only worked at Silas Memorial for a year, but he'd had previous hospital experience and had fit in well. Liam Sommers had been the social worker for the AIDS unit at the time of Paul's arrival, and Paul had begged to take over that assignment with such fervor that Liam had agreed. Joelle and Liam had speculated that Paul was gay. He was a stunningly handsome man, always neatly tailored, with stylishly short black hair, green eyes and a sexy crooked smile, and everyone knew he had once modeled for a department-store chain. But they soon realized, especially after meeting Paul's fiancée, that he was quite straight, and that his interest in AIDS patients was born of his compassion for them, nothing more.

Liam, who covered the emergency room, as well as the oncology and cardiac units, was Paul's opposite, at least physically. His hair was light brown and on the long side. It had a bit of wave to it, and it grazed the top of his ears and the nape of his neck in a way that Joelle found appealing. His eyes were a pale, pale blue. The few times Joelle had seen Liam in a suit, he'd looked almost silly; this was a man cut out for T-shirts, maybe a Hawaiian-print shirt or plaid flannel in cooler weather. He had a warm, white smile that had been all but absent this past year. She missed seeing it across the table from her at lunch.

Since starting to work at Silas Memorial nearly ten years earlier, Joelle's assignments in the hospital had been the Women's Wing and general surgery, but she and Paul and Liam covered for one another as needed. When one of them had too much on his or her plate, the other two would pitch in, so they always tried to keep one another abreast of their cases.

"How is your day going?" Liam asked her as she took a bite of liver. It was not too bad with the onions to mask the flavor.

"Okay, except for a stillbirth. It's their second."

"Second child or second stillbirth?" Paul asked.

"Second stillbirth. With no apparent cause." She ran her fork through the dull green, obviously canned, spinach. "It's gotten to me, for some reason." She wished she could tell them, but knew it would be a long time before she revealed her pregnancy to anyone. She would hold out as long as she could before letting the rest of the world in on the unplanned, and possibly reckless, choice she had made.

"Why do you think?" Paul asked.

She shrugged, cutting another piece of liver.

"Because you struggled with fertility yourself," Liam offered. "Of course it gets to you."

"That's probably it," she said, willing to allow Liam that explanation. "And what are you two dealing with today?"

The men took turns discussing their cases, and Joelle listened as she forced down the liver, bit by bit. The three of them used to be jocular with one another, but a pall had settled over them a little more than a year ago, when Liam's wife, Mara, suffered an aneurysm while giving birth to their first child. In the days following the birth, Silas Memorial's nurses and doctors, various technicians and even the custodial staff, would come up to Liam during lunch to ask him how his wife was doing. Gradually, their concerned questions slowed, then stopped, as word got around that Mara would never recover. Only people very close to Liam bothered to ask anymore. Mara had been moved from the hospital to a rehab center, then soon after into a nursing home as it was determined that rehabilitation would not help her. They had found an excellent nursing home for her; Liam and Joelle and Paul certainly knew which homes were the best in the area.

But sometimes Joelle wondered if it mattered. Although Mara seemed strangely content, even joyous at times, a phenomenon which her doctors described as euphoria brought on by brain damage, she did not know that the little boy who visited her with Liam was her son. Joelle, herself, stopped by the nursing home at least once a week, and although Mara was full of smiles and looked delighted to see her, she didn't seem to understand that Joelle had once been her friend. Nor did she recognize her own mother. She welcomed everyone, from her child to the electrician, into her room with equal pleasure.

She knew Liam, though. It was obvious in the way she lit up when he appeared in her doorway at the nursing home, and in the sounds she made, like a puppy whose owner had returned after an absence. Joelle was not certain if Mara's surprising good cheer made it easier or harder for those who loved her to cope with her condition. Mara had never been the sort of woman one would describe as perpetually cheerful, and her simple happiness made her seem like a stranger. It had been only in the last few months that Joelle could drive away from the nursing home after a visit without crying in her car.

Mara had been Joelle's closest friend for years. A psychiatrist in private practice, Mara had specialized in psychological problems related to pregnancy and childbirth, and Joelle would bring her in as a consultant from time to time on her hospital cases. She'd been drawn to Mara the instant she met her. Two years older than Joelle, Mara had worn her straight dark hair to her shoulders, and her nearly black eyes were intense against her fair skin. She was a remarkable mixture of qualities and interests: young doctor, novice folk musician, churchgoing Roman Catholic, yoga instructor and avid runner who had participated in three marathons and was fluent in several languages. Although Mara was the consummate professional while at work, once she and Joelle were alone, she slipped easily into girl talk, the sort of sharing of intimacies that created a treasured and unbreakable bond. It was Joelle who had introduced Mara to Liam, after he started working at Silas Memorial, and she couldn't have been more pleased when those two people she cared about began to love each other.

Lord, she missed Mara! She had no one to turn to with the dilemma she was facing, no one she could safely tell about her pregnancy. Least of all the baby's father, even though he was sitting right across the table from her.

CHAPTER TWO

At five o'clock, Liam said good-night to the staff in the emergency room and left the hospital. It had been a long day; his pager had gone off so often for the E.R. that he'd had little time for oncology or cardiology, and he would have to spend more time in those units tomorrow. To make matters worse, this week was his turn to be on call, so he wasn't able to turn off his pager as he walked across the employee parking lot to his car. He alternated nighttime and weekend coverage with Joelle and Paul. The overtime pay was decent, but the "every third week" schedule had just about done him in this year. He'd been trying to persuade management to hire another social worker, someone who would only cover evenings and weekends, but there was no money for that. Joelle had volunteered to do an extra week on call every month to help him out, but he didn't think that was fair, even though he had a year-old child to take care of and she did not.

On a couple of occasions, he'd called Joelle, either to take a middle-of-the-night case at the hospital for him or to ask if she'd watch Sam while he took the case himself, but he wouldn't be calling her anymore. As of two months ago, he'd felt unable to ask her for a favor or see her outside of work in any capacity, or—God forbid—be alone with her. It was okay when Paul was with them, but alone, he found himself unable to make eye contact with her, as though he was embarrassed or ashamed. And he was both.

So now, those dreaded middle-of-the-night E.R. calls meant that he had to awaken Sheila, Mara's mother, and ask her to come over and stay with Sam while he went to the hospital. Sheila was a great sport, though. She lived less than a mile from Liam, in a two-story house Mara had always called "the pink house" because of its cotton-candy color. The pink house was just a block from Monterey State Beach, where Sheila often took Sam, bundled up against the cool air, to watch the kites zig and zag through the sky. A widow who had retired several years earlier from the Monterey Institute of International Studies, where she'd taught Russian, Sheila took care of Sam every day while Liam was at work, and she never complained when he had to ask her to come at one or two in the morning, as well. She also, unfortunately, had to help Liam with his mortgage. Monterey housing was horrendously expensive, and without Mara's handsome income from her psychiatric practice, he could not possibly have kept his three-bedroom, cottage-style home. He was dependent on Sheila in many ways, which was both a blessing and a curse. Liam's own family—his parents and older sister—lived three thousand miles away in Maryland. Although they kept in frequent touch with him, there was little they could do to help him financially.

He drove straight from Silas Memorial to the nursing home in Pacific Grove, a ten-minute ride in decent traffic. Once in the parking lot, he spotted Sheila and Sam sitting together on the concrete bench outside the entrance. He waved to them as he pulled into a parking space, a smile forming on his lips. He could actually *feel* the unfamiliar change in his face; his smile muscles were atrophying from disuse.

The grounds of the nursing home were truly lovely, beautifully landscaped and vibrantly green and alive. That was one of the reasons Liam had been drawn to this place, why he had selected it over the others. It was also cleaner and brighter inside, and he and Sheila and Joelle had eaten a meal there and found the food to be both palatable and nicely presented. He remembered those days of searching, of weighing the aesthetics of various homes, and thought of how naive the three of them had been. None of that mattered to Mara. Very little mattered to her anymore.

Liam walked up the pathway from the parking lot to the home, and Sam tottered toward him as he neared the bench. *The cutest child on earth,* Liam thought, not for the first time. Sam was small for his age, a doll-like fourteen-month-old little boy, with curly blond hair that was certain to darken as time wore on, and Mara's dark eyes and fair skin, which would always need protection from the sun. Sam wore a constant smile. He had no idea that his birth had brought about such tragedy. Liam hoped that, somehow, he'd be able to protect his son from making that connection, at least until he was much, much older.

When he walked quickly like this, filled with excitement at seeing Liam, Sam looked as though he might topple over at any second. Sometimes he did, but this time he made it all the way to Liam without a hitch. Bending over to pick him up, Liam planted a kiss on his cheek, breathing in his scent—which was all too quickly changing from baby to little boy—before settling him into his arms. He knew Sam would only remain there for a moment. Sam loved his newfound skill of walking, and Liam missed the closeness of holding him for more than a minute at a time. It was going to be hard to let go of his son, bit by bit over the years, as his development demanded. There were days when Liam felt as though Sam was all he had left in the world.

"We had such a wonderful day," Sheila said, standing up from the bench and brushing a lock of blond hair away from her face. The warm breeze blew it back again, along with a few other wayward strands. In the sunlight, Liam could see the subtle crow's-feet at the corners of Sheila's eyes, reminding him that she had turned sixty the week before. She'd had a face-lift at fifty-five, and while she was a stunning woman, her skin smooth and barely lined, there was something in her face that told her age. Only in the last year had he noticed that. Everyone involved in Mara's care had aged: Sheila, Joelle, Mara, himself. This year had stolen something from each of them.

"Oh, yeah?" Liam sat down on the bench. "What did you do today, Sam?" he asked, and Sam squirmed to get out of his father's arms and back on the sidewalk without answering. Sam was not very verbal yet, still speaking in one- or two-word sentences, but ever since discovering his legs, he'd been impossible to keep still. Liam didn't know how Sheila kept up with him all day.

Liam watched his son as he explored one of the light fixtures that lined the sidewalk near the ground. Sam banged it with the flat of his hand, as though trying to make it do something, and Liam turned his attention to his mother-in-law.

"How are *you* doing, Sheila?" he asked her, and she smiled.

"He's my world, Liam," she said, nodding toward Sam. "He's the joy that helps me deal with the sorrow. I don't know what I would do without him."

Liam nodded. He understood completely. Standing up, he held his hand out to Sam. "Let's go see Mom," he said, and Sam tottered over to him, slipping his tiny hand into Liam's.

The foyer was bright from two huge skylights overhead, and the place smelled truly clean without being antiseptic. It was actually Joelle who had first recommended this nursing home to him. He remembered her sitting at the desk in her tiny office, tears running down her cheeks, as she called around looking for the best place for Mara. It had been a terrible day, a giving-up day. After four months in the intensive-care unit of the hospital, a short coma, two surgeries and a fruitless stint in rehab, Mara's doctors had said they should begin looking for a home. He'd felt paralyzed at first, and Joelle had taken over. There was rarely a day that he walked into this building without thinking of her with silent gratitude.

Mara's room was at the end of the hallway, where he had insisted she be placed because the room possessed two huge windows, one of which overlooked the beautiful green courtyard with its white gazebo. He had visited Mara every single day since she'd been moved here nine months earlier—except for the day after he and Joelle had slept together. He couldn't bring himself to visit Mara that day, to see the innocent wonder in her face and experience her joy at seeing him. He'd been filled with guilt and anguish that he and Joelle had crossed that line. He was disgusted with himself for wanting it to happen, for allowing his heart and body to overrule his mind.

Mara began to make her "happy sounds," which Joelle affectionately called her puppy squeals, as soon as the three of them stepped into her room, and Liam immediately broke into the upbeat voice he had mastered for these visits.

"Hi, Mara!" he said as he walked toward her bed. He bent over to kiss her on the lips, then lifted Sam and put him on the edge of the bed.

"We should get her up in the chair," Sheila said, but an aide passing by in the corridor must have overheard her, because she peeked around the doorway.

"She was up for a while this afternoon," she said. "It's better if she stays in bed for your visit today."

Liam was secretly glad. Getting Mara from the bed to the chair was an ordeal, and he felt certain she didn't like the manhandling it necessitated, because she would lose her smile during the process. Mara could only control her head and her right arm. She couldn't speak, and her brilliant mind, or at least most of it, was gone.

"Okay," Liam said. "We'll let her rest in bed while we're here."

Mara's smile widened, as though she understood him. He still felt love from her. She couldn't express it except with her smile and her squeals and the light in her eyes when he walked into her room, but he knew it was there, and he felt both honored and burdened by that fact. Not even Sheila, her own mother, could elicit that demonstration of recognition from her. Nor could Joelle, who Mara had known and adored years longer than she'd known Liam. And certainly not Sam. Oh, Mara now recognized Sam and sometimes even seemed to enjoy his company, despite the fact that she'd never cared much for children, but she hadn't a clue that the little boy was hers. Sometimes Liam found that unbearably painful. He so longed to share Sam, his antics and his development, with Mara. With the Mara of the past. His loving, beautiful, fully functioning wife.

They spent half an hour with Mara, telling her about the day, how Sheila had taken Sam to the beach and allowed him to remove his shoes so the waves could tease him with the frigid water, how Liam had handled a difficult case in the E.R. He never talked down to her, and he always hoped that, if he spoke about a case that had a meaty psychological component, he might tap into the part of Mara's brain that had once come alive with the challenge of helping a deeply troubled patient. Then they focused on Sam, who often grew impatient with the chatter. The little boy needed action. They played huckle-buckle-beanstalk, "hiding" the small pot of silk daisies that ordinarily rested on Mara's night table in various places around the room. They made sure the daisies were always in plain sight, but it still took Sam minutes to find them each time, and he would let out a yelp and holler, "huh-buh-besawk!" when he did. It made them laugh, made Mara's smile grow wider, although Liam doubted she understood the game. After the fourth time they hid the flowers, Liam noticed Mara's eyelids growing heavy and knew she'd had enough of her visitors for today.

"Let's go," he said to Sam, lifting him into his arms.

Sam let out a sound of pure desolation, pointing to the daisies as Sheila placed them back on Mara's night table. "Huh-buh-besawk," he said, but it came out as a grief-stricken moan.

Liam grinned and kissed his temple. "Sorry, sweetheart," he said. "We can play some more when we get home."

"And someday, maybe Mommy will be able to play it with you, too," Sheila said, and Liam gritted his teeth. He hated it when she talked like that. Hated her denial of Mara's condition, although to tell the truth, he had a bit of it himself. When Sam was old enough to understand, he would have to put a stop to Sheila's verbal wishful thinking.

He leaned over to kiss Mara on the cheek. Her eyes were now closed, and he knew she was no longer aware of his presence.

They walked through the corridor toward the foyer, stopping briefly to speak with one of the nurses about Mara's medical treatment, and as they were walking out of the building, Joelle was walking in. Thursday night. Joelle always visited Mara on Thursday nights. He'd forgotten and hadn't been prepared to see her, and now, his defenses down, he felt a rush of pure love, gratitude and, yes, the adrenaline that accompanied desire. Followed quickly by guilt, the impulse to run from her rather than to her.

"Hello, Joelle," Sheila said with the cool edge to her voice that Liam had noticed recently when she spoke to—or about—Joelle. He worried that, somehow, Sheila knew that he and Joelle had become very close. *Too* close.

Sam instantly reached toward her, and Liam transferred the little boy from his arms to hers, his hand accidentally brushing her breast as he did so. He flinched inwardly at the touch, but Joelle pretended not to notice. She nuzzled Sam's neck.

"Hello, sweetie pie," she said. "How's my boy?"

She smiled at Liam, but quickly riveted her gaze on Sheila, and Liam understood. She, too, felt the discomfort, the danger, in looking directly at him.

"How's Mara this evening?"

Stupid question, Liam thought. Everyone knew how she was. The same as she'd been for months. But they all played the game, anyway.

"She's full of smiles, as usual," Sheila said.

"I'm afraid we wore her out, though," Liam added. "I'm sorry. I forgot it was Thursday."

"That's all right," Joelle said as she handed a squirmy Sam back to his father. "I'll just sit with her. Hold her hand."

"That would be nice," Sheila said, and she proceeded past her through the doorway.

"See you tomorrow," Liam said, following his mother-in-law outside.

Once on the sidewalk, he set his son down, and Sam started his toddling exploration of the landscaping.

"What's with you and Joelle?" Sheila asked as they walked toward the parking lot.

"What do you mean?"

"I've picked up a little ice between the two of you lately."

"Your imagination," Liam said, but he was certain he heard some satisfaction in Sheila's voice. He recalled some of his mother-in-law's recent comments about Joelle: "She only comes to see Mara once a week," she'd say. "And to think they had once been best friends!" Or, "I didn't like that shirt Joelle was wearing today. It makes her look fat."

Liam buckled Sam into the car seat, then stood up to give his mother-in-law a quick hug. "Thanks," he said.

"My pleasure."

"Hope I don't need to call you again tonight." He opened the driver's-side door.

"I'm available if you need me, dear," she said, the warmth back in her voice. She waved bye-bye to her grandson through the car window, then turned to walk toward her own car.

Liam pulled into the street, turning in the direction of home, knowing he'd have to fix something to eat once he got there and feeling overwhelmed by the thought of that simple task. He hated this depressed feeling that had come over him lately. He'd made it through an entire year without Mara, the Mara he'd known and adored, and he'd been depressed, yes, certainly, but still strong and resilient. The one-year anniversary, though, had kicked him in the back of the knees. Two months ago had been Sam's first birthday, the date that would always mark the moment Mara lost her body and mind, if not her spirit. The day that everything changed. *Forever,* said her doctors. She would never be the same. She would never be the woman he had fallen in love with.

He'd celebrated Sam's birthday with Sheila and Joelle, none of them mentioning the other event marked by that date. There was something about a year that made it so final. A year of growing as a person, as a doctor, as a first-time mother. It had all been snatched away from Mara. And from him.

But despite his aversion to Sheila's veil of denial, he would not allow himself to give up hope, and he pulled into his driveway with new determination. Once he'd fixed supper, washed the dishes and settled Sam into bed for the night, he would do what he'd been doing ever since the day of his son's birth: he would log on to the Internet and visit the Web site where people had written anecdotes about their friends and relatives who had suffered an aneurysm. And there he would find stories of hope. Stories of miracles. They would make him believe, if only for a moment, that the wife he still loved would one day be able to hold her son in her arms.

CHAPTER THREE

Joelle listened to a novel on tape as she drove toward Berkeley and her parents' home. She kept having to rewind it, because her mind was wandering, and finally she turned the tape off altogether. Fiction no longer seemed as gripping to her as her own life.

It was her father's birthday, and she'd promised to make the two-hour drive to Berkeley to help him celebrate. *Celebrate* was probably the wrong word. It was to be a quiet dinner, just her parents and herself. Her parents weren't much for birthdays. Gifts, for example, were not allowed. She had received no birthday gifts from her parents in all the thirty-four years of her life, although she'd received many gifts from them at other times. Her parents didn't believe in giving because you were expected to, but rather because you were moved to. Nor did her parents believe in celebrating holidays. No Christmas. No Hanukkah. They attended some tiny Berkeley church, the denomination of which Joelle could never remember, that honored the sacred spirit in all of nature, and Joelle was never surprised to find a pot of dried leaves or a bowl of shells or fruit on the so-called altar in their so-called meditation room. No one was allowed in that room unless they were there to meditate. For two people who eschewed society's rules and traditions, Ellen Liszt and Johnny Angel had created plenty of their own.

That was the way Joelle had been raised. She'd lived the first ten years of her life as Shanti Joy Angel in the Cabrial Commune in Big Sur. It was a time she remembered with remarkable clarity: eating a strictly vegetarian diet, worshiping nature, learning not to play too near the edge of the cliffs, the way some children learned not to play in the street. Growing up there, she'd taken the magic of Big Sur for granted. Sometimes now, though, she remembered it with longing. She missed the view of the bluffs carving their way through the blue and green water, the dark, cool forest, the ubiquitous fog that washed over them in the morning and late afternoon, which made games of hide-and-seek thrilling and scary. You never knew who or what was mere inches away from you. Her mother and a few of the other parents had taught the children in one of the cabins, the commune's one-room schoolhouse, and by the time Joelle entered public school, she had been far ahead of her classmates.

She had been grateful, then, that she'd spent ten years in the commune. Her life there had given her skills that other children did not seem to have. She could talk with anyone, of any age group, about nearly any subject. The commune had provided her with nonjudgmental acceptance and plenty of fuel for her imagination. It had taught her to take care of other people, and she was certain that was one reason she'd become a social worker.

Somehow, though, over the last twenty-four years, she'd picked up the mores and conventions of the outside world and had made them very much her own. Maybe it was the talk she'd had with her parents when she turned thirteen, three years after they left the commune, that had influenced her. For some reason, her parents began confiding in her then, apparently deciding that thirteen was the appropriate age for that sort of conversation. They had believed in free love, they told her, the sharing of partners, as well as of food and clothing and chores, and that had been fine for both of them at first. But they began to feel that age-old emotion they had been trying to suppress for a decade: jealousy. As the feeling ate away at each of them, they decided it was time to leave, to rejoin the world. Maybe the way of the commune had not been intended for a lifetime, after all. Yet, although her parents were able to fit in easily in Berkeley, with its counterculture and free thinkers, Joelle doubted they could have adjusted to any other area of the country. In many ways, her parents, who had never married, were still the people they had been at Cabrial Commune.

Ellen and Johnny had accepted the fact that she wanted to change her name when she left the commune, although they never called her Joelle themselves. She'd combined her parents names, John and Ellen, and resurrected her father's surname of D'Angelo. That her father still went by Johnny Angel seemed perfectly natural to Joelle, until she really stopped to think about it. Then, the goofy charm of it, of picturing her teenage father taking that handle for himself, made her smile.

Her father, now fifty-three years old, managed a coffee shop near the university, while her mother was a weaver, a beader, a massage therapist, a tarot-card reader and a part-time auto mechanic at the gas station near their house. And somehow, she managed to incorporate her varied talents into a business that brought in more money than Joelle's father and his coffee shop.

Her parents had been on her mind a good deal these past two days. She supposed that was natural: If you learn you're about to become a parent, you begin viewing your own parents in a new light. But that wasn't the only reason she'd been thinking about them. She was beginning to toy with an idea, a way to have the baby and avoid hurting anyone in the process—with the possible exception of herself. She could leave the Monterey Peninsula. Leave Silas Memorial, her condominium in Carmel, everything. Leave that part of her life behind, move someplace else, have her baby, raise it in her new home, and no one in Monterey would ever have to wonder how she came to be pregnant and who the father of her baby might be. Most importantly, Liam would not be faced with a dilemma he could not possibly resolve. It was the right time to make such a move, she thought, and not just because of the baby. She'd lost her two closest friends in Liam and Mara; her other friendships in the area were shallow by comparison. So, she could move someplace new, where she could start over and build a fresh network of friends for herself.

It would be best, she thought, if she moved where she knew someone, and Berkeley, with her parents nearby, was a logical choice. Maybe she could even live with them for a period of time. She wasn't sure how she felt about that, but tonight was not going to be the night she decided. She needed to sit alone with the idea of leaving Monterey for a while, just as she needed to keep her pregnancy a secret.

She arrived at her parents' house just shy of six. She'd spent her teen years in this house in the Berkeley foothills, but as an adult, she saw it through different eyes. The house was diminutive and absolutely charming. It resembled a Mexican adobe, with its straight, angled roofline. The stucco was painted a color that fell somewhere between blue and white, and deep blue tiles flanked the front door and the large arched window of the living room.

Joelle parked in the driveway and walked across the small half circle of green grass to the front door, which was, as always, unlocked.

"Hello!" she called as she stepped into the small foyer.

"We're in here, Shanti," her mother called from the kitchen.

The kitchen was at the rear of the house, and she walked into the room to find her father in an apron, skewering vegetables for kebabs, and her mother in jeans and a T-shirt, stirring a pitcher of lemonade. Both her parents were slender, sharp-featured and gray-haired, and as usual, they looked so happy with their lot in life that she couldn't help but smile at seeing them.

"Hey, baby." Her father set down the skewer he was working on, wiped his hand on the dish towel hanging from the refrigerator door, and pulled Joelle into one of his familiar bear hugs.

"Happy birthday, Dad," she said, her head resting against his shoulder.

"Thanks for coming, honey," he said, emotion in his voice. He was not a typical male, never one to hide his feelings, and she adored him for that.

"Shanti, I want to show you something." Her mother grabbed her hand as soon as Joelle had let go of her father. "You've got to see what I made."

She led Joelle out the back door and down the steps to the small yard.

"Look," she said, pointing. "Up there."

Joelle raised her eyes to see a birdhouse atop a pole in the center of the yard. She walked toward it for a closer look. The little house was an exact replica of her parents', and she laughed.

"How did you do that?" she asked. "It's adorable."

"Oh, a little bit of paint and plaster and ingenuity. I'm hoping it will attract some songbirds." Her mother stood next to her, her arm around Joelle's shoulders, and Joelle suddenly felt her eyes begin to tear. Would she ever be able to give her child the unconditional love and devotion that her parents had lavished on her? She slipped her arm around her mother's waist and rested her head on her shoulder with a sigh.

"What's that about, love?" her mother asked.

"Just...a long week," she said. "Glad to be up here with you and Dad. That's all."

"That's plenty," her mother said, giving her shoulders a squeeze.

She stayed in the yard for a while, surreptitiously wiping the tears from her eyes as her mother led her around the garden, telling her what vegetables and flowers she was planting this year. For the first time, Joelle thought it would be nice to have a small yard of her own, someplace where she could watch things come to life. She had never cared about that before, but suddenly she felt a need to dig in the earth, to get her hands dirty.

"Come and get it!" her father called from the patio, where he was grilling their dinner.

Vegetable kebabs, Joelle thought with a smile as she and her mother crossed the yard to the patio. What would her parents say if she told them she'd eaten liver this week?

They sat at the rickety, aging picnic table on the patio, talking about Joelle's old Berkeley friends as they ate, running down the list of who was living where and doing what. Joelle slipped inside her own head as they talked, wishing she could tell them about her pregnancy, even if she was not ready to talk about a possible move to Berkeley. She knew they would not chastise or judge her, and they would support whatever choices she made for herself. They had been an incredible help to her during the divorce from Rusty, even though they had never understood her desire to marry him in the first place. He was too conservative, they'd said, too rigid, and ultimately, they'd been right.

Her parents' solutions to her problems, though, were often not "of this world." Her mother would probably load her up with herbs and teas and tell her which acupressure points she should stimulate, perhaps even talk her into having her tarot cards read. Joelle wasn't ready for all that, and so she wasn't ready to share her bittersweet secret with them. Instead, she found herself telling them about the patient whose baby had been stillborn.

"I feel terrible for her," she said after describing the woman's situation. Again, she felt her eyes burn with tears, and she knew that this time her parents noticed.

"You see things like that every day, honey," her father said gently as he rested his empty skewer on the side of his plate, and Joelle thought he was eyeing her suspiciously. "You don't usually get so upset over them."

"I know," she admitted. "I don't know why this time it's so hard for me. Maybe because they had fertility problems, and I can relate to that."

"How did this baby die?" her mother asked, pouring more lemonade into her glass.

"They don't know why it happened," Joelle said.

"I just wondered if it might have been the cord. You know, like it was with you."

Joelle shook her head with a smile. Leave it to her mother to imagine a metaphysical connection between this woman's loss and her own problematic birth. She waited for the next words, wondering which of her parents would say them first. Her father, most likely.

"You should get in touch with the healer," he said.

Bingo.

"I knew you were going to say that, Dad." She smiled at him with a mixture of affection and annoyance.

"So why don't you ever take my advice about contacting her?" he asked.

"You know why." She didn't want to get into this with her parents tonight. To her way of thinking, healers were right up there with UFOs and magic tricks. "It's hardly my role, as a medical social worker, to suggest that anyone engage the services of a healer," she said. "That's all."

Her mother leaned forward, the expression in her blue eyes both serious and sincere. "If you'd been there the day you were born, you wouldn't be so skeptical," she said. "Well, you were there," she added, "but you know what I mean."

"Mom, I started breathing because I was lucky," Joelle said. "Or maybe Carlynn Shire was holding me in a position that stimulated my taking in air. I doubt anything magical happened."

"And what about all those other people she healed?" her father asked.

"You remember Penny, don't you?" her mother asked, mentioning the name of one of the women who had lived in the commune.

"Penny was gone by the time Joelle was old enough to know her," her father said.

"Oh, that's true." Her mother laughed. "She was only there about a year. Maybe even less. But, anyway, she'd lost her voice, and Carlynn gave it back to her. There were many other times she healed people. And there was that little boy who was written up in *Life Magazine.*"

Joelle was afraid they might pull out the old issue of *Life,* which they'd found in a used bookstore and kept preserved in a plastic wrapper. She vaguely remembered them showing her the yellowed article at some time over the years. Long before Joelle's birth, Carlynn Shire had supposedly healed a sick little boy, who turned out to be the son of someone who worked on the magazine. That someone wrote a glowing article about her, which apparently launched Carlynn Shire's fame and fortune.

Sliding the vegetables off one of the skewers, she listened to her parents tell their stories about Carlynn Shire, and quite unexpectedly, she saw Liam's face in her mind. She saw him with Mara in the nursing home, where he would touch his wife with affection, making himself smile at her when he felt anything but happy. It broke Joelle's heart to see him that way. There had always been so much love in Liam's eyes when he was with Mara, and that love was still there these days, although Mara could not return it with anything more than puppy squeals. Then there was Sam and his ingenuous acceptance of his mother just the way she was. Soon, he would realize what he was missing. Soon he would be old enough to be embarrassed about it.

She'd lost track of the conversation and nearly jumped when her mother put a hand on her arm. "Are you with us, honey? You look like you're a million miles away. What's troubling you, love?"

Joelle drew in a long breath. "I was thinking about Mara," she said. "If anyone deserves a miracle, it's her."

"Mara's perfect for Carlynn Shire to work with," her father said.

Joelle felt like screaming in frustration at his one-track mind, but she managed to make her voice even as she responded. "You haven't seen Mara since the aneurysm," she said. Her parents knew Mara quite well. Over the years, Joelle had brought Mara to Berkeley with her several times. "The doctors say she'll be this way forever."

Her father leaned toward her. "What do you have to lose by going to see Carlynn Shire?" he asked.

"I'd feel like an idiot," she replied.

"And if there's the slightest chance Mara could be helped," her father said, "wouldn't that be worth feeling like an idiot?"

"Of course, but..." She shook her head. "I doubt people can just call her up and ask her to heal someone."

"But if you told her who you were," her mother said. "If you told her you were that baby she saved in Big Sur thirty-four years ago, I bet she would—"

"Although," her father interrupted, "she might not want to be reminded of that time."

"Why not?" Joelle was puzzled.

"Because of the accident," her mother said.

"Oh." Joelle had heard the story any number of times, but she had never really listened. She knew what she was risking by asking her parents to repeat it to her once again—they would go on and on and on—yet suddenly she had a real desire to know.

"Remind me," she said. "What happened, exactly?"

"Carlynn and her husband—"

"Alan Shire." Joelle recalled his name from the previous recitations of this tale.

"Right. They were both doctors. And Carlynn had the gift of healing. Alan Shire didn't, but he was very interested in that sort of phenomenon. So they founded the Shire Mind and Body Center to look into the phenomenon of healing."

Joelle knew the center still existed and was somewhere in the vicinity of Asilomar State Beach. It was viewed with skepticism by the medical establishment and with total credibility by California's alternative practitioners.

"Yes," her mother said, "but they didn't call it that back then. What was it called?"

Her father looked out toward the new birdhouse for a moment. "The Carlynn Shire Medical Center," he said.

"Right," said her mother. "It was just getting off the ground then. Penny Everett showed up at the commune one day, without a voice. She came there to get away from stress, because her doctor said that was what was causing her hoarseness."

"She went on to be in *Hair*," her father added.

"Who did?" Joelle was getting confused. "Carlynn?"

"No, Penny," her mother said. "And she knew she couldn't get a part in *Hair* if she had no voice. She'd been an old friend of Carlynn's, and so she called Carlynn and asked her to come heal her voice. Carlynn dropped everything and came down to the commune."

"Of course," her father added, "we always believed some other force brought her there right at that time, because it was just the day after she arrived that you were born. If she hadn't been there, you wouldn't be here now."

The thought made her shudder despite her skepticism.

Her father continued. "So, she'd been there a few days when—"

"A whole week," corrected her mother. "That's why Alan Shire and her sister were so freaked out."

"Whatever," her father said. "She'd been there a while, and of course we had no phone or any way for her to reach her family without leaving the commune, so I guess her husband and sister got worried about her and drove down to Big Sur to find her." He looked at his wife. "What was the sister's name?" he asked her.

"Lisbeth."

"Oh, right. Alan Shire and Lisbeth, the sister, got a cabin over near Deetjen's Inn—remember Deetjen's?"

Joelle nodded quickly, wanting him to get on with the story.

"They checked into the cabin," he said, "then started looking for the commune. We weren't the only commune in Big Sur, as I'm sure you remember, and they probably didn't know where to start looking. It was dark, I guess, by the time they got to the right one."

"Actually, it was only Alan who got there," her mother said. "The sister had stayed behind in the cabin."

"That's true. And Carlynn was in Penny's cabin then, but she'd been in our cabin just an hour or so earlier. Rainbow." He grinned. "Remember it?"

"Sure." She smiled at the memory of the small, dark cabin. She could smell it right at that moment—the scent of ashes mingled with the earthy, musky odor inevitably present in a wooden cabin surrounded by trees and fog. What a strange existence she'd had for the first ten years of her life!

"We'd had her come over to Rainbow a couple of days after you were born because we thought you were running a fever," her father continued.

"*You* thought she had a fever," her mother corrected him.

"I still think she did," her father said. "I think it disappeared as soon as Carlynn touched her."

Even Joelle's mother shook her head at that, but Joelle felt moved. Her father had always been a nurturer, and she liked to picture him, a kid of nineteen, skinny little Johnny Angel, aching with worry over his baby girl.

"Well, anyhow," her father said, "she went back to Penny's cabin after curing you—" he winked at her "—and Alan Shire showed up and spirited her away without letting her even say goodbye."

"And the next day, Carlynn and her sister were driving on Highway One, looking for a phone or a market or something, and they didn't know the roads, and they flew off the side of the cliff in the fog. The sister, Lisbeth, was killed, and Carlynn nearly died herself."

"Scared the shit out of us because we knew that could happen to any one of us on those roads," her father said. "Those of us with vehicles, anyhow. We all felt terrible. Carlynn had helped Penny and had saved your life, and yet her own sister died without her being able to do a thing about it."

"I know Penny felt terrible," her mother said. "If Carlynn hadn't stayed with her so long at the commune, her sister would never have had to come to Big Sur to find her."

"It was so long ago, though," her father said. "I doubt someone of Carlynn's...you know, internal resources, would still be grieving over something that happened that long ago."

"How old is she now?" Joelle asked.

"Well, she must have been in her mid-thirties then," her mother said, "so that would put her at about seventy by now."

"You know, I really wish you could go see her." Her father dabbed his lips with a cloth napkin before resting it on the table. "Whether you ask her for help with Mara or not, she'd probably feel great seeing you. Knowing that you're alive, that something good came out of that time at the commune, even though it meant the loss of her sister. That you're the wonderful person you are because of her."

Her eyes burned again. What was wrong with her? Was this part of being pregnant, growing weepy over every little thing?

She set her own napkin on the table. "I'll think about it, Dad," she said, and to her surprise, she knew she meant it.

CHAPTER FOUR

The social work department had not been given much space in the hospital. Located on the second floor, it consisted of one large room divided into four small offices, or "cubbyholes," as the staff referred to them. The largest of the cubbies was the central office, where the coffeepot, mini-refrigerator, watercooler, mailboxes and reception desk were located. The three other offices were aligned in a row, separated only by paper-thin walls, through which a whisper could be heard if someone was really trying to listen.

For that reason, Joelle waited until she had the social work offices to herself before making the call to Carlynn Shire. She could hear Maggie, the department's receptionist/secretary/office manager, talking to her boyfriend on the phone in the central office, but both Paul and Liam were in other parts of the hospital, and she wanted to take advantage of the quiet. Dialing the number for the Mind and Body Center, she wondered if Carlynn Shire would really remember an infant she had "saved" more than thirty-four years before.

"Shire Mind and Body Center." The voice that answered the phone was that of a very young woman.

"Hello, my name is Joelle D'Angelo." Joelle heard Liam step into his office next to hers as she was finishing the sentence. *Drat.* Swiveling her chair to face the far wall, she lowered her voice. "I was wondering if I could speak with Carlynn Shire," she said.

There was a moment's hesitation on the other end of the phone.

"Carlynn Shire doesn't actually *work* here," the young woman said.

"Oh," Joelle said. "I thought..."

"She's retired. You might catch her at some kind of function or whatever, but she's almost never actually here."

"I see." Joelle wondered whether to dig further. She needed to use the bathroom very soon. In just this past week, she'd learned the location of every public and staff rest room in the hospital. She'd had some teasing of nausea, as well, and couldn't even think about the liver she'd eaten the week before without gagging. It had been only a little over a week since she'd learned she was pregnant, before which she'd felt completely well, which made her wonder how many of her symptoms were psychological.

"Well, I'd still like to talk with her," she said. "Could you tell me how to reach her?"

"I can't give out that information."

"How can I get a message to her?"

That hesitation again. "Hold on a sec," the young woman said.

Not too long, please, Joelle thought, squeezing her legs together. She could hear Liam on the phone in his office, and the sound of his voice made her want to weep. *Everything* made her want to weep these days. Liam hung up his phone and left his office, much to her relief, and she heard his footsteps travel down the hall.

In the old days, before the night that had ruined their friendship, he never would have come and gone from his office without ducking into hers for a quick hello. Often, he'd ask if she wanted to go for a hike the following weekend, sometimes with Sam in a carrier on Liam's back, sometimes without.

The last hike they'd been on, shortly before Sam's birthday, had been at Point Lobos. The hike had been, she'd thought later, a turning point for both of them, a warning they'd chosen to ignore. They'd hiked together many times, both of them finding the exercise a great outlet for the stress they were under and an opportunity to talk. But on this hike, something had been different. Sam had not been with them, and when Liam held her hand to help her climb a boulder or cross a dry creek bed, she'd felt something new in his touch.

That morning, she'd given him a book of meditations related to the loss of a loved one, and he'd brought it with him on the hike. They sat on a rock, back to back, while he read aloud from it. They were high above the Pacific, and below them, cormorants flew from rock to rock and sea lions floated and bobbed in the water. Oh, what a strange mixture of emotions she'd felt that day! Surrounded by all that nature had to offer, she'd listened to Liam read about feelings they both shared over Mara's illness. Those words, and the warmth of his back against her own, had made her both tearful for all that Mara was missing and filled with joy that she, herself, was alive and healthy. Afterward, Liam plucked a small yellow flower from some ground cover and slipped it into her hair, the tips of his fingers sending an electric thrill through her body as they brushed against the shell of her ear.

"That's probably an endangered flower," she'd said, but she picked one of the pale yellow blossoms and slipped it behind his ear, as well. They'd held hands as they walked along the smoother part of the trail, neither of them addressing the fact that the way they were relating to one another went beyond the sharing of grief to something more.

Joelle thought she could wait no longer for the bathroom. She was about to hang up when the voice of another woman, sounding slightly older than the first, came over the line.

"I understand you want to speak with Carlynn Shire?" the woman asked.

"Yes, I would."

"What is this regarding?"

Joelle hesitated. *I want her to cure a friend,* sounded ridiculous if not downright presumptuous. "I wanted to talk with her about a friend of mine who's very sick and—"

"She doesn't take special requests any longer," the woman said. "She hasn't for years. I'm sorry."

"Wait!" Joelle said, afraid the woman was about to hang up on her. "I, um, Car...Dr. Shire saved my life many years ago, when I was born, and I just wanted to meet her and...reconnect, I guess."

"What did you say your name was?"

This time, Joelle said, "Shanti Joy Angel," and she was willing to bet the woman didn't bat an eye as she wrote down the information. She probably heard similarly eccentric names all the time in her business.

"And when did she save your life?"

"Thirty-four years ago. I was born on the Cabrial Commune in Big Sur, and she happened to be there visiting a friend. I wasn't breathing when I was born. My parents said she saved my life."

There was a long silence from the other end of the phone, and Joelle hoped the woman was jotting down the story.

"Give me your number," the woman said, "and I'll pass the message along to Dr. Shire. It'll be up to her whether she gets in touch with you or not."

"Sure, I understand." She gave the woman both her work and home numbers and hung up, wondering why she was now feeling an almost desperate need to speak with Carlynn Shire. Her father's words were still in her mind: *If there's the slightest chance Mara could be helped, wouldn't that be worth feeling like an idiot?*

CHAPTER FIVE

Carlynn Shire stood in front of one of the massive bookshelves in the mansion library, her head cocked slightly to the side so that she could read the titles as she searched for one of the books on seals. In recent years, she hadn't had much time to think about things as frivolous as the seals that swam in the ocean behind the mansion, but now, with so little time left to her, she was hungry to study them as closely as she had when she was a child. Funny how late in life you treasure those simple pleasures that were important to you growing up, she thought, when you all but ignored them in adulthood. Suddenly, when you knew your life was nearing its end, those simple things seemed most important of all.

The phone rang on the broad desk at the other end of the library, and Alan, who was sitting in his desk chair reading the *Wall Street Journal,* pressed the button for the speakerphone.

"Shire residence," he said.

"Alan?" It was Therese, who ran the Mind and Body Center so efficiently that it was rare for her to call them anymore. Carlynn turned at the sound of her voice.

"Hi, Therese," Alan said. "How are you?"

"I'm fine, thanks. I have a message for Carlynn."

"I'm here, Terry," Carlynn said, taking a few steps toward the desk to sit on the arm of the sofa. "You're on the speakerphone. What's the message?"

"Sorry to bother you with this," Therese said. "A woman called, wanting to talk with you. She has a sick friend she wanted you to see. I told her you don't do that anymore, but she said she knows you. Well, sort of knows you. She said you saved her life when she was a baby. On a commune in Big Sur."

Carlynn and Alan exchanged looks. It was a moment before Carlynn spoke again. "What was her name?" she asked.

"Shanti Joy Angel," Therese said.

"Ah, yes," Carlynn said, her eyes still on Alan's.

"You recognize it?" Therese asked. "It must have been a long time ago."

"A time I'll never be able to—"

"Call her back, Therese, and tell her what you told her the first time," Alan said, leaning toward the speaker. "Carlynn doesn't treat people anymore."

Carlynn looked at Alan with annoyance. "Wait a minute, Therese," she said as she picked up the receiver. "I'll see her, if she's willing to come here." She wasn't looking at Alan, but she heard him blow out his breath in annoyance and knew he was wearing a scowl.

"You will?" Therese sounded surprised.

"Yes." She picked up a pen and pad from the desk and leaned over, ready to write. "Give me her number and I'll have Quinn call her and set something up." She jotted down the number. "Thanks," she said. "How are things going over there?"

"Great," Therese said. "I'll fill you in at the meeting next week. And how are *you* doing, Carlynn?"

"Okay, dear," Carlynn said. "I feel much better than I did when I was on all those poisons they were giving me. We'll see you next week, then."

She hung up the phone and let her gaze rest on Alan's stunned face.

"Why in God's name would you do that?" he asked.

"I'm dying, Alan." She folded her arms across her chest. "What do I possibly have to lose?"

"You know as well as I do what you have to lose."

He was afraid, and she felt sudden sympathy for him. He had always been afraid. Leaning over, she gave him a soft hug and a peck on the cheek. "I may be old, and I may be dying, but I'm not senile," she said. "I won't do anything that would hurt us. You know that."

Using her cane, with which she had a love-hate relationship, she walked from the library into the massive living room and through the French doors to the broad terrace behind the mansion. The air was warm, almost balmy, and it held the faint salt smell of the Pacific mingled with the lemony aroma from the cypress trees surrounding the mansion. She rested her cane against one of the patio chairs and walked to the edge of the terrace to be as close to the water as she could get. What a glorious day on her beloved Cypress Point! The indigo sea beneath the vivid blue sky was framed by the cypress, which grew so close to the terrace she could reach out and touch the coarse leaves. Lifting her arms, stretching them wide, she drew the world into an imagined hug.

She should be at peace now, in this paradise that was her home, as she neared the end of a long-enough life. She should be able to embrace the world with abandon, to visit the seals on Fanshell Beach with nothing else on her mind but their huge dark eyes and shimmering bodies. But peace was elusive, and the reason for that was no mystery to her. Thirty-four years was a long time to be haunted by something. The guilt and sorrow and wretched sense of loss remained tangled up in her heart and her mind. Was she to die still burdened by her memories of that time?

Shanti Joy Angel. How could she ever forget that name? The

three words alone pulled her back to Big Sur. She didn't care what Alan had to say about it, she would see the young woman. She was not much of a believer in fate or in things happening for a reason, but this seemed a sign, something she shouldn't ignore. Perhaps it was a coincidence that the baby from Big Sur had called her at this moment in her life, when the peaceful pull of death was thwarted by her preoccupation with her sins.

Or, perhaps, it was a gift.

CHAPTER SIX

Cypress Point, 1937

"We live on the Circle of Enchantment, girls," Franklin Kling said. He was standing on the terrace of the mansion, smoking a cigar as he looked out at the Pacific, his seven-year-old twin daughters, Carlynn and Lisbeth, on either side of him.

"What's that mean, Daddy?" Carlynn asked.

It was a moment before Franklin responded. He didn't want to speak again for fear of breaking the spell that had come over him as he stared out to sea. The view was bordered on all sides by the deep green of the Monterey cypress trees, which clung to the rugged bluffs along the coastline. The crimson sun was just beginning to sink, inching closer to the water, and the air was clear, although all three of them knew the fog would soon be rolling in. This clarity on a late-summer afternoon was rare. Franklin felt at peace, except for one thing: Presto, the family's huge, red dog, was not out here with them. Presto was always with the children, whether they were here on the terrace or up in their rooms. This evening, though, the dog was asleep in the kitchen. Asleep for an hour—or maybe for all eternity. Franklin didn't want to think about it. He would have to address the topic later, but for now he just wanted to enjoy the view, his cigar and his daughters.

"That's another name they sometimes call the Seventeen Mile Drive," he said, glancing down at Carlynn. "You don't realize. You go on about your days as though you lived someplace perfectly average. As though you lived in Iowa City, for heaven's sake." Franklin had grown up in Iowa. "But you actually live in paradise. And every once in a while, it pays to stop and think about it." He looked out at the sea again. "The Circle of Enchantment," he repeated.

"What does enchantment mean?" Carlynn asked.

"It means...captivating," Franklin tried, then shook his head. "No, beyond captivating. It means...it means drawing you in, in a magical sort of way. Think of all the amazing things you can see here. You girls don't know any different, of course, since you've always lived here. Spoiled, you are." He chuckled and puffed at his cigar. "Where I grew up, it was flat and cornfields for miles and miles. Nothing to rest your eyes on. Here, just driving from the store, you go through the forest—"

The girls shivered. They thought the forest was spooky.

"—and you have one magnificent view after another of the ocean. Some people never see the ocean in their whole lives, and you live right smack on it. There's that one cypress down the road, the one that juts out of the rocks, standing all by itself, just trying to hang on, trying to keep growing, high above the water, and those ghost trees, all bare and gnarled up and leaning back from the wind. Fighting the wind. Everything around here is fighting to keep going."

Carlynn and Lisbeth could feel the power of the place they lived. They understood it better than their father knew. They never took it for granted. Right now, they could feel the mansion at their backs, its cold gray stucco exterior rising above them, high above the ocean and the cliff that held it precariously in place. They knew that next to the mansion, beyond the cypress and chaparral, was Fanshell Beach, where their father often took them to see the seals or comb the beach for shells. Sometimes he'd take them to a different beach, where they could explore the tide pools, the wondrous worlds filled with tiny sea animals and underwater gardens.

Pelicans often made their gawky way across the sky behind their house, and in the winter, whales swam right through their backyard. Sometimes they had nightmares about the whales, or at least, Lisbeth did. Very little ever seemed to bother Carlynn. Although they were physically identical, right down to the unruly cowlick on the crown of their heads which their mother, Delora, complained about as she tried to force their pale hair to behave, they were two different girls. And Delora made sure the world knew it. She refused to dress them alike, or send them to the same school, or, if truth be known, treat them equally. Carlynn's hair was long, its platinum waves cascading down her back, but Delora kept Lisbeth's hair cut short, the curls bouncing around her face when she walked.

Carlynn was in the second grade at the Douglass School, a private school in Carmel. The Mediterranean-style building was nestled in a stand of tall trees, and in addition to academics, it offered tennis and badminton, drama classes and riding lessons. Carlynn always had a healthy, rosy glow to her cheeks.

Lisbeth, on the other hand, attended Esley Rhodes School, a less prestigious private school not far from her sister's, but a world apart in amenities and in the quality of the teachers. Carlynn's teacher had taken her class to the opening of the Golden Gate Bridge in May, but Lisbeth's teacher would never have thought of such a thing. Franklin ended up taking Lisbeth himself, not wanting her to feel left out of that celebration. The girls didn't know the difference between their schools, at least not at the age of seven, but anyone familiar with the educational institutions in the area would know that Carlynn was getting the better education. And anyone who spent more than five minutes with Delora knew the reason for that difference.

Franklin rested his hand on the back of Lisbeth's head. "And you two are also wonders of the Seventeen Mile Drive," he said. "Twins. Perfectly look-alike little girls. Wish your mama didn't insist on chopping off your hair, Lizzie."

"I look like Shirley Temple, though," Lisbeth said so quietly she could not be heard above the sound of the ocean. She was the quiet twin, a shyness borne of her uncertainty about her worth. People always spoke with wonder about Carlynn's ethereal hair and barely noticed Lisbeth's. But Rosa, their housekeeper, had told Lisbeth her haircut made her look like "that adorable Shirley Temple," and Lisbeth carried that description of herself in her heart.

Franklin Kling tried to be fair to both girls. Perhaps he went overboard in his caring for Lisbeth, he realized, because he had to make up for the little concern his wife showed her second daughter. That's what Delora Kling always called Lisbeth— "my second daughter," as if Lisbeth were years younger than Carlynn instead of a half hour. Delora might as well have said "second-best." That was what Franklin heard, what made him bristle each time she said those words, and he feared that's what Lisbeth heard as well.

Delora had not known she was carrying twins when they checked into the hospital seven years ago. She'd been thrilled at being pregnant and cheerier than usual during those nine months. Ordinarily, she tended toward a moodiness that Franklin found hard to predict. Together, they'd fixed up one of the up-stairs bedrooms in the mansion as a nursery, buying beautiful furniture and pasting up wallpaper that was both pink and blue, ready for any eventuality. But Delora had not counted on the possibility of two babies. Before she and Franklin got married, they'd talked about having a family, and she'd made it very clear she wanted only one child. "I barely have what it takes to be a mother at all," she'd said in an honest assessment of her abilities, as well as of the amount of love she had to give. "So, promise me you'll be happy with only one."

He had promised. He'd loved Delora, loved the spark in her when she was happy, and she had been happy most of the time back then, when he was first falling in love with her. It had been easy for him to dismiss her infrequent dour moods as aberrations. But her parents, with whom they'd first lived in the mansion, were killed in a car accident shortly after he and Delora were married, and since that time, she'd been depressed more often than not.

Delora's delivery of Carlynn had been remarkably smooth, given that the baby was her first, and she'd even refused the twilight sleep her doctor had offered her. She and Franklin had already selected a name for the child if it turned out to be a girl. Delora wanted to name her after her beloved parents by combining their names: Carl and Lena. Franklin had said little in the matter; he was an easygoing man and he hoped that, through this child, Delora might finally be able to lay her grief over her parents' deaths to rest. It didn't occur to him until later that she was trying to re-create her own family—a father, mother and one doted-on child, all living together in the family mansion on the Circle of Enchantment.

Franklin had paced dutifully in the waiting room while Delora was delivering, and he'd been overjoyed when a nurse came out to tell him about the birth of his daughter.

"But we're not done, yet." The nurse had smiled at him. "There's another one."

"Another one?" He had not understood.

"You are going to have twins."

He'd sat down at that, amazed, grinning, and forgetting Delora's staunch opposition to having more than one child. What was taking place in the delivery room, though, would forever color his wife's feelings toward her children. Carlynn had slipped easily into the world, causing her mother the least pain necessary. But the second baby had struggled. She was breech, "backward from the start," Delora would say later—and often. Delora writhed in pain, finally begging for the twilight sleep which promised her relief. When she awakened, she discovered she had been cut open to deliver this second daughter. Every tiny movement, every flick of a finger or blink of an eye, made her cringe with pain. For days the unexpected baby went nameless, and while Carlynn took quickly to the breast, Lisbeth could not get the knack of it, as if she was somehow able to discern, to feel, her mother's disdain for her. Sometimes, Franklin watched her struggle with the nipple, and it seemed to him that the tiny infant was so afraid of doing anything to upset Delora that, in her anxiety, she simply could not get the sucking right. Franklin understood his daughter's anxiety all too well. He experienced it much of the time around Delora himself.

In those first few days in the hospital, when he bottle-fed the nameless infant while Delora nursed Carlynn, Franklin decided he would like to name the baby Lisbeth after his own mother, who was still living at the time. Delora did not get along well with his mother, and he doubted she would agree to the name. When he broached the subject with her, though, Delora said, "I don't care what we name it," and he'd recoiled in horror.

"Name *her,*" he said, thinking protectively of the little white-haired angel he held in his arms.

The nurses told him Delora's antipathy toward the second twin would pass in time. She would love both her babies equally, they said. Right now she was in too much pain to think about anyone other than herself. They did not know, and neither did he at the time, what Delora had known all along: she truly had room enough in her heart for only one child.

Lisbeth didn't help matters. She was a difficult baby, colicky and forever waking her sister with her howling and fussing. But Franklin often blamed himself for Delora's attitude toward the little girl. He never should have named her Lisbeth, because it set up yet another negative association between the infant and something Delora loathed: his mother. He should have let *Delora* pick a name. Make that baby hers.

"Mr. Kling?"

Franklin turned now to see Rosa at the door to the terrace.

"Supper," Rosa said, her voice still tinged with a Mexican accent, although she had been in this country three decades. "Come inside, girls, and get washed up."

Dinner was served in the grand dining room, which looked out over the sea. Rosa served them, as she had served Delora's family before Franklin had moved in. She was not the best housekeeper in the world, but she had a warmth about her that had charmed Franklin from the start. He liked that she treated the twins equally, and she had even complained to him once, with apologies for overstepping her role, that she thought it unfair that only Carlynn went to the Douglass School while Lisbeth did not.

Over dinner, Delora questioned Carlynn about her day at school, while Lisbeth nibbled her food, a small shadow in the room. When Delora stopped for breath, Franklin broke in.

"Who wants to go sailing with me tomorrow?" he asked and saw the instant sparkle in Lisbeth's eyes. He'd asked the question just to bring that joy into her face.

"I do!" she said.

"How about you, Carlynn?" he asked his other daughter.

Carlynn shook her head. "No, thank you," she responded, as he knew she would. Carlynn had hated the water ever since their sailboat capsized in Monterey Bay a couple of years earlier. The girls had been wearing life jackets, but the water was freezing and the whole experience had been frightening, particularly for Carlynn. Lisbeth still loved to sail, but Carlynn decided she would never go on the water again. That was fine with Franklin. Carlynn had many opportunities for adventure at school, and he wanted Lisbeth to have one for herself. A pastime she could love, at which she could learn to excel.

At the end of the meal, Delora looked across the table at Franklin, and he knew she was asking him if they should remain in the dining room to tell the girls about Presto. He mouthed the word *library,* and Delora stood up.

"Let's go into the library, girls," she said. "Your father and I want to talk with you."

Franklin led his family across the foyer into the library, dreading the conversation he knew was coming.

Delora and Carlynn sat on the love seat near the window, while Franklin and Lisbeth opted for the wing chairs. The girls looked apprehensive. They were rarely invited to participate in family discussions such as this.

"You tell them, Franklin," Delora said.

Franklin looked from one daughter to the other. "Presto is very sick," he said.

Both girls glanced in the general direction of the kitchen, where they knew Presto slept by the stove. Neither of them spoke.

Clearing his voice, Franklin continued. "I'm afraid he's going to die."

"No!" Carlynn cried, instantly in tears, and Delora pulled her close, trying to smooth her unsmoothable hair.

"Hush, darling," she said. "It will be all right."

Lisbeth's hands were locked on her lap and she sat motionless, quiet. But her eyes glistened.

"Tomorrow," Franklin said, "we will take him to the veterinarian to have him...put down."

"Killed?" Carlynn wailed. "Please don't, Daddy. Mommy?" She looked at her mother with hope.

"He's suffering, Carlynn," Delora said. "He's having trouble breathing, and you know how he can hardly walk these days."

"He's nearly blind," Franklin added. "And we want to end his misery, Carly. It's not fair to make him go on like this when we can help him die, so he doesn't have to be in pain any longer."

Carlynn nestled against her mother's breast, sobbing quietly now, and Franklin saw the tears in Delora's eyes. She was not an insensitive woman, just limited in her capacity to love. Lisbeth's mouth was downturned and quivering, as though she was struggling to control her emotions, and a fat tear spilled from each of her eyes. Franklin walked over to the ottoman in front of her chair and sat down on it. Leaning forward, he covered her hands, still folded in her lap, with his own.

"Are you all right, Lizzie?" he said.

Lisbeth nodded, biting her quivering lip. She was brave. Stoic. He felt a lump in his throat. No one appreciated this child except him.

But that was not exactly true. Carlynn drew away from her mother to see the pain in her twin sister's face. Jumping up from the love seat, she ran across the room to hug her. "I won't let them do it, Lizzie," she said, as though she had forgotten she was only a child.

But Lisbeth knew the limitations of a seven-year-old. She nodded, as if she was humoring her sister, but Franklin saw that the sorrow never left her eyes.

That night, Carlynn slept on the kitchen floor, her arms locked around Presto's failing body. Franklin and Delora tried to force her to come upstairs to bed, but she wouldn't budge from the dog's side.

"Let's let her be," Franklin finally said to his wife. "Let her have one last night with him."

Delora agreed. She watched as Franklin covered the little girl with a comforter, squatted down to kiss the top of her head, and stroked Presto's side. Then he and Delora went to bed.

The dog's rasping breaths could be heard throughout the mansion. Carlynn spent the night whispering words to him, of comfort or love, or pleading, no one really knew, but the fur on his neck grew wet from her tears.

In the morning, everyone in the house awakened to the sound of Presto's barking. They came downstairs to find him sitting up next to Carlynn, his breathing even and strong. Carlynn put her arm around the dog's broad shoulders.

"Presto's hungry," she said simply, and Lisbeth ran over to embrace first the dog, then her sister.

The vet would later say that he must have misdiagnosed Presto's condition, that he had judged it to be far more serious than it actually was. Maybe that was so.

And maybe it wasn't.

CHAPTER SEVEN

The call came just as Joelle walked in the door of her condo that evening. Dropping her purse and appointment book on the kitchen counter, she picked up the receiver.

"Hello?"

"I'm trying to reach Shanti Angel." It was the voice of an older, possibly even an elderly, man—a deep, rich voice with an edge of refinement.

"This is Shanti," she said.

"I'm calling you for Carlynn Shire," the man said. "She got a message that you would like to meet with her?"

"*Yes,*" she said, "I would."

"And you have some special connection to her?" he prompted, and she repeated the story of her birth to him.

"Well, Dr. Shire said that if you'd be willing to come over to the house, she'd be happy to talk with you."

"Does she remember me?" Joelle asked.

"She says she does."

Joelle couldn't help but smile. "I'd be happy to come to her home. Just tell me where and when."

"She could see you next Tuesday at noon."

That would be right in the middle of her workday, but she didn't dare ask for a different time.

"That will be fine," she said. "What is the address?"

"Are you familiar with the Seventeen Mile Drive?" he asked.

"Yes," she said. Everyone knew the Seventeen Mile Drive. The Carmel entrance was not that far from her condominium. She'd only been on the drive a few times, though, since there was a fee for the privilege of entering it. It was visited mainly by tourists who wanted to view the wonder-filled coastline of the Monterey Peninsula—and by the residents lucky enough to live along the route.

He gave her the address, telling her the house was near Cypress Point. This would be no simple "house," she thought.

"When you turn into the driveway," he continued, "you'll need to press the buzzer on the column to your left. You'll see it. I'll open the gate to let you in."

"Thank you."

"Oh, and just let the fellow who takes the toll for the Seventeen Mile Drive know that you're coming here, to the Kling Mansion," the man added. "I'll let him know to expect you. You won't have to pay."

"Thanks," she said. "That will be great."

She hung up the phone and wrote down the appointment time in her book. It would be interesting to meet Carlynn Shire, if nothing else, and it would be fascinating to hear her side of the dramatic story of her birth. She would tell Carlynn about Mara and see what she had to say. But she wouldn't tell Liam what she was doing. He would think she'd gone off the deep end.

And, she thought, *he might be right.*

The following day, Joelle found herself sitting at the nurses' station in the maternity unit next to Rebecca Reed, the perinatologist in charge of the department, as they both wrote notes in medical charts. Joelle wished she could tell Rebecca about her pregnancy. From the corner of her eye, she watched the doctor's slender hand move across the page as she wrote, her handwriting far neater than most of the other physicians' in the hospital. Even when she wrote, Rebecca had an air of confidence, of taking charge. She was thirty-nine and beautiful, her long blond hair pulled back from her face with a clip at the nape of her neck.

Rebecca had helped Joelle find a fertility specialist when she and Rusty were going through their failed attempts at conception, but, although Rebecca was a skilled and respected physician, she possessed little warmth. She was not a nurturing sort of doctor, not a hand-holder. Joelle would have loved it if, right then, as they were sitting side by side, she could have confided in the doctor. She couldn't bring herself to talk with her that easily, though. Joelle could converse with almost anyone, but she'd never felt completely comfortable around Rebecca. The few times they'd been at parties together, small talk had been awkward and difficult.

Still, until she moved away, which she had definitely decided to do, she wanted Rebecca to be her obstetrician. Her plan was to tell the doctor when she was twelve weeks pregnant, at the end of her first trimester. Joelle, herself, would have scolded any woman who waited that long for a first prenatal appointment, but she simply didn't want to let anyone in on her pregnancy until it was absolutely necessary.

Rebecca's pager went off, and she took the time to close the medical chart in which she was writing and carefully cap her pen before removing the pager from the waistband of her skirt to check the display. Reaching for the phone on the counter, she glanced at Joelle.

"It's the E.R.," she said, and Joelle nodded.

Writing her own notes, Joelle listened to Rebecca's end of the phone conversation, wondering if the case might be something in which Liam would need to be involved. She couldn't tell, since Rebecca was doing more listening than talking.

Rebecca hung up the phone. "Have to run," she said, standing up. She smoothed her skirt with both hands, then picked up her notebook and pen. "They're paging Liam, Joelle, but you might eventually need to be involved in this. A car accident's coming in. A pregnant woman, thirty-eight weeks, and her husband. Husband's okay, but the woman isn't expected to make it. I'll have to meet them in the E.R. to see if we can save the baby."

"Let me know if the baby ends up coming here," Joelle said. If the child survived, it would most likely be rushed to the neonatal intensive care unit, and the case would certainly become hers.

Right now, though, it was Liam's. She pictured Liam trying to handle a situation in which a wife dies, a baby lives, and a husband grieves. Standing up, she closed the medical chart and rested it back on the lazy Susan. Too close to home for him, she thought. This would kill him. She headed down the hall in the direction of the emergency room.

CHAPTER EIGHT

Liam was about to leave the E.R. to head up to the cardiac unit when Rebecca Reed whisked past him. She touched his arm as she rushed by.

"Don't go yet," she said. "We'll need you."

"What's going on?" He heard the sirens outside the doors of the E.R., but Rebecca didn't stop to answer him. Typical Rebecca.

One of the nurses who had overheard their conversation stopped briefly near Liam as she headed toward the front door.

"It's a car accident," she said, glancing in the direction of the ambulance. "Husband is all right, but the wife went through the windshield and died on the way in." She started walking again, then added over her shoulder, "And she's pregnant."

Liam stood near the corridor that led from the E.R. to the rest of the hospital and felt the numbness come over him. This happened to him every once in a while. It was not an emotional numbness, although he supposed that was part of it. Instead, it was a literal paralysis that started in his feet and rose to his chest until he could barely pull any air into his lungs. He stood there feeling thick and stupid and wanting to escape. He could leave and pretend he had not been caught in time to handle this case, to deal with the husband who was "all right." That husband would never be all right again.

Unable to move, he watched as they wheeled the woman into the E.R. toward one of the treatment rooms. Except for one streak of dried blood on her temple, her injuries were strangely invisible, and her belly was huge. Her husband walked next to the gurney, limping, perhaps from an injury suffered in the accident, and clutching his wife's lifeless hand. They were both in their thirties, Liam guessed.

One of the nurses left the side of the gurney to step over to Liam. "Take care of the husband, okay?" she said, and he wondered if she could see the panic in his eyes. "He's physically fine, but emotionally—"

"I'll do it."

Liam turned at the sound of the voice behind him. Joelle.

"I heard what was happening," she said, touching his hand, then quickly drawing her fingers away. "Since the baby will eventually be in my unit, I thought I'd come down and take over. If that's all right with you, Liam."

He doubted his face could mask the gratitude he felt. She knew. She'd heard about the case, and she knew he would not be able to handle it. And she'd come.

"Thanks," he said, or tried to say. His mouth was too dry to get the word out, but Joelle had already moved past him.

Still holding his wife's hand, the man tried to stay with the gurney as the staff wheeled it through the doors to the treatment room, but the nurses shook their heads at him and told him to let go. Liam watched as Joelle took the man's arm, speaking quietly to him. Finally, he let go of his wife's hand and stood next to Joelle, wearing that shocked, this-can't-be-happening-to-us look on his face that Liam knew all too well. Joelle and the husband watched the doors to the treatment room swing shut, and Liam turned away before he saw any more.

* * *

"What shall we do tonight, Sam?" he said as he drove out of the nursing home's parking lot, hours after the situation in the emergency room. He glanced in the rearview mirror at his son, who was buckled into the car seat. Sam did not answer him. He was seemingly fascinated by the handle of the door, poking it, patting it, and Liam smiled.

He was better now. He and Sheila and Sam had had their visit with Mara, and he'd managed to block the incident in the E.R. from his mind. Whenever it threatened to slip in, he thought of Sam. The ruse—replacing a negative thought with a positive—worked every time. Almost.

Now came his favorite part of the day, his time alone with Sam. Sam was pure joy. He knew nothing of sorrow, nothing of the sad circumstances of his birth. Liam checked the rearview mirror again, enjoying the traces of Mara he could see in his son. He had her incredibly dark eyes and fair skin, but more than that, he had Mara's spirit. It was obvious in the way he took on every new challenge with optimism and excitement.

Liam pulled into the carport of his cottage and lifted Sam out of the car seat. The maid would have come today, he thought. Good. He liked the powdery-fresh smell and the sense of order she left behind. Sheila paid to have her come once a week—one more thing for which he was beholden to his mother-in-law.

He and Sam ate dinner, then went out in the small backyard to pull a few weeds in the garden. At least Liam pulled weeds, while Sam pushed his tot-size lawn mower back and forth over the lawn. Then, while it was still light out, Liam got the bubble solution and the huge bubble wand Joelle had given them from the kitchen. He sat on the patio and blew bubbles for Sam to pop and chase in his gawky toddling run. Every time a fresh bubble slipped from the wand, Sam laughed, a tinkly, golden sound that made his eyes crinkle and showed his pearly little teeth, and Liam felt like blowing bubbles forever just to see that happiness in his son's face.

But finally he noticed it was growing dark out, and he screwed the lid on the bubble solution. Sam's face fell in disappointment.

"Let's play with the blocks," Liam said quickly, standing up, and the little boy brightened and headed for the back door.

Inside, Liam dumped the round canister of large, colored blocks onto the carpeted living-room floor, and Sam instantly grabbed one and set it in front of him, then reached for another. They'd played with the blocks nearly every night this week, and Liam could see Sam's abilities growing. The first night, Sam had just watched Liam build a tower, then gleefully knocked it over. But the past few evenings, he was building towers himself. Well, not towers, exactly, but he was piling one block on top of another, at any rate.

"Let's see how many blocks you can stack tonight, Sam," Liam said. "Last night you got to three before they fell down. Remember? One, two, three." He showed him his three fingers, then the three blocks, but Sam seemed disinterested in the number game. He was building, and in a moment he had three blocks stacked, if a bit precariously.

"That's fantastic, Sam," Liam said, and handed him one more. "Can you put this one on the pile? That would make four."

Sam clumsily set the fourth block on the pile, and the stack quivered for a moment, then tumbled over, making him laugh.

They played a few minutes longer, but then Sam stepped over the blocks and fell hard into Liam's lap.

"Oh, you wanna wrestle, do you?" Liam said, lying back on the carpet. Sam crawled on top of him, letting himself roll and fall and climb, using Liam's body as a jungle gym. Liam had to do very little. He thought about all the toys Sheila had bought her grandson, which were piled up in Sam's room and in the corner of the den. Totally unnecessary, Liam thought. All this kid needed for entertainment was a dad lying on the living-room floor.

"Aya-pane!" Sam said, patting Liam's knees.

"You want to be an airplane?" Liam said. "Well, I don't know about that. Do you know how to fly?"

"Aya-pane!" Sam giggled as he pounded harder, his hands a mere feather's weight against Liam's knees.

"Ok, Sammy-Bananny, you asked for it. Assume the position."

Sam leaned against Liam's shins, and, holding the little boy's hands, Liam raised his legs into the air. Making airplane noises, he flew his son this way and that, while Sam laughed and shrieked, his tiny hands gripping his father's for dear life.

"Uh-oh!" Liam said. "We're hitting turbulence. It's going to be a bumpy flight."

Sam let out an anticipatory squeal even before Liam started the bouncing motion with his legs. Turbulence was great for his own abdominal muscles, he thought to himself. Good thing, too, since he hadn't been to the gym in over a year.

Finally, he lowered his legs and Sam fell on top of him with a thump.

Liam groaned. "Rough landing," he said.

"More Dada," Sam said, begging for more even though he was lying, exhausted, on his father's stomach.

Liam laughed. "That's enough turbulence for one night," he said. "I think it's bath time, now."

Sam stood up. "Bose!" he said.

"Right. We can play with the boats in the tub." Suddenly tired, Liam needed a few token tugs from Sam to get him on his feet.

He gave Sam a bath, then brought him into his own bed so they could look at a book together. Liam rested on a stack of pillows piled against the bookcase that served as a headboard, Sam on his lap, as they turned the pages. Finally, after two picture books, in which Sam had to name every single item in every single picture, most of them in a language only Liam could understand, the little boy's eyelids began to droop.

Liam set the books on the night table, settled lower into the pillows and turned his sleepy son so that he was resting against his chest. He kissed the top of Sam's head through the blond curls, the scent of baby shampoo comforting in his nostrils. He felt like hugging him tightly, but didn't dare for fear of waking him. When Sam was still like this, Liam felt a fragility in him, a need to protect him, always, from anything that might hurt him.

"I love you, Sam," he whispered into his son's clean hair.

If only he could share Sam with Mara. He wanted that more than anything. Of course, he *did* share him with her, as much as was possible. But when he was honest with himself, he had doubts about what sort of mother Mara would have been. She'd never had an interest in children and had been nothing but candid with him about that fact. Maybe he was kidding himself to think she would have been as smitten by Sam as he was.

He'd told Mara about Sam's first steps and his first words, but Mara had only smiled her simple smile, the same expression she would have offered if he had said that Sam had been hit by a car. Once, he'd put that theory to the test by telling Mara he had some sad news.

"Your mother died," he said.

Mara smiled.

"She was in a car accident."

Smile.

"I made that all up, honey," he said quickly, upset with himself for even putting the awful thought into words. "Your mother will be here to visit you tomorrow, as usual."

Mara's constant smile, though, encouraged Sam to relate to his mother, and for that Liam was grateful. How long would that last, though? For how long would Sam be able to relate to her so easily, so unassumingly? Liam thought of the future—the first day of school, Sam's teen years, his graduation, his leaving home, his wedding. When he pictured himself in the future, he was completely alone with his son.

He would always have a wife whom he loved, but who could never truly be a wife to him. Not in any way. She could not be a friend in whom he could confide or a partner with whom he could share life's joys and sorrows. Nor could she be a lover to hold him close, to touch his body the way he hungered to be touched. He still reached for Mara in the middle of the night sometimes, only to find the cool, empty space on the bed where her body should have been. Confused for a moment, he'd turn on the light and then remember, and he'd want to scream and punch the walls. He had lost so much.

Sometimes, people who didn't know what had happened, people in the music world, perhaps, would ask him why Sommers and Steele was no longer performing, and he'd have to explain. He and Mara had formed their little two-person folk group shortly after meeting, and they'd been fairly popular on the local club circuit. They both sang quite well, especially together, and they both played acoustic guitars. Mara would play the piano, as well, when one was available. People had commented on how well matched they were. Joelle had known that even before he and Mara had met. If it hadn't been for Joelle, the two of them never would have been together. Liam told himself that he didn't regret their meeting, that a few years with Mara was worth what he was going through now, but he wasn't sure. He never sang these days, not even in the shower. He hated the sound of his voice alone. It had been Mara's harmony that had made his voice whole.

Liam breathed in the scent of Sam's hair again. He should get up and carry him into the nursery, but he felt weighted down on the bed, and he remembered the case in the E.R. What would he have said to that devastated man if Joelle had not rescued him? *At least your wife died.* That's what he would have liked to say, and the thought made him feel instantly guilty. It was true, though. At least that man would have a fresh start. He had the hope of happiness. Liam would have explained to him that the baby would become his world. His reminder of his wife, his source of laughter and hope. But he knew those words would not have been helpful. Mara used to say she thought therapists who had "been there," who had experienced the issues their clients were struggling with, were rarely as helpful as those who had not. They'd argued about that. An intellectual argument, the sort that was frequent between two bright and opinionated people. Now, though, he understood what Mara had meant. When he visited her earlier that evening, he even told her she'd been right, but her vacuous smile let him know she didn't understand his words, much less the meaning behind them. He told her he would have been of absolutely no help to that man. He might even have done some harm, if not to the widower, then to himself, by trying to handle that family's crisis.

Thank you, Jo.

Joelle had been so wise to know how that case would have affected him, and so truly loving to come down to the E.R. to save him from it.

He would not have been able to survive this past year without Joelle. Their relationship had been one of respectful co-workers and good friends before Mara's aneurysm, but Joelle quickly became his main source of support afterward. She shared his grief. She could get inside it with him because she loved Mara, too. She understood the reality of what was happening. She knew what the future held for Mara, as well as for him, and she let him talk about it, opening the door to his fury, and sometimes his tears. Not like Sheila, who never, not once during the past fourteen months, acknowledged Liam's dilemma of having a wife, yet having no wife.

"Because she's Mara's *mom*, Liam," Joelle had said to him. "She's too busy seeing what's happening to her daughter. She can't see how it's affecting you. Give her time."

But he feared Sheila would never understand, no matter how much time passed. She had cared for her cancer-ridden husband for five years at home before his death, sacrificing her needs to take care of his, and Liam knew Sheila expected nothing less of him.

Liam and Joelle had never directly addressed what was happening to their relationship, but they grew closer over the months, stopping in each other's offices at work for a bit of conversation and talking on the phone every night. Most of the time, he would call her. Other times, it would be the reverse. Either way, those calls became a routine, and if for some reason he wasn't able to talk to her before going to bed, he would lie awake for hours before he could fall asleep.

They taught each other to smile and laugh again. To a grieving person, nothing was more seductive than laughter. Then there were the hugs, of course, the comforting embraces between good friends. At some point, though, those hugs became longer, tighter, followed by lingering touches. Her fingers would slide over his shoulder or wrist, his hand would brush an eyelash from her cheek.

God, he missed her. He missed talking to her every night. There was a vacuum around him at night now, after Sam fell asleep and he was alone with his thoughts.

He looked over at the phone on the night table, then shook his head. If only he hadn't allowed things to get out of hand, he could still have that friendship with her, that wonderful relief of confiding in someone and being heard. But there was no going back. He knew better than that. Just eating lunch across the table from her in the cafeteria set up a guilty longing in him. He loved Mara deeply, but sometimes what he felt for Joelle went even deeper, and that scared him.

Reaching behind him to the bookshelf, his fingers found the book of meditations she'd given him. He leafed through it, Sam still asleep on his chest, looking not for a particular meditation, but for the picture he kept tucked between the pages. The photograph made him smile when he found it. He and Joelle had taken Sam to the Dennis the Menace Playground, more for their entertainment than Sam's, because he was far too young to make good use of the park. Most of the photos from that day were of Joelle and Sam together, but in this one, Joelle was alone. She sat cross-legged on the ground near the playground's giant black locomotive, grinning, her chin raised in a way that gave her a teasing, insolent look. Like Mara, she was dark-haired and dark-eyed, but that was where the comparison ended. Joelle looked like a kid. She'd worn her thick dark hair in braids that day, and her grin in the picture was wide and uninhibited. She was not a kid, though, but a flesh-and-blood woman, with a woman's body and a woman's heart.

Liam glanced at the phone again. What would it hurt if he called her to thank her for coming to the E.R.?

No, no, no.

He nearly sprang from the bed as though he'd touched a live wire. Lifting Sam into his arms, he headed toward the nursery. He would have to take something to help him sleep tonight. Otherwise, chances were good he would do something else he would regret.

CHAPTER NINE

Cypress Point, 1946

Carlynn Kling had a gift, there was no doubt about it. By the time she was fifteen, nearly everyone on the Monterey Peninsula had heard of her. Some believed in her unique abilities; some didn't. But believers or not, everyone knew that Carlynn Kling was not your average fifteen-year-old girl. In addition to her gift of healing, she was a stunning beauty, slender and very blond, who turned the heads of everyone who saw her.

Lisbeth Kling, on the other hand, seemed nearly invisible in her averageness. By fifteen, she was old enough to pick her own style of dress and hairdo. She chose to wear her hair exactly as Carlynn did—in the style of Veronica Lake, parted on the side, with long, flowing blond waves that partially blocked the vision of one eye. But Lisbeth had gained weight since becoming a teenager, and although she emulated Carlynn's style of dress and hair, she did not project the same attractive and confident image. She envied Carlynn, a jealousy that might have turned ugly and set sister against sister, had the love between them not been so strong.

Every weekend, Delora drove Carlynn to the Letterman Army Hospital in San Francisco, where the teenager made her "rounds." They visited the patients, some of whom had lost limbs, some of whom were dying, and some who would make a full recovery in time. Carlynn touched them and talked to them, amazing even her mother with her composure and poise in the midst of such a horrific setting. Often, Carlynn eased the men's pain, and sometimes she caused their wounds to heal faster. She seemed fascinated by the medical history of each man, and she questioned any nurse willing to talk with her to glean more information about the soldiers. She'd want to know the extent of their injuries and what sort of treatment they'd been given, and she'd listen closely, asking intelligent and appropriate questions. Soon, she had the nurses, themselves, requesting that she see specific patients.

Of course, none of the physicians had any faith in Carlynn's gift, and she made her rounds not in any formal capacity, but merely as a visitor. The soldiers knew that when she touched them, though, something happened. There was magic in her touch, they said, and in her words. Her voice was soft and even, and occasionally it rang out with laughter. The anguish that the solders' war experiences had left inside them seemed to dissipate during Carlynn's visits. The doctors, though, joked that any girl as beautiful as Carlynn was sure to have a healing effect on young men deprived of women's company for so long.

Lisbeth knew, probably better than anyone, that it was truly Carlynn's touch that made the difference to those men. She possessed the same voice as her sister, and except for her weight, a very similar beauty, yet she knew that if she were to walk through the VA hospital, enter those rooms, touch those men, she would not have the same impact on them. She would be useless. That was how she felt much of the time. Useless. Invisible. At least, in everyone's eyes save her father's.

Franklin did not like Delora drawing so much public attention to Carlynn's gift. He knew his daughter's healing ability was real; he had seen too many examples of it to deny it. She had once cured an excruciating case of shingles that had cropped up on his back. He would never allow her to heal his colds or headaches because it seemed wrong to him to accept the gift from his own daughter. But the shingles had made him desperate, unable to sleep or even sit in a chair without gritting his teeth against the pain, and he would have done anything to end that anguish.

But Franklin worried the outside world would see Carlynn as mentally ill or, worse, as a charlatan, and he was also concerned that Lisbeth suffered from spending so much time in her sister's shadow. The girls still attended separate schools with qualitatively different activities and benefits, and he sometimes worried that the way he and Delora were raising them was akin to an experiment: take two identical twins and treat them differently, giving them different life experiences and different schooling, to see what would happen. What had happened was that Carlynn was confident, outgoing, and an outstanding student, while Lisbeth was quiet, unsure of herself and barely scraping by in school. She was not fat, exactly, but pudgy in all the wrong places, and he knew that she ate when she was sad, which was much of the time. It tortured Franklin that he had allowed this to happen to the daughter who had been the one he had named, bottle-fed, bathed and cuddled.

The twins were planning their sixteenth birthday party, to be held in the mansion, with different levels of enthusiasm. Carlynn was excited; Lisbeth, apprehensive. *Sweet sixteen and never been kissed,* one of their housekeepers teased them several days before the party. The adage held true for Lisbeth, but not for Carlynn, who had written her boyfriend's name at the top of the guest list, hoping that she'd be able to drag him into the cypress trees for more of those delicious kisses.

Carlynn's guest list had twenty names on it, all of them friends from her posh high school, but Lisbeth had added only four names to the list, four quiet wallflowers, much like herself.

The night of the party, the living room and dining room of the

mansion were decorated with reams of colored crepe paper and
helium balloons, and popular music played on the phonograph.

Carlynn introduced her friends to Lisbeth, one by one. How
obvious it was that Lisbeth hated introductions! She wore a
frozen smile on her face as Carlynn's friends marveled over the
duplicate of their classmate, though they quickly saw the differences in their personalities. They were nice to Lisbeth after
their initial stunned surprise, asking her questions about being
a twin, but when the questions stopped, Carlynn could see Lisbeth had no idea how to prolong the conversation. She grew quiet
and uncomfortable and eventually she and her four girlfriends
drifted into one corner of the living room, where they could listen to the records and watch the world go by.

Carlynn's boyfriend, Charlie, was there, and at first Carlynn
could not take her eyes off him. She thought he looked like a
rugged Gregory Peck, with dark hair and tanned, smooth skin,
and when Nat King Cole started singing "I Love You For Sen-
timental Reasons," Charlie held her very close as they danced
in the living room. Carlynn, though, was no longer thinking only
of going off into the cypress trees with him, because her eyes
and her thoughts were on her sister. Lisbeth's lack of poise in
social situations was both annoying and embarrassing, but Carlynn could not help feeling sorry for her. She wished shyness
were something she had the ability to heal.

They were dancing to Perry Como's "Prisoner of Love" when
a scream came through the open French doors leading from the
living room to the terrace. Everyone stopped what they were
doing to look in the direction of the sound.

Suddenly, Jinks Galloway appeared on the terrace. His shirt
was partially unbuttoned, a smear of dirt across the white fabric, and his blond hair hung damply over his eyes.

"Penny's hurt!" he said. "She fell."

Everyone rushed toward the moonlit terrace, Carlynn in the
lead. Reaching the edge of the terrace, she carefully peered over

the side. Penny Everett, Carlynn's closest friend from school, was about ten feet below, lying precariously on the broad crown of a Monterey cypress. She was awake and alert, but grimacing with pain. Her blouse was entirely unbuttoned, her bra almost luminescent in the moonlight, and her blond hair was spread around her head like the arms of an octopus.

"What's going on?" Franklin, who had been kindly staying out of the way of the party, must have heard Penny's scream and was now walking onto the terrace.

Carlynn leaned far over the edge. "Button your blouse, Pen," she whispered, and Penny managed to get one button through its buttonhole before Franklin got a look at her.

"How'd you get down there, Penny?" he asked, then turned to Carlynn. "No one's drinking here, are they?" he asked.

That had been part of the agreement, and Carlynn quickly shook her head, although she wouldn't have put it past Jinks to have smuggled in his own bottle in his jacket pocket.

"All right, Penny," Franklin called down to her. "Hold still. I'll come around the house and see if I can get you from below."

Penny nodded. "My leg..." she said.

Her leg was twisted into an awkward and unnatural angle against the nearly black branches of the cypress. Probably broken, Carlynn thought.

Jinks and Charlie accompanied Franklin around the outside of the house until they reached the area where Penny was stranded. The tree on which she'd fallen was low to the ground, and after a few minutes they were able to jostle her free, although not without eliciting cries of pain from her. Gently, they rested her in the small clearing near the house. By that time, nearly all the guests were in the yard observing the scene, and Carlynn rushed toward her friend, dropping to her knees at her side.

"Penny," she said, taking her friend's hand, "does anything hurt besides your leg?"

Penny shook her head. Her blouse was still only partially buttoned, and Carlynn was certain her father had figured out that Penny and Jinks had been petting at the time of the fall. She was relieved to see, though, that Penny's leg now lay flat and straight against the ground.

"Where does it hurt?" Carlynn asked, trying to button Penny's blouse with her free hand. Penny was shivering, and Carlynn motioned to Charlie to take off his jacket.

"Above my knee," Penny said. "I think it's broken. Is the bone sticking out?"

Carlynn rested Charlie's jacket over Penny's chest and arms, then carefully raised her friend's skirt a few inches above her knee. She was relieved to see there was no blood or protrusion of bone beneath her stocking. She looked up at her father. "Get the boys to leave," she said, pointing behind her. "Or at least get them far enough back that they can't see."

"We need to get some ice on her leg." Jinks looked pale and anxious in the moonlight. "Maybe take her to the hospital."

"Not right now," her father said, and Carlynn was grateful that he understood what she'd meant and what she was intending to do. "Come on, fellas, let's give Carlynn some room."

Penny understood, too. On one occasion, she had accompanied Carlynn and Delora to Letterman Hospital and had seen with her own eyes the marvels Carlynn could achieve.

As the boys moved back to join the others, Carlynn slipped her hands beneath Penny's skirt, unhooked her stocking from the garter belt and pulled it from her leg, while Penny winced with pain. Resting her hands on the skin above Penny's knee, Carlynn looked into her eyes.

"Is this where it hurts?" she asked.

Penny nodded. "Yes, but a little more to the side."

Carlynn shifted her hands slightly, and Penny nodded. "That's it," she said. "I think I heard it crack when I fell, Carly. Ugh."

"Does it hurt a great deal?" Carlynn could already feel the area beneath her hands growing warm from her touch, and she knew that was a good sign.

"It's horrid," Penny said.

"And just what were you and Jinks doing on the terrace?" Carlynn asked with a grin.

"You mean—" Penny managed a smile "—this is God punishing me?"

"You never know," Carlynn said. "You are the rowdiest of my friends—do you know that, Pen?"

"But you love me anyway."

"Yes, I do. Very much." She looked earnestly into Penny's eyes. "Even though you've probably gotten me into big trouble with my father."

"Sorry." Penny giggled, the lightness of the sound encouraging to Carlynn's ears.

She continued talking with her friend, keeping her hands on her leg, for another fifteen minutes. Finally, Penny said, "This is so strange. It's not hurting. At least not while I'm lying still."

"Move it then, with my hands still on it. Slowly. See if you can bend your knee."

Penny bent her leg. "My God, Carlynn, it doesn't hurt. Just feels a little stiff."

"Do you think you can stand on it?"

She helped Penny to her feet and accepted the grateful hug she offered. The guests cheered from behind them, as though they were witnessing an injured player rise from the ground on a football field.

"Can you walk?" Carlynn asked. Penny began to carefully move toward the house, leaning against Carlynn, just in case. "Now," Carlynn said as they neared the rear door, "we really *should* get some ice on it. No point in getting too cocky about all this."

After the party, Carlynn and Lisbeth sat on the edge of the cold stone terrace, their legs dangling over the side, bundled up in jackets against the chill. Behind them, in the house, they could hear the tinkle of glasses and clatter of plates as Rosa and the other servants cleaned up. Fog was rolling in over the Pacific, but they could still see the lights of a boat that must have been quite close to shore.

"We shouldn't be out here," Carlynn said. "We're both going to get sick, sitting on the terrace in the cold."

"You can heal us, then," Lisbeth said, and Carlynn looked at her quizzically.

"That sounded snide," she said. "Did you mean it that way, Lizzie?"

It was a moment before Lisbeth answered. "Sorry," she said. "I just...it still amazes me, that's all. How do you do it?" She turned to her sister. "How did you fix Penny's leg?"

It was not the first time Lisbeth had asked Carlynn about her healing skills, but this time the tone of her voice was marked more by envy than curiosity.

"I don't understand any more than you do, Lizzie," Carlynn said. "Maybe Penny's leg wasn't really broken. Maybe she just scared herself when she fell."

"I saw it. It was twisted up."

Carlynn gently let one of her feet touch one of Lisbeth's. "I have to be touching the person," she said. "At least I know that much. But other than that, what I do doesn't seem like anything special. I'm not a magician. It's just that when I'm touching a person, I think only about him or her. I try to send them all my love, everything good that's inside me. I concentrate really hard."

"It's amazing," Lisbeth said, shaking her head in quiet wonder.

"Do you remember Presto?" Carlynn asked. "The night before he was going to be put to sleep?"

"Of course." Lisbeth nodded. Presto had lived for three more years after that night.

"All night long I lay next to him with my arms around him, and I prayed. I just kept hoping and praying he would get well."

"Is it praying, then?" Lisbeth asked. "Is that what you're doing?"

"Not always. I've sort of experimented with it," Carlynn admitted. "Sometimes I pray. Sometimes I just think as hard as I can about the person I'm touching. It doesn't seem to matter what I do. The only thing I know for sure is that, afterward, I'm more tired than you can imagine."

Lisbeth knew this. She had seen her sister after her visits to Letterman Hospital. It was all Carlynn could do to drag herself upstairs to bed, and she would sleep so deeply that nothing could wake her for hours.

"You must be tired now," she said.

Carlynn nodded, then rested her head on Lisbeth's shoulder.

"I wish you could talk more easily to people, Lizzie," she said. "They won't bite."

"Well, I can't," Lisbeth said a bit defensively. Then she sighed. "It's just one more thing you can do better than I can."

The following day was a glorious clear Sunday, and Franklin invited his daughters to go sailing with him. Only Lisbeth accepted, just as he'd expected. As he'd hoped. He'd observed his less popular daughter at the party the night before and wanted some time alone with her.

They set sail on the bay in his small sloop, and he allowed Lisbeth to take over once they'd motored away from the pier. The sea was calm, a sheet of pale aquamarine glass, but there was a good headwind, and Lisbeth showed real skill as she tacked far out into the open bay.

"You're getting very good at this, Lisbeth," Franklin said.

"Not very hard today," she said. "The water's so smooth." But she was smiling at the compliment all the same. She leaned back on her hands, eyes closed, her pretty face turned up to the sunlight.

"Did you enjoy the party last night?" Franklin asked.

"Yes," she said without opening her eyes.

"What did you like about it?"

She shrugged. "The music, I guess."

Franklin licked his lips, letting a silence form between them as he tried to think of what he could say next.

"I have the feeling it was not much fun for you, honey," he said finally, and then quickly added, "And that's all right. I never much enjoyed parties either when I was your age."

She opened her eyes to look at him. "You didn't?" she asked.

He smiled. "I was actually a lot like you, Lizzie. My brother— your uncle Steve—was always the popular one, the one who commanded attention. He was more intelligent than I was, better-looking and far more interesting to the girls. I was the shy one, always afraid to say anything in case I sounded stupid."

She looked surprised. "But you're *much* smarter and nicer than Uncle Steve," she said, then added, "No offense. I know he's your brother."

He laughed. "That's my point, sweetheart. As I grew up, I got more confident. What I was like when I was sixteen didn't matter anymore."

Lisbeth looked out to the vast Pacific, where the air was growing hazy with fog, a crease between her eyebrows.

"You'll blossom, Lizzie. Someday. It can't be rushed, and you'll need to be patient. But you have a lot of happiness ahead of you, and you'll probably appreciate it more than Carlynn, because she's known nothing else."

Lisbeth smoothed her hand across the gunwale. "I don't really want Carlynn to be unhappy, though." She looked past the sails at her father.

"It's not an either-or thing, honey," he said. "You can *both* be happy. There's not a finite amount of happiness to be divided between the two of you, where if you get more, she gets less." He leaned toward her. "You and Carlynn are so lucky to have each other," he said. "Other friends will come and go, for both of you, but you'll always be there for each other."

"She's so pretty," Lisbeth said, fishing, he thought, for a compliment.

"She could use a few more pounds, if you ask me," Franklin said, taking her bait, and Lisbeth smiled at him.

"Thanks, Daddy," she said and leaned back on her arms to face the sun again.

Lisbeth felt the slight sting of a sunburn on her face as she helped her father moor the boat to the pier. She'd hated to come in, hated to put an end to her time with the one person who seemed to value her more than Carlynn, but the fog was getting closer, and both she and her father knew how quickly it could surround them out on the bay. She walked ahead of him as they made their way over the dunes to the car. A couple of young boys were playing on the dunes, running and jumping and shrieking, and when she heard the *thud* behind her, she guessed it was just one of the boys leaping from the dune, so she didn't bother turning around.

"Hey! Girl!" one of the boys cried out.

Still, she didn't turn, figuring the boys were planning to play some sort of joke on her.

"Girl! Your father!"

She turned at that and saw her father lying several yards behind her, on his back in the sand.

"Daddy!" she cried, racing back to him. Kneeling next to him, she rested her hand on his heart but could feel no beating against her palm. His face was the color of the old ashes in the fireplace. She turned to the boys who were watching, stock-still, from the dune.

"Get help," she said. "Hurry!"

She rested both her hands on his chest, holding them there, praying to God to save him. Squeezing her eyes shut, she tried to send her love into her father, but knew she should have questioned Carlynn more about her ability to heal the night before. What had she meant when she'd talked about sending "everything good" inside herself into someone? How did she do that? *How?*

She held that position, crouched over her father, telling him out loud that she loved him, while his face turned from ash to white. She could hear the sirens in the distance, but by the time the ambulance pulled into the small parking lot, she knew it was too late. Her father, her champion, was gone. It was, in some ways, his own fault, she thought. He had taken the wrong twin sailing with him.

CHAPTER TEN

Joelle turned off Highway One and quickly found herself in a line of five cars, all of them waiting to enter the gate to the Seventeen Mile Drive. When she reached the tollbooth, she smiled at the young man waiting for her money.

"I'm Joelle D'Angelo," she said. "I'll be visiting Dr. Carlynn Shire."

He checked a list inside the booth, then looked up. "Go ahead," he said.

She looked ahead of her, but wasn't certain if she should take the road to the left or the right.

"Which way do I go?" she asked, and he pointed to her left.

"The Kling Mansion is that way," he said. "Just past Cypress Point."

"Thanks." She started driving again. She passed the lodge at Pebble Beach, where the road was clogged with cars and golf carts and tourists, and after a few minutes she came to a spit of rugged land that jutted out into the northern end of Carmel Bay. If she'd had binoculars—and the time to stop—she thought she might be able to see across the bay to her condominium from there. *Damn.* How could she possibly leave Monterey?

She could probably hide her pregnancy until she was four or five months along, she thought. She'd seen young women come into the maternity unit who had hidden their pregnancies right up until the end, not wanting their families to know, so surely with some loose clothing and by keeping more to herself, she should be able to pull it off. She wanted to hold out as long as she could and keep working, because she doubted she'd be able to find a job as a five-or-so-month-pregnant woman, and she'd need every cent she could hang on to when she moved.

She didn't think she could handle living with her parents for more than a week or so. They were wonderful people, but they would drive her crazy long before the baby was born. If she could afford an apartment in proximity to them, though, that might work. She'd thought of her friends who lived in different parts of the country, wondering if living near one of them might be feasible. Her college roommate lived in Chicago and had two little kids, so she would be a great resource. But Chicago? After Monterey? She was going to have to let go of her need to live someplace perfect. That could not be her priority right now.

But Joelle forgot that promise to herself as she passed the lone cypress, where it rose out of the rocky coastline. Within a few minutes, the road slipped from the open, oceanfront vistas into a dark, thick grove of Monterey cypress. Finally, she spotted the turnoff to the Cypress Point Overlook. Pulling her car to the side of the narrow road, she checked her directions. The house should be ahead and to the left, and she lifted her gaze to see a gray stucco mansion nestled in a stand of cypress. Letting out her breath, she stared at the large, Mediterranean-style building, with its red tile roof and seemingly flimsy hold on the edge of the bluff. What a setting! A car honked as it passed her on the too-narrow curve, and she put her foot on the gas pedal, drove forward a short distance and turned into the gated driveway of the Kling Mansion.

The stone post to which the gate was attached bore a touch-pad of numbers with a buzzer beneath it. She pressed the buzzer as she'd been directed to do, and the gate slid open with a barely audible grinding of metal on metal. She drove into the estate, its thick, emerald-green landscaping enveloping her, and parked her car close to the mansion. There was a stone path leading from the driveway to the house, and she walked up to the huge double doors. Although a mother-of-pearl doorbell graced the wall next to the door, she opted to use the heavy dolphin-shaped knocker for the sheer pleasure of lifting it and letting it fall.

After a moment, a woman drew open the massive door. She wore a lavender dress, her gray hair pulled back in a bun at the nape of her neck, and she smiled at Joelle, her eyes crinkling behind narrow, stylish wire-rimmed glasses.

Joelle held out her hand. "Dr Shire?" she asked.

"No, dear," the woman said, but she squeezed her hand with a smile. "I'm the housekeeper, Mrs. McGowan. And you must be Shanti." There was a touch of Irish in her voice.

"Oh," Joelle said. "Yes. I have an appointment with Dr. Shire."

"Come in, love." The woman stepped back to let her in, then guided her through a beautiful foyer with a terra-cotta-tiled floor into a living room dominated by a fireplace so enormous, Joelle felt as though she'd stepped into the mansion in *Citizen Kane*. At one end of the room, huge arched windows and a set of French doors looked out onto a terrace, and beyond that, framed by windswept cypress, lay the blue Pacific.

"This is breathtaking," Joelle said, her feet sinking into a rich, red oriental carpet.

"I'll tell Dr. Shire you're here," the housekeeper said. "Make yourself comfortable."

"Thank you."

The woman disappeared from the room, and Joelle thought she should probably take a seat on one of the love seats or the sofa, but she was drawn to the rear of the room and the view.

Looking through one of the arched windows, she could see that the edge of the stone terrace was irregular, cut at rough angles to match the rugged coastline. There should be different words to describe the smidgen of ocean she could see from the balcony of her condominium and the expanse of water and greenery that could be seen from this mansion, she thought. The word *view* simply could not cover both extremes.

Toward the side of the terrace, she spotted a man whose back was to her. He was a gardener most likely, a black man with graying hair and pruning shears in his hands, and he was working on a shrub of some sort. A younger man was grooming something below the level of the terrace. She could just see the top of his head. What a fabulous place to work! But the evidence of servants and caretakers distressed her somehow. Carlynn Shire obviously had plenty of money, and that made Joelle think of her as a con artist, making millions off the desperation of the sick.

"Hello!" The voice came from behind her, and she turned around to see a small woman walk into the room, one hand on a cane.

Joelle smiled at her uncertainly. "Hi," she said. "Dr. Shire?"

"Yes." The woman held out her hand. "Please call me Carlynn."

Joelle shook her hand. "How do you do?" She was surprised to see the cane and the frailty of the woman. This was a healer?

"Have a seat," Carlynn said, pointing to the sofa adjacent to the windows.

Joelle sat on the sofa, and Carlynn took a seat in the leather armchair, lifting her feet onto its matching ottoman with surprising energy and resting her cane against the chair's arm. There was a spryness just beneath the surface of her fragility, as though the woman's body was not quite ready to give in to whatever nature and age had in store for it. Her voice had a lyrical quality, and her gray hair was cut in a short, youthful bob with deep bangs. Her blue eyes were lively, and she wore a short-sleeved navy-blue blouse with a pink-and-blue scarf tied around her neck. There was a bit of dirt on the knees of her pale blue slacks, and Joelle wondered if she might have been help-ing the gardeners in the yard. She looked the type who would not mind getting her fingernails dirty, but would her body allow her to crawl around in a garden? All in all, Carlynn Shire was nothing like Joelle had expected. Somehow, the mystical, gifted woman described by her parents had sounded tall and sinewy and mysterious. There was nothing mysterious about the sev-entyish woman sitting in front of her.

"So." Carlynn leaned forward in her chair. "You are little Shanti Joy."

"Yes." Joelle smiled. "But I go by Joelle D'Angelo now."

Joelle thought she saw understanding in the older woman's smile. "When did you change your name?" she asked.

"When I was ten. My parents and I left the Cabrial Commune then, and even though we were living in Berkeley, the name Shanti was just a bit much for me." She grinned. "So I took a combination of my parents' names. John and Ellen."

"Ah," Carlynn nodded. "That's how I came by my name, too. Only Carlynn is a combination of my grandparents' names—Carl and Lena."

Joelle cocked her head to one side. "Do you remember when I was born?" she asked.

"Yes, certainly."

"Do you think you really healed me, or do you think I sim-ply started breathing, finally? Forgive my skepticism."

"It's difficult to know, Joelle," she said, using her chosen name easily. "I put my hands on you. You began to breathe, whether it was a coincidence or not. Neither you nor I will ever know. But here you are, alive, looking lovely, and that's what matters."

"I guess so," Joelle said. "But just in case it was a true...heal-ing, I'm glad you were there."

"I am, too." Carlynn narrowed her gaze at her. "But what brings you here now?" she asked.

"I have a friend," Joelle began. "Mara. She had an aneurysm

that left her with severe brain damage. She's in a nursing home, and she's not expected to regain any more of her functioning. I know it's a long shot, especially since I am, as I already pointed out, a skeptic—" she smiled at Carlynn "—but I thought it was at least worth talking to you about it, because there's no other hope. Do you think there's anything you could do for her?"

She expected Carlynn to smile with sympathy and tell her, as the woman over the phone had already made clear, that she no longer took special requests for healings. So she was surprised when the older woman settled back in the leather chair as though expecting a long conversation and said, "Tell me more about this friend of yours."

Joelle was not certain what to say. What information would help a healer? "Well, she was a psychiatrist, and she—"

"No," Carlynn interrupted her, but her voice was soft and kind. She stood up and, without her cane, walked slowly across the room to sit facing Joelle on the sofa. "Tell me about Mara through *your* eyes, Joelle," she said. "What was *your* experience of your friend?"

Instantly, Joelle pictured her best friend in a collage of images. Laughing with her on a hike, talking with her about a case in the hallway of the Women's Wing, holding Liam's hand as she struggled to give birth to her son, lying in the nursing home asleep, her jaw slack, her head rolled forward.

Mara.

Joelle was going to cry. The sensation came over her suddenly, and she felt the liquid burn in her eyes, the swelling of her nose. She pressed her hand to the side of her face.

"I'm sorry," she said as a tear slipped over her fingers.

"Nothing to be sorry for." Carlynn stood up again and walked over to the end table near the leather chair for a box of tissues, which she brought back to Joelle, setting it between them on the sofa. "She's obviously someone you care for deeply," she said, taking her seat near Joelle again.

Joelle could only nod, pulling a tissue from the box and pressing it to her eyes. "She was my best friend." She choked the words out, and Carlynn nodded.

"Take your time," she said.

It was another minute before Joelle could continue.

"I started working as a social worker at Silas Memorial ten years ago, when I was twenty-four, just out of graduate school. I was pretty green. The opening they had was in the maternity unit, so that was where I landed. The second day that I was there, I was given this difficult case." Joelle smiled to herself. "At least, it seemed difficult to me back then. It was a woman who had lost a baby and was slipping into severe postpartum psychosis. I needed to get a psychiatrist in for a consultation. Someone recommended I contact Mara Steele, so I called her, and she came in to see the patient. I couldn't believe it when I saw her. That she was an M.D., I mean. She was only twenty-six years old, but she was one of those kids who just flew through high school and college and then on to medical school."

Carlynn nodded. "She already sounds quite special," she said.

"Yes," Joelle agreed. "Her expertise was in working with maternity issues—pregnancy loss, infertility, neonatal intensive care, that sort of thing. She was drawn to that type of work, even though she never wanted a baby of her own.

"Anyhow, it was late in the day after she'd seen the patient, and she suggested we get something to eat and discuss the case over dinner. Dinner lasted four hours." Joelle smiled at Carlynn with the memory. She and Mara had talked about the patient, yes, but that conversation had segued into everything else under the sun. Joelle told her about Rusty, whom she had married only weeks before. How she had met him in graduate school, how he had dropped out to pursue a career in computers. He was making more money than she would ever make as a social worker, and she knew it had been the right move for him: he'd never been cut out for working with people. Rusty and machinery were a far better fit. She'd been attracted to his intelligence, and perhaps, as she later admitted to herself, to the fact that her parents thought he was completely wrong for her. She should have listened to them.

Mara had talked about her lack of a social life. The previous years had been dedicated to her education and to getting a private practice off the ground, and she'd had little time for men. Joelle knew that Mara would have trouble finding a man who was not threatened by her intelligence, education and beauty. Back then, Mara had worn her shimmery dark hair to her shoulders. She had intense, large, dark brown eyes, clear fair skin, and was undeniably extraordinary-looking. Sitting with Mara in the restaurant that night, Joelle had felt physically small, girlish and simple, although Mara did nothing to intentionally cause that feeling in her. She treated Joelle as a peer, and by the end of the evening, they had made a date to go hiking together over the weekend.

"We hiked for hours that Saturday, and we got so close, closer than I've ever been with another friend," Joelle said to Carlynn. "I knew I could tell her anything. I really admired her and held her up on a pedestal, but as time went on, our friendship became much more of an equal partnership. She was like a sister. I'd never had a sister, and Mara met that need for me and then some." Joelle hoped that the mention of a sister would not bring back bad memories for Carlynn, but it was the truth. The forever bond that sisters possessed best described what she'd had with Mara.

She noticed, with embarrassment, that she had twisted the tissue into a long rope, and she set it down on her lap. Did Carlynn really want to hear all this?

"Have I told you enough?" she asked the older woman, who shook her head.

"You're just getting started," Carlynn said.

That pleased her, because she was finding an unexpected comfort in this telling.

"I fixed her up with her husband," Joelle said. "There was this guy who started working in the social work department a few years after Mara and I had become friends. His name is Liam. He's attractive, smart and just a nice guy—" she felt her cheeks growing hot and quickly continued "—and he played folk music semiprofessionally at some of the clubs in town. Mara was also into folk music. She played guitar and she sang, but just as a hobby. I knew Liam was single and hoping to meet someone, but he seemed resistant to being fixed up. So I had a party and invited both of them. I told everyone to bring musical instruments, even if it meant a comb with tissue paper over it, which it did in my case." Rusty had hated the idea. He'd endured the get-together rather than enjoyed it. Remembering how poorly he'd fit into her social scene made her cringe.

"So everyone came," she said, "and we had a great time. By ten o'clock, Liam and Mara were singing and playing their guitars together, which was exactly what I'd hoped would happen, and by midnight they were off in another room, working out different songs, teaching each other their favorites. By one o'clock, they'd put down their guitars and were deep in conversation. Everyone else had left, so I just closed the door to the room they were in, while Rusty and I cleaned up and went to bed. They were gone in the morning, but that was the start of their relationship."

Liam and Mara had thanked her over and over again once they realized her role in bringing them together. They'd never stopped thanking her.

"I'm telling you way too much," Joelle said.

"No, honey, you're not." Carlynn moved a bit closer and took her hands, holding them on her knees. The older woman's hands were delicate and bony, with a yellowish cast to the dry, warm skin. "Tell me about their wedding," she said.

"Well," Joelle said, feeling only a bit awkward with the new intimacy between herself and the healer. "They were married a couple of years later, on the beach at Asilomar. I was their matron of honor." She recalled her happiness at seeing her two friends together, a happiness that was tinged with envy because she knew she and Rusty would never have the sort of relationship Mara and Liam enjoyed. "They started playing together at clubs then. They called themselves Sommers and Steele, and they had a real following."

Occasionally, she would be in the audience at a club where they were performing, and they would play the song they'd written for her—a funny, poignant song of teasing gratitude for fixing them up—that would make her blush and the audience laugh.

"Mara didn't want to have children, as I mentioned. It was the one thing we were always in disagreement about, because I wanted children so badly and Rusty and I couldn't seem to get pregnant." For a moment, the sense of fullness in her belly teased her, but she tried to ignore it. "Mara was afraid. I mean *deeply* afraid. She had dreams that things would go wrong if she got pregnant or that she'd inadvertently harm her baby because she couldn't take good care of it. Her work focused on everything that could go wrong with pregnancy and childbirth. Day in, day out, that's what she dealt with, so naturally, that affected her. Plus—" Joelle looked through the arched window at the cypress trees "—she really wasn't crazy about kids to begin with. We'd be someplace, the mall or somewhere, and I'd be oohing and aahing over a toddler or a baby, and she'd look right through them. If you talked to her about her goals, they would all be oriented toward her career. But Liam wanted children, and I know it was a source of tension between them, because I'd get dragged into it from time to time." She looked apologetically at Carlynn. "I'm really rambling," she said.

"That's good." Carlynn gave her hands a squeeze. "Keep on rambling."

Carlynn might not be able to heal anyone, Joelle thought, but she certainly had the patience of a saint.

"I saw Mara socially," she continued, "even after she was married. We still got together a couple of times a week. We took an aerobics class, and later on, yoga. We went out to dinner or lunch, and I would hear her side of the having-children issue, her fears and concerns. Then at work, Liam would tell me how much he longed for a child. I have to admit, I could relate to Liam's longing more than I could to Mara's fear, although I certainly understood it, given the work she did."

Joelle stopped talking for a moment, looking out the arched window again, where the old gardener was sweeping the terrace.

"I think," she said finally, "that I pushed her too hard." She looked at Carlynn. "I'm afraid I talked her into it. To getting pregnant."

"It's not talking that gets one pregnant," Carlynn said with a smile.

"But I kept telling her that everything would be all right. That she could go to Rebecca Reed, the best OB in town, and that she would love her own child, even if she'd never cared about other peoples' children. Liam and I both pushed her. And she loved Liam so much..." Her voice cracked, but she got control of herself quickly. "She wanted to please him. So she finally got pregnant, and her pregnancy turned out to be really easy, and I think she was actually starting to look forward to the baby. And, partly because I work in the maternity unit, and partly because I was a very close friend to both of them, they invited me to be in the delivery room with them when the baby was born. They were going to be in the family birthing room, which is a very homey environment."

Carlynn nodded.

"Everything was fine at first. But as things progressed, Mara suddenly started screaming that her head hurt. She was grabbing her head." Joelle's tears started again at the horrific memory, and she removed one of her hands from Carlynn's to pull another tissue from the box. "It was terrible," she said, not bothering to raise the tissue to her eyes. "She had a convulsion, and then she was unconscious. Liam and I didn't know *what* was going on. They rushed her into the operating room and performed a C-section, then they took her upstairs to X ray to get an MRI or a CAT scan, I don't remember which. We were hoping, Liam and I, that she had just passed out from the pain, but deep down we knew it was something more. Something terrible. I think we both knew that Mara's worst fears were coming true."

"How terrible for all of you." Carlynn clutched her hand, her smile completely gone.

"I feel guilty," Joelle said. "And Liam feels even worse. He's lost a wife, her son has no mother. I've lost my dearest friend, and her patients have lost their doctor. One of them committed suicide when she learned that Mara was never coming back to her practice."

"Were you ever able to get pregnant yourself?" Carlynn asked. "Do you have children?"

Joelle shook her head. "No, and it finally split my husband and me up. We were divorced two years ago."

"I'm sorry," Carlynn said.

Joelle waved away her sympathy with her free hand. "We were never a good match," she said. "The infertility just brought us to the end of our marriage sooner than we would have reached it otherwise, but I don't think children would have saved our marriage."

"And do you have a boyfriend now?"

The question seemed far off the subject, but she shook her head, anyway. "No." She smiled weakly. "I'm just taking things one day at a time."

"And now Mara is...what sort of condition is she in?" Carlynn asked.

"She's in a nursing home because they gave up on her in rehab. She can't do anything, really, and they never expect her to be able to. She can use one arm and move her head, but that's about it. The thing is, she smiles a lot. She smiles more than she did when she was..." She almost said alive, but caught herself. "Than she did before. Sometimes, when someone has brain damage, it can cause them to feel unnaturally high—"

"Euphoric." Carlynn nodded, and Joelle remembered that she was talking to a doctor.

"Right. And that's what's happened in her case. Which is both a blessing and a curse. At least she's not suffering. But we want her back. Liam and I. And her little boy, Sam, who is such a doll." She pressed the tissue to her nose, afraid she was going to start crying once again.

"I'll see her," Carlynn said.

"You will?" Joelle was surprised. "Thank you!"

Carlynn squeezed her hand again, then let go and stood up. "I don't know my schedule yet for the next few weeks, but if you could call me in a couple of days, I should be able to set up a date to see her. And you'll go with me, of course, all right?"

"Yes, that would be—"

They both turned at the sound of footsteps entering the room. A tall, elderly man with a wild shock of white hair stood in the doorway.

"Hi, dear," Carlynn said. "Joelle, this is my husband, Alan." She walked over to the armchair and picked up her cane, then started toward the man.

Joelle stood up and walked to the doorway to shake Alan Shire's hand. He was unsmiling, staring at her with frank curiosity. He looked as though he was in his eighties, at least a decade older than Carlynn.

"Hello," she said. "I was just about to leave. I came to ask Carlynn if she would see a friend of mine."

Alan raised his eyebrows at his wife. "And you said?" he asked her.

"It's a very special case," Carlynn said. "Especially since Joelle was the baby born at that commune down in Big Sur. Remember?"

He looked at his wife stupidly, as though not understanding

her words, and his lips were turned down in a scowl. Then he shifted his gaze to Joelle, forcing her to look away in discomfort. He was odd, she thought. Perhaps he suffered from Alzheimer's. Whatever his problem, he was hardly a good advertisement for Carlynn's ability to heal someone with brain damage.

Carlynn walked her out to her car, where she shook Joelle's hand, pressing it between her own.

"You call me in a few days, honey," she said.

"I will." Joelle got into her car and turned it around in the wide driveway, catching sight of Alan Shire's stern face at the front window as she passed. She waved at him, but received no response. Surely he was suffering from dementia. But whatever the cause of his reaction to her visit, she quickly forgot about it as she left the driveway and pulled onto the Seventeen Mile Drive. She could still feel the warmth of Carlynn's hands.

CHAPTER ELEVEN

Three days after visiting the Kling Mansion, Joelle sat in her office writing a report on a patient, keenly aware that on the other side of the thin wall dividing her office from his, Liam was talking on the phone. Although it was difficult to make out exactly what he was saying, it was clear he was arranging home health care for one of his patients. His voice was cordial and calm, not too deep, not too high, and she realized how much she missed hearing him sing. She didn't think he had picked up his guitar once since Mara's aneurysm.

Tonight she planned to call Carlynn Shire to schedule the visit with Mara. She was firm in her decision to keep Liam from learning about the woman's involvement. He would either scoff at her foolishness or simply forbid her to subject Mara to more unnecessary treatment. She didn't know which reaction she would get from him, but one thing was certain: he would not think that involving a healer was a good or useful idea. She knew herself that it was impossibly out of character for her to even consider it.

Carlynn Shire had been charismatic in a quiet, peaceful way. If anyone had told Joelle that she would sit for a half hour or more, holding someone other than a lover's hands while revealing her feelings, she would have cringed at the thought. Yet having Carlynn hold her hands had been comfortable as well as comforting. Joelle was a trained counselor; she knew all about active listening, and she knew that Carlynn's attentiveness had gone way beyond the norm, even after Joelle had rambled on far too long. How good it had felt to pour out all of Mara's story and her involvement in it to another human being! Of course, she had not poured the part that desperately needed pouring. And that she could never do.

Mara would have been the one person to whom Joelle could have confessed what she'd done. She could have told Mara that she was in love with her best friend's husband and that she was torn apart with guilt over having slept with him while her friend lay helpless in a nursing home. If Mara were well and could serve once again as Joelle's confidante—and the husband in question were, of course, not Mara's—how would she respond to that revelation? What would she say? What guidance would she offer? Mara was big on morals and ethics, but then so was Joelle. She had never done anything so flat out wrong in her life, and the experience was still tangled up in her mind and her heart. How could she regret that night, when they had comforted one another in the deepest way a man and woman could? Yet, if it cost her their friendship, and it certainly seemed to have done that, she would regret it always.

Lifting her fingers from the keyboard of her computer, she rested her hands on her belly, uncertain if the slight rise of flesh beneath her palms was the growing fetus or the product of not working out. Ten and a half weeks now. Last night, observing her body in a full-length mirror, she'd noticed that the blue-green veins in her belly and breasts were clearly visible beneath the skin, and her waistline was just starting to thicken. How long would it be before people began talking about her behind her back? She could imagine the social work department's receptionist, Maggie, saying to Liam, "Gee, Joelle's gettin' a little chunky, isn't she?"

The intercom on her desk buzzed, and she lifted the phone to her ear.

"There's a doc here to see you," Maggie said.

A doctor? Her first thought was that Rebecca Reed had somehow guessed she was pregnant and wanted to have a heart-to-heart talk with her.

"Who is it?" Joelle asked.

"Your name again?" Maggie asked, her voice muted a bit, and Joelle couldn't hear the doctor's answer. Then the receptionist was back on the line. "Dr. Alan Shire."

What was Carlynn Shire's odd, elderly husband doing here? She remembered him from the other day at the Kling Mansion, when he'd looked at her with a confused disapproval that she'd guessed to be a symptom of dementia. She certainly could not have him come back here to her office, where Liam might be able to overhear their conversation.

"I'll be right out," she said, then hung up the phone and got to her feet.

Though quite old, Alan Shire was an imposing figure in the small reception area of the social work department. He seemed taller than he had in the high-ceilinged living room of the mansion, his hair looked whiter but less disheveled, and the expression on his face was not one of confusion, but rather of deep and genuine concern. She reached her hand toward him.

"Nice to see you again, Dr. Shire," she said. His hand felt large and strong in her own. "We'll be in the conference room," she said to Maggie. She led her visitor down the narrow hallway to the comparatively large room at the end, the one room that was truly soundproofed from the rest of the social work office.

"Please, have a seat." She motioned to one of the tweed and wood chairs surrounding the long table and sat in the chair adjacent to him. "What can I do for you?" she asked.

He leaned forward in the chair, his long arms resting on the table, the fingertips touching. "I've come to appeal to your good judgment as a social worker," he said.

She wished he would smile or show some lightness in his face. He had probably been handsome as a young man, although right now he looked worried and tired. In no way, though, did he look confused or slow or demented.

"What do you mean?" she asked.

"My wife...Carlynn...is retired," he said, his blue eyes locked on her face. "She's done no work for the center for nearly ten years, and it's been wonderful to see her so relaxed and free." He did smile a bit now. "She dabbles in the garden. She takes care of the house," he said. "There's little for her to worry about. When she was involved with patients, though, she always carried their problems around with her, trying to figure out how to help them. I don't want to see her in that position again."

"I understand," she said. "But, Dr. Shire, I don't think I twisted her arm. I simply told her about my friend, and she said she would like to meet her." She tried to remember their conversation, examining her approach to determine if she had been coercive in any way. Unless tears could be counted as coercion, she could not see that she had.

"Yes, of course she would say she would help," he said. "Carlynn's a very caring person. She doesn't like to see anyone suffer if she thinks there's some way she can help. But you have no idea what healing takes out of her. It's frightening, really. She's exhausted afterward, sometimes for days. I'm concerned about her."

For some reason, she did not believe him. There was nothing in his demeanor to suggest he was lying to her—in fact, he seemed nothing if not sincere—yet his words struck her as less than honest. Perhaps it was his own needs that would not be served if Carlynn were to get involved in healing again. Perhaps he had grown tired of sharing her with the rest of the world.

But then she remembered the cane. The woman's frailty.

"Is she ill?" she asked.

He hesitated a moment before answering. "Yes, she's quite ill, actually," he said. "She needs her rest. And I would hate to see her go through that sort of all-consuming exhaustion that results from her healings."

"I understand," Joelle said. She wanted to ask him what was wrong with Carlynn, but thought better of it. Suddenly, she recalled her parents' one concern about her contacting the healer: seeing Shanti Joy might trigger unhappy memories of Carlynn's sister's death.

"I was a little worried, anyway," she said to Alan. "I was afraid that seeing me might remind her of when her sister died, since my birth and her sister's death both took place in Big Sur, just days apart."

He actually lit up, his eyes wide. *"Yes."* He nodded. "That's another concern I have. I didn't know you knew about her sister, because you were...well—" he grinned, his teeth still white and straight and obviously his own "—just a couple of days old. I don't know if you realize what a toll that accident took on Carlynn, herself, both physically and emotionally." He licked his dry lips. "I'm just so afraid that—"

Joelle held up her hands to stop him, knowing now she had no choice but to agree to his wishes. She would have to give up the fantasy of Carlynn healing Mara to save the elderly couple from painful reminders of the past, as well as from an exacerbation of Carlynn's illness. It shouldn't be that hard to let go of the idea; only two weeks earlier, she'd scoffed at it. Yet, she felt undeniable despair at losing the hope, no matter how slim it had seemed.

"I understand," she said. "I won't call her. But will you let her know that? That I've changed my mind? Or would she be upset that you came here?" She felt as though she was probing a bit too deeply into their relationship.

"Oh, no, she won't be upset," he said, standing up. "I'll let her know we talked, and you decided against it. She'll understand. I think she knows that she was promising something she really shouldn't at this time in her life."

His words made her wonder if perhaps Carlynn had sent him here to do her bidding for her.

Alan Shire shook her hand again, bowing slightly. "I'm very grateful to you for being so understanding."

"No problem," Joelle said. "Thank you for coming in."

She led him back to the reception office, where Liam was collecting his mail from the wooden mailboxes on the wall. She pointed Dr. Shire in the direction of the elevators, then checked her own mailbox, although she had already emptied it earlier.

"How's your day going?" she asked Liam.

"Good," he said, barely glancing in her direction as he sorted through the mail in his hands. "Yours?"

"Fine," she said.

"That's good." He turned and headed out the door into the hall.

Walking toward her office, she bit back tears over the emptiness of the perfunctory exchange. No smile from Liam. No "Let's get a cup of coffee on our break." Nothing. She had truly lost him.

The only part of him she had left was growing inside her.

CHAPTER TWELVE

San Francisco, 1956

Lisbeth turned off the Dictaphone and pulled the two sheets of white paper, along with the carbon paper, from the typewriter. Opening the medical chart on her desk, she carefully attached the typed report to the prongs at the top of the manila folder, tossed the overused piece of carbon paper in the trash can, then filed the copy of the medical report in the four-drawer gray metal filing cabinet on the other side of the room.

At the sound of the tinkling bell hanging from the front door, she looked across the counter between her small office and the waiting area to see a young mother walk into the room, her six- or seven-year-old son at her side.

Lisbeth glanced quickly at the appointment book, then looked up as the woman approached the counter.

"Good morning, Mrs. Hesky," she said. "And good morning, Richard. How are the two of you today?"

"We're fine," the woman said. "Just here for Richie's booster shot."

"Ah, yes." Lisbeth could see by the stark white, unsmiling expression on Richard's face that he was not looking forward to getting a shot. That was the only thing she disliked about working in a pediatrician's office—it was filled with scared little children. Lloyd Peterson was known as one of the kindest pediatricians in all of San Francisco, but that made little difference when he had a syringe in his hand.

"Have a seat," Lisbeth said. "Dr. Peterson will be with you in a moment."

She moved Richard Hesky's folder from her desk to the table near her office door, where Lloyd would know to look for it, then began to file the stack of folders he'd left her from the day before.

This office was very much hers. Lisbeth had been working for Lloyd Peterson for six years, ever since her graduation from secretarial school, and his office had been in complete disarray when she'd arrived. His previous secretary had been eighty years old at the time of her retirement, and she must have had failing vision, because the charts were misfiled and there was simply no system to the running of the office. Lisbeth had relished the challenge of bringing order to the place, and Dr. Peterson often told her he couldn't do without her.

She loved working in a medical office. She had no fear of blood or broken bones or germs, only a fascination for the miracles modern medicine could perform. Like the new polio vaccine. Yes, the shots hurt and the children cried, but, oh, what lifesavers they were! She was always picking Dr. Peterson's brain about the various medical conditions of his patients.

She looked over the counter to the waiting room, where Mrs. Hesky was engrossed in a magazine. Richard was ignoring the toys in the play area as he sat in a chair next to his mother, swinging his legs in an anxious rhythm, and Lisbeth could almost feel his fear from her desk.

"Richard," Lisbeth said, and he looked over at her. "Come here for a minute, please."

The little boy glanced at his mother, who nodded, then walked very slowly toward the counter. Lisbeth leaned toward him, as though telling him a secret.

"There's a trick to making a shot barely hurt at all," she said. "Want to hear it?"

He nodded, his brown eyes huge.

"Wiggle your toes when you're getting it," she said.

"Wiggle my toes?" There was the hint of a smile on his face.

"Yes, absolutely." She nodded. "Now, it's hard to wiggle your toes when you have your shoes on, so tell Dr. Peterson you have to take your shoes off first, okay?"

"Does it really work?" He looked so hopeful, Lisbeth wanted to reach across the counter to hold his little face in her hands and give him a kiss on the forehead.

"I promise," she said. "But you have to wiggle them *hard*."

"Okay." He nodded conspiratorially, then trotted back to the seat next to his mother.

The wiggling *would* work, she knew as she returned to her filing. The children focused so hard on moving their toes that the shot was given before they even realized what was happening. Dr. Peterson thought she was a genius for coming up with the technique.

The real medical genius in the Kling family, though, was Carlynn. She was in her fourth year of medical school at the University of California, spending almost all her time this year at San Francisco General Hospital, a few blocks from Dr. Peterson's office. Lisbeth had wanted to go to medical school—or at least to nursing school—herself, but she'd panicked at the thought of college, fearful that she would not get in, or once in, that she would not be able to keep up. She felt angry at herself for not working harder throughout her school years, and she was angry at her parents for providing her with what she had long ago realized was the lesser education. Sometimes she was angry at Carlynn, as well, although she knew the situation was not truly her twin's fault.

So, she'd opted for secretarial school instead, hoping to work in a medical setting. She did not regret her choice; there was no one better at whipping an office into shape, and for the first time in her life she felt valuable. She was full of innovative ideas to make Dr. Peterson's office run smoothly, and was often asked by other physicians to train their secretaries and receptionists in some of the methods she used.

She had followed Carlynn to San Francisco, although not without her sister's encouragement. Carlynn may have been smarter, more beautiful and better educated, but she was still Lisbeth's twin, and the love between the two of them, though sometimes tinged with resentment or annoyance, was strong. They met at least once a week for lunch, and occasionally saw each other on the weekends, although this year Carlynn's free time outside the hospital was quite limited.

Carlynn had told her she'd have time for lunch today, though, and Lisbeth was supposed to meet her at noon at a delicatessen halfway between the hospital and Dr. Peterson's office. It was now eleven, and although she was looking forward to the time with her sister, she wished Gabriel would hurry up and call. What if he called at ten to twelve? Then she'd only have a minute to talk to him before turning the call over to Dr. Peterson.

Gabriel Johnson was Dr. Peterson's tennis partner. He usually called Dr. Peterson on Tuesdays and Thursdays to make sure their schedules would allow them to meet on the doctor's private tennis court for a game after work. Of course, Lisbeth was always the one to answer the phone, and lately, Gabriel had been keeping her on the phone for a while. One time, for thirty minutes! He asked her questions about herself and seemed genuinely interested in her answers. He told her he'd heard about her reputation as an "office manager," and she'd loved that he used that term instead of "secretary." She was so much more than a secretary, and he seemed to know that. Although she'd never met him, sometime in the last few months she'd started fantasizing about him, wondering what he looked like. She pictured him looking like Rock Hudson, although his voice was deeper. Or maybe he was blond, like James Dean, his hair sun-streaked from the tennis courts.

The last time he called, Gabriel had asked her if she played tennis.

She'd looked down at her lap, where her white uniform stretched across her soft thighs. "No," she'd said. "I did when I was a child, but not in years."

"I'll have to get you out there someday," he said. That was the closest he'd come to actually suggesting a date between the two of them, and it both elated and troubled her. How could she ever let him see her?

"Maybe," she'd said.

"What do you like to do for fun?" he asked.

I eat. That would be the honest answer.

"Oh, I like the water," she said. "I used to like to sail." She hadn't sailed since that fateful day with her father, but it *was* something she missed.

"Aha!" Gabriel said. "Did Lloyd mention that I have a sailboat?"

She was embarrassed. She did recall Dr. Peterson mentioning that fact, perhaps as long as a year ago. Would Gabriel think she was hinting at a commonality between them? She would never know, because right at that moment Dr. Peterson had walked into her office, and she'd had no choice but to turn Gabriel over to him, saving her answer to his question for the next time he called.

Now Dr. Peterson stepped into her office again and picked up Richie Hesky's chart.

"Let him take off his shoes," Lisbeth whispered to him, and Lloyd Peterson smiled his understanding at her. "Are you playing tennis tonight?" she asked, trying to sound casual, hoping it was not obvious to him that she was yearning for Gabriel to call.

"Not tonight," he said, leafing through Richie's chart. "Gabe's tied up in meetings." He poked his head around the corner of her office into the waiting room.

"Richard? Come with me, son."

Well, darn. No chance to talk to Gabriel today. She was being ridiculous, anyway; she was hardly in his league. Gabriel was the chief accountant at San Francisco General. He was certainly older than she was, maybe by many years. And the truth was, if she had an opportunity to meet the man, she would turn it down. That meeting, she knew, would put an end to their long phone conversations.

At twenty-six years of age, Lisbeth weighed two hundred pounds. Although she had a few girlfriends who worked for other doctors in the area, she still found most of her solace in food. She'd given up trying to emulate Carlynn's style of dress, and she wore her short blond hair in petal curls she set with bobby pins every night before going to bed.

Carlynn, on the other hand, was the same one hundred and fifteen pounds she'd been when she graduated from high school, and just last week she'd started wearing her long hair in a new do called a French twist, which she said kept it out of her way when she was working. She looked, Lisbeth thought, sophisticated and beautiful, and there were times, mostly in private, when Lisbeth had difficulty keeping her jealousy of her sister in check.

At eleven forty-five, Lisbeth left the office and walked the few blocks to the deli where she was to meet Carlynn. She was first to arrive, as usual, and as she carried two ham and cheese sandwiches from the deli counter to one of the small tables by the window, she hoped her sister would show up. Carlynn's hospital schedule was not often predictable, and on a couple of occasions Lisbeth had watched the hands on the clock above the deli counter tick by as she gave up on her sister and ate lunch alone.

Today, though, Carlynn arrived at ten after twelve, and she was breathless, probably having run from the hospital.

She kissed Lisbeth's cheek, then took a seat across the table from her.

"I talked to Mother last night," Carlynn said, pulling one of the sandwiches to her side of the table.

"Is her eyesight any better?" Lisbeth asked.

"She said it's still fuzzy. I gave her the name of a doctor to see in Monterey. I wish I could be there to go with her, but I really can't get away."

Delora had been complaining about problems with her vision, asking Carlynn to come home and "heal" her. Carlynn didn't have time to breathe, much less make the trip to Cypress Point, but Lisbeth supposed it was only a matter of time before her twin would go, and she would have to decide if she wanted to accompany her or not.

Lisbeth always had mixed feelings about going home and rarely dared to go alone, needing Carlynn to serve as a buffer between Delora and herself. Delora would always shake her head in disgust as soon as Lisbeth walked in the front door of the mansion, and she'd badger her constantly about her weight, insulting her in front of the servants and anyone else who happened to be present. Lisbeth usually brought hidden food home with her because she didn't dare eat as much as she wanted to at mealtimes, when Delora watched her every mouthful from across the table.

Yet there was nowhere in the world that stirred Lisbeth's heart more than the setting of her childhood home. In spite of the strong pickle-and-coleslaw smell of the delicatessen, it took her only a second to conjure up the scent of the sea and the cypress trees and the way the air felt when a blanket of fog rolled over the house. Cypress Point was as familiar to her as her own face— and far better loved. She knew she would accompany Carlynn if she decided to go home. Spending a few days at Cypress Point was worth any humiliation her mother might dish out.

"So." Carlynn swallowed a bite of her sandwich and smiled at her. "How are you? You're hair looks pretty."

"Thanks," Lisbeth said, touching the waves, wondering if

they looked any different today to elicit Carlynn's comment, but guessing that her sister was just being nice. "I'm fine. I'm reading *Peyton Place*. Have you read it?"

Carlynn shook her head. "I wish I had time to read something other than medical journals," she said. "I'm swamped. Penny Everett was in town the other day and I couldn't even make time to see her."

"What's she doing these days?" Lisbeth remembered Penny primarily from the night ten years ago, when she'd fallen off the terrace at Cypress Point while necking with her boyfriend. Carlynn, though, had kept in touch with her old friend.

"She's living in Chicago, singing with a choral group that does classical music. Oh!" She interrupted herself, setting her sandwich on the plate and picking up her purse. "Before I forget," she said, drawing her wallet from the purse. "Let me pay you for my sandwich. I got a check from Mother, so I can give you some money."

Delora sent regular checks to Carlynn, but none to Lisbeth, saying that Lisbeth was on her own since she had elected not to go to college. She had paid for Lisbeth's secretarial school, but the money for her had stopped the moment she'd graduated. Delora, however, still sent Carlynn far more than she needed for her school and living expenses, and Carlynn insisted on giving her a portion of it. Lisbeth had long ago stopped arguing about it. She needed the money and figured she deserved it just as much as Carlynn did.

"Thank you." She accepted the bills from Carlynn and slipped them into her own purse.

"Did the man call today?" Carlynn asked. "Dr. Peterson's tennis partner?"

Lisbeth shook her head, her cheeks turning pink. She'd told Carlynn about Gabriel's phone calls, nearly every word of them. But she had not told her his name or that he worked at SF General. Carlynn might try to get a look at him then, and Lisbeth didn't want to hear that he chewed his nails at his desk or was only five feet tall. She preferred her fantasies to reality.

"No, he didn't," she said with a scowl. "They're not playing tonight, so I probably won't get to talk to him until Tuesday."

"Oh, I'm sorry to hear that," Carlynn said. Despite her beauty, Carlynn had no more dates than Lisbeth, and she didn't even have the time for fantasies. She was married to medical school.

Lisbeth would have liked to talk more about Gabriel, but Carlynn suddenly set down her sandwich and turned to look out the window, letting out a great sigh.

"I don't think I can eat," she said.

"What's the matter?" Lisbeth asked.

Carlynn returned her gaze to her sister, the gleam of tears in her eyes. "Oh, this little girl at the hospital."

Lisbeth could have guessed. Carlynn was way too soft. "Carly, honey, you're not going to survive being a doctor if every patient upsets you so much," she said.

"I know, I know. And it's getting harder every day." She leaned across the table as though someone might overhear her. "The more I get to actually work with patients, the harder it is for me not to...you know...help them in my own way."

Lisbeth knew her sister had been careful to keep her gift under wraps at the hospital. She did not want to be seen as different or better than the other students, and she certainly didn't want to be thought of as crazy.

"What's wrong with the little girl?" Lisbeth asked.

"She has a very serious case of pneumonia, probably fatal because it's complicated by a congenital deformity of her lungs." Carlynn looked down at her sandwich, her nose wrinkled. "She's eight, and she's dying. We visit her on rounds every day, and one or two of us listen to her lungs and talk about her as though she wasn't there, and just watch her die." Carlynn looked pained, and Lisbeth wondered, as she had a number of times before, if being a doctor was going to take too much out of her sister.

"And you think you can help?" Lisbeth asked.

"I think I should at least try. But I don't dare. I've thought of sneaking into her room at night, but if I got caught I'd have a hard time explaining what I was doing there. She's still conscious and able to talk. She'd tell someone I'd been there."

Lisbeth knew that Carlynn had, on a few occasions, been able to spend enough time with a patient to touch him, or, as she would say, to "send her energy coursing through his body," but she'd done it quietly, surreptitiously, and only with unconscious patients. She'd told Lisbeth about overhearing a few of her fellow students talk about how strange she was, and Lisbeth knew she was terrified of fueling that assessment of her.

"You have to find a way," Lisbeth said. She knew her sister would never be able to live with herself unless she did.

"How?" Carlynn wrapped up her sandwich, probably saving it for later. Lisbeth's was already gone.

"What about during those rounds you were talking about?" Lisbeth asked. "Can you get near her?"

"Only if the teaching physician chooses me to listen to her lungs. But that would only take a few seconds."

"Not if you can't seem to hear well. Maybe your stethoscope is broken, or for some other reason you need to listen harder and longer than the other students."

Carlynn rolled her eyes. "They'll kick me out of med school," she said. "They already think I'm weird."

"Let's see." Lisbeth lifted her hands, palms up, in the air. "On the one hand, you'll be seen as weird, but the girl might live. On the other hand, you'll be seen as a good and normal doctor, but the girl will probably die."

"Ugh." Carlynn wrinkled her nose again. "Don't say it that way."

"I'm sorry." Lisbeth felt contrite, but only to a degree. "I don't mean to put more pressure on you, honey," she said, "but you went into medicine because you wanted to use your gift. Medical school has been relatively easy for you. You whizzed through all the chemistry and biology courses and whatnot. The hard part for you will be finding a way to combine all that training with what you have naturally. What you never had to go to school to learn."

Carlynn stared at her a moment, then let out her breath.

"You're right," she said. "You're the only person who really understands me, Lizzie, do you know that?"

Carlynn and her fellow medical students, all of them men, made their rounds with Dr. Alan Shire, the teaching physician on the pediatric floor, that afternoon. Although there were a couple of other female medical students in Carlynn's year, the group doing their pediatric rotation was, except for her, composed entirely of men, and that was enough in itself to set her apart from them.

The flock of students moved from patient to patient, and Carlynn grew increasingly anxious as they neared Betsy's room. Although she was still not certain what she would do when they got there, she knew Lisbeth was right: She had to at least make an effort to help the little girl in a way none of the other physicians would even know to try.

Carlynn did not for a moment believe she was any smarter than her twin, but Lisbeth's intelligence was far more down to earth, more in the realm of common sense, than was her own, and sometimes she actually envied that. Carlynn could solve complicated mathematical equations, but when it came to the simpler matters in life, she was often stymied. She wondered if her sister knew how much she depended on her counsel, on the wisdom Lisbeth barely knew she possessed.

Working for Lloyd Peterson had been wonderful for Lisbeth, and Carlynn had loved watching her sister's confidence grow over the past few years. If only her body had not grown with it. Her obesity—for that was, she had to admit, the word for Lisbeth's weight problem—had become an armor around her, protecting her from...Carlynn wasn't sure. Rejection? Love? Even Carlynn's psychiatric rotation had not given her answers to Lisbeth's situation. Whatever the problem, Carlynn had never spoken to Lisbeth about it. Lisbeth got enough negative feedback from their mother and the rest of the world. Carlynn wanted to be her one safe harbor, and she prayed she was not actually doing her sister a disservice by ignoring the problem.

Finally, Carlynn, her fellow students and Dr. Shire reached Betsy's room, but they did not go inside right away. Dr. Shire turned to the group outside Betsy's door.

"This eight-year-old female's condition has deteriorated markedly since our rounds this morning," he said. He discussed the little girl's most recent vital signs and lab results, none of which held out much hope for her recovery. Carlynn did not ordinarily find this particular doctor heartless, but she thought he seemed pleased to have such a serious case to show them. She appreciated the fact, though, that Dr. Shire discussed the child's condition with the students *outside* the patient's room. So many of the doctors spoke in front of the patients, as though they were deaf as well as sick. As though they were not human beings with feelings. She liked Dr. Shire's respect for his patients and the way he treated her like any other student, instead of someone who was less than competent by virtue of being a female. Frankly, she liked everything she knew about Dr. Shire, and she was hoping he would invite one of the students to listen to Betsy's lungs and heart. She was counting on it, and she planned to be the first to volunteer.

Inside Betsy's room Carlynn stood with her fellow students in a semicircle around the child's bed as Dr. Shire listened to the little girl's lungs. She was ready to raise her hand the moment he asked for a volunteer, but she could feel the perspiration forming in her armpits. Did she dare do something in front of Alan Shire and the other students? She knew the male med students already found her a bit peculiar, and not just for being a woman in a man's profession. They would chat among themselves about a particular patient, sharing their uncertainties—and, in some cases, their arrogance—but Carlynn always stood apart from them, both literally and figuratively, as she tried to think of a way to heal. Would it work if she simply poured healing thoughts into a patient as she stood in the room? she'd wonder. She'd experiment often with her gift, and she was doing so right now as she stood at the foot of Betsy's bed.

"How are you feeling this afternoon, Betsy?" Dr. Shire inquired, but the little girl did not respond or even look in his direction. Her gaze was fastened to some point in space, and she was as pale as her pillowcase. Carlynn could hear the rasp of her breathing. She was definitely worse than she had been that morning.

Dr. Shire took Betsy's blood pressure and reported the numbers to the group. Then he straightened up to his full, lanky height and motioned toward the door of the room.

"All right," he said, "let's move on. We're running late today."

Carlynn froze. They couldn't leave. Not yet.

"Dr. Shire?" she asked as the students began to walk past her. "May I listen to her lungs for a moment?"

He hesitated, and the other students waited for him to say they didn't have time, but the doctor studied her, an odd, inquisitive expression in his eyes, and she did not turn away.

"Yes, Miss Kling, you may."

There was a groan from some of the students, but Dr. Shire moved close to the patient again as Carlynn approached the head of Betsy's bed. She didn't care what anyone thought of her. What mattered right now was the life of this little girl.

Carlynn smiled at the youngster, hungry to touch her. Sitting on the edge of the bed, she reached for the girl's hands instead of for her own stethoscope.

"Hi, Betsy," she said. "I'm going to listen to your heart and your lungs, but first I wanted to talk to you for a moment."

Oh, it was hard to send her energy when she was so aware of

the men behind her! Each of those young men would have simply moved toward Betsy, stethoscope in hand, leaning over the
child without making eye contact with her, concentrating on the
bruits and rubs they would hear through the cold metal disk. If
she had her own way, if she could design her intervention any
way she liked, she would spend a long time talking with a patient, then a long time touching them. But with Dr. Shire and
the students at her back, she did not have the luxury of time. So
she struggled to do both: talk and heal.

Betsy was with her, though. Everyone else in the room might
have been a million miles away, but Betsy was right there. Her
gaze, previously vacuous, now locked onto Carlynn's eyes, and
her delicate damp hands relaxed in her gentle grasp.

"What do you want to talk about?" Betsy asked in a small,
hoarse voice.

"About how strong you are." Carlynn expected to hear Dr.
Shire interrupt her at any moment, but she continued, smiling
at the girl. "You're very strong. Even though you are quite sick,
you still have the strength to ask me what I want to talk about.
You're an amazing and very brave girl." She kept her eyes glued
to Betsy's, glad the students and Dr. Shire could not see the in-
tensity of the shared gaze. She did not want to let go of the
child's clammy little hands. Any minute Dr. Shire would tell her
she was wasting time, but she tried not to think about that.

"You have warm and pretty hands," she said. She heard the
students stir behind her and imagined they, too, were waiting,
hoping, Dr. Shire would interrupt her so they could get on their
way. "I'd like to listen to your lungs now," Carlynn said. "Would
that be all right with you?"

Betsy nodded and, with some effort, rolled onto her side, accustomed to the drill. Carlynn rested her stethoscope against the
child's back, but it was merely for show. She placed her hand
flat over the disk, her other hand on the girl's rib cage, just
above her stomach. Closing her eyes, she breathed, imagining

every molecule of her breath flowing through her hands and into the child. She held the position as long as she could without attracting any more attention than she already had from those behind her. As soon as she stood up, she almost keeled over from a sudden weakness in her own body, and she could not help but smile. The weakness was telltale: she had made a difference in this little girl's condition.

"Feel better, sweetheart," she said, resting her hand lightly on Betsy's head. Then she turned away, ignoring the looks from her fellow students.

Dr. Shire cleared his throat. "All right, then," he said. "Let's move on."

Carlynn was last to leave the room. She looked back at Betsy, whose eyes were still on her, and smiled at the little girl, as though they shared a secret. In a way, they did.

Later that afternoon, Dr. Shire paged her over the hospital intercom. It was the first time she had heard herself paged, and it took her a minute to realize that it was *her* name ringing out through the corridors of SF General.

"Miss Kling," Dr. Shire said when she called him on the phone in response to the page. "Do you have a moment to meet me in the cafeteria for a cup of coffee?"

It was an odd invitation, and she swallowed hard, wondering what sort of reprimand he would give her for her behavior in Betsy's room earlier. "Yes," she said. "I can be there in a few minutes."

He was waiting for her in the corner of the doctors' cafeteria, two cups of coffee on the table in front of him.

"Cream or sugar?" he asked, rising as she approached the table. He was being remarkably kind for someone about to chew her out.

"Black," she said, although she wasn't much of a coffee drinker. She knew this meeting was not about coffee, anyway.

Dr. Shire smiled at her, and she began to relax. "The patient we saw on rounds this morning, the little girl, Betsy, appears to be recovering," he said.

"How wonderful," Carlynn said.

"Yes," he said as he stirred his coffee, "how wonderful...and how strange. I listened to her lungs while we were on rounds, as you know, and they were crackling and wheezing and generally—" he looked perplexed "—the lungs of a dying child. I just listened to them a few minutes ago, and they are now very nearly clear."

"That's amazing," she said. "The antibiotic must have—"

"She's been on an antibiotic since the beginning," Dr. Shire interrupted her. He looked down at his cup of coffee. "Miss Kling...Carlynn," he said, "I've been observing you. I know that you are not the...usual medical student, and not just because you are a woman. You are very bright and very knowledgeable, that's for certain, as are most of your fellow UC students. But you deal with the patients in a much more personal way than most of them do. Than most doctors do, don't you?"

"I think it helps to view a patient as a human being rather than merely as a diagnosis. We should treat them the way we would want to be treated."

"Yes, yes, of course." He waved his hand through the air. "But it's more than that, isn't it?" He tilted his head, his eyes on hers as he waited for her answer.

"What do you mean?" she asked.

"You have some sort of...for want of a better word...*gift,* don't you?"

It was Carlynn's turn to stare into her coffee cup. "I'm still not sure what you—"

"I think you understand me," he said. "You weren't just listening to Betsy's lungs this afternoon, were you? As a matter of fact, I'm not sure you listened at all."

She felt herself color. "Of course I listened," she said, uncertain if she was being chastised.

"Carlynn...please be honest with me." He leaned forward. His blue eyes were clear and lovely, his long face handsome. "If you're doing nothing special, at least nothing that you know of, just tell me and I'll drop it. But the truth is, I have a great deal of interest in other ways of treating patients. Other than the usual, that is. I've studied Edgar Cayce and other purported healers, and I've come to believe there's something to it. But if I'm wrong about you, I apologize and—"

"You're not wrong," she said. Her hands began to tremble, and she lowered them from her coffee cup to her lap. Not since those long-ago days when her mother had dragged her from soldier to soldier in Letterman Hospital had she let the outside world in on her secret.

He looked excited. "Then Betsy, and Mr....I don't remember his name...the man with nephritis, and that woman with what we thought was a brain tumor...they all got better unexpectedly. Did you have a hand in that?"

"I may have," she said. "I never really know. Sometimes I'm able to do something, and sometimes I'm not."

"Tell me everything," he said, shoving his coffee cup away from him with disinterest. "Tell me how you do it. What you're feeling. Is religion involved in some way? Are you praying?"

His sudden enthusiasm freed her tongue. Suddenly she was the teacher and he the student. "I don't know how I do it, and no, religion is not involved, at least not religion as we usually think of it."

"Do you feel it happening?" he asked.

"I'm still not certain what the *it* is, but yes, I do feel something happening. A surge of some sort. And I feel..." This was hard to explain. "I feel as though something's been taken out of me and given to them."

"You nearly fainted after you examined Betsy this morning, didn't you?" he asked.

"I felt weak. I don't know if I was going to faint, though. I never have." She launched into the explanation of how she treated a person, an explanation she had given only a few others over the years. She felt not only safe with Dr. Shire, but thrilled that he might give her the opportunity to work in her own way with the patients she saw.

It grew dark outside the cafeteria windows as she told him about her childhood and how she first became aware of her gift, and about how she had determined she should keep quiet about it once she was in medical school, so as not to be seen as a kook.

"You were wise to do that, Carlynn," he said soberly. "I've kept my own interest to myself, and I have to admit, I am incredibly thrilled to discover someone I can talk to about it."

"Dr. Shire—"

"Alan. Call me Alan."

She smiled at him. "Alan. Is there a way...I mean, if I see a patient whom I think I might be able to help...can you arrange it so that I can have more time with them? I've had to do this so surreptitiously."

"Yes," he said. "We'll work it out. But we have to be cautious. You must know that the other students and some of the staff talk about you. They know you're different. They just don't understand in what way yet."

"I know."

"Right now they think it's because you're a woman and you have this nurturing side to you that can't resist sitting and chatting with patients." He grinned at her, his teeth straight and white. "We'll let them think that for now."

"One thing about...what I do..." She shook her head. "I don't understand it. Why does it work sometimes and not others?"

"I don't have the answer, but I'd be happy to share some of the books I'm reading with you. I have a library on the subject."

"Oh, I'd love to see it!" she said.

"Then you will. It's at my house, though. Do you mind that you'll have to come over and—"

"No. Of course not."

"We'll have to keep that quiet, as well, you understand. A female medical student and a physician... People would really talk then."

She suddenly had a thought. "Do you have this...this gift, too, Dr. Shire? Alan?"

"No," he said. "I don't, but I wish I did. I've wondered if any ordinary person could develop it, but I've come to think not." He ran a hand through his light brown hair and shook his head. "I just have a deep belief that we're missing the boat somehow in medicine, Carlynn." He looked her squarely in the eye. "I'd love for you and me to be partners in trying to find it."

CHAPTER THIRTEEN

Sam ran into Liam's arms on the sidewalk outside the nursing home, and Liam lifted the little boy up and gave him a kiss on the cheek. Leaning back in his arms, Sam placed his two small palms on Liam's cheeks.

"I love you, Dada," he said, clear as day. They were his new words, and he used them frequently, but always appropriately. Delighted, Liam hugged him tighter. At fifteen months, Sam was either getting bigger, or Liam was getting weaker, because he could really feel the weight of his son in his arms now. Before, carrying Sam had been like holding a pillow filled with feathers.

"I love you, too," Liam said, but before he had a chance to truly savor the moment, Sam began wriggling to be let down again. Reluctantly, Liam lowered him to the ground and took a seat on the bench next to Sheila.

"How are you, Sheila?" he asked, his eye still on his son.

Sam began running in circles around the white wishing well, which stood on the lawn near the sidewalk. He could actually run now, not very steadily, but with some genuine speed, and Liam grinned as he watched him chase his invisible prey.

"Oh, I'm all right." Sheila sounded tired. She rubbed her hand on the back of her neck and rolled her head on her shoulders. "Sam and I had a bit of a rough day," she added. "He had his first spanking. At least, his first from me."

"What?" Liam turned to look at her, unable to hide the shock in his face. Sheila did not seem to notice, though.

"He threw a tantrum in the grocery store." Her eyes looked tired as she watched Sam lift himself awkwardly to his tiptoes as he tried to peer over the edge of the well. "He's advanced for his age, I guess." She chuckled. "Moving into the terrible twos at fifteen months."

Liam tried to stay calm, afraid that if he let her see the anger building inside him, she wouldn't tell him the truth about what happened.

"What do you mean by tantrum?" he asked.

"Oh, you know. The usual." She glanced at him. "Or maybe you don't know, not having had a child before. He was grabbing things he thought he wanted from the shelves, yelling his head off when I took them away from him. He sat down on the floor in the middle of the aisle and wouldn't stop screaming."

"He probably just needed a nap." Liam watched Sam drop into a sitting position and begin slapping his hands against the stucco of the wishing well. He tried to picture Sheila hitting the little boy in the middle of the grocery store. *Hitting* him. For being a normal fifteen-month-old boy. Liam clenched his fists in his lap.

"He'd already had a nap," Sheila countered. "He was just being a bad boy. I told him if he didn't settle down, he'd get a spanking. And he kept right on screaming. So, when we got home I turned him over my knee."

Liam practically jumped from the bench, turning to face Sheila with his hands held in front of him, fingers spread as though he was trying to keep himself from strangling her.

"Not okay!" He said the only two words he seemed able to

force from his mouth. "That's not okay, Sheila! I don't want anyone hitting my son. *Ever.*"

"Oh, Liam, I didn't *hit* him. I didn't leave a mark on him." She put one hand over her eyes to block out the sun as she looked up at him. "I *spanked* him. Parents have been spanking their kids since Adam and Eve. Weren't you ever spanked?"

"No. I wasn't." His voice was growing louder, and a woman walking up the path to the nursing home glanced at him as she passed by. He didn't care who heard him. "Not ever," he said. "It's barbaric. It teaches children that violence is a solution. How could you do that to him? How could you hurt him? You, who made me baby-proof every inch of my house? He—"

"Liam, you're really being silly." Sheila wore a patronizing smile he wanted to wipe from her face. "I gave him a few gentle swats on his bottom while he was turned over my knee. How else can you teach a fifteen-month-old right from wrong? You can't explain it to him."

"Do you honestly think he had a clue why he was being punished?" Liam asked. He paced three feet in one direction and three feet back, pounding his fist into the palm of his other hand. "He misbehaved in the grocery store for whatever reason. For a reason our grown-up minds can't fathom. For reasons that had meaning to him. Then you warn him you'll spank him, when he hasn't ever heard the word before. And then you do it when you get *home*. How is he supposed to make a connection? I mean, even if it could possibly be considered an appropriate form of punishment?"

"Well, he knows the word now." Sheila pursed her lips. "He'll know what I mean the next time I say it."

"There won't *be* a next time, Sheila." Liam stopped pacing to look at her. "I mean it. This is absolutely nonnegotiable. No one is hitting Sam."

"When they're too young to reason with, there's no other way to—"

"*I* turned out all right," he said. "My parents somehow managed to teach me right from wrong without resorting to...the humiliation...the physical violation of smacking the crap out of me. And Mara would never approve."

"Oh, for heaven's sake," Sheila said. "You're overreacting, Liam. I didn't smack the crap out of him, and you know it. And, as for Mara, she was spanked any number of times."

She was? He hadn't known that. They had never gotten around to discussing how they would discipline their child.

"It doesn't matter," he said. "I still don't think she would approve."

Sam suddenly ran over to him and wrapped his arms around Liam's leg, clinging, obviously aware that something was wrong between his father and his grandmother. Liam rested one hand on top of Sam's head.

"Look," he said to Sheila, attempting to lower the angry pitch of his voice, "I appreciate all you've done for Sam. But please, just promise me you won't hit him again."

"I can't promise that, Liam," she said. "I think you're being absolutely ridiculous."

"I don't want you hitting him!"

Sam let out a wail and clung harder.

"Then I just won't take care of him anymore," Sheila said, standing up. "You can find someone else to do it. And you can pay for it yourself."

Liam closed his eyes in frustration. "That's not what I want," he said. Bending over, he lifted Sam into his arms again, and this time the little boy buried his face against Liam's neck.

"Then I'll spank him when he needs it." Sheila folded her arms across her chest.

Liam couldn't respond. He felt helpless and realized that, if he tried to say something, anything, more to Sheila, his voice would break. He pressed his cheek against Sam's head.

"When Mara is well enough," Sheila said, "she'll agree with me. I can assure you of—"

"She's never going to get well, Sheila!" he said angrily, eliciting another cry from his son, but he couldn't stop himself from spitting the words at her. "Don't you understand that?" he asked. "*Never.* She is in this nursing home for the rest of her life. She's never going to understand that Sam is her son. She doesn't even know you're her mother."

Sheila's face was red, her cheeks puffed out as though they might explode. Turning on her heel, she walked back down the pathway toward the parking lot.

Liam sat on the bench, his body shaking, and watched her go.

"It's okay, Sam," he whispered, and the little boy relaxed against his neck once more. "It's okay, sweetheart."

Although he couldn't see the parking lot because of the landscaping, he heard Sheila's car door slam and the engine turn over, and he felt pleased that she was leaving. He would have to find a way to repair the damage he'd just done to his relationship with her, but he didn't want Sheila in Mara's room with him and Sam today.

"I'm sorry you had a rough day, Sam," he said, rocking the boy a little. "I'm so sorry."

Damn, this was hard! There was so much he wanted to talk to Mara about, so much he *needed* to talk to her about. He wanted to tell her what Sheila had done to Sam, to ask if, perhaps, Mara *did* approve. How did she feel about it? Maybe he had projected his values about parenting onto Mara, since she could no longer speak for herself.

He wished he could tell Mara that her mother was stuck in denial. That he was, too, at times. It was so comfortable there, in that imaginary place where there was always hope. Hope was both friend and enemy, he knew: it kept him going, but it also prevented him from planning realistically for the future. And in his darkest moments, he was certain Mara's future was in that bed in the nursing home. He honestly didn't know how to plan his life around that indisputable fact.

* * *

When he and Sam arrived home after their visit with Mara, they played with blocks and read books. All the while, Liam had only one thing on his mind: he wanted to talk to Joelle. He told himself it would be a mistake, but the thought would not leave his head.

He managed to avoid calling her until after he'd gone to bed that night, when the image of his confused baby son being turned over Sheila's knee filled his mind. Without stopping to think, he lifted the receiver from the night table and dialed Joelle's number.

"Hello?" Her voice was thick, and he knew she'd been sleeping.

"I'm sorry to wake you," he said. "I just have a quick question."

"What is it?" She sounded instantly awake. He pictured her sitting up in bed, her long, dark hair messy from sleep and her heart beating quickly as she realized it was him on the phone.

"Do you know how Mara felt about spanking?" he asked.

There was a beat of silence on Joelle's end of the line. "I...I don't know specifically," she said, "but my guess is she wouldn't want to handle discipline that way. Are you having some trouble with Sam?"

He laughed, the sound almost alien to his ears. It had been a long time since he'd laughed about anything with Joelle, but he quickly sobered. "No," he said. "I'm having trouble with Sheila. She spanked Sam today."

"What happened?"

"He was screaming in the grocery store," he said. "It doesn't really matter what happened. He's a baby. He can't do anything bad enough to merit a spanking."

"You sound so upset." The tenderness in her voice made the muscles in his chest contract.

"I *am* upset," he said. "But then I realized I had no idea how Mara would feel about it. About spanking."

Another beat of silence. "Hon," Joelle said, and he felt close

to tears at her use of the affectionate term. "It doesn't really matter how Mara would feel about it. What matters is how *you* feel."

"I can't stand the thought of anyone hurting him," he said,
squeezing his eyes shut.

"Then don't let them," she said. "He's *your* son. You make the
rules."

"I..." If he said another word, he was going to cry. "Thanks,"
he said quickly. "I've got to go. I'll see you at work." He hung
up abruptly. He pictured her staring at her phone with a puzzled
look on her face, wondering if she'd said something to make him
hang up like that. He'd wanted to ask her more questions. How
did he stop Sheila from hitting Sam, for example, when he was
completely dependent on her in so many ways? But he'd been
afraid that any more conversation on the subject, any more
words of loving comfort from Joelle, would definitely start his
tears, and that would put an end to his carefully maintained defenses. It had happened before, and he feared it could happen
again, because what he really wanted, what he *desperately*
wanted, was to have her here in bed with him, holding her close,
his hands tangled in her hair, one of her legs nestled between
his, all night long.

CHAPTER FOURTEEN

It was obvious to Joelle that Liam was avoiding her the following day. He'd not been in his office when she arrived at work, and he skipped out early from the peer supervision meeting he, Joelle and Paul held each week in the conference room. But Joelle had even bigger things on her mind than Liam's phone call of the night before.

As of today, she was twelve weeks pregnant, and she was finally going to say those words out loud to someone other than herself. She found it difficult to concentrate on the patients she saw in the maternity unit that morning, because she was on the lookout for Rebecca Reed, who never seemed to be in the corridor or at the nurses' station the same time she was. In the afternoon, Rebecca would be seeing patients in her office, and although that office was in the maternity unit, she would be too busy to take time out for Joelle.

Her pregnancy was still quite easy to hide. She definitely had a rounded belly, and she'd bought a few loose-fitting dresses and tops to wear, so that when she truly had to wear baggier clothing, the change in style wouldn't be so obvious to her co-workers. She no longer needed to use the bathroom every few minutes, but she was beginning to get a strange achy feeling in her groin that made her glad she was finally going to see a doctor. She had to know her baby was all right.

She didn't spot Rebecca until nearly noon. The doctor was talking with Serena Marquez at the nurses' station, a stack of patient charts in her arms. Joelle greeted the two women briefly, not wanting to interrupt their conversation. Taking a seat at the counter, she hoped Serena would leave the station before Rebecca did, and she was in luck. One of the nurses asked Serena to check on a patient, leaving Rebecca and Joelle alone at the counter.

Rebecca sat down, opened one of the charts she'd been carrying and began to write. Almost immediately, Joelle moved to the seat next to her, and Rebecca looked over at her with a quick smile before returning to her notes.

"Sorry to interrupt, Rebecca," Joelle said, "but would you have some time today to talk with me? Maybe after you're done seeing your patients this afternoon?"

"Do you have a problem patient?" Rebecca asked without taking her eyes or her hand from the chart.

"Yes," Joelle said. "Me."

Rebecca stopped writing. She looked at Joelle, her eyebrows raised and frank curiosity in her face. "Sure," she said. "I'll be done around five. Can you come to my office then?"

"Thanks," Joelle said. "I'll be there." She stood up and started walking toward the cafeteria, thinking she would go to Rebecca's office a bit *after* five in the hope that the doctor's staff would have left by then. The fewer people who saw her there, the better.

She spotted Liam sitting alone at their usual table near the cafeteria window and took a seat across from him, glad he had not skipped lunch in an effort to avoid her.

"Where's Paul?" she asked as she opened her napkin and rested it on her lap.

"He's swamped," Liam said. "He'll be late."

He'd sounded so miserable on the phone the night before, so distressed at the thought of Sam being hurt. He had to have been in a deep, dark crater to have called her. Awkward though it had been, she'd been thrilled he'd turned to her the way he used to.

"How are you?" she asked him as she raised her glass of milk to her lips.

"I'm all right." He looked directly at her, his eyes a little red and swollen. "Sorry I bothered you last night," he said.

"It was no bother, Liam," she said. "Did you decide how you're going to handle the situation with Sheila?"

"I've got it covered, thanks." He tore open a packet of sugar and poured it into his coffee, a barely perceptible tremor in his hand. *Like hell he had it covered,* she thought.

"Oh, sweetie." She leaned toward him, wishing she could touch that trembling hand. "Let me help you. You don't need to—"

"Hi, Paul," Liam interrupted her, looking above her head, and she turned to see Paul about to set his tray on the table.

"Will this day never end?" Paul said as he lowered himself into the chair.

"What's going on?" Liam asked with sudden enthusiasm, as though he wanted nothing more than to talk with Paul about his cases.

"Three new AIDS admissions, one of them a fourteen-year-old girl," Paul said. "Two child abuse cases. One little boy about to die. You know, the usual."

"I might be able to help you out later," Joelle said to Paul. Her load today was comparatively light.

Liam began questioning Paul about the details of his cases, exhibiting insatiable curiosity that Joelle knew was born of his desire to avoid talking about his own problems, and she grew quiet. As soon as she had finished eating, she excused herself and went up to the general surgery floor to see if she was needed there. It was too hard to be around Liam when he was shutting her out, cutting himself off from the friendship she still longed to give him.

That afternoon, she whisked through her referrals, then helped Paul with his cases, not allowing herself any free time. She did not want that much time to think. At five o'clock, someone else would finally know what was happening to her body. The contents of her mind and heart, though, would have to remain hidden.

At quarter after five, she sat down in the chair across the desk from Rebecca Reed and offered the doctor a weak smile.

"Thanks for seeing me," she said.

Rebecca shoved aside a stack of charts to give Joelle her full attention. "So," she said, "what's up with you?" Even at the end of a long day, the doctor's blond hair was still neatly, sleekly, pulled back into a clasp at the nape of her neck, and her face looked freshly scrubbed, her skin smooth and glowing.

Joelle had spoken about her personal problems once before with Rebecca, many years earlier, when she and Rusty had been unable to conceive. Rebecca had been her usual cool and clinical self, giving Joelle the names of several fertility specialists, spelling out their credentials and offering her own opinion of each of them, but she'd offered Joelle no words of sympathy, no hand-holding, and Joelle had not expected any. That was not Rebecca's style. She did not expect any sympathy now, either. What she needed was excellent clinical skills embodied in a woman who was certain not to either meddle or gossip.

"I have to ask for complete confidentiality," Joelle began, and Rebecca smiled.

"Is there any other kind?" she asked.

Joelle could not smile back. "Right. I guess not," she said. She looked squarely at Rebecca and took in a breath. "I'm pregnant," she said.

Rebecca raised her eyebrows and for a moment seemed speechless. "Wow," she said, leaning back in her chair. "Wow."

"Lousy timing, isn't it?" Joelle asked.

Rebecca folded her arms across her chest and shook her head

in what Joelle thought was wonder. "Well, there was a time when I would have congratulated you on this news and broken out the Perrier," Rebecca said, "but I'm not quite sure what to say right now. Is this good news for you or not? Or would you prefer not to discuss it?"

"It's a...mixed blessing, I guess." Joelle ran her fingertips over the smooth edge of Rebecca's desk. "It wasn't planned. I'm not married, of course, and I have no plans to be. But still—" she looked at Rebecca "—you know how much I wanted a baby."

"When was the first day of your last period?" Rebecca asked.

"My periods are so irregular," Joelle said. "I couldn't begin to tell you. But I do know that I'm exactly twelve weeks pregnant as of today."

"You know the moment of conception, then, huh?" Rebecca smiled, almost warmly.

"Yes."

Leaning forward, Rebecca rested her elbows on her desk. "If *conception* actually occurred twelve weeks ago, that would probably make you around fourteen weeks pregnant."

"*Fourteen weeks?* What do you mean?" Joelle asked.

"We count from the first day of your last period. Usually, that's a couple of weeks prior to the actual date of conception."

"I never knew that," Joelle said, bewildered to suddenly find herself two weeks further along than she'd thought she was. "I've worked in the maternity unit all these years and never knew that."

"Well, it's the ultrasound that will give us the most accurate reading on how far along you are." Rebecca cocked her head to one side. "I just need to make sure you know you can still have an abortion at fourteen weeks."

Joelle shook her head. "How could I do that after trying for so long to get pregnant?"

"Yes, of course," Rebecca said. "I just want to be sure you know your options."

"I do," Joelle said. She glanced at the wall of framed diplomas near the window of the office. "I wanted to ask if you would be my obstetrician," she said.

Rebecca nodded. "Of course." She looked at her watch and stood up. "How about we start right now. Do you have time for your first prenatal exam?"

Joelle was relieved. That was the invitation she'd been hoping for. She needed to know the baby she'd been neglecting, at least from the perspective of prenatal care, was healthy. "I haven't felt any movement," she said, getting to her feet. "If I'm fourteen weeks, shouldn't I be feeling something?"

"Not yet, but you will soon enough." Rebecca guided Joelle toward one of the small examination rooms. "Let's see what the sonogram tells us."

Rebecca left her alone in the room, where Joelle undressed, put on a blue gown and climbed onto the table.

In a moment, Rebecca returned to the room. After a gentle examination, she began to squeeze warm gel on her stomach.

"I've been having some pain down here." Joelle moved her hands along either side of her groin. "A pulling sort of feeling."

Rebecca nodded. "Ligament pain," she said. "That's normal." She began sliding the transducer back and forth over Joelle's belly as an image formed on the monitor.

Joelle had never been able to make out those blurry fetal pictures, but Rebecca was an excellent interpreter.

"This is the head," she said, pointing to the image in the center of the screen. "These little buds will become his or her arms and legs. Look, you can see one of the hands already. And most importantly, here's the heart."

"Oh!" Joelle lifted her head to get a better look at the pulsing speck of life on the monitor. "How beautiful! How big is it?" she asked. "The baby? The fetus?"

"About three and a half inches long," Rebecca said. "And you are most definitely fourteen weeks, Joelle."

"Oh, God." She closed her eyes and let her head fall back on the small, flat pillow. "I feel so guilty for waiting this long to see you. To get prenatal care. Fourteen weeks!"

"Would you like a due date?" Rebecca did not seem to be listening to her ruminations. Instead, she was fiddling with a chart on the counter.

"I figured it would be in mid-January," Joelle said.

"How about January first?" Rebecca said. "A New Year's baby."

A New Year's baby. It would be just her luck to make the papers as having the first baby of the new year.

"You won't be able to keep this a secret too much longer," Rebecca said.

Joelle looked at her. "I plan to move before it becomes that apparent," she said, then added quickly, "Please keep that between you and me, Rebecca. No one knows. I haven't turned in my resignation or mentioned it to anyone yet."

Rebecca frowned as she slipped the transducer back in its holder. "What are you talking about?" she asked. "You can't leave. You're an institution in the Women's Wing."

"Thanks," Joelle said, staring at the ceiling, "but I want to go."

Rebecca wiped the gel from her stomach with a towel. "You don't need to name names," she said, "but could you please tell me if the baby's father will be involved during this pregnancy? Will you have support from him? Does he live somewhere else? Is that why you'll be moving, to be closer to him?"

Joelle shook her head. "No," she said. "The father won't be involved."

He's married, she wanted to say. *He's overwhelmed by life already. I can't burden him with one more thing. He can barely look me in the eye, much less be a father to my child.*

"Where are you going?" Rebecca asked as she helped Joelle to sit up.

"I don't know yet," Joelle said, turning to dangle her legs over the side of the table. "Someplace I can start fresh with this baby."

"Are you running away from something?" Rebecca probed.

"I don't know." Joelle shrugged. "No. Yes. Maybe." She smiled an apology at the doctor for being so evasive. "The important thing is, can you be my obstetrician until I leave, Rebecca? I mean, without telling anyone? Or will that put you in too much of a bind?"

"I'll be your doctor," Rebecca said. "But people love you here, Joelle." It seemed odd to hear the word *love* come from those ordinarily cool and dispassionate lips. "I hope you have a very good reason for going."

"Yes," she said. "I do."

As she was unlocking the outside door to her condo that evening, Tony, one-half of the gay couple who lived downstairs, poked his head out his front door.

"Joelle!" he said. "Come join us for dinner. We made stuffed portobello mushrooms and we got carried away. There's more than we can eat."

"Oh, thanks, Tony." She smiled at him with a shake of her head. "Not tonight, I'm afraid."

"Well, we'll save you some, then," Tony said, disappearing inside his condo again.

She walked up the stairs and into her own condo, remembering the last time she'd eaten with her neighbors. She'd made a huge pot of fish stew and invited Tony and Gary over to help her eat it. The three of them had stayed up half the night, drinking a little too much and singing oldies off-key. She liked those guys. They were by no means her closest friends, but they had potential. If she were staying in the area, maybe they would have liked being honorary daddies. Maybe even her labor coaches.

You've been watching too many sitcoms on TV, she told herself as she lifted the telephone receiver to check her voice mail. She had one message, the mechanical voice told her, and she pressed her code to hear it.

"Hello, Joelle, a.k.a. Shanti Joy," a woman's voice said.

Joelle frowned. Carlynn Shire?

"This is Carlynn Shire," the woman said, answering her question. "I've been thinking about you, and was wondering why I haven't heard from you. How is your friend doing? Would you still like me to see her? If you would, give me a call." She left her number, and Joelle wrote it down on the cover of a catalog resting on the kitchen counter.

How strange, she thought with a bit of annoyance. Apparently Alan Shire had neglected to tell Carlynn he had asked Joelle not to call her. Yet, she was pleased to hear the older woman's message.

Setting down her purse and appointment book, she dialed the number.

"Shire residence." It was a man's voice. For a moment she was afraid it might belong to Alan Shire, but then she remembered the man who had called to set up her first meeting with Carlynn. This was most certainly *his* voice.

"This is Joelle D'Angelo," she said. "May I speak with Carlynn Shire, please?"

"Please hold for a moment," the man said, and several minutes passed before Carlynn came on the line.

"Hello, Joelle!" she said. "How are you?"

"I'm all right, Carlynn, but I have to say I was surprised to hear from you."

"Why is that?"

Joelle sat on a stool at the counter. "Maybe you didn't know this," she said carefully, "but your husband contacted me. He told me you were retired and having some health problems and would rather not be seeing people. That's why I didn't call. I didn't want to bother you again."

There was a moment of silence on the line. "Alan called you?" Carlynn asked.

"No, he came to see me at the hospital where I work."

"And he said...?"

"He said you're retired and ill, that healing takes too much out of you, that—"

"Oh, horsefeathers," Carlynn said. "He's an old worrywart, isn't he? He's right that I'm retired, and he's right that I'm ill, and there are few cases I'd be willing to take on these days, but you touched me with the story of your friend Mara. I would truly like to see her, Joelle."

"Thank you," she said, liking Carlynn a great deal for remembering Mara's name. "But, Carlynn..." She hesitated, wondering if she should bring this up. "Another thing your husband said concerned me. He said that talking to me would remind you of... I know you lost your sister right around the time I was born."

"That was a very long time ago, Joelle." Carlynn sounded completely unconcerned by the matter. "It overjoys me to see that a life I touched back then has flourished in spite of what I lost. So put that right out of your mind."

"All right, I will," Joelle said, thinking that Carlynn seemed quite capable of making her own decisions in the matter, despite her husband's concerns.

"Okay, then," Carlynn said. "So, dear, when shall we see your friend?"

CHAPTER FIFTEEN

Carlynn found Alan sitting at the table on the terrace, his feet up on one of the other chairs, a book in his lap, although he was not reading. Instead, his gaze was fixed on the gardeners working in the side yard.

She sat down on the other side of the table, and Alan glanced at her, then nodded in the direction of the yard.

"Crazy old man," he said.

"What?" she asked. "Who?"

"Quinn," he said.

She followed his gaze to one of the taller cypress trees, and saw the elderly man standing on a ladder, his head buried somewhere beneath the branches of the tree. She could see his weathered dark hands working the pruning shears. She shook her head.

"He can't hold still, can he?" she said with a smile. "Quinn!" she called. "Come down from there. You're going to kill yourself."

He did not respond, and she knew that he had either not heard her or was going to pretend that he had not. She knew Quinn would rather die by falling out of a tree than by the slow, miserable route she seemed compelled to endure.

"I need to talk with you, Alan," she said, shifting her gaze back to the terrace.

"Should you be out here in the sun?" Alan turned to ask her, his eyes masked behind his sunglasses.

"I don't plan to be out here long," she said. "I just wanted to understand why you would talk to Joelle D'Angelo behind my back."

"Who?"

"You know who. The social worker who wanted me to see her friend. Why are you interfering in my business?"

"I think it's my business, too, don't you?" he asked. The sunlight on his head made the thick shock of his hair even whiter.

"Not really," she said.

"Well." He closed his book and set it down on the table. "I went to see her because A) you're not well, and B) you're not thinking straight."

"I know I'm not well," she said, "but there's nothing wrong with my thinking."

"There has to be if you're willing to take on a healing," he said. "For the last ten years I haven't had to worry about you. I don't want to start that up all over again."

"You're operating out of fear, Alan," she said. He always had. "I know your intentions are good and that you're trying to protect me. To protect all we've built together. But this girl—Joelle—needs me."

"And without you, what will happen to her? Will she explode? Die? What? You're not going to heal her friend. There's nothing in the universe that can be done to help a woman that brain-damaged. You're just giving Joelle false hope."

"It's not her friend I'm interested in." She looked down at her hands. They were not so yellow today, or perhaps it was the sun that made them look a bit less like the hands of a woman dying from hepatitis. "I've been thinking a lot about my sister lately," she said. "I may be going to see her soon." She smiled, knowing she would irk Alan with that sort of talk. She'd always liked the open-ended nature of spiritual questions, while Alan, ever the physician, had no patience for them.

"Well," Alan said, "if you see her, send her my regards."

Carlynn leaned toward him across the table. "I'm not particularly proud of the life I've led, Alan," she said. "I need to find a way to set it right."

"And this is it?" he asked. "Helping the social worker's friend?"

"Yes," she said, rising to her feet. She rested one hand on his shoulder and bent low to buss his temple. "Please don't worry," she said. "I'll be very careful. I promise."

CHAPTER SIXTEEN

Joelle slowed her car to skirt a golf cart parked at the side of the road. She and Carlynn were driving north along the Seventeen Mile Drive, heading toward Pacific Grove and the nursing home. "Was Alan upset about you coming with me today?" she asked as they passed the pricey and beautiful Inn at Spanish Bay.

"You have to forgive Alan," Carlynn said, without answering the question directly. "He's very overprotective of me."

"Has he always been that way?" Joelle took her eyes from the road to glance at the older woman.

"Not in the beginning," Carlynn said. "But once people began going to great lengths to try to see me, hoping I could heal them, he really worried that I was either overdoing it, or that some loony person might try to kidnap me or heaven knows what."

Joelle smiled to herself. It was funny to hear someone who claimed to be a healer refer to anyone other than herself as loony.

"Are you...forgive me for prying," Joelle said. "Is your illness very serious?"

Carlynn nodded. "I have hepatitis C," she said. "Apparently I contracted it thirty-four years ago, when I was hospitalized after the accident and needed a transfusion. But it was silent until a couple of years ago."

Joelle remembered that hepatitis C was serious, but knew little more than that. "What about treatment?" she asked.

"I'm done with that," Carlynn said. "I had a couple of rounds of the best drugs medicine has to offer, but the side effects were horrendous and the treatment simply didn't work for me. I could go through it again, but frankly, I'd rather live a comfortable six months or so then a miserable year or two."

"I'm sorry," Joelle said. "It sounds as though it's been pretty frustrating for you."

"Well, I feel fairly good these days," Carlynn said with a nod. "So much better than I did when I was taking those drugs. Then I could barely get out of bed."

"Seeing Mara might tire you out terribly, though." Joelle suddenly wondered if she should have paid more attention to Alan Shire's concerns.

"I'd like to do some good before I die," Carlynn said.

"You've already done a great deal of good, though," Joelle said.

Carlynn smiled and turned to look at her. "I want to see Mara, Joelle," she said firmly but kindly. "And that's the final word on the subject."

She obviously didn't want sympathy, so Joelle changed the subject.

"How long have you and Alan been married?" she asked. They were nearing the Pacific Grove gate, and Carlynn waved at the toll taker as they passed by.

"Forty-three years. We met when I was in medical school. I was keeping my abilities to myself back then, but he sensed there was something different about me."

Joelle glanced at her again and saw that she was smiling, perhaps at the memory. Today, Carlynn wore a yellow T-shirt beneath denim overalls, a blue-and-yellow-striped scarf tied at her neck, tennis shoes and small, round sunglasses. She looked very thin, yes, and her skin was probably more yellow than it should be, but otherwise it would be hard to guess that this was a woman with a terminal illness.

"I envy you for being married so long to someone who cares enough to protect you," Joelle said as she turned in the direction of the nursing home.

That coy little smile again. "Yes, I've been lucky. And I'm sorry about your divorce. It must have been difficult for you."

"Yes, it was," she said. "I think I told you that we were unable to have children. So, my husband found someone he *could* have children with."

"Oh, my, I am sorry." Carlynn shook her head. "Alan and I could have no children, either, so I know how you must have felt."

"But Alan didn't leave." Joelle turned the corner into the parking lot of the nursing home.

"No, I think our generation was quite different from yours. And Alan and I were bound together by so much... So very much." Carlynn looked lost in her own thoughts for a moment, then she suddenly sat up straight in the seat. "Is this the nursing home? Let me shift my mental gears, then," she said, taking off her sunglasses and folding them in her lap. "Let me sit quietly. I want to get ready to meet your Mara."

Joelle parked the car and turned off the ignition. "Shall I leave you alone?" she asked.

"Just for a few minutes," Carlynn said. "I'll open my door so I don't suffocate." She giggled like a little girl as she opened the passenger-side door.

"There's a bench by the front door of the building," Joelle said. "I'll meet you there, all right?"

"Fine." Carlynn leaned her head against the headrest, folded her hands around her sunglasses in her lap, and closed her eyes.

Joelle walked slowly up the path to the bench near the front door of the nursing home. This whole situation was starting to feel a bit hokey to her now. The so-called shifting of mental gears, the sitting quietly to prepare herself for meeting Mara. The healer herself dying of hepatitis. Maybe Alan Shire had been trying to protect Joelle from being suckered. Whatever. It was too late now to change her mind.

She hoped she had timed the visit accurately. It was nearly five. She knew Liam would be visiting Mara alone today, without Sam and Sheila, and even if she and Carlynn spent a full hour with Mara, they would still have time to get out of the nursing home before he arrived. As long as Liam was not early, they would be all right.

Joelle did not understand why, but Sheila had turned cold to her recently. She and Sheila and Liam had been a real team after Mara became ill, working together to get her the best care possible. Sheila would often call Joelle for her opinion of a particular doctor's suggested treatment or of a nursing home's skill level, and sometimes she'd simply call for consolation or to chat. Joelle had felt like a true member of the family. Although she couldn't pinpoint the moment she'd noticed a change, Joelle no longer received phone calls from Sheila. As a matter of fact, Sheila barely even spoke to her when they bumped into one another, not even offering her a smile. Joelle had called her once, a couple of months ago, to ask if she had done something to offend her, and Sheila pretended she had no idea what Joelle was talking about. That left very little room for resolving the situation, and Joelle had given up.

Carlynn walked up the path toward her, using her cane, with only a hint of a limp in her gait. Joelle drew in a deep breath. *Sorry if I'm making a big mistake, Mara.* She stood up and led the older woman into the home.

Mara's bed had been cranked up into a sitting position, and she looked exactly the way Joelle hated to see her look. She was asleep, her face slack, aging her fifteen years. Her mouth hung open a little, a rivulet of saliva trickling down her chin, and her short hair, which Joelle cut herself once a month, was disheveled from the pillow.

Joelle took Carlynn's arm at the door of Mara's room. "She'll smile when she wakes up," she whispered. "She'll look as though she knows who I am, but I don't believe she does."

Carlynn nodded and followed Joelle into the room.

Joelle sat on the edge of Mara's bed, while Carlynn stood off to one side.

"Mara." Joelle touched the pale hand where it rested on the covers. "Mara? It's Joelle, sweetie."

Mara's long, dark lashes fluttered open, and she smiled the instant she saw Joelle.

Joelle took a tissue from the box on the nightstand and wiped Mara's chin with it. "Mara," she said, "I'd like you to meet a friend of mine, Carlynn Shire."

Mara didn't shift her gaze from Joelle until Carlynn moved closer to the bed, stepping into her field of vision. She looked at Carlynn, that vacuous but eternally happy expression on her face. Carlynn had to be taken in by her beauty, Joelle thought, by the remarkable change in Mara's face once she was awake and alert, if *alert* was the right word to use. Her black eyes were extraordinary, and even the messy haircut looked stylish on her.

"Hello, Mara." Carlynn gently lifted one of Mara's hands.

"Would you rather she be in her wheelchair?" Joelle asked, standing up from the edge of the bed.

"No," Carlynn spoke to Mara, "let's leave you in bed, where you're probably more comfortable."

Joelle sat in the chair near the night table, while Carlynn rested her cane against the table and took her place on the edge of Mara's bed.

"My, you're very beautiful," Carlynn said. "I've spoken with Joelle, and she told me all about you. How deep your friendship is with her. How much she loves you. You are a much-loved person."

Mara merely blinked her eyes. Joelle was certain she had no understanding of Carlynn's words.

"Would you like to have a gentle massage of your hands?" Carlynn asked, but Mara's expression didn't change.

"I think she would," Joelle said. "I've done that for her sometimes." She realized as she spoke that it had been a long time since she'd given Mara a massage. She used to rub her all over with moisturizing lotion, and it had made her feel as though she was at least trying to help her friend. Sometime in the past year, she'd given up. Did Liam still do that, massage Mara, touch her that way, with gentleness? She hoped so.

Carlynn reached into her large handbag and brought out a bottle of lotion. Joelle craned her neck to see the label, expecting the lotion to contain special herbal ingredients or at least *something* out of the ordinary, but it was a plain pink bottle of baby lotion.

Carlynn poured some of the lotion onto her own palm, then gently lifted one of Mara's limp hands and began a slow, tender massage. Joelle remained quiet, not even watching the two women after a while, just listening as Carlynn spoke to Mara in an even, almost hypnotic, tone.

"This feels so good, doesn't it, Mara?" Carlynn asked. "Yes, you like the way it feels. You like to be touched with caring, I think. You can tell the difference if someone cares or not. You are very wise that way."

After a while, Carlynn stopped talking and Joelle looked up to see Mara's gaze fastened on the older woman. There wasn't a sound in the room, and Joelle looked at their hands. One of Mara's hands lay limp in Carlynn's, but the fingers of her right hand, her so-called "good" hand, were moving against Carlynn's palm. She was massaging her! Could it possibly be? She didn't dare stand up to see, but something was happening between Mara and the healer. Something Joelle was not a part of.

Mara's eyes gradually fell shut and her breathing grew even, but Joelle felt certain that her face lacked the flaccid, droopy look of her usual sleep. Her facial muscles looked merely relaxed rather than limp and wasted.

Carlynn turned to smile at Joelle, then silently replaced the cap on the baby lotion. She was getting up from the bed when Liam walked into the room.

"Joelle!" he said, stopping short. He looked at Carlynn, then back at Joelle. "I didn't expect to see you here."

Of course he hadn't. She had told him she was leaving work early to go to a doctor's appointment.

"Liam, this is Carlynn Shire," she said, motioning toward the older woman, hoping he wouldn't recognize her name.

"Hello, Carlynn." He reached out to shake her hand, then frowned. "Are you the Carlynn Shire of the Shire Mind and Body Center?" he asked.

"Yes." Carlynn smiled warmly at him, reaching for her cane. "Although I'm retired now."

Joelle saw his jaw muscles tighten beneath the skin of his cheeks and knew he was angry. He controlled himself, though, as he turned toward her.

"How is she today?" he asked, but there were a dozen other questions in his eyes.

"I think she's doing very well," Joelle said, wanting to get Carlynn and herself out of the room as quickly as she could. "Carlynn gave her a hand massage, and now we're on our way out."

Mara opened her eyes again, and when she saw Liam she let out the little squeal of childish joy that she seemed to save only for him. She raised her one good arm an inch or so off the bed, and he moved toward her, leaning over to kiss her unresponsive lips. Then he lifted one of her soft, baby-lotioned hands and held it tightly against his hip as he turned to Joelle.

"Could I speak with you a moment before you go?" he asked.

Damn. "Sure," she said. "Carlynn, would you mind waiting in the hall for me?"

Liam waited until Carlynn had left the room.

"What's going on?" Liam asked, the words coming out slowly and deliberately as he worked to keep his voice calm. Joelle knew he would not raise his voice around Mara.

"I...could we talk about this later?" she asked.

"You bet we can," he said. "I'll call you tonight."

"All right." She picked up her purse and left the room. She'd wanted to hear those words from him for over three months now. *I'll call you.* This was one call, though, she was not looking forward to.

Both she and Carlynn were quiet for the first mile or so of the drive back to the mansion, and Joelle was barely aware of the older woman's presence. Liam was furious with her, and rightly so. She should not have brought Carlynn to see Mara without his permission. She'd crossed some ethical boundary, perhaps, one she couldn't identify but knew was there. Otherwise, she wouldn't have hidden the visit from him.

Until Mara's aneurysm, she had rarely, if ever, seen Liam angry. She'd certainly witnessed his frustration over some of the cases in the hospital, when he was helpless in the face of whatever fate had planned for a particular patient, or when he felt he could help someone but the policies of the hospital or some other bureaucracy got in his way. He felt the plight of his patients deeply, much as she did. They had learned together over the years how to walk the line between distance and overinvolvement with their patients, how to maintain enough objectivity to be able to help, without losing their humanity in the process. It was something they used to talk about often—the broad philosophical aspects of their work. She'd loved those talks, and their relationship had been strong enough to allow them to disagree with one another without breaking down. That, she knew, was no longer true.

They reached the Pacific Grove gate to the Seventeen Mile Drive. The man at the tollbooth waved them through, and once on the Drive, Carlynn finally spoke.

"I think I can help Mara," she said. "There is still a great deal of energy and grace left in your friend. I think I can tap into that, but it will take time."

Joelle thought back to what she had witnessed in the nursing home. "She was massaging your hand, wasn't she?" she asked.

"It seemed that way to me." Carlynn smiled.

Joelle knew she would never be able to bring Carlynn back to the nursing home now that Liam had seen her there and had reacted the way he did. But she didn't want to address that with Carlynn just then.

"I honestly thought she looked better by the time we were ready to leave," Joelle said.

"Well, of course, we'd both like to think that. Only time will tell if we're fooling ourselves or not. It doesn't always work, Joelle. You must understand that."

Joelle laughed. "It's harder for me to accept that it sometimes *does* work," she said. She glanced at Carlynn. "Do I pay you per visit or...?"

"You don't pay me at all," she said. "I'm retired. I only work when I truly want to. And from what you've told me, Mara is worth my time and energy."

"Thank you," Joelle said.

They fell silent again as they drove past the entrance to the Spyglass Hill Golf Course. After another minute or two, Joelle pulled into the driveway of the Kling Mansion and started to press the buzzer on the stone pillar.

"3273," Carlynn said.

"What?" Joelle asked.

"That's the code. Just press 3273."

Joelle did so, and the gate slid open. She pulled all the way up the driveway and stopped the car near the house.

Carlynn made no move to get out of the car. Instead, she looked at Joelle. She was no longer wearing her sunglasses, and her gaze was steady and, somehow, disquieting. "There's much you haven't told me, isn't there?" she asked.

"What do you mean?" Joelle put the car in park and took her foot off the brake pedal.

"I mean, with Liam. With you and Liam, perhaps?"

Joelle thought back to the scene in Mara's room, wondering what Carlynn had gathered in those few awkward moments. She was about to tell the older woman she was imagining things, but found herself nodding, instead.

"Yes," she said.

"Come in." Carlynn nodded toward the house. "Turn off your car, come inside, and let's talk."

Obediently, Joelle turned off the ignition, stepped out of the car and walked with Carlynn up to the front door of the mansion.

Mrs. McGowan, the housekeeper with the Irish accent, greeted them at the door and took Carlynn's handbag from her.

"Have you two met?" Carlynn looked from the housekeeper to Joelle.

"Yes, indeed." The housekeeper smiled. "She thought I was you at first."

Carlynn laughed at that, and Joelle blushed.

"We're going in the library for a little chat," Carlynn said to Mrs. McGowan. "Please let Alan know we'd rather not be disturbed."

"Would you like something to nibble while you're there?" the housekeeper offered.

"Please, dear." Carlynn then took Joelle's elbow and walked slowly with her through the living room and into the library. A large room, though not nearly as big as the living room, the library had one wall of windows looking out on the sea and cypress, and three walls covered from floor to ceiling with books.

Joelle sat at one end of the leather sofa, while Carlynn sat at the other, turning to face her. Behind Carlynn's head, Joelle could see the evening fog rolling in, pink-tinged from the falling sun.

"So, tell me," Carlynn said, folding her hands in her lap once again. "Tell me what made you freeze up when Liam walked into the room."

"Did I freeze up?" Joelle asked.

"You did, indeed." Carlynn wore a small frown.

"I hadn't told him I'd contacted you to see Mara," Joelle said. "He's even more skeptical about healers than I am, so I hadn't really wanted him to know."

Carlynn tipped her head to the side. "And what else?"

"What else is that...I'm in love with him." She blurted out the words, but Carlynn did not look the least bit surprised.

"Yes," the older woman said gently. "I know."

"How could you possibly know?"

"Because it was written all over your face when he walked in and when you watched him kiss his wife," she said. "I didn't need to possess any special gift to see that."

Joelle shut her eyes and covered one side of her face with her hand. She felt exposed. "It's so complicated," she said.

"Tell me."

Lowering her hand from her face, Joelle leaned back against the cool leather of the sofa, letting out a sigh. "Well," she said slowly, "I told you how I fixed them up, right?"

Carlynn nodded.

"At that time, I just liked Liam a great deal, and I loved Mara."

"Yes, she was your closest friend," Carlynn said. "Your confidante. A sister you never had." It had been weeks since she'd last spoken to Carlynn about this, but the woman seemed to remember their conversation well.

"Right." Joelle nodded. "And they were so very wonderful together. They were perfect. I had no bad feelings about it at all...well, except a bit of envy because I knew how good their marriage was and how lousy mine was. My ex-husband and I would go out with them from time to time, but Rusty, my ex, just didn't fit in. He was very quiet. Into computers. Into working with machines instead of working with people, the way Liam, Mara and I were. After Rusty and I divorced, Mara and Liam were very good to me. They always included me in parties they had, and they asked me out with them now and then, even though I was single." Other couples with whom she and Rusty had been friends had faded away, but not Mara and Liam. "Mara and I still had lunch together once a week or so, and we'd go hiking every once in a while. She never let her marriage cut into our...girl-time." Joelle shook her head. "I miss her so much," she said.

"I'm sure you do," Carlynn said, and it suddenly occurred to Joelle that Carlynn had lost a flesh-and-blood sister, a twin. She probably understood completely what Joelle's life was like now that Mara was no longer an active, contributing part of it.

There was a knock on the library door.

"Come in," Carlynn said, looking past Joelle to the door.

The elderly man Joelle had previously seen working in the garden entered the room, bearing a tray of sandwiches and iced tea. He lowered it to the coffee table in front of them.

"Thanks, Quinn," Carlynn said. "This is Joelle, by the way, a new friend of mine." She motioned toward Joelle. "Joelle, this is Quinn."

"Hello, Quinn." Joelle nodded a greeting at the man.

"How do you do," he said, then turned to Carlynn. "Do you need anything else?"

"No, thank you," Carlynn said. "You're a love."

Quinn turned and started for the door, smiling at Joelle as he passed her, and she thought, although she was not certain, that he winked at her before shuffling away.

God, he seemed far too old to be working! And Mrs. Mc-Gowan had to be near seventy. Joelle doubted there would be many people willing to hire such old-timers. It was kind of Carlynn to keep them on.

Carlynn picked up one of the small plates with its crustless white-bread sandwich and handed it to Joelle, who took it, although she was not hungry. The filling was chicken salad. She could smell it as she rested the plate in her lap.

"You were telling me about your relationship with Liam and Mara," Carlynn prompted, handing her a glass of iced tea.

Joelle set the tea on top of a wooden coaster on the coffee table and looked out the window. "After Sam was born," she said, "and Mara had the aneurysm, it was Liam and I who stayed by her bedside in the hospital. She was in a coma for a couple of weeks, and we sang to her. At least Liam did." She remembered him bringing his guitar into his wife's hospital room, singing some of the songs he and Mara had often performed together, while Joelle stroked her arm or combed her hair. "I read to her, or just talked to her. We took turns being with her, along with Mara's mother, Sheila, and Liam and I really started leaning on each other. He included me in all the decisions he needed to make about her. Her rehab. What nursing home to put her in. I felt like I was part of the family."

"You were," Carlynn said, swallowing a bite of her sandwich.

"I helped him with Sam." She broke into a smile at the thought of the little boy. "He's a treasure, Carlynn. You've never seen a cuter child. I love him to pieces, and I don't know what Liam would do without him." She bit a small corner from her sandwich, then swallowed it before continuing. "I tried to help Liam deal with all the mixed emotions he was having. He'd essentially lost a wife and gained a son. But he'd been the one who'd wanted the son in the first place, not Mara, so of course he felt terribly guilty." She lifted her sandwich toward her mouth again, then set it down without taking a bite. "Liam and I talked every single night on the phone. Every night."

"You're using the past tense."

Joelle nodded, sighing. "About three or four months ago, Sam had his first birthday. And, of course, that was also the one-year anniversary of Mara's aneurysm. I helped Liam and Sheila celebrate Sam's birthday, then afterward I was alone with Liam at his house, Sam was in bed, and we were both so upset. We'd been getting closer and closer all year. I knew we loved each other very deeply." She was confident of that fact. Confident that Liam had loved her as much as she did him. "And that night, it just...got out of hand."

"You made love," Carlynn said, and Joelle nodded. She stood up, struggling against the memory and unable to look at Carlynn at that moment. She walked over to the window to see that the fog had obliterated the view of the ocean and was now teasing the branches of the cypress trees behind the mansion.

"I went home afterward," Joelle said, still facing the window. "I couldn't get Mara's face out of my head. I knew how she felt about fidelity. My God, we'd talked about that sort of thing so often. We both felt so strongly about it, about the sanctity of marriage and wedding vows. I couldn't believe what I'd done. I was like a teenager who didn't know any better. Who didn't know that A would lead to B and on and on and on."

She walked back to the sofa and sat down again, looking at the magazines arrayed neatly on the coffee table without really seeing them. "The next day," she said, "he called me and said he felt worse than ever, that we never should have done that, that he was sorry, that we had to stop spending so much time together, that he still had a wife he loved. Etcetera."

"Oh, I'm sorry, Joelle. How painful for you."

"I knew he was right. And yet...to just cut off our relationship like that. It was all I had left."

"And all he had left, too."

"He has Sam," she said, and started to cry. "And now I'm cut off from both of them."

"But you work together, don't you?"

She nodded. "Every single day. And we have meetings together, and help each other out on cases, and eat lunch together with Paul, the other social worker, and we don't ever really look each other in the eye. It's torture."

"I'm sure it is."

"And there's more," Joelle said.

"Yes." Carlynn wore a sympathetic smile.

"I'm pregnant."

Carlynn nodded. "I know."

"How could you have known that?" Joelle's hands flew to her belly. She'd thought she had hidden her pregnancy well.

"I'm a good guesser."

Joelle thought something other than guessing was at work here, but she continued. "Fifteen weeks pregnant. I thought about an abortion, but I've wanted a baby so long."

"And Liam doesn't know?"

"He has no idea."

"When will you tell him?"

"I don't plan to," she said. "I'm going to leave before my pregnancy becomes too obvious. I'll move away. I'm not sure where I'll go yet. Maybe to Berkeley where my parents live."

"Isn't it unfair of you not to let Liam know?" Carlynn leaned toward her on the sofa.

Joelle shook her head. "There's nothing he can do about my being pregnant except feel worse than he already does, Carlynn," she said. "He can't marry me."

"Do you really want to leave Monterey?" Carlynn asked her.

Joelle hesitated a moment before answering. "Honestly, no. I love it here. But maybe I can come back someday." She let out her breath, looking up at the ceiling. "This doesn't have to be forever."

"Does Liam still perform his music?" Carlynn asked the question, seemingly, out of the blue.

Joelle shook her head. "No. I don't think he's picked up his guitar since Mara went into the nursing home."

"Well." Carlynn set her sandwich plate on the coffee table. "There is one thing I know for absolute certain about you, Joelle." There were tears in Carlynn's eyes as she moved closer to Joelle, wrapping her thin hand around Joelle's where it rested on her knees. "You are a tremendously noble human being."

"Why do you say that?"

"Look at what you're doing, honey. You love this man so deeply that you want to find a way to heal his wife, to return his wife to him, because you know that's what will make him truly happy. Even though *you* love him. Even though you're carrying his *child.* You've placed his happiness above your own. Few people would do that."

A bit embarrassed, Joelle looked at her uneaten sandwich resting on the coffee table. "It feels good to love someone that much," she said, her voice a near whisper. "It's the only thing that feels good about this whole situation."

"The next time I visit Mara," Carlynn said, "I'd like Liam to be there, as well. Can you arrange that?"

Joelle grimaced. "I'm not even sure how he's going to react to your being there today, Carlynn," she said. "But I'll ask him."

"Good." Carlynn patted her hand and stood up. "Now you'd better get out of here before the fog socks you in."

Joelle nodded, although she was thinking it might not be that bad to be stuck in the mansion with Carlynn.

At the front door, she kissed Carlynn's cheek.

"Thanks so much," she said, opening the door and walking outside. The world was filled with translucent gray air, but all Joelle could think about was that she had a new confidante. An unexpected confidante.

Although she was not very far from Carmel, the fog obscured parts of the road, and she had to drive slowly. She felt trapped inside her car with nothing but the memory of that night with Liam.

She and Liam had sat with Sam on Liam's bed, looking through a picture book with the little boy and singing him silly songs, like "Itsy, Bitsy Spider" and "Pat-a-Cake," and Sam didn't care a bit that Joelle couldn't carry a tune. He giggled and let her nibble his fingers while he cuddled with her and his dad. When Sam grew tired, Liam carried him into the nursery and tucked him into his crib, but Joelle stayed where she was on Liam's bed. She was looking forward to talking with Liam about the day, and if she realized the sofa in the living room would be a more appropriate place for such conversation, she did not let herself think about it.

Liam came back into the room and fell forward onto the bed, his head resting on his folded arms. Joelle lay down as well, on her side, propping her head up by her elbow. Liam's face was turned toward her, but he was not looking at her. Instead, he seemed to be staring into space. The light on the night table caught the pale blue of his eyes, and she wanted to touch his cheek, the place where the long, sexy crevice formed when he smiled, but she kept her hands to herself instead.

"What are you thinking about?" she asked him.

He licked his lips. "About you, actually," he said. "About how great you've been this year. How I couldn't have made it without you. How good you are with Sam. How much I need those late-night phone conversations with you. How incredible you've been at helping me deal with all the nuts-and-bolts issues around Mara—the nursing home, dealing with her doctors, the whole gamut. You took so much of the pressure off me by being there."

"I'm glad," she said, touched.

With a sigh, Liam rolled onto his back and stared at the ceiling. "We've been grappling with this mess for a year," he said. "One long fucking year." He never swore, and the sound of the word coming from his mouth made her wince. "My beautiful wife is a... Oh my God. She's just gone. I don't know who that person is inside that screwed-up body, but Mara's not in there anymore." He squeezed his eyes shut. "Why didn't I listen to her, Jo?" he asked, turning his head to look at her. "Why did I talk her into having a baby? It wasn't my body that had to go through it. If I'd only listened...really let myself *hear*...how afraid she was. How much she didn't want to have a child. She knew it was the wrong thing for her. She knew it." His chin quivered, and Joelle pressed her hand to the side of his face.

"Shh, sweetie," she said. "She made the choice. She—"

"It was *my* choice," he said, his voice breaking. "*You* know it and *I* know it. She did it for me. She had a selfish side to her, I know that, but she would have done anything for me. I took the person who loved me more than I ever deserved to be loved, and I begged her to do something she knew was wrong for her. She had a gut feeling about it, Jo."

"I know," she said. "But—"

"I *destroyed* her." He began crying in earnest, like a child might cry, with rivers of tears and shaking shoulders, and Joelle wrapped her arms around him and held him tight, as though trying to keep the parts of him together. "I *killed* her, Jo," he said.

"Liam, no," she said, her own tears beginning to mix with his because she knew his words were, if only in his own heart and head, the truth.

It was a long time before his crying subsided. They lay together, holding each other tightly, and soon all that was left of his tears was an intermittent tremor that passed through his body beneath Joelle's arms.

Suddenly, he opened his eyes to look at her. Really look. She felt him explore every cell on her face as he lifted a long, thick strand of her hair from where it lay against her breast and draped it over her shoulder. "Thank you for being with me," he said. "I love you."

"And I love you." She stared into his eyes for a moment before leaning forward to kiss him, and she was not surprised when he met her halfway. The kiss was long and deep and started a hunger in her body she had not felt for years. He leaned away from her, only to return for another kiss a second later, and when she slipped her tongue between his teeth, he groaned.

She was wearing a long, loose skirt, and as he rolled on top of her, he carved a place between her legs with his own, until she could feel his erection press against her through their clothes. Kissing her harder and deeper, he rocked against her until she was on fire. Reaching her arms behind her, she grabbed the edge of the bookshelf headboard, then felt his teeth and tongue against the flesh on her throat. His hand tugged her blouse from her skirt and slipped beneath the silky fabric to gently squeeze her breast

through her bra. She could hear the ragged edge of his breathing...or maybe it was her own that she heard. She needed his
mouth on her breast. It was not a wish, not a want, but a *need.*

Letting go of the headboard, she reached for the placket of
her blouse, and with one quick tug tore it open, the fine mother-
of-pearl buttons pinging softly as they hit the hardwood floor
of the bedroom. She arched her back as Liam slipped his hands
behind her to unhook her bra. He lowered his head to her
breasts, his long hair brushing her chin and her chest, and the
moment his mouth circled one of her nipples, she cried out,
her body exploding with an orgasm delivered to her through
three layers of fabric. Then she was the one who was sobbing,
holding on to him as if afraid to let go, her breathing hitching
with her tears.

Slowly, Liam raised himself to his knees above her. Taking
her hand, he pressed it to the bulge of his penis beneath his
slacks, which were still zipped, still belted. He looked at her with
the eyes of a man who had not known physical love in a year.

"Please," he said.

Slipping out from under him, she guided him down onto the
bed where she had been lying. While he watched, she removed
her buttonless blouse, then her bra, her skirt, her panty hose, until
she was naked, standing next to the bed. The night-table lamp
was still on, and she knew her body was not slender and perfect
like Mara's, but she didn't feel at all self-conscious. Instead, she
felt loved. Liam's face was serious, his gaze held fast to her eyes,
as though it was not her nude body he wanted but something
deeper inside of her.

Climbing onto the bed, she straddled him and began to un-
button his shirt. He kept his eyes on hers as he ran his hands
slowly up her thighs. Bare-chested, he relaxed as she explored
his throat and chest and stomach with her tongue and lips.
Slowly, and with his help, she finished undressing him, then
leaned over to feel the heat of his penis against her cheek be-

fore closing her mouth around it. He groaned again and began moving with her, tangling his fingers in her long, thick hair.

"Come here," he said after a few minutes. "Let me come inside you."

She lifted her head, her hair falling over her breasts and his thighs, and moved up the bed until she could slip down on top of him.

"You feel so good," he said, and he was rocking again, not thrusting the way she was used to, but moving in a way that made her forget everything outside her own body. He held her hips tightly against him when she came this time, and the explosion of his own release quickly followed.

Lying next to him afterward, exhausted and chilled, she pressed her lips to his shoulder. "I love you," she said, but there was no reply.

She didn't feel it yet herself, but she knew it was coming. The guilt. She feared, though, that it had already found Liam. Without a word, he slipped out of the bed, leaving her skin cool where his body had been touching hers. He reached for the afghan that lay across the end of the bed and covered her with it, tucking it all around her as though he truly cared that she be comfortable and warm. He leaned over, and she felt him brush her hair from her forehead with his hand, then kiss her lightly on the temple. She heard him walk into the bathroom, then into the guest room, closing the door behind him. And she knew that she had both found and lost something, all in the same moment.

CHAPTER SEVENTEEN

Liam wondered if Joelle was simply ignoring his calls. He'd been trying to reach her since seven, when he'd arrived home from his visit to Mara. He left her one more message, calling her from the phone in his bedroom.

"Call me no matter what time it is when you get home," he said.

There was no point in going to bed yet because he knew he would not be able to sleep until he'd spoken to her, so he walked into the den and sat down at the computer desk. Once online, he navigated to the Web site that contained the essays—sometimes uplifting, sometimes heartbreaking—about aneurysm survivors. His jaw ached from clenching his teeth all evening, and he tried to relax as he looked through the Web site, but within moments he'd realize his jaw was clamped tight again.

There were no new essays on the site, even though he hadn't visited it in a few days, and he tried to read some of the older stories, but it was a struggle to find one that could still hold his interest. Those stories had offered him such hope in the beginning. They were written not only by the families of patients, but often by the patients themselves after they'd come back from the brink. In the beginning, he'd imagined Mara one day adding her own essay to the site, but that fantasy had evaporated along with his dreams for their future together.

He knew the essays by heart, and he had analyzed them. They fell into two broad categories: Either the patient had died within a few days, or they had begun their recovery. Sometimes that recovery was rapid, sometimes it was slow and involved many steps backward, but it always headed in the direction of redis-covered health. None described the limbo that had become Mara's existence. He'd longed to find a story like Mara's: a young woman, alive but not truly living, who'd left her husband with a small child and no promise of a future. If he found such a story, he would have written to that husband to ask him how he was handling the situation. How did he get up and keep going every day? How did he face his own future? How did he feel in the middle of the night when he woke up and reached for his wife, his lover, only to remember that she was lying in a nurs-ing home and could offer him nothing more than a vacant smile?

How did other men in his position manage this? At the age of thirty-five, was he to have only his fantasies—and his own hand in the dark—as his wife and lover for the rest of his life? Would this man Liam searched for, but could not find, give in to temp-tation the way he had with Joelle?

In those moments when he could step back, away from the pain and the loss, he would ask himself if there might be a reason for what had happened to his family. What was he to learn from this? But he could see no lesson here. Just a cruel joke by a cruel god.

He recalled working with the husband of an Alzheimer's pa-tient a couple of years ago. The man had been in his sixties, and he had slept with an acquaintance, a one-night stand. "I needed to know I was still a man," he'd said.

Liam had maintained his professional composure, remaining nonjudgmental as he helped the man talk through his feelings of loss and grief. Personally, though, he had recoiled from the man's words: "I needed to know I was still a man." To himself, he'd thought, *Selfish bastard. Whatever happened to your vow of "in sickness and in health"?*

When he thought of that man now, he knew he had been of little help to him. He hadn't understood what it was like to lose that part of oneself. Not just sex, but the intimacy that accompanied it, the waking up together with stale breath and bad hair, and feeling love in spite of it all.

His head began to ache as his thinking turned in circles. If he hadn't pushed Mara to have a child, she would be well. She'd still be that healthy, vibrant, bright, talented woman with whom he'd fallen in love. But then he would look at Sam and wonder how he had ever existed before having this child. Sam was a miracle wrapped up in flesh and blood, and the thought that he and Mara might never have created him was unthinkable. And yet, if Sam did not exist, Mara would be well. He could get lost in those thoughts, spinning in a circle that had no end.

He'd picked up Sam at Sheila's that evening after visiting Mara. Once or twice a week, he wanted to visit his wife alone, so Sheila would keep Sam longer. Thank God, he'd been able to work things out with his mother-in-law. They'd had a long lunchtime meeting the day after the spanking incident, when their heads had been cooler and their hearts more in sync, and they'd worked out a compromise: Sheila would not, under any circumstances, spank Sam. Instead, she would call Liam when she had a disciplinary problem, and they would think of a solution together. He'd asked Sheila to reward Sam's good behavior and not focus too much on the bad. Although she'd looked annoyed at taking parenting advice from him, the plan seemed to be working. He had not heard from Sheila again about the matter in the two weeks since their conversation.

His phone rang, and he quickly logged off the Internet and picked up the receiver.

"Hello?"

"Hi." It was Joelle's voice, and he felt the return of anger in a rush.

"What do you think you're doing?" he asked.

"I spoke with Carlynn Shire about Mara, and—"

"Why? You've always pooh-poohed the idea of Carlynn Shire," he said, truly bewildered by Joelle's behavior. "Your parents—"

"I can't explain it," Joelle interrupted him. "I just wanted to talk with her about the situation, and when I did, she thought she might be able to help. I didn't think it would hurt to at least let her meet Mara."

"I can't believe I'm hearing this. You're the one who's always saying she's probably a quack, that she didn't really save your life."

"I know. But what if I was wrong?" Joelle asked. "Mara believed so strongly in the power of the mind to heal the body. You know that. Don't you think she would have wanted us to try everything we could?"

"Mara *has* no mind," Liam said, and then winced. That was not true. At least, he didn't want it to be true. "I think it's abusive," he said. "You subjected Mara to something she didn't ask for. I don't like the idea of some stranger coming in there and—"

"Mara hasn't asked for *any* of the treatment she's received," Joelle reasoned. "She's dependent on those people who love her to make treatment choices for her."

She was right, of course, but that didn't stop him.

"I don't want you bringing *anyone* to see Mara without my permission," he said.

"Didn't you notice Mara seemed a bit more alert when you were there?" Joelle asked.

He scowled into the phone. "No, I didn't. As a matter of fact, I think she was completely worn out from her visit with you and Carlynn Shire. She didn't touch her, did she?"

"She massaged her hands with baby lotion."

Why that seemed like such an invasion, he couldn't say. He felt as he had when Sheila told him she'd spanked Sam. Mara was as trusting and vulnerable as a little child, ignorant of everything going on around her, and she would smile through any assault.

"She thinks she can help, Liam."

"That's utterly ridiculous."

"You may be right, but she's a truly nice woman and maybe she can do something we don't understand. What would it hurt to let her try? She wants to see Mara again. And she asked that you be there, as well."

"The answer is no, Joelle," he said. "No, I won't be there, and no, you may not bring her to see Mara. Please don't ask me again. I have enough to deal with right now." He hung up the phone without saying goodbye.

He walked from the den to the bedroom, still angry, and with an added sense of having escaped from a great threat. If he yelled at Joelle, if he was cruel to her, as he thought he had been on the phone, he was safe. That aching longing he had for her, the love and admiration, didn't exist when he was chewing her out. And he thought, now, that he would be able to sleep tonight.

Around three in the morning, though, he woke up with a start, feeling much as he had the night after they'd made love, when he'd turned away from her with the hope of saving himself.

CHAPTER EIGHTEEN

San Francisco, 1956

Lisbeth was terrified. Dr. Peterson had borrowed Gabriel Johnson's tennis racket the day before and now wanted her to return
it to him at San Francisco General. That was why she was locked
in the stall in one of the first-floor ladies' rooms at the hospital
during her lunch break. The tennis racket rested against the tiled
wall while Lisbeth stared at herself in the mirror, trying to get
her breathing under control.

What would she say to him? She'd never had a problem talking to him over the phone, and lately their conversations had
grown even longer. But over the phone her voice did not give
away her size.

She thought about Gabriel often when she was in bed at night,
and she talked to him in her head all the time when she was
alone. She told him everything about herself, which made it hard
for her to remember that he did not actually know her as well
as she felt he did.

A few weeks ago, he'd suggested she call him Gabriel instead
of Mr. Johnson.

"I'd feel strange calling you by your first name," she'd said.

"I want you to," he'd answered in that deep voice that she loved. He had this way of making her feel like his equal, as though that was very important to him. As though the chief accountant of a big hospital and a medical secretary were on the same level.

"Okay, Gabriel." She'd smiled, relieved, actually, since she called him that in her imagination all the time and was always afraid she'd slip while talking to him on the phone.

Her fantasies of Gabriel had become so intense, such a glorious part of her quiet existence, and she feared they would come to an end once he saw her. Touching up her makeup in the ladies'-room mirror, she pressed powder to her forehead and nose and rubbed a circle of rouge onto her cheeks. She didn't want to look as though she'd made herself up especially for this meeting, so she skipped a fresh application of lipstick. She patted her petal curls into place. It was a stylish haircut, but what did it matter when the face that it framed was as round as a bowling ball? In her fantasies, she would meet Gabriel Johnson after losing sixty or seventy pounds. When, exactly, that would be she didn't know. In the past six months, she'd added another ten pounds to her two hundred, and she was beginning to have difficulty finding a uniform for the doctor's office that fit her.

She thought of simply leaving the racket with someone at the hospital's reception desk, but as much as she didn't want to be seen by Gabriel, she was longing to see him, to see the man who had facelessly filled her fantasies and her dreams for the past year and a half.

The woman at the information desk was an elderly volunteer, and the name tag attached to her collar read Madge.

Lisbeth smiled at her. "I'm looking for Gabriel Johnson's office," she said.

"Is he the bookkeeper?" the woman asked.

"The chief accountant. Yes."

"That's the business office." The woman pointed a misshapen finger toward the bank of elevators in the corridor. "Second floor. Take the elevator and turn right, and his office is there on the corner."

Lisbeth felt nauseous in the elevator, and she knew the perspiration was returning to her nose and forehead. By the time she turned the knob of the door to the business office, her hand was shaking.

There was no one sitting at the reception desk when she walked into the business office. She stood, waiting, for an uncomfortable moment, the racket at her side, before spotting an open door halfway down a narrow hallway.

"Hello?" she called, hoping the person in that office would hear her, but there was no response.

She walked down the hall and knocked on the open door, peering inside the room at the same time. A colored man sat at a desk, and he looked up at the sound of her knock.

"Excuse me," she said. "I'm looking for Gabriel Johnson."

The man had been writing something, but now he set down his pen.

"I'm Gabriel Johnson," he said.

"No—" She stopped herself. She wanted to tell him that he couldn't possibly be Gabriel. She wanted to tell him he was wrong, or to ask him if he was playing some sort of trick on her. But that voice. She recognized it, the depth and gentleness of it. She was stunned beyond speech, though. Gabriel—*her* Gabriel—was colored?

"Ah, I see you have my racket," he said, standing up. "You must be Lisbeth."

"Yes." She tried to smile, holding the racket toward him. Her fantasy instantly evaporated, leaving a huge empty space inside her chest. She refused to think of herself as a bigot, but a romance with a colored man was out of the question. Her knees were full of jelly, and she was glad when he motioned toward the chair opposite his desk.

"Please, sit down, Lisbeth."

She handed him the racket, then sank into the chair. Suddenly, she understood why Gabriel played tennis on Dr. Peterson's private court. He would not be welcome at most of the courts around town.

Gabriel sat down again, resting his racket on the desk. He smiled at her, and she saw so much in that smile. She could see an apology there, and understanding, along with a deep well of sadness.

"I should have told you in our phone conversations that I was a Negro," he said.

"Well," she said, "I should have told you that I was fat." The words were out of her mouth before she could stop them, and she laughed out loud at herself.

Gabriel laughed, too. In fact, he roared, then shook his head, taking off his horn-rimmed glasses to wipe his eyes. "I would say you are every bit as lovely as your voice," he said.

What else could he say? she thought. He was trying to take the awkwardness out of the moment. She was certain, though, that he felt the same sting of disappointment at seeing her that she felt at seeing him.

"Hey," he said suddenly. "I wanted to show this to you." Lifting a framed photograph from his desk, he handed it to her. It was a picture of a sailboat, and it looked very much like the sloop her family had once owned. She looked from the picture back to him.

"Is this yours?" she asked. "The boat you told me about?"

He nodded. "What do you think?"

"It's a beauty," she said. "It reminds me of the boat my father used to take me out on."

"I love it," he said, taking the picture back from her and placing it again on his desk. "I feel so free out on the water."

She remembered that feeling well, although she'd not experienced it in a long time. "Where did you learn to sail?" she asked.

"My father taught me, too," he said. "On an estuary in Oakland."

She remembered him telling her he was originally from Oakland, but now she pictured his childhood home in the section of that city where the colored people lived.

"Is that why you went in the navy?" she asked, recalling that he had told her he'd served in the war.

"Yes," he said. "You have a good memory. And I recall that you grew up along the Seventeen Mile Drive. And you have a twin sister."

"Right."

"Identical or fraternal?"

"Identical," she said, although it felt like a lie, since she was nearly twice her sister's size.

"Amazing to think there are two of you." He smiled. "Are you alike in other ways, as well?"

Lisbeth bit her lip. She did not want to talk about Carlynn. She did not want to draw attention to the twin who had always received it. Yet, she longed to pour her heart out to this man who seemed so interested in her. She drew in a breath.

"We are nothing alike," she said. "Carlynn's a doctor. She graduated from medical school last June, and now she's an intern here at SF General."

"So, you both have an interest in medicine."

It seemed ridiculous that he was comparing Carlynn's being a doctor to her being a secretary in a physician's office, but he was actually right. She loved it when Dr. Peterson talked to her about his patients, especially when he spoke of those he seemed unable to help, and she often pressed him for the medical details of those cases. Sometimes, she wanted to ask Carlynn to come over and just sit with one of those patients in the waiting room, just touch his or her hand gently, to see if perhaps she could make a difference.

"Yes, we do," Lisbeth said. "But I could never be a doctor."

"Why not?" Gabriel asked.

"I'm just not...as smart as she is. I know that supposedly we have the same brain. But somehow...she's just smarter than me, that's all. We went to different schools." She didn't want to sound small and bitter. Besides, education was not the primary difference between herself and Carlynn. "And she has this...ability..." She spoke slowly, not certain how much to say. Carlynn was still very secretive about her gift. "She will be a gifted physician," Lisbeth said simply.

"I don't think you give yourself enough credit," Gabriel said. "Whenever I talk to you, I'm struck by how concerned and well educated you are about Lloyd's patients."

"Thank you," she said, touched by his kindness. Then, suddenly, she shook her head.

He leaned forward on his desk. "Why are you shaking your head?"

Don't cry, she told herself. *Don't cry in front of him.*

"It's just that—" She stopped herself short. Could she say this to him? She had little to lose at this point. "You're so nice. And I...talking with you on the phone...I've allowed myself to imagine...well, we have common interests, and so I allowed myself to foolishly think we might..."

"Me, too." His smile was warm, his teeth very white against his milk chocolate-colored skin, and he suddenly looked beautiful to her. "Though I guess I knew that when you met me, it would be over. I'm a Negro, to begin with. I'm what...ten years older than you?"

"I'm twenty-seven," she said.

He groaned. "Eleven years older, then."

And I'm fat, she wanted to add, but managed to stop herself.

"Is it impossible?" he asked.

She raised her eyes quickly to his. "You mean...?"

"Is it impossible for us to go out together?" He looked ill at ease for the first time, and she felt like hugging him to make him comfortable again. "I mean," he continued, "how would you feel about that? Would it be awkward for you to be seen with me?"

She shook her head. "No." She hoped she was being honest in her answer. "No. I wouldn't care."

"What about your family?"

Oh, God. "My sister wouldn't care," she said, hoping that was the truth, as well. "But my mother..." Her voice trailed off.

"Your mother?" he prompted.

"She thinks...well, she sees..." She started to say colored people, but he had referred to himself as a Negro, and she decided she should use his language. "She sees Negroes as servants or manual laborers."

He nodded. "Not unusual," he said, and she picked up a hint of some old, deep anger in his voice.

"But—" she shrugged with a laugh "—she already detests me, so I guess I shouldn't worry about that."

"Detests you? Why on earth?"

"I...oh, it's a long story."

He suddenly picked up his phone and pressed the intercom button.

"Nancy?" he said. "No interruptions."

Hanging up the phone, he stood and closed his office door until it was almost completely shut, but not quite, and she was grateful for his sense of propriety. He sat down again.

"When is Lloyd expecting you back?" he asked.

She looked at her watch. "At around one," she said.

Gabriel picked up his phone again, and with a jolt, Lisbeth noticed he was missing two fingers on his left hand, both the pinkie and ring fingers. They'd been sliced off right down to his hand, and she wondered what he had been through. Had he lost them as a child or an adult?

Gabriel dialed a number. "Lloyd? It's Gabe," he said. "Lisbeth Kling is here and she'll be late getting back to you. Yes, it's my fault. I need to keep her here a while longer. We have some things to discuss." He smiled across the desk at her. "Sure, thanks." He hung up the phone and leaned back in his chair.

"Now we have time for your long story," he said.

She told him everything, letting out the secrets and sadness of her childhood years. She spoke of her love for her sister despite her feelings of bitterness and resentment, emotions she usually tried hard to keep hidden. She cried, but only a little, when she spoke about how hard it was to go home these days. She *needed* to spend time at Cypress Point, she told him, the way someone else might need food or medicine, but she had not yet figured out a way to prevent her mother's insults from ruining those visits for her.

Never before had she chronicled the hurt in her life in quite this way. She'd never allowed it to spill out to another soul. Gabriel's face was full of sympathy and understanding, and she had the feeling he had experienced the same sort of ostracism she had. Not from a mother, perhaps, but from the world at large. Somehow, though, he had overcome it, and she wondered if he might be able to teach her how to do the same. His gentleness, his attentive listening, was seductive and comforting, and by the time she had finished her story she was in love—with Gabriel the man, not Gabriel the fantasy.

"Don't answer now," he said as he walked her to the door after their long conversation. "But I would love to go out with you. Sailing, or out to dinner, or just about anywhere. Do you have a phone?"

"I can only use my landlord's phone in an emergency," she said, thrilled, but by this point, not surprised, by his invitation. "I can call from Dr. Peterson's office, though."

Stepping back to his desk, Gabriel jotted down a phone number on a piece of paper and handed it to her.

"I'm giving you an open invitation," he said. "If you decide you want to go out with me, please call. I'll leave it up to you."

"Dr. Kling. Call the front desk." The voice came over the hospital loudspeaker, and Carlynn looked up from the chart on which she was writing. She was accustomed to being paged these days, now that she was an intern. The pages were often from Alan, of course, but he was good about using the paging system for business only, keeping their personal relationship out of the hospital. They had been dating for six months now, and after their initial conversation about her "gift," Alan had found ways to bring her in on cases. A couple of times he'd even spirited her into patients' rooms in the middle of the night so that she could sit with them while they slept, her hands on their bodies. She'd discovered, though, the mere touching of the patients alone did not seem nearly as effective as when she was able to look into their eyes and speak with them. She and Alan were both fascinated by trying to determine when her skills would work and when they wouldn't. What made the difference? She truly could not say.

In front of others, they were Dr. Shire and Dr. Kling, but they often couldn't wait until the end of the day, when they could discuss cases, pore over Alan's books on the subject of healing, and sometimes, when the serious business of medicine was set aside, laugh together. Alan was fairly good-looking, but he was more scientist than Prince Charming, and she was no empty-headed fairy-tale damsel. Their brains and their passion for their work drew them together and solidified their relationship, so that when they finally did sleep together, it was almost as an afterthought. There was love between them, of that Carlynn had no doubt, but it was not a romantic love, and she told herself that was fine. Next to Lisbeth, Alan was her best friend, the person with whom she could be entirely honest about her gift. If they ever married, something they had spoken about a time or two, he would make a wonderful father, and she was longing to have children. She could ask for little more than that.

Quickly, she finished writing her note in the chart, then picked up the phone to dial the operator.

"This is Dr. Kling," she said when the operator answered. She waited to hear her say that Dr. Shire was on the line for her, but the operator surprised her.

"Lisbeth Kling on the line for you," the operator said.

"All right." Carlynn frowned, a bit concerned. It was rare for Lisbeth to disturb her at the hospital. "Put her through, please."

"Carly? I'm so sorry to bother you at work."

"That's all right. What is it? Are you okay?"

"I'm here in the hospital. I'm fine, though," she added quickly. "I came here on business for Dr. Peterson, and I need your advice, Carly. Do you have some time?"

Carlynn looked at her watch. "I'll meet you in the front lobby in five minutes," she said, then hung up the phone.

The lobby was large, in need of new furniture and very crowded, but she quickly spotted her sister near the entrance and sat down next to her on one of the sofas. "What's going on?" she asked.

"I met him," Lisbeth said. Her face glowed with excitement. "Dr. Peterson's tennis partner."

"You did?"

"Yes. But I need to talk to you about him."

Carlynn glanced at her watch again. It would soon be time for afternoon rounds, but she would just have to be late. She moved closer to her sister.

"Talk to me, then," she said.

"Oh, Carlynn," Lisbeth grabbed her arm. "He's wonderful."

Despite her concerns, Carlynn couldn't help but grin at the rare joy in her twin's face. "Go on."

"I had to bring his tennis racket to him. Dr. Peterson had borrowed it. I was so nervous!"

"And what happened?"

"He was absolutely the best, Carlynn. Just as nice as he's been on the phone. I talked with him in his office for over an hour, and he asked me out."

"Hurrah!" Carlynn clapped her hands together, but she felt fear mixed with her joy. Whoever he was, he'd better not hurt her sister. Lisbeth was not stupid, but she could be very vulnerable, a dreamer filled with longing. It was far too easy for her to be taken advantage of. "What's his name?"

"Gabriel Johnson." Lisbeth looked at her expectantly. "Do you recognize it?" she asked.

Carlynn frowned. "No. Should I?"

"He's the chief accountant here."

"Here?" Carlynn asked. "He works here? You've been talking to him on the phone for over a year. Why didn't you ever tell me he works here?"

"Because I didn't want you to go peek at him and tell me something about him that would wreck my..." She lowered her voice. "My idea of what he looked like." She started to laugh.

"What's so funny?"

Lisbeth shook her head, but she was still grinning. "Oh, Carlynn," she said. "Here comes the problem."

"What?"

"If you go stop by the business office, you'll see."

"Tell me!"

"He's colored."

Carlynn caught her breath. The first thought in her head was "You're kidding," but that was not what Lisbeth needed to hear. She wasn't certain *what* she should say to her sister. She could think of no colored professionals working at the hospital, but then recalled noticing a nice-looking Negro in the corridor once or twice, a man obviously not a patient, carrying a briefcase. He was missing fingers on his left hand.

"Carlynn?" Lisbeth sounded worried.

Carlynn laughed. "You caught me off guard there," she said. "I might know who he is. Is he tall and good-looking? Is he missing two—"

"That's him!" Lisbeth nodded.

"I've never spoken to him, but he looks nice," Carlynn said. "He's a lot older than you, though, I think, but then Alan is ten years older than me, so I guess I can't say anything about that."

"But Alan isn't colored."

She knew Lisbeth was waiting for her opinion of her dating a Negro. "Does it matter to *you* that he's colored?" she asked her.

"I really like him, Carly," Lisbeth said.

"Then go out with him." Carlynn was unsure if that was the right advice, but she'd never heard such joy in her sister's voice before.

"What about Mother?" Lisbeth asked.

"What about her? Mother won't like anybody we pick. She doesn't even like Alan. No one's good enough for me, in her eyes."

"Well, maybe she'll think a colored man would be just perfect for me, then," Lisbeth said.

Carlynn laughed, but without much spirit. "Look," she said, "it doesn't matter what Mother or anyone else thinks. Not even me. None of that matters, Lisbeth, if you really like him. You can't live your life trying to please everyone else." Mother, she thought, must never know. Perhaps this man would just be the start of dating for Lisbeth. Perhaps Mother never would have to know that Lisbeth had seen him. "So, did you accept his invitation to go out?"

"I'm supposed to call him," she said. "He left it up to me to decide if I wanted to or not. He understood that I might feel...uncomfortable."

"Do you?"

"I think he's the most. He sails, Carlynn. He has his own boat."

This was one unusual Negro, Carlynn thought. She knew how much Lisbeth loved sailing. "Then call him," she said. "Do you want Alan and me to go out with you the first time? A double date? As long as it's not on a boat, that is."

"Oh, would you?"

"Of course." It was strange. She had been intimately involved with Alan for half a year, yet she had no idea how he would feel about a white woman dating a colored man.

"How *are* things with you and Alan?" Lisbeth asked, as though she felt rude for having focused the conversation on herself.

"Great," Carlynn said, and they were. But just then she wanted to feel some of the passion that Lisbeth clearly felt. She wanted a man whom she could be certain was in love with *her,* not just with her gift.

CHAPTER NINETEEN

There was no better way to let you know you had no friends than spending a birthday alone, Joelle thought. It was early Saturday morning, July fourteenth, and she was seated in front of her computer checking housing prices on the Internet. She had looked at Berkeley and Chicago and was now surfing through a real estate site for the third city she'd added to her list, San Diego, since a social worker she'd known from Silas Memorial was living there. It would be best if she could stay in California, she thought, so that she wouldn't have to worry about getting a social-work license in another state.

She'd decided she'd rent when she first moved, putting her condo on the market and using her savings for her expenses until it sold. At that point, she could decide if she wanted to buy something in her new town. Right now, though, she couldn't imagine taking that permanent a step. It was hard for her to picture herself living anywhere but here.

She was sixteen weeks pregnant and still able to hide her belly, although that feat was getting more difficult by the day. If anyone wondered why she now fancied loose jumpers and tunic tops, no one said a word. At least, not to her. She would have to leave within a month, though, to be able to keep her secret, and she worried that waiting that long might be pushing her luck.

Happy birthday to me.

"Feeling a little sorry for ourselves, are we?" she said out loud as she clicked the "rentals" button on the real estate page. She was now officially thirty-five years old. She'd hear from her parents sometime during the day, of course, but knew she would receive no card from them and certainly no gift. She and Mara used to take each other out to dinner on their birthdays, just one of several rituals they'd had. No one at work had said a word to her about her birthday yesterday, but, of course, she hadn't re-minded anyone, either. The only people who were showing any serious intention of acknowledging the day were Tony and Gary, who had invited her for dinner, an invitation she'd accepted be-cause she knew she would be depressed tonight if she didn't have something to do. They would make a cake and fuss over her, and she would be eternally grateful for their kindness.

She planned to visit Carlynn that afternoon, and thought she might tell *her* that today was her birthday. It was possible Car-lynn might even remember, since she'd actually been there at Joelle's birth. That thought made her laugh out loud, but then she realized that the thirty-fifth anniversary of Carlynn's sister's death was also this week, so perhaps she would keep her mouth shut about her birthday, after all.

After her phone conversation the week before with Liam, Joelle had called Carlynn to tell her she'd been, essentially, forbidden to bring the healer to visit Mara again. She wanted to say to the older woman, "But I'd still like to see you sometimes. Can we be friends?" but she'd felt awkward making that statement. It was Carlynn who said it for her, as she seemed to read her thoughts.

"Then *you* come see me," Carlynn had said with certainty. "We never know how these things work. Perhaps Mara can get better through you, if you occasionally visit with me."

The concept made even less sense than Carlynn being able to heal Mara by actually touching her, but Joelle was not about to argue. She visited the mansion the following day, and she and Carlynn walked around the grounds. Carlynn seemed in good shape and good spirits, and did some of the walking without her cane. Quinn, the elderly black man, was helping some strapping young men with the yard work, and Alan was not at home, a fact that secretly pleased Joelle. Although maybe he wouldn't mind her being there now that she was not asking Carlynn to heal Mara.

Mrs. McGowan made them a picnic lunch, which they took to Fanshell Beach, practically next door to the mansion. They sat on rocks under the shade of a cypress, not too far from where the harbor seals basked in the sun, and ate little crustless sandwiches and talked and talked and talked. Carlynn described what it had been like growing up in the mansion. She spoke about her life as a twin and the close bond she'd had with her sister, as well as the guilt she felt over having been the beloved twin while her sister suffered neglect. She told Joelle about healing the family dog when she was a child, without even knowing what she was doing.

Carlynn wanted to know exactly what Liam had said to Joelle on the phone the night after her visit to Mara, and Joelle told her how furious he had been.

"He's still angry with me," she said, remembering how coolly he'd treated her at work this week. "He's completely changed from someone who loved me—and I know he truly did—to someone who seems to despise me."

"I doubt that," Carlynn had said.

"You didn't hear him on the phone," she said simply.

It was nearly noon when she had finished searching the Web, and she was about to get dressed for the visit with Carlynn when her phone rang. Checking the caller ID display, she recognized Liam's number. She hesitated only a moment, then pressed the talk button on the receiver.

"Liam?"

"I'm sorry to disturb you on a Saturday," he said. "I'm on call, and I just heard from the cardiac unit. One of my patients isn't doing well, and they want me to come in to be with the family. Sheila had to go to Santa Cruz for the day. Her sister's sick up there, so I have no one to leave Sam with. Is there a chance you could watch him?"

He had to feel like a heel asking her for a favor after the way he'd treated her this past week, but she wouldn't rub his nose in it. This was a professional call, and although it would mean canceling with Carlynn at the last minute, there was no question that she would do as he asked. Besides, she could think of no better way to spend the afternoon than with Sam.

"I'll be right over," she said.

She called Carlynn from the cell phone in her car as she drove over to Liam's.

"Ah," Carlynn said, and she actually sounded a bit pleased. "I understand. No need to apologize. We'll get together another day. And Joelle?"

"Yes?"

"Happy birthday, dear."

Liam was waiting on his front porch with Sam in his arms, and when he handed the baby to her, she was surprised at how heavy Sam had become.

"Thanks," Liam said. "I'll call you when I know what time I'll be back."

"I'll take my cell if we go out," she said.

She and Sam stayed on the porch until Liam had pulled out of the driveway, and she was relieved that Sam did not seem distressed as he watched his father drive away. It had been a while since she'd spent much time with the little boy, and she hadn't been sure how he would react to being left alone with her.

Pulling open the screen door, she walked inside the house. Before she did anything else, she wanted to get her fill of just holding Sam in her arms, so she sat on the sofa with him and began nuzzling his delicate little neck.

"Sammy, Sammy, Sammy!" she said, and he giggled, squirming as she tickled his neck with her lips. "What shall we do today, sweetie pie?"

The sun was shining outside the living-room windows, and the sky was a cloudless, vivid blue. "Let's not waste our time inside," she said. "Who wants to go tide pooling with me?"

"Me!" He wriggled from her arms to stand in front of her on the floor, his little hands on her knees. "Me, me, me!"

"Do you even know what a tide pool is?" she asked.

He nodded. "I go bool," he said.

"Not a pool, silly. A tide pool."

"Tybool."

"Right! Let's go." She stood up and headed for the mudroom, where she knew she would find an extra car seat and where the cupboard above the laundry sink would hold some sunscreen. Sam followed close behind her, trying to grab her leg as she walked.

"We go tybool!" he said.

Once in the car, Joelle drove to a parking area along the coastal trail. She got Sam out of the car seat and watched with trepidation as he ran toward the rocky beach. Maybe this was not such a good idea. She hadn't realized how mobile Sam was these days.

They spent an hour exploring the tide pools, and Joelle thought Sam enjoyed himself almost as much as she did, although she was certain he was tired of hearing her say, "Don't touch," by the time they were ready to leave.

Liam called her cell phone as she was driving back to his house.

"I'll be another hour," he said. "Is that all right?"

"No problem. We're on our way back from the beach, and I think you-know-who is ready for a nap."

"Okay," Liam said. "I usually put him in his crib with a couple of books. He entertains himself until he falls asleep."

"All right," she said. "Thanks for the tip."

She changed Sam's diaper when they got back to the house, then laid him in his crib with a couple of picture books. She doubted the books were needed, though, because Sam was ready to crash. Standing over the crib for a moment, she stroked her fingertips over his blond curls. *Mara,* she thought, her eyes filling just a bit, *I wish you could enjoy your beautiful baby boy.*

In the kitchen, she poured herself a Coke, then noticed the yellow envelope propped against the phone on the counter. The envelope read *Joelle* in Liam's handwriting. Picking it up, she tore open the flap. Inside was a card, the sort you would send to a child for her birthday, with a big-eyed puppy and kitten on the front. Below the animals were the words *For A Special Girl.* She opened it to find the verse, *Says the Little Kitty, and Puppy, too, There's no Other Girl as Nice as You! Happy Birthday!* It was signed, *Love, Liam and Sam,* and simple and silly though it was, it put a grin on her face. She could picture Liam and Sam picking the card out together.

She wandered aimlessly around the house for a while, sipping her Coke, looking at the framed pictures of Mara that were scattered here and there, noticing the dust on the guitar case standing in the corner of the living room and the ever-growing pile of Sam's toys in the den. Finally, she found herself in the doorway to Liam's bedroom. She stared at the bed, trying both to remember and forget the night she had slept in this room. Liam had made the bed in a hurry this morning, the green-and-white-striped coverlet pulled up sloppily above the pillow. The blue afghan, which matched nothing else in the room, and which Liam had tucked around her nude body before moving to the guest room, hung over the footboard of the bed.

On the bookshelf behind the bed she spotted the book of meditations she'd given him. It was lying flat on the shelf, separate from the other books, as though Liam read from it often. She walked into the room and sat down on the bed, pulling the book from the shelf, remembering their Point Lobos hike and how close she'd felt to him as he'd read aloud from the book.

As she opened the book, a photograph fell from between the pages, and she felt a chill when she saw the picture of herself. She knew when it had been taken—the day she and Liam discovered Sam was far too young to appreciate the Dennis the Menace Playground. The photograph was no more than five or six months old, yet it looked worn, as though it had been handled a great deal, and Joelle bit her lip. She felt as though she was peering inside Liam's soul, a place she had no permission to see.

Oh, Liam.

Closing the book, she returned it to the shelf behind his bed and stood up. That's when she felt it. Not a fluttering, as she'd expected, but more like a bubble. She rested her hand on her stomach as the bubble moved again, and she smiled to herself.

She was not alone today, after all.

CHAPTER TWENTY

San Francisco, 1956

The air was cool and damp on Fisherman's Wharf, but the huge iron cauldrons offered bursts of crab-scented warmth as Carlynn and Alan walked toward the restaurant where they were to meet Lisbeth and her date. Although it was autumn and the sky was dark, the well-lit wharf was crammed with people, some of them eating shrimp and crabmeat from little paper trays as they strolled.

Carlynn spotted Lisbeth standing in front of Tarantino's, and she took Alan's arm and pointed.

"She's here first," she said with a grin. "Do you think she's a little anxious?"

"Can't blame her," Alan said. "This is her first date in a while, isn't it?"

"In her *life,*" Carlynn corrected, then more to herself than Alan, "My poor sweet sister." She bit her lip as they neared Lisbeth, who looked beautiful in a blue coat that matched her eyes. Lisbeth was big, yes, but her legs were shapely, if not slender, and she was wearing adorable strappy black heels that must have been murder to walk in all the way from the cable car. Her blond hair, with its carefully constructed waves and curls, so perfectly framed her face that Carlynn thought she might have her own hair cut that way. *No,* she told herself. She should let that cute style be her sister's.

Lisbeth waved as soon as she saw them.

"She's terrified," Carlynn whispered to Alan, waving back. "Look at her." Lisbeth's face wore a smile that was only skin deep; Carlynn could see the apprehension just below the surface.

"Oh, God, I'm so glad you're here!" Lisbeth said, clutching her sister's gloved hands in her own.

"You look beautiful," Alan said, bussing Lisbeth's cheek, and Carlynn loved him for his kindness.

"Thanks," Lisbeth said. "What time is it, though? He's not here yet." She tried to peer through the throng of people.

"It's just seven, honey," Carlynn said. "Relax."

"Boy, does that shrimp smell good." Alan eyed one of the women walking by with a little tray of shrimp. "It's making my mouth water."

"Do you know him, Alan?" Lisbeth asked. "Gabriel? From the hospital?"

"I've seen him around, but no, I don't know him person-ally," Alan said. "I asked around a bit, though, did a bit of checking, and—"

"Alan, you didn't!" Carlynn scolded him.

"Yes, I did," he answered.

"What did you say to the people you asked?" Lisbeth looked worried. "Will it get back to him?"

"I was very discreet," he said. "I just tried to find out what kind of fellow he is. Make sure he's not a womanizer, that's all."

Carlynn knew Alan had worried, not so much that Gabriel might be a womanizer, but that he might want to be seen with a white woman to raise his status. "Lisbeth could be ruining her life if she goes out with him," he'd told her. "White men might not want her if they find out." Carlynn had to admit she'd had the same concern.

"Well, what did you learn?" Lisbeth asked.

"That he was married before."

"He's *divorced?*" Lisbeth looked brokenhearted.

"No, he's widowed. He was married to a woman—a Negro woman, in case you're wondering—and she died five years ago of breast cancer."

"Oh!" Lisbeth's hand flew to her mouth. "Oh, how sad. Poor Gabriel."

"He apparently was very attentive to her and cared for her himself as much as he could. And he hasn't dated since. At least not according to my source."

"Who was your source?" Carlynn asked, curious.

"None of your business," he answered, but he winked at her, and she was certain she knew. Alan was friends with Lloyd Peterson, Lisbeth's boss and Gabriel Johnson's friend and tennis partner.

"Poor Gabriel," Lisbeth said again, her eyes full of sympathy.

Carlynn studied the faces of the tourists as they strolled past the restaurant eating cocktails, laughing and talking, and it was a moment before she became aware of the fact that every single face she could see in front of her—every one!—was white. Gabriel Johnson would feel out of place here, she thought. He managed at the hospital, though, and he was out of place there, as well. He was probably well accustomed to feeling that way.

Lisbeth spotted him first. "There he is," she whispered, grabbing Carlynn's arm again with quiet excitement.

Carlynn looked through the crowd to see Gabriel walking toward them, his dark face standing out from the pale faces of the tourists. When he saw Lisbeth, he broke into a grin and waved, and the color in Lisbeth's cheeks grew brighter and her eyes glowed. Carlynn thought she had never looked prettier.

Gabriel took Lisbeth's hand and gave it a gentle squeeze. "It's so good to see you again," he said.

"You, too." She smiled. The two of them looked positively lost in one another.

"Yoo-hoo," Carlynn said. "Remember us?"

Lisbeth laughed. "Gabriel, this is my sister, Carlynn, and her boyfriend, Alan Shire."

"Drs. Shire and Kling," Gabriel said, shaking Alan's hand and nodding to Carlynn. "We've crossed paths in the hospital from time to time. Good to finally meet you both."

"Please," Alan said. "Call us Alan and Carlynn."

Carlynn studied his face. She had honestly never thought before about colored men being handsome or ugly or anything in between, the way she did when she saw a white man. But looking at Gabriel through Lisbeth's eyes, she could see how attractive he was. He wore his hair very short, close and tight to his scalp. His face was fairly long and thin, and he wore horn-rimmed glasses that made him look very serious, but that could not quite mask the sparkle in his dark eyes.

"Let's eat," Alan said, and he motioned toward the door of the restaurant.

The hostess led them to the upper story of the restaurant, to a table in the darkest corner, away from the windows and the other tables, and Carlynn couldn't help but wonder if Gabriel's presence had something to do with her choice.

"We'd prefer a table by the window," Alan said, not moving to sit down.

"Certainly, sir," the hostess said, as though she wondered why she hadn't thought of that herself. She led them to an empty table next to a window. Alan thanked her, and the four of them sat down.

Carlynn felt her own anxiety mount as other diners glanced in their direction, but Lisbeth did not seem to care a bit. She and Gabriel were already chatting, their heads close together as they laughed about some subject that had meaning only to the two of them. Carlynn wondered if she and Alan were needed here at all.

Their table overlooked the harbor. It was dark outside, but they could see the wharf lights reflected off the boats lined up along the pier.

"Thanks for getting us this table, Alan," Lisbeth said, straightening in her seat as though realizing she and Gabriel had been rude to ignore him and Carlynn. She giggled a little, still amused by her conversation with Gabriel, and Carlynn thought she had never heard that girlish sound from her sister, not even when they were children.

They ordered cioppino all around, and talked about the hospital. Alan and Gabriel had been at SF General for about the same length of time and knew many people in common, so Carlynn and Lisbeth listened as they asked each other about various incidents that had taken place at the hospital. Occasionally, the men included Carlynn or Lisbeth in their discussion, but only due to the demands of good etiquette. The women didn't belong in this conversation, and that was all right. They smiled at each other as Gabriel and Alan exchanged stories and laughter. The bond between the two men could not have developed more quickly, Carlynn thought, if they had been locked together in a prison cell.

Once their huge bowls of cioppino arrived at the table, the men turned their attention to the food. Gabriel buttered a piece of sourdough bread, holding the slice in his right hand and using the knife with his left, deftly maneuvering it despite the missing fingers.

"You and Alan are both lefties," Carlynn said.

"Well," Gabriel smiled, "I *was* left-handed before this happened." He nodded toward the injured hand. "I still use it when I can. I can write with it, but I can't hold a racket. I had to learn to play tennis right-handed, which is still a challenge, as Lloyd Peterson can probably tell you."

"What happened?" Lisbeth asked the question neither she nor Alan dared to.

"I was at Port Chicago," Gabriel said.

"My God." Alan, his spoon halfway to his mouth, sat back in his chair.

Carlynn exchanged an ignorant glance with her sister. She knew something big had happened during the war at Port Chicago, a town about fifty miles north of where they were now sitting, but she and Lisbeth had been young and well-protected teens at the time.

"What was it like?" Alan asked.

Gabriel worked a clam free of its shell. "It's not the best dinner-table topic," he said, looking apologetic.

"I want to hear," Lisbeth insisted. "Unless...of course, if you're uncomfortable talking about it."

"Do you know what happened at Port Chicago?" he asked Lisbeth.

Something bad, Carlynn would have answered, but her sister surprised her.

"An explosion of some sort?" Lisbeth asked. "Some men were loading explosives onto a ship and something went wrong?"

Gabriel nodded. "Something went very wrong." He sipped from his drink, then continued. "I joined the navy in 1943. They'd only opened their ranks to Negroes the year before, but I felt it was my duty to volunteer. I already had a degree from Berkeley, and I was married." He looked at Lisbeth, touching the back of her hand gently with his fingertips, and said only to her, "Which is something I'll tell you about later."

Lisbeth nodded.

"I loved to sail, and I wanted to go to sea," Gabriel continued. "I went through boot camp and training school and then off to Port Chicago, where I expected to ship out. But when I got there, I found out the navy wasn't letting Negroes into combat. Instead, they put us on the loading docks, loading munitions onto ships, with no special training whatsoever. We knew it was dangerous, but I don't think we had any idea how much so."

"All the men doing the loading were Negroes," Alan added as he reached for another piece of bread. "And the guys supervising them were white, if I remember correctly."

"That's right," Gabriel said. "And there was some wagering going on among the white officers as to whose division could load the most munitions in the least amount of time. So, as you can imagine, safety was sacrificed for speed."

"Were you actually on the pier when it happened?" Alan asked.

"No." Gabriel shook his head. "I wouldn't be sitting here if I had been. I'd been working the night shift for months, and I don't remember why, but I got moved over to days just the week before. Someone was watching out for me, though I sure don't know why I was spared and three hundred other fellows weren't." He set down his spoon. "I was in the barracks, about a mile from the pier, and we heard a huge explosion and saw a white light through the windows. We started to run out, but a second explosion hit, this one even bigger, and the next thing I knew, my buddies and I were flying all over the place, the walls tumbling down on top of us. Outside, it was like firecrackers going off, and the sky was yellow. That's the last thing I remember—that yellow sky. I woke up in the hospital like this." He held up his hand. "And I knew I'd been very, very lucky."

"You weren't one of the men in the mutiny trial, were you?" Alan asked.

"What was the mutiny trial?" Carlynn asked as she slipped a clam from its shell.

"No, no," Gabriel said. "I received a medical discharge, so I was spared that, too." He turned to Carlynn. "The Negro seamen were sent right back to doing the same type of work, with no extra training, no counseling to help them deal with what they'd been through, and some of them refused to do it. The white officers testified against them, and they were convicted of mutiny."

"Would you have been one of them if you hadn't been discharged?" Lisbeth asked. Her bowl of cioppino was still full, and Carlynn wondered if she was too nervous to eat.

"I don't know the answer to that one, Lisbeth," he said. "I was angry. I had a degree from Berkeley, and I wasn't the only one of those men who had tried to make something of himself and been treated more like an animal than a human being. I think if they'd made me go back, yes, I would have fought it. At least I hope I would have had the guts to stand up to the navy."

It was hard for Carlynn to imagine life through his eyes. She'd known men in the service. They'd moved about freely, specializing in any area they chose for the most part. How humiliating it must have been for Gabriel, with his educational background, to be told he wasn't the right color to fight for his country. She wanted to offer him sympathy, but he didn't seem to need it. His left hand had been blown to bits, and he'd learned to use his right hand. He'd lost his wife, and he'd survived and moved on. She felt joy for her sister that she had found such a fine man.

Gabriel suddenly looked a bit uncomfortable at having consumed so much of the attention at the table. "Let's move on to a more pleasant topic," he said, looking directly at Carlynn. "You two truly do look alike," he said, lifting a scallop from his bowl. "It's hard to say which of you is more beautiful. Are you interested in sailing as much as Lisbeth is, Carlynn?"

"No," Carlynn said with a shudder. "That was Lisbeth's passion."

"We went out with our father one time," Lisbeth explained, "and capsized. Carlynn got stuck underneath the boat for a bit, and she decided sailing was not her cup of tea."

Gabriel winced. "I don't blame you for that," he said to Carlynn.

"Lisbeth was a much better swimmer than I was," Carlynn said.

"The same thing happened to my sister and myself when we were kids," Gabriel said. "We were sailing on this estuary in Oakland when we capsized. She was stuck underneath for a couple of minutes. I dived under and got her, and she wasn't breathing when I brought her to shore."

"What happened?" Lisbeth asked.

"Well, she was essentially dead," Gabriel said. "But my great-grandmother was there. We were having a picnic, and all the aunts and everyone were with us. Granny grew up in the South, in Alabama, and she was a healer."

Lisbeth and Carlynn exchanged quick glances.

"One of my aunts did mouth-to-mouth on her, but it didn't work. Then Granny came over and held on to my sister's shoulders, and said, 'In the name of Jesus, child, breathe!'"

His voice rose, and when a few of the diners turned to look at him, he grimaced. "Sorry," he said to his tablemates with a laugh. "I got carried away. Anyhow," he continued in a softer tone, "my sister started breathing. In a few minutes, she was good as new."

The three of them stared at him in silence.

Gabriel looked at Lisbeth. "Did I say something wrong?" he asked. "I'm sorry I shouted."

Lisbeth touched the back of his hand. "That's not it," she said. "You didn't say anything wrong."

Carlynn was ready to explode with questions, but Alan beat her to it. He leaned forward in his chair. "Tell us more about your granny," he said.

Gabriel didn't answer. Instead, he looked at them suspiciously, and Carlynn wondered what they were giving away on their faces.

"What's going on here?" he asked.

"Please," Carlynn said. "Just tell us about Granny."

"Well, she had a reputation," he said slowly, leaning back in his chair, still obviously confused by whatever strange hunger he saw in their eyes. "She always fixed me up when I was a kid."

"Do you mean she cleaned your cuts and put Band-Aids on them?" Alan asked.

"Or did she use herbs or her own special poultice?" Carlynn added.

Gabriel shook his head. "No. If I had a cut or hurt myself she would hold me, or put her hand on the place that had been injured, and she'd go into a trance of some sort and talk about God and Jesus, and I'd be better. Everyone in the family turned to her when they were sick. Even the neighbors. Even the *white* neighbors. I remember wishing she was still alive when I lost my fingers, although I'm not sure she could have done much about that." He smiled.

"What was the most remarkable healing she ever performed?" Lisbeth asked.

"I think bringing my sister back from the dead was pretty remarkable," Gabriel said. "But she also cured a neighbor boy's polio."

"Was this polio diagnosed by a physician?" Alan asked.

"Yes. And it was very obvious that he had it. He needed to use an iron lung sometimes. But Granny actually moved into his house, into the same room he lived in, and she'd pray with him and...I don't know what-all she did, but that kid was cured in a month's time."

Alan turned to look at Carlynn, and she could see the question in his eyes. *Can we tell him?* he was asking her. They couldn't keep hounding Gabriel with their own questions without telling him why they were filled with curiosity. She liked Gabriel, but she'd only known him for slightly more than an hour. And he worked at SF General, and he also liked to talk a lot. Who might he tell?

Lisbeth caught her eye, giving her the slightest of nods.

"All right, I'm beginning to feel left out here." Gabriel set down his spoon, but the frustration in his voice had a playful edge to it. "You three are communicating with each other word-lessly, back and forth across this table, and I would love to know what the secret is."

Carlynn took in a breath. "Can you keep this quiet?" she asked him.

"Of course."

"I seem to be able to heal people sometimes," she said. "I don't know exactly how it happens, but that's why we're asking you questions about your great-grandmother. We're all very interested in the phenomenon."

"My." Gabriel looked a bit stunned. "I wasn't expecting that. Tell me more. How do you do it? Who have you healed?"

The three of them started talking at once, and the conversation lasted into dessert. They speculated about everything. Could his great-grandmother have cured the neighbor of polio *without* living in his room with him? And what did invoking the name of Jesus have to do with her healing?

"I think it's all the same thing," Alan said finally. "Whatever your great-grandmother did and what Carlynn does is connected. It's not the religiosity involved. But maybe it does have to do with faith. I just don't know."

Gabriel looked at Lisbeth. "You must have this ability, too," he said. "After all, you have the same genetic makeup as your sister. Have you ever tried?"

The color rose to Lisbeth's cheeks. "I don't have it," she said with certainty. "There must be something more than genes at play."

Gabriel covered her hand with his. "I guess one healer in a family is enough," he said.

By the time they left the restaurant, Carlynn had the feeling she'd known Gabriel for years instead of hours. He fit in well with the three of them, and his adoration and admiration of Lisbeth was clear.

"Can we give you a lift home, Lisbeth?" Carlynn asked.

"I was hoping to have the honor of driving Lisbeth home," Gabriel said before Lisbeth could answer.

"I'd like that." Lisbeth easily put her hand through Gabriel's arm, and the two of them started walking down the wharf together, and this time Carlynn didn't even notice that Gabriel's face was not like any of the others.

CHAPTER TWENTY-ONE

Midmorning found the Women's Wing bustling with activity. Two sets of triplets had been born overnight in addition to twice the usual number of single births, one of them to the wife of a popular local sportscaster. Newspaper reporters and photographers clogged the corridor, where a security guard was doing his best to keep them from disturbing the patients. The nurses were frantic, and extra staff needed to be called in. Although it was nearing the end of July, the weather was still unseasonably hot for Monterey, and the air-conditioning in the Women's Wing was not working properly. Engineers trying to fix the problem added to the mayhem in the hallway. Some of the rooms were ice-cold, the mothers and babies bundled in blankets. At the other end of the corridor, perspiration dripped from the new mothers' foreheads as they nursed their nearly naked infants.

Joelle did not feel well. She had picked up a stack of twelve referrals from the social work office earlier that morning, and so far had managed to see only one of the patients on her list. That case had required her to make over a dozen phone calls, and as she leafed through the remaining referrals, she hoped the rest of them would not be so labor intensive. She really wanted to go back to her office, put her head on her desk and fall asleep.

For the past couple of days, she'd been having pain low in her belly. It was subtle at first, and she'd mentioned it to Rebecca the day before when they passed each other in the hall. Rebecca said it was most likely more of the same ligament pain that had been bothering her for the past month. "Don't be concerned about it unless it gets worse," she'd said.

Well, it *was* getting worse, although Joelle wondered if it was the chaos in the Women's Wing that made everything about this day seem unbearable. She was certain, though, that the pain had been sharper when she woke up this morning, tugging at her groin along her right side. Plus, she'd been unable to eat breakfast. She'd made her usual oatmeal and strawberries, but when she sat down at the counter in her condominium and looked into the bowl, she'd felt nearly overwhelmed by queasiness. She was supposed to have lunch with Carlynn that afternoon and would have to cancel with her once again if she didn't start feeling better soon.

Leaning against the wall of the corridor, trying to stay out of the way of a guy with a newscam, she studied the next referral on the top of the pile. It was for a twenty-four-year-old woman who did not want to see her baby, and her room was, unfortunately, in the hot end of the maternity unit. Joelle started down the hall, trying not to limp or wince as she walked, but unable to find a gait that didn't increase the pain in her side. Rebecca had probably been right. Every step would pull on the ligament, wouldn't it? Still, she made a bargain with herself: if, after seeing this patient, the pain had not lessened, she would find Rebecca and have a discreet chat with her about it.

Stopping outside the patient's room, she had to read the referral once again, despite its simplicity. Her brain felt foggy, and she'd already forgotten why she had to see the woman in room 23.

The woman was alone in the room, in the bed nearest the window. Her eyes were closed, her head turned toward the window, and Joelle stopped first at the foot of her bed.

"Hello, Ann," she said. "Are you awake?"

The woman slowly opened her eyes and turned her head toward her. She was a striking young Asian woman, most likely Chinese-American, with long, straight black hair. The expression on her face was flat and lifeless, however, and the whites of her eyes were so pink they nearly glowed. Joelle recognized the look. She'd been in this business long enough to know that it meant one of two things. She glanced at the referral again, and saw that Ann's baby was a girl. That fact alone was probably responsible for driving Ann into the depths of depression.

Joelle stepped around to the side of the woman's bed and sat in the chair between the bed and the window, wincing as she did so from the cramping in her belly. Would ligament pain cause cramping? For the first time she wondered if something might be wrong with her baby.

"Hi," she said again, trying to concentrate on the woman in front of her. "I'm Joelle D'Angelo. I'm a social worker here in the maternity unit, and your nurse asked me to visit you because she's concerned about how sad you are."

The woman turned her head away from her so that her perfect profile was sharp against the pillow. "You can't help me," she said in a voice that only hinted at a Chinese accent.

"I'd like to understand what has you so down, though," Joelle said. "Sometimes new mothers feel terrible because of the hormonal changes that occur after pregnancy, and—"

"That's not it." Ann spoke into her pillow.

Joelle felt the nausea returning, rising up from somewhere low in her gut, washing over her slowly, the way it had when she'd looked at the bowl of oatmeal. It was so hot in the room. She wasn't sure she could make it through this interview.

She licked her lips and tried again. "Your nurse told me you gave birth to a healthy baby girl during the night," Joelle prompted, and she knew immediately she'd hit the real reason for Ann's depression. The woman turned her face toward her, tears spilling down her cheeks.

"My mother-in-law will never forgive me," she said. "It's the second girl. My husband is so angry. He won't even come in to visit me."

Joelle barely heard her last words. She was going to be sick. Standing up quickly, she managed to say, "Excuse me, I'm sorry," to the woman before fleeing from the room.

All she wanted was to make it to the rest room in the nurses' lounge, halfway down the hall, but the colors and smells and motion in the corridor made her dizzy, and she knew she would never reach the lounge in time. Ducking into one of the patient rooms, she was relieved to see that the bathroom serving the two beds was free, and she managed to close the door behind her before vomiting into the toilet.

Flushing the toilet, she stood up and leaned back against the wall. What a lousy time to run out on that mother! What a horrible thing to do to the poor woman. But her thoughts quickly returned to her own pain, which was still there, burning and cramping, and the bathroom felt like a sauna. Could it be her appendix? she wondered, but the pain now seemed too high on her side for that.

Wetting paper towels with cool water, she pressed them to her forehead. Did she have a fever, or was it the lack of air-conditioning that was making her so hot? Either way, something was definitely wrong with her. A summer flu, maybe. Whatever it was, she didn't dare try to go back to Ann's room. She'd have to fill one of the nurses in on the situation and see if someone else could take over for her. Right now all she wanted to do was find Rebecca.

She rinsed her mouth out with cool water and looked at her watch. It was nearly eleven. Rebecca should be finished with her rounds by now and in her office.

Leaving the patient room, she headed down the long corridor toward Rebecca's office, the pain in her belly jarring her with every step. Someone behind her called her name, but she didn't bother to turn around. They would have to get along without her for a while.

She was nearly crying by the time she reached Rebecca's office, and she felt the two patients in the waiting room staring at her as she limped toward the reception counter.

"LuAnn, I need to see Rebecca," she said to the receptionist, who was writing something on a form.

LuAnn glanced up at her, then back at her notes. "She's with a patient, Joelle," she said, but then her head jerked up again as if the sight of Joelle's sweaty face had just registered in her brain. "You look terrible!" she said, setting down her pen. "What's the matter?"

"I'm not sure. I'm sick. Let me go into one of the examination rooms, please. Then tell Rebecca I'm here."

LuAnn's eyes flew open. "Are you *pregnant?*" she whispered.

"Shh." Joelle pressed a finger to her lips, but she knew the gesture was futile. So much for her plan to escape Monterey before anyone knew. She had the feeling that, whatever was going on with her body, today was the day everyone would learn that unmarried, unattached Joelle D'Angelo was more than four months pregnant. And if everyone knew about it, Liam would, as well.

"Go in the first room," LuAnn said. "I'll let Reb know you're here and that you look like hell."

In the small examination room, Joelle could not decide whether to sit, stand or lie down. No position offered relief from the pain, and every movement felt as though it was tearing something loose inside her. She thought she should try to undress so that Rebecca could examine her. Her red-checked jumper could stay on, but she should at least get her panty hose off.

She was leaning against the examining table, the room spinning around her, one leg of her panty hose off and the other on, when Rebecca stepped into the room.

"What's going on?" Rebecca asked, taking Joelle's arm as if to steady her.

"The cramping is worse," Joelle said. "And I've been throwing up. I'm dizzy. I'm hot. I think something's really wrong, Rebecca."

"Can you get up here?" She patted the table with her free hand.

Joelle nodded and managed to climb onto the step, then turn around and sit down gingerly on the edge.

"Are you all right?" Rebecca asked, her hand still on Joelle's arm and a look of concern in her eyes. "Do you need a basin?"

"I don't think so," Joelle said. "It hurts, though, Rebecca. I don't think it's ligament pain anymore."

"No, I don't either." Rebecca helped Joelle lie down. She pulled off the remaining leg of her panty hose, setting them on the chair in the corner, before picking up the receiver of the phone on the wall.

"I need to get a CBC on a patient, stat," she said into the phone. Then she was back at Joelle's side, pressing her fingers on her belly, and Joelle tightened her abdominal muscles to keep her from pushing too hard.

"Extend this leg out," Rebecca said. "That's it, all the way."

"It hurts," Joelle said. "Oh my God, Rebecca!" She tried to sit up. "I just realized I haven't felt the baby move yet this morning!"

"I think the baby's okay," Rebecca said. "She or he is probably just giving you a break, since you have so much else to deal with right now." Rebecca took her temperature, but Joelle did not need a thermometer to know she had a fever.

"I'm going to do a sonogram," Rebecca said as Gale Firestone, a nurse Joelle knew well, walked into the room. Joelle saw the sharp look of astonishment on Gale's face at the sight of her rounded belly, but the nurse got her surprise quickly under control.

"Sorry you're not feeling well, Joelle," she said as she set up the phlebotomy tray on the counter.

"I think you've got a case of appendicitis," Rebecca said. She turned on the ultrasound monitor. "But I'd like to rule out a cyst and a few other things just to be sure."

Joelle closed her eyes as Gale drew blood from her arm, but opened them again to watch the screen while Rebecca moved the transducer over her belly.

"I don't see a cyst," Rebecca said. "But I do see a healthy baby. Not too sure of the sex yet, though."

"It's okay?" Joelle asked. "It's moving and—"

"There's the heart," Rebecca said, leaning back so Joelle could see the screen, and she spotted once again that reassuring flutter of life inside her.

"Thank God," she said, lying back again.

"I'll call you with this," Gale said to Rebecca as she carried the tube of Joelle's blood out of the room.

"Make it fast," Rebecca said, and Joelle could feel her urgency.

Rebecca gently wiped the gel from Joelle's stomach, then lowered her dress back over her thighs.

"Do you want to sit up or stay like that?" she asked.

"I don't want to move any more than I have to," Joelle said. She looked at Rebecca. "Now what?" she asked.

Rebecca's gaze settled on the small, shaded window of the room, and Joelle recognized that look on the obstetrician's face: she was thinking through her options.

"I'd really like to get an MRI," Rebecca said, "but I'm concerned about wasting time. I'm ninety-five percent sure it's your appendix, and we don't want it to rupture. That's not something we need, with you pregnant."

"Is that serious?"

"It could be quite serious," Rebecca said. "Let's see what your white blood count tells us and go from there." She moved toward the door. "Do you need a blanket?" she asked, her hand on the doorknob. "It's cold in this part of the building."

"No," Joelle said. "Just hurry back, please."

She must have dozed off, because the next thing she knew, Rebecca was telling her to sit up.

"What's happening?" Joelle tried to sit up with Rebecca's help and let out a yelp as the pain cut into her side again. "Did the blood work come back?"

"Yes, and it confirms my suspicions. I'm sending you upstairs for an emergency laparotomy. Dr. Glazer will perform it. You know him, don't you?"

Joelle nodded as she carefully lowered herself from the table onto the step. "What about the baby?" she asked. "What about the anesthesia? How will that—"

"It will be fine," Rebecca said. "And I'll be there, keeping an eye on the baby the whole time."

Joelle suddenly realized that Gale was in the room, moving a wheelchair close to the step she was on. With Rebecca's help, Joelle lowered herself into the chair, nearly doubled over with pain.

"I'll take her up," Rebecca said to Gale, and the nurse held the door open while Joelle was pushed out into the hallway of the office. When they neared the door to the corridor of the Women's Wing, which they would have to pass through to reach the elevators, Rebecca leaned over and whispered in her ear.

"This means the end of your secret, you know that, don't you?"

Joelle nodded. "Not important," she said, and it wasn't. Not anymore. She just wanted to get through this crisis with both herself and her baby intact.

Rebecca wheeled her through the Women's Wing, which passed by her in a blur. She could hear the word *pregnant* following her down the hall, being spoken in surprise and disbelief, and she knew she would be the subject of that day's gossip in the hospital.

It wasn't until she was on the operating table, the IV in her vein, a sedative fog washing over her, that she suddenly remembered walking out of the room of her patient. She tried to sit up. "I need to—"

"Lie down, Joelle," someone said.

"But the patient I was seeing. Someone needs to see her. I ran—"

"We'll take care of it," someone else said.

They wouldn't know what the problem was. She had to tell them. But she felt herself sinking, floating away.

"Girl baby," she said slowly. "She had a little girl."

CHAPTER TWENTY-TWO

Liam entered the social work office to find Maggie sitting on the edge of her desk, her legs dangling over the side. She was engaged in excited conversation with Paul, who was standing at the watercooler.

"Did you hear?" Paul asked him as soon as he'd set foot in the room.

"Hear what?" He reached toward his overflowing mailbox on the wall.

"Joelle's in surgery," Maggie said.

Liam's hand froze in the air, and his heart made an unexpected leap into his throat. *"Why?"* he asked, lowering his arm to his side.

"Appendix, they think," Paul said. "But she's also—get this—*pregnant.* Do you believe it?"

"Pregnant?" he asked, feeling stupid. "She's not even involved with anyone."

"I know," said Maggie, "and it's pretty amazing after all her hassles with fertility. But maybe she had one of her eggs fertilized in a test tube by a sperm donor or something, and then had it implanted. You know how much she wanted a baby, and she knows all the right doctors to do something like that."

He shook his head. "She wanted a baby when she was *married*," he said. "But not now." Could Maggie be right? Might Joelle have taken extraordinary measures to have a child? It didn't sound like the Joelle he knew, but then he hadn't been close to her the past few months. Still, he hoped against hope that was the answer, because the only other possibility was one he didn't want to think about. "How far along is she?" he asked.

"Not sure," Paul said.

"I heard someone in the maternity unit say she was four months," Maggie said. "I *thought* she was putting on weight."

Four months? Liam's mind raced. Sam was sixteen months old. So, his birthday would have been—

"Excuse me?" The three of them turned to see a small, thin woman leaning on her cane in the doorway. She looked vaguely familiar, and Liam guessed she was the wife of one of the patients he'd worked with in the cardiac unit.

"Can I help you?" Maggie scooted off the desk, smoothing her skirt and attempting to look professional.

"I'm looking for Joelle D'Angelo," the woman said. "We have a lunch date."

Carlynn Shire. He recognized her now as the woman he'd discovered in Mara's room with Joelle a couple of weeks earlier.

"Dr. Shire." He held out his hand to her. "We met at my wife's nursing home. I'm Liam Sommers."

"Yes, Mr. Sommers." She smiled and held his hand for a moment before letting go. "And you were not at all pleased to see me there."

Liam looked at Paul and Maggie, who were staring at him with frank curiosity. Paul probably recognized the Shire name from the Mind and Body Center, but Maggie would not have a clue.

"Listen," he said to the healer, taking her elbow. "Why don't you and I go into the conference room for a minute? I'll tell you what's going on with Joelle." He led her through the short, narrow hallway leading into the conference room and closed the door behind them.

The woman sat down at the long table and looked up at him with concern. "Is Joelle all right?" she asked.

"She's in surgery for appendicitis," he said, taking a seat across the table from her.

"Oh, my goodness." Her hand flew to her mouth. "Has it ruptured? That could be terribly dangerous in her—" She stopped herself from saying more.

"In her condition," Liam finished the sentence for her. "You know that she's pregnant?"

"Yes, I know," she said, and she was eyeing him so intently that he was afraid to ask her his next question.

"Do you know if it...if the baby..."

"It's yours," she said bluntly.

He looked away from her, shaking his head. "Man, oh, man," he said, rubbing his forehead with his fingers. "Why didn't she tell me?"

"Well, I think she had a few very good reasons," she said. "At least, they seemed good to her. One, she knew you've been overwhelmed dealing with your wife and son. And two, you haven't...been inviting her to share much with you lately, have you?"

"I don't know what you mean." He looked across the table at the diminutive, gray-haired woman, trying not to turn away from her penetrating blue eyes.

"You've been pushing her away," Carlynn said.

"I haven't been pushing her away," he said, but he knew she was right. He sank lower into the chair. "Maybe I have. I'm angry at both of us for allowing ourselves to get so close. We can't let it happen again."

"It happened. Guilt does no one any good."

He studied her for a moment. "Is Joelle losing her mind?"

he asked. "What on earth can she possibly think you can do for my wife?"

"Mara belongs to Joelle as well as to you, Liam," Carlynn said. "They were extremely close friends, and Joelle suffered a loss as great as your own. She needs to grieve in her own way. If bringing me in helps her, I don't understand why you should object."

"Because I don't believe there's anything you can do to help my wife," he said, biting off the words. "I think...what you're all about is a...a crock of bull. Sorry. But that's what I think."

She looked unoffended by his words. "I'm not a quack, Liam," she said. "Not a charlatan. The truth is, sometimes I can help, and sometimes I can't. Often, the help doesn't come in the form we expect it to."

"What do you mean?" he asked

"I mean, that sometimes getting well, *physically* well, is not the true goal of healing."

"Then what the hell is the point of it?"

Carlynn Shire stood up and rested her hands on the table, leaning toward him. "Do you love Joelle, Liam?"

He felt his jaw tighten at the intrusiveness of the question. "That really isn't any of your business."

She didn't respond, but didn't let him loose of her gaze, either.

"It doesn't matter if I do," he said.

"Do me a favor, Liam," she said, sitting down again. "Describe Joelle to me."

"You already seem to know her very well," he said.

"I want to hear *your* description of her, though," she pressed him. "I want to see her through your eyes."

He sighed. Why was he giving this woman so much control over him?

"She's very capable," he said. "Compassionate. Caring. Ethical."

"Moral?"

"Yes, absolutely. And so am I," he insisted. "We didn't plan

this to happen, Mrs....Dr....Shire. We didn't mean it to happen."
God, that sounded trite.

"I know," she said. "Go on."

He sighed again, giving in. "She's nurturing." He could see
Joelle, back in the days when their friendship had been close
and warm, sitting across the cafeteria table from him. She'd
looked girlish, with that long thick dark hair and heavy bangs
above her brown eyes. "Very cute," he said. "And open. *Extremely* open, especially with me." He shook his head. "It's hard
to understand how she could have kept this from me. She tells
me everything."

"*Used* to tell you everything," Carlynn Shire corrected him.
"She didn't ever want you to know about the baby. She planned
to leave before you found out."

"Leave?" He frowned. "You mean, leave Silas Memorial?"

"No, leave Monterey," she said. "Leave her life here. Have
the baby someplace else so you would never have to be burdened by it."

He winced. "I can't believe she would leave without telling
me about..."

"I believe," she said gently, "that you've treated her like an
evil person. Like someone you need to avoid."

He started to object, but she was right, wasn't she? If he
avoided Joelle, he could avoid temptation and never have to face
his own weakness.

"Do you have any idea how much she loves you?" Carlynn
asked him.

He stared at her, uncomfortable with her questions and with
how much she seemed to know about his relationship with Joelle.

"She loves you so much that she came to me, hoping that,
somehow, she could give you your wife back. Despite how desperately she wants you for herself. Despite the fact that she's
pregnant with your child."

His throat tightened, and he stood up quickly to rid himself of the emotion. Folding his arms across his chest, he leaned against the wall.

"What am I supposed to do?" he asked. "*Yes,* I love her. But I'm married to a woman I also love, who will never be able to love me back, but who still needs me. Who still lights up when I come into her room. Who, if she were still...whole...would trust me to be faithful to her, to take care of her forever. Do you blame me for pushing Joelle away? For trying to avoid the one person who can turn me into a man I'd have no respect for?"

"You're alive, dear." There was sympathy in Carlynn's eyes as she rose to her feet. "You're alive, and Joelle is alive."

"And so is Mara. So is my son!"

"What pain you carry." Carlynn Shire shook her head sadly as she moved past him to open the conference-room door. "Think about something, Liam," she said before stepping into the hallway. "Think about how much harder it is to carry that pain alone than it was when you shared it with Joelle."

CHAPTER TWENTY-THREE

Joelle opened her eyes, then shut them again. Her eyelids were too heavy, the lights too glaring. The surgery was over and she was in the recovery room; she remembered that much. Rebecca had told her that a few minutes ago. Or maybe a few hours. She wasn't sure. Her baby was all right, Rebecca had said, also telling her that she had an incision in her right side, but Joelle was unaware of any pain. Just a dragging tiredness and some nausea that made her want to lie very, very still.

Rebecca had said something about monitoring the baby's heart rate with a Doppler, making sure she didn't have contractions brought on by the surgery. She remembered the doctor standing next to the bed, delivering all this information to her. But something was different now, and it took her a minute to realize that the curtains were pulled around her bed, and that she wasn't alone. Slowly, she turned her head to the left to see Liam sitting next to her, his face solemn.

"How do you feel?" he asked, his voice quiet. His arms were folded on top of the bed rail, his head resting on his hands.

She swallowed. "Okay." It hurt to open her eyes wide enough

to look at him, but she could see him press his lips together. He looked away from her, then back again.

"When exactly did you plan on telling me?" he asked.

"Never," she whispered. Her voice was hoarse, her throat dry.

"*Jo.*" He reached over to smooth her hair back from her face, and she closed her eyes to savor the touch. "I'm sorry," he said. "This must have been a terrible few months for you."

She turned her head away from him as her tears started.

"I'm sorry if I've been cold," he said, the backs of his fingers brushing a tear from her cheek. "If you've felt as though I was pushing you away."

"No one knows, do they?" She turned toward him, wondering if, while she had been in surgery, the truth might have somehow come out.

"Just you, me and Carlynn Shire."

How did he know she'd confided in Carlynn? She looked at him quizzically.

"She came up to the office looking for you."

"Oh, our lunch date."

"I told her you were in surgery, and we had a talk."

"A good one?" she asked.

"Depends on your definition of good," he said dryly. "She told me you were planning to move away."

She nodded, and he looked incredulous.

"How could you even think of doing that, Joelle?" he asked. "You love it here. This is your home."

"I wanted to avoid what I knew would happen if I stayed," she said. "What is happening right now—you having one more gigantic problem to deal with."

"I'm a big boy," he said. "I can handle it."

"I know you can," she said. "I just didn't want you to have to. Not when I had the power to do something about it."

"Did you consider abortion?" he asked, then quickly shook his head and placed the tips of his fingers on her lips before she could respond. "I'm sorry. Of course you wouldn't, and I understand that, Jo. I do. I'm sorry."

He was so contrite that she felt sympathy for him.

"It's okay," she said.

"Listen, I don't want you to move away on my account, all right? Please. You're not going anywhere. I'll help you however I can, short of..."

"Short of admitting that it's yours?" she asked.

"Let me think about it, please. I can't make a decision about that right now."

"That's all right," she said. "I didn't plan on letting anyone know, either. I'm just as much in the wrong as you are, you know, and I don't want people watching us, judging us."

"I'm afraid you're already being judged, kiddo," he said.

"But people know I wanted a baby," she reasoned, "and that I might have gone to extraordinary lengths to have one."

He nodded. "We'll talk more about it later, when you're not groggy from anesthetic. And I'm not still in shock. Okay?" He took her hand. "When you're up to it, and if you still want to," he said, "you're welcome to bring Carlynn Shire back to see Mara. Not that I believe for a minute she can heal her, but it's not fair for me to stop you. Mara was your best friend, too."

"Thank you. And will you be there?"

"If you insist." He smiled at her, but there was a deep sadness in his eyes. Lifting her hand to his lips, he kissed it. "I care about you, Jo," he said. "You know that. But I'm married, and as long as Mara is alive, I'm her husband. I love her."

"Me, too," she said.

"I'll be there for you in whatever way I can. But...we can't get that close again."

"I know." She nodded.

"I'll help you support the baby financially, of course."

"You're having a hard enough time with money as it is," she said. "I don't expect Sheila to pay child support for my baby."

He said nothing, and she knew she had bruised his ego. She said the word, "Sorry," but it came out as a whisper, and she wasn't certain if he'd heard her or not.

"Do your parents know?" he asked.

She shook her head. "No. They don't know I've had surgery, either."

"Would you like me to call them for you?"

"Would you, please? But don't tell them about the pregnancy, okay? I'd rather do that myself. Tell them I'm fine, not to come down, not to worry, not to—"

"I'll take care of it," he said.

He bent over to kiss her on the forehead, and the gesture reminded her of all the times she'd seen him bend over to kiss Mara in her bed at the nursing home. Mara, though, he would have kissed on the lips.

Liam called her parents from his office. He knew John and Ellen, having spent time with them over the years, when they came down to visit Joelle. They had even come to his wedding, the only guests who took to heart his and Mara's request for no gifts.

It was John who answered the phone, and Liam told him about the appendectomy, feeling as though he was lying because of what he was omitting from the story.

"We're on our way," Joelle's father said after Liam had delivered the news.

"No, don't come," Liam said. "She asked me specifically to tell you not to come. Right now she's well taken care of. Everyone here knows her and will keep an eye on her." He recalled one of the nurses telling him that Joelle might be out of work for six weeks. "I'm not sure what her recovery will be like, though," he said to John. "She'll probably need some help when she gets home. That might be a better time to come down."

"Will you keep us posted?" John asked.

"Yes, and she should have a phone in her room later," Liam said. "I'll call you when I get the number."

That seemed to satisfy her father. Liam hung up the phone and sat staring at his blank computer screen.

Why hadn't they used a condom? Two social workers, two intelligent people in their thirties. Two idiots. Yet, she had been so famously infertile, and they both knew the other was disease-free. A condom, had they stopped to think about using one, would have seemed superfluous. But if they *had* stopped to think, it wouldn't have happened at all. And he knew they had both carefully, intentionally, not stopped to think.

He'd needed Joelle so badly that night. He'd needed to know he was still a man, just like that sixty-year-old man he'd seen who had the wife with Alzheimer's. He should have found a prostitute instead, if that had been so damn important to him, not someone he loved who could be hurt by his stupid need to prove his virility.

He would visit Mara that afternoon. She would make her puppy-dog squeals when he walked into the room, and he knew exactly what she would be saying with those sounds. *I remember you*, she would say. *You're the one who loves me. You're the one I can trust, no matter what. You're my husband, in sickness and in health.*

CHAPTER TWENTY-FOUR

San Francisco, 1957

Lisbeth sat on the cabin top of Gabriel's sloop, munching on a pear. For the first time in her life, she did not crave candy and ice cream and cookies. Although she was dressed in knee-high rubber boots, bib overalls over a jersey, a yellow slicker, hat and gloves, she could actually *feel* the difference in her body beneath all that gear. Certainly, she was still larger than she wanted to be, but there was some unmistakable definition to her waistline, and although her hips and thighs were hardly slender, she could fit into the overalls without looking like an elephantine version of the pear she was eating. She had forgotten how it felt not to be tired all the time from carrying around so much extra weight.

She and Gabriel had been going together for six months, but they'd only been able to start sailing about a month ago, when the wintry San Francisco cold began to soften around the edges, and they could get out on the water without either freezing or capsizing. Their inability to sail had not interfered with their dating, however. They'd explored San Francisco together as though they were tourists, and met often for dinner at a restaurant after work. They had a few favorites, especially in the primarily Italian North Beach area where Gabriel lived, where the beats read their poetry in the coffeehouses, and where no one looked twice at a Negro man and a white woman walking or dancing together. She learned to play whist and bridge in the dark, smoke-filled clubs, and she fell in love with jazz and rhythm and blues.

She and Gabriel could talk all day and all night and never run out of things to say. He told her about growing up in the English Village section of Oakland, where a white Realtor had purchased the house his family had wanted and then transferred the title to Gabriel's father, which had been the only way a Negro family could get into that neighborhood. His mother had been a housekeeper, his father a porter on the Southern Pacific railroad, where just about every man Gabriel knew worked. His father had died on one of the trains when Gabriel was eleven years old, killed by a fellow crew member during a game of craps.

Gabriel's family had little money after that, and he'd worked his way through school and college. He'd met his wife, Cookie, at Berkeley, and they'd been married eight years when she discovered the lump in her breast. By the way Gabriel spoke of his late wife, Lisbeth knew he'd adored her, yet she never felt he was comparing her to Cookie. Gabriel knew how to focus on the future without letting the past get in the way, and he was teaching her, through his example, to live the same way. The fact that they both had suffered in their childhoods and their early adult years certainly drew them together, but it was their yearning to create a future that would be peaceful, bright and full of love that sealed that bond.

Dating Gabriel was not without its problems, though. Lisbeth had to find a new place to live after her landlord kicked her out the night she'd brought Gabriel up to her room. She'd only wanted to get him out of the rain while he waited for her to get ready for their date, but the landlord was livid, the tendons in his neck taut as ropes beneath his skin. He had teenage children, he yelled, as if she didn't know, didn't hear them playing Elvis on the phonograph at all hours of the night and day. He did not want them to witness interracial dating, and he couldn't have a colored man in his house. So she left, finding an apartment in North Beach, four blocks from Gabriel's, with a phone that was available for her use anytime she wanted. Her landlady was a boisterous Italian woman who didn't care a whit what color Lisbeth's friends were, and whose house always smelled of tomatoes and olive oil and oregano.

Now that Lisbeth no longer spent her free time huddled in her room eating, the weight dropped off her without her even trying. Diets had not been what she'd needed. All she'd really needed had been the unconditional love of a man, and that she had found in Gabriel.

She loved being out on his boat more than she enjoyed dining with him or listening to music or dancing, because out here they were alone. There was never anyone staring at them, never a look of disapproval or shock from a stranger, as there was sure to be when they ventured out of North Beach. Occasionally, someone would make a disparaging comment loud enough for them to hear, using language that belonged in a sewer, and it would only make Gabriel hold her hand tighter. Sometimes, he would apologize to her, as though the rudeness of others was his fault, and that irritated her no end. He had nothing to apologize for.

At least once every couple of weeks they got together with Carlynn and Alan. They were a compatible foursome, and they'd play bridge at Alan's apartment, or go to a movie, or meet at Tarantino's for cioppino. Conversation often seemed to turn to the topic of healing. Gabriel had even taken the three of them to Oakland to meet his mother, who remembered more than he did about his great-grandmother, and who filled their heads with stories they would never have believed, were it not for Carlynn.

"So, Liz," Gabriel said now, once they were sailing smoothly downwind. "When is Alan going to pop the question to your sister?"

"This weekend," Lisbeth said, licking a bit of pear juice from her thumb. "They're going to Santa Barbara, and he plans to ask her sometime while they're there."

Alan had shown her the ring, a beautiful large diamond in a white-gold setting, and told her his plans. Lisbeth had been surprised at being taken into his confidence, but Alan had been anxious to tell her. He was a brilliant physician but a bit stuffy and private, and to see that sense of romance and excitement in him had touched her.

"Any chance she'd turn him down?"

Lisbeth laughed. "What do you think? She loves him to bits, and she's dying to have babies." Carlynn had found the right man, of that Lisbeth was certain. They were both bright, intense people with a passion for science and medicine and a shared curiosity about Carlynn's ability to heal. Lisbeth herself would not have been happy with a man like Alan—not that Alan would have been happy with her, either. She needed someone like Gabriel, whose great joy in living was written all over his face.

Lisbeth was careful never to bring up the subject of marriage with Gabriel, although that was certainly where she hoped their relationship was headed. She was afraid he might think she was pressuring him, though. They had only been going out for six months, she would remind herself. Alan and Carlynn had known each other three times that long.

"Carlynn's not a virgin," Lisbeth said suddenly, shocking herself more than she did Gabriel. She clapped her hand over her mouth. "I can't believe I just told you that."

He raised his eyebrows at her. "And how did you find that out?" he asked.

"She told me a couple of weeks ago when we were driving home to see Mother. We had a very long, sisterly conversation in the car." Despite her mother's usual criticism, the visit to Cypress Point had been wonderful. She'd felt whole to be back at the mansion, nourished by the scent of the sea and the cypress. She wished Gabriel could visit the mansion with her sometime, but knew that would never be possible.

"Were you shocked?" Gabriel asked her.

Lisbeth gazed in the direction of Angel Island. *We've been lovers a long time now,* Carlynn had told her, and Lisbeth had sensed that her sister was moving far, far ahead of her. Somehow, all of Carlynn's medical skills, all her education and everything else she had accomplished that Lisbeth had not paled in comparison to this. Carlynn knew sex. Lisbeth had thought about the way Gabriel kissed her, his hands running up and down her arms or through her hair, never moving anyplace she could interpret as pushing her into something she might not want to do.

"No, I wasn't shocked. But I was—" she lowered her gaze from Angel Island to Gabriel's attentive face "—jealous," she admitted, feeling the color rise into her cheeks.

"You mean, you want to make love with Alan?" Gabriel teased her, and she threw the rest of her pear at him.

"Don't make this so hard for me, Gabe," she pleaded.

"Sorry." He smiled at her. "Is that something you want, baby?" he asked.

She loved it when he called her baby. "Don't you?" She bit her lip, waiting for his answer. She'd wanted him to make love to her when he'd been nothing more than a voice on the phone.

Gabriel let out a long groan, leaning back in the boat and looking up at the sky. "Hell, *yes,*" he said. "But I've been trying to be a gentleman."

"Well, stop it." She giggled.

"I will, if you insist." He glanced toward the shore, then grinned at her. "Think we should go in?" he asked. "Have you had enough sailing for today?"

She laughed. "We just got out here," she said. "Besides, we can't do it yet," she said. "I have to get a diaphragm first. Carlynn told me about a doctor I can go to."

"I could use a rubber," Gabriel said, and she laughed again at his sudden enthusiasm.

"I didn't even think you *thought* about sex," she said. "That's what I told Carlynn."

He groaned again. "Why'd you tell her that, Liz? Now she's going to think I'm queer."

"Not for long she won't." She smiled coyly at him, enjoying the banter, but she hoped she wasn't giving him the impression that she wanted sex for the sex alone. "I wouldn't do it with someone I didn't love, Gabe," she said, the smile no longer on her face. "I only want to do it with you."

"I know that, baby," he said, his face just as serious. "And if I didn't feel the same way about you, I wouldn't have waited this long."

That night, they made love in the double bed in his North Beach apartment. She'd been nervous at first, but Gabriel had taken his time. She'd read about sex, but he knew more than had been written in the books she'd analyzed until the pages had started to fall out. Or maybe it was love that had been missing in those books, maybe the men in those stories did not take the time to teach, and to learn, what pleased him, and what pleased his lover.

She remembered something she'd heard one time: sex would either make a relationship better or it would make it worse, but it would not leave it unchanged. She was certain it could only make what she and Gabriel had better, but when they had finished making love, Gabriel rolled onto his back and lit a cigarette, blowing the smoke toward the ceiling, following it with his gaze. She knew something was wrong.

"What is it?" she asked, resting her hand on his bare chest.

He blew a smoke ring, then spoke without looking at her. "I'm afraid of costing you," he said. "Costing you way too much." He rolled his head on the pillow to look at her, and in the smoky, dark room, without his glasses on, he looked like a stranger.

"The whole world's not like North Beach, you know," he said. "You haven't even told your mother about me."

"Yes, I have," she said, already distressed by the tenor of the conversation. "At least, she knows I'm going with someone named Gabriel. I'll tell her the rest when I have to."

"I don't want to be a 'have to' for you, Lisbeth," he said. "It makes me feel like a burden."

"I didn't mean it that way."

"I know you didn't. But that's the way it is, isn't it? That's the reality."

"It doesn't matter what my mother thinks, Gabe," she said. "She hasn't truly been a part of my life for a long time."

"But you still visit her, and Cypress Point is still important to you. I know you love it there." He stubbed out his cigarette in the ashtray on his windowsill and rolled over, bracing himself on his elbows to look down at her. "I've taken you to Oakland," he said. "I've introduced you all around, to my family and my neighbors. I showed you the house where I grew up and the places I hung around. What can you show me from *your* child-hood? I can't meet your mother, can't set foot in the house you adore unless I pose as a delivery boy, can't walk through your old neighborhood without scaring people out of their wits."

"I don't care about that, Gabe," she said fervently, worried that she was lying to herself as well as to him. "I'd give all that up for you in a heartbeat."

"I don't know that I should let you," he said, sitting up and leaning back against the wall.

Lisbeth felt something precious slipping from her grasp. "Are you saying you want to break up with me?" She started to cry, silently, not wanting him to know.

"No," he said. "I *don't* want to break up. But I'm not sure about our future, together, Liz."

Before they'd made love, he'd been full of tender words for her. Now he sounded as though he was pulling away, ready to end what they'd nurtured together for the past six months. And suddenly, she thought she knew the reason why.

"Was I not as good as your wife?" she asked, unable to hide the tears in her voice. "In bed, I mean. Not as good as the other women you've had?"

"What?" He looked truly surprised. "Oh, Lizzie. Oh, no, baby." He moved toward her, pulling her up by her shoulders until she was in his arms. "You were perfect," he said. "I didn't mean that at all. I'm just thinking ahead, that's all. Thinking about...how hard it could be to be married. How hard it would be on our children. I'm sorry, baby." He lowered his head to the hollow between her throat and shoulder. "I'm sorry."

She felt his tears on her shoulder then, and he pulled her even closer to him, so close she could barely breathe, and that was where she wanted to be. Always.

Although Carlynn was thrilled to be engaged to Alan, she knew there was trouble ahead and that it would take the form of Delora Kling. As soon as Carlynn told her mother about the engagement, Delora started planning.

"We'll have the wedding on the terrace," Delora said. "The weather in September should be ideal for it to be outdoors. I heard a harpist the other day who would be perfect. Wouldn't that be lovely, dear? It's so rare to hear a harpist at a wedding. Of course, if we have it here, that will limit the number of guests we can have. Would you prefer it to be in one of the cathedrals instead?"

Carlynn *did* want to be married at Cypress Point, but she also wanted Lisbeth to be her maid of honor, along with Penny Everett as her bridesmaid. And Lisbeth was attached at the hip to Gabriel, as she should be. Carlynn had no problem with that—she adored Gabriel—but Delora was sure to have a fit if her "second daughter" showed up with a Negro by her side.

She and Lisbeth were closer than ever as they talked over wedding plans and shopped for the wedding gown and bridesmaids' dresses. Lisbeth looked fabulous these days. She was only two sizes larger than Carlynn, and Carlynn persuaded her to try on wedding gowns, as well as the bridesmaid's dress. She told Lisbeth that it would help her see how a dress would look on her to see it on her twin. But really, she'd just wanted Lisbeth to enjoy the thrill of seeing herself in a wedding dress. Only later did she think it might have been a little mean of her to make Lisbeth see herself as a bride without a wedding of her own in sight.

Lisbeth fell in love with one of the dresses. She couldn't stop fingering the lace and looking behind her at the long train, and she spent a long time admiring herself in the mirror before she took it off. She tried to persuade Carlynn to try it on, as well, but, although Carlynn also loved the dress, she had never seen Lisbeth so enamored with an article of clothing.

"No," she said, selecting her second choice for herself. "That one will be yours someday."

They left the bridal shop and began walking toward the bus stop.

"I guess, if Gabe and I ever get married, it won't be at Cypress Point," Lisbeth said as they walked.

Carlynn heard the wistfulness in her sister's voice. She had no doubt that Lisbeth and Gabriel would be together for the rest of their lives, no doubt that they were meant for one another, and yet there would always be that extra burden for them to carry. They would never have the freedom to live their lives as she and Alan would.

"Honey," she said, putting her arm around her sister's shoulders as they walked. "We have to have a serious talk about my wedding."

"You mean about having Gabriel there, don't you?" Lisbeth asked, and Carlynn knew her sister had been expecting this conversation.

"Yes," Carlynn said. "Alan and I want him there. He will be your guest. I'm going to insist upon it. It's my wedding, after all."

Lisbeth looked at her with affection, but there was doubt in her eyes. "It's at Mother's home," she said. "Mother will make the rules."

"I've been thinking about it, though," Carlynn said. "Maybe we're not giving Mother enough credit. I don't think she's a racist, exactly. It's just that all the Negroes she's ever known have been servants or waiters or other service people. She never had an opportunity to meet them under any other circumstances. We really don't know how she'll react. We're guessing. Maybe you should just show up with him. If we act like there's nothing amiss, what's she going to say?"

Lisbeth was quiet for a moment. "I couldn't put Gabriel in that position."

Carlynn sat down on the bench at the bus stop. Lisbeth was right. That would be unfair to Gabe, and unnerving for the rest of them as they awaited Delora's reaction.

"What if Mother knows, and says it's all right?" Carlynn asked. "He'd come then, wouldn't he?"

"Of course, and that would be wonderful," Lisbeth said. "It would also be a miracle, though." She ran a hand through her blond curls, which she now wore looser and longer, in a style that was so flattering Carlynn wished she'd discovered it first.

"Well, I'm going to talk with her about it," Carlynn said.

"Good luck," Lisbeth said. She didn't sound at all optimistic.

Carlynn called her mother that evening from the phone in her bedroom, and Delora immediately launched into a litany of problems she was having making arrangements with the photographer and the caterer. Carlynn listened patiently, and when Delora stopped to take a breath, she said, "I need to talk with you about something, Mother."

"Don't tell me the wedding's off," Delora said. There was more of a warning in her voice than there was sympathy.

"No, of course not. Nothing like that. I just wanted..." she hesitated. "You know, of course, that Lisbeth will be bringing her boyfriend."

"Yes, I have his name on the list. Gabriel, isn't it? Shall I put him at the head table, next to Lisbeth?"

"That would be perfect, Mother. But I thought it would be best if you knew a little bit about him before the big day." Carlynn screwed up her nose as she spoke. She hated this. Gabriel's color should not be an issue, and she felt as though she, herself, was making it one.

"Well, tell me about him, then," her mother said. "Where is his family from?"

"Gabriel's a fabulous person, Mom," Carlynn said, avoiding the question of family, "but I thought I should let you know ahead of time that he's a Negro, just so you wouldn't be surprised when you saw him."

There was a long silence on the phone line, and Carlynn wondered if her mother had fallen into a dead faint.

"This figures," Delora said finally, in disgust. "Lisbeth goes out with no one her entire life, and then when she finally does, it's with a colored man. Well, it's out of the question, Carlynn. He can't come here."

"It's my wedding, Mother."

"And it's my house and many of my friends will be here, and I just won't have it, Carlynn."

Carlynn ran her hand over the chenille spread on her bed, trying to think of a different approach. "Mom, he's really a lovely man," she said. "He—"

"I don't care if he's president of the United States, he's not coming here."

Carlynn gritted her teeth. "Lisbeth loves him, Mother. And he loves her. Doesn't that count for something? He's a professional. An accountant at SF General."

"So he thinks he can get a white woman, then? Because he's

an accountant? He's going to lower Lisbeth to his level, that's all he's going to do. And Lisbeth is going to let it happen."

Carlynn let out her breath. How was she supposed to respond to that?

"If you think I'm going to have someone like that at one of my parties, especially on the arm of one of my daughters, well...I wouldn't dream of putting any of my guests in that uncomfortable position."

"It's not *your* party, Mother. It's *my* wedding. And it's Lisbeth you're putting in an uncomfortable position. You're making her unwelcome in the home she grew up in."

"I never said she wasn't welcome. *She* can come. But she'd better be alone."

"Mother..." Carlynn's voice trailed off in frustration.

"You know, I sometimes wonder if that girl is actually mine. I was asleep when they cut her out of me."

"Don't be ridiculous."

"Oh, I know she looks just like you, but you're a true Kling, with elegance and bearing and intelligence..."

Carlynn rolled her eyes.

"...but, somehow, Lisbeth turned out to be nothing but trash. Fat trash. I just can't believe she's doing this to me. To our family." Her mother was weeping now, and Carlynn ignored her tears.

She thought of telling her that any differences between her twin daughters were of her own creation, but wisely bit her tongue. "She's not fat any longer, and you know it," she said instead. "You saw her just a few weeks ago. She looks great. Give her some credit. She gained weight because she was miserable, but with Gabriel, she's happy. She's lost seventy pounds so far, and you didn't even compliment her on it when you saw her."

"I don't care if she disappears," her mother said angrily, and hung up the phone.

Carlynn stared at the phone in her hand a long time before placing it back in the cradle.

Lying down on the bed, she continued the conversation with her mother in her mind. She thought of telling her that she envied what Lisbeth had with Gabriel. There was an adoration between Lisbeth and Gabe, a love so caring and tender, it sometimes made her feel weepy to be around it. She knew Alan loved her, but it was different. She supposed that she, as a physician, did not invite the sort of attentive devotion that Lisbeth received from Gabriel. She couldn't help but wish, though, that Alan would touch her more often, hold her hand in public and talk with her about his deepest secrets and feelings, the way Lisbeth said Gabriel spoke to her.

Rolling onto her side, she felt a pang of guilt for wanting Alan to be someone he was not. He would make a wonderful husband and father, and that's what truly mattered. And he *did* adore her, in his own way. She was never quite certain, though, if it was her gift or herself that he treasured most.

Carlynn and Alan met Lisbeth and Gabriel at Tarantino's the following night. It had become their favorite restaurant for a double date, despite the fact that the diners around them were mostly tourists. The sun had not yet set, and from their table near the window, they could see the boats in the harbor and gulls flying above the green water.

She'd told Alan about her conversation with her mother and about Delora's unwillingness to have Gabriel at the wedding.

"How bad has her eyesight gotten?" Alan had asked, only half joking.

"Not *that* bad," she'd replied.

They'd gotten serious then, weighing their options and coming up with the only solution that seemed both fair and feasible.

Now, after they'd ordered their cioppino, Carlynn looked at Alan, who nodded at her, letting her know it was time to tell Lisbeth and Gabriel the decision they had made.

"There's been a change of plans," Carlynn said.

"Regarding?" Gabriel was lighting a cigarette, but his eyes were on Carlynn.

"The wedding," Alan said. "We've decided not to get married at Cypress Point, after all. We're going to have a smaller wedding right here, in the little Episcopal church near my row house."

"What?" Lisbeth was clearly astonished.

"It will have to be a different weekend than we'd planned," Carlynn said, "because the church doesn't have our date open, but—"

"Stop this," Gabriel said softly, and they all turned to look at him.

"Stop what?" Lisbeth frowned.

Gabriel tapped the ash off his cigarette as he seemed to collect his thoughts, then he looked at Carlynn. "I know you're making this change because of me," he said, "and I don't want you to do that."

"Oh, no," Lisbeth said, understanding dawning in her eyes.

Alan licked his lips. "Look, Gabe," he said, resting his arms on the table so he could lean closer to Gabriel. "You're right that you're the catalyst for the change. But please understand that your friendship and your presence at our wedding are much more important to us than where we get married."

Carlynn gratefully squeezed Alan's knee beneath the table. How could she ever have wished for someone better than this gallant man?

"You spoke to Mother?" Lisbeth looked at Carlynn.

Carlynn nodded. "She reacted as you guessed she would," she said. "And Alan and I are not willing to have Gabriel excluded or to have anyone feel uncomfortable at what is supposed to be a happy occasion."

Lisbeth turned to Gabriel. "Oh, Gabe," she said. "I'm sorry my mother is so impossible."

Gabriel took another drag on his cigarette, blew the smoke into the air, then turned to Lisbeth. "Your mother called me," he said.

"Oh, no." Carlynn grimaced.

"How would she know where to reach you?" Lisbeth asked.

"I'd told her that he was the accountant at SF General," Carlynn said. "I'm so sorry, Gabriel. I had no idea she'd call you."

"Not your fault," he said quickly to Carlynn, then leaned back, saying nothing as their waiter set plates of salad in front of each of them.

When the waiter had walked away, Gabriel continued. "She told me I wasn't welcome at the wedding," he said. "But she had a great deal more to say than that."

"She is a class-A bitch," Carlynn said too loudly, and a diner at the next table turned to glare at her.

"What else did she say?" Lisbeth looked worried.

Gabriel stubbed out his cigarette and covered Lisbeth's pale hand with his dark one. "She made me realize that the cost of us being together would be even higher than we imagined. She said that she would cut you completely out of her life if you continued to see me, that you'll never be welcome at Cypress Point again, ever, whether I'm there with you or not."

Lisbeth leaned forward. "I've told you, I don't care about any of that," she said, tears filling her eyes. "Do you think in a choice between you and my mother, she stands a chance?"

Carlynn was furious with Delora. How could she hurt Lisbeth this way? Lisbeth adored Cypress Point, and her mother knew it.

"She said that," Gabriel continued, "if we were ever to get married, she'd cut you out of her will."

Lisbeth blanched at that. "She wouldn't do that," she said. "Her money was also my father's money, and no matter what she thinks of me, *he* loved me and would have wanted me to have it."

"I don't believe Mother would really cut her out of the will," Carlynn agreed. "I think she's just saying that to try to control her. That's the way she is." She wasn't sure, though, and she knew quite well what Lisbeth might be giving up for love: millions of dollars and her share of the mansion she adored.

"You know, Liz, I'm just a guy from Oakland," Gabriel said.

"There are plenty more men out there who are better than me, and who would cost you nothing. If I truly love you, and I sure do, how can I let you lose so much?"

"I want *you,*" Lisbeth said.

"And I want you, too." Gabriel said, tightening his grip on her hand. "I just need to be very sure you know the risks of being with me."

"I do," Lisbeth said.

Carlynn felt her eyes burn.

"Your wedding—" Gabriel looked at Alan and Carlynn "—will be at Cypress Point. Lisbeth will be a beautiful maid of honor, and you will have pictures taken that you'll show me when you get back to San Francisco. And I'll be very sad to miss your special day, but the four of us can have a separate celebration when you get back." He looked at the three of them one by one. "All right?"

"Thanks, Gabe," Alan said, nodding. Beneath the table, he took Carlynn's hand and held it tighter than he ever had before.

CHAPTER TWENTY-FIVE

"Here you go, honey." Joelle's mother handed her a glass of fresh lemonade, then sat next to her father at the small table on the balcony of the condominium.

"Thanks, Mom." Joelle was in the lounge chair, where she'd planted herself an hour ago, after her parents brought her home from the hospital. It had been three days since her surgery, and she felt remarkably well. There wasn't much pain, but she was tender and shaky, and she felt a need to move cautiously. The baby had been quiet during her hospital stay, but he or she was active today, the moving-bubble sensation filling Joelle's belly a couple of times an hour.

Joelle took a sip of cool lemonade, then set the glass on the flat arm of the lounge chair. "I need to talk to you two," she said, not completely sure she was ready to have this conversation.

Her parents turned in their chairs to face her.

"What's up?" her father asked, reaching for a tortilla chip from the bowl on the table. He was wearing sunglasses, and she wished she could see his eyes.

"I'm pregnant," Joelle said.

There was a moment of silence on the balcony.

"Oh, honey." Her mother scraped her chair across the floor of the balcony to move it closer to the lounge. She put her hand on Joelle's arm, her face impassive, unreadable, and Joelle felt some sympathy for her. Ellen didn't know whether she should be happy for her daughter or not, and she was waiting for a cue from Joelle.

"It's good and bad news," Joelle said, "as you can probably guess."

"How far along are you?" her father asked.

"Eighteen weeks," she said. "Almost nineteen."

"Wow," said her mother. "You're barely showing."

"I haven't emphasized it," Joelle said. "I've tried to wear loose, nonmaternity clothes, but it will be impossible to hide soon. And, anyway, now everybody knows."

"You poor thing," said her mother. "You had to have your appendix out while you were pregnant!"

"Well, fortunately, everything turned out okay," she said.

"Who's the father?" her dad asked.

"That doesn't matter," her mother said quickly. "What matters is that you're going to have a baby. Something you've wanted for so long. Something you thought was impossible."

She imagined her mother was thinking the same thing as her colleagues—that she had gotten herself artificially inseminated or perhaps had found an egg donor. Something out of the ordinary, since everyone knew the struggle she and Rusty had had trying to conceive.

"I want you both to know the truth," she said, longing to tell them. "But please keep this to yourselves." Who would they tell, anyhow?

"Of course," said her mother.

"Liam is the baby's father."

"Liam!" Her mother leaned back in the chair, surprise clear on her face. "I thought you and Liam were just friends."

"We are." She sighed and shook her head. "We spent so much time together when Mara got sick. And we became very close.

One night...we made love. Just that one time, but..." She nodded toward her stomach. "That appears to have been enough."

"Why does it have to be a secret?" her father asked.

Her mother turned to him. "Because Liam is married to Mara," she explained as though he were senile. "He's so committed to Mara. I'm actually surprised he would..." Her mother didn't finish her sentence, but Joelle knew where she had been heading.

"But not surprised that I would?" she asked, then was instantly annoyed with herself. Her mother had meant nothing by her comment, and Joelle knew it. It was simply the truth. Anyone would be surprised that Liam had made love to another woman.

"That's not what I'm saying," her mother said.

"I know. It's just...it's a mess, Mom. We didn't use birth control because neither of us figured I could get pregnant. And you're right. Liam is completely and utterly committed to Mara."

"Well, so are you," her father said, rushing to her defense.

"What does Liam have to say about all this?" her mother asked.

Not much, she thought, feeling the unwelcome anger that had been teasing her lately. "He didn't know until the appendectomy, when word finally got around that I was pregnant," she said. "I was never going to tell him." She smiled at them. "Actually, I was thinking of leaving here. Moving to Berkeley to be near you two, or to San Diego to be near another friend, where I could start a new life. Then no one here would have to know."

Both of her parents stared at her in silence. "To spare Liam from having to deal with the whole thing," her mother said. It was a statement rather than a question, and Joelle nodded.

"He's so screwed up, Mom," she said.

Her father shook his head. "You've always wanted to save everybody, Shanti," he said. "Even when you were a kid, you'd take the blame for things the other kids did. Do you remember that?"

"Only once," Joelle said, remembering the time she'd claimed she'd set fire to a flowering shrub near the cabin that served as the schoolhouse. She knew the parents of the boy who had actually set the fire would punish him far more severely than her parents would punish her.

"I can think of at least three or four times," her father said.

"Are you still planning to move?" her mother asked.

Joelle shook her head. "No. There's not much point to it now that the cat's out of the bag. Liam and I are going to have to figure out how to handle this without creating more of a mess than we already have." So far, though, Liam had shown little evidence that he planned to join her in that task.

While she was in the hospital, Liam had been careful to give her the attention befitting a friend with whom he'd worked for many years and about whom he cared a great deal, and nothing more than that. Paul treated her similarly. She doubted anyone's suspicions had been raised. She wondered if, now that she was home, she would hear from Liam or if he would continue his policy of no longer calling her at night. Perhaps that would be wise. They would inevitably grow closer with each call, as they had before. She would love to have those calls again—she needed more support from him than she was getting—but that much contact could only lead them down the same slippery slope.

"What do *you* want, honey?" Her mother touched her arm again. "What do you wish would happen?" There was such love in her mother's eyes that Joelle had to look away from her.

She bit her lip. "I want what I can't have," she said, her voice breaking, and she began to cry.

"She's tired," her father said, talking about her as if she were not sitting just three feet from him.

"Dad's right, hon." Her mother leaned forward to stroke her hair. "How about a nap?"

Joelle nodded, letting her mother help her to her feet. She *was* tired. She reminded herself of Sam, when he'd gone too long without a nap and simply could not maintain his good disposition one minute longer.

She slept for hours, awakening to the unmistakable smell of her mother's vegetable soup. Although her bedroom door was closed, the aroma still found its way to her bed, and it filled her with longing for her childhood, when everything had seemed so simple and good.

Slowly she got out of bed, her right side aching a bit. She combed her hair in the dresser mirror, thinking that she should tell her parents she'd finally gotten in touch with Carlynn Shire. They would love to hear that she and the healer were becoming friends, and that Carlynn would soon be working with Mara in earnest, for whatever that was worth.

Slipping on her sandals, she walked from her bedroom to the kitchen.

"That smells so good, Mom," she said.

"I thought you might like some soup, even though it's warm outside," her mother said.

"You're exactly right," Joelle said, leaning against the breakfast bar. "My stomach still feels a bit queasy."

Her father came up behind her and put his arm around her waist. "I've been thinking, Shanti," he said. "Good and good and good can't possibly equal bad."

"What do you mean?" she asked him.

"You're a good person," he said. "And so is Liam, and so is Mara. There's no way something bad can come from anything the three of you do."

She was touched by his rationale, and she rested her head on his shoulder. "You're so sweet, Daddy," she said. "I'm glad you guys are here."

Her father looked at her mother. "Hey," he said, "remember Shanti's cypress in Big Sur?"

"Yes, of course!" her mother said. "I'd forgotten all about that." She looked at Joelle. "Do you remember? You're supposed to take a cutting from it for each child you have. You know, plant a new tree for the new baby."

She knew what they were talking about: the Monterey cypress planted on top of her placenta. To be honest, though, she did not recall anyone ever talking about taking a cutting from it to plant a tree for a new baby.

"I don't have to bury the placenta under it, do I?" She tried to keep the teasing tone out of her voice, but wasn't sure she had succeeded. She decided she would wait a while before admitting to them that she'd contacted the healer. She could only handle so much of her parents' eccentricities at one time.

"No, of course not," her father said. "We'll go down and get you a cutting from it."

"She really should get it herself," her mother argued.

"You guys are too much." Joelle laughed. "Is the soup ready yet?"

As she lay in bed that night, Joelle found herself thinking of Big Sur and the Cabrial Commune. It was more the smell of her mother's vegetable soup than the discussion about the cypress that brought the memories to mind, and she felt a yearning to go back there, to the place she'd spent her first ten years of life. The troubles of the outside world had been nonexistent there, and the world inside the commune consisted only of friends and forest and fog. It was the place where her father and the midwife, Felicia, had taken the time to dig a hole and plant a cypress to ensure her future. She knew exactly where her cypress was planted—near the northwestern corner of the cabin that served as the schoolhouse. Each of the kids who'd been born at the commune knew which cypress was theirs, and all mysticism aside, it had been a pretty nice custom.

She'd been to the Big Sur area several times in the last twenty-four years, but never to Cabrial. Rusty had shown no interest in visiting the place where she'd grown up, and each time they drove down Highway One to Big Sur, she would pass the dirt road leading to the commune with an unspoken longing.

Maybe, after she had the baby, she would go.

CHAPTER TWENTY-SIX

San Francisco, 1959

"She's my right arm," Lloyd Peterson said, his hand on Lisbeth's shoulder. "I'm not sure if I can get along without her that long."

He was looking across the reception desk at Gabriel, who had come to the office as they were closing up to plead with Lloyd to let Lisbeth take a vacation. Lisbeth had already told Gabriel she could not possibly take a whole week away from the office in the middle of the summer, when she was the only girl working, but Gabriel was not one to give up easily.

"You need a break," he'd told her as they walked back to his place from the cinema the night before. "You work too hard." They'd just seen *Some Like it Hot,* during which Gabriel had whispered to her that he'd take her over Marilyn Monroe any day. Those flattering words were still on her mind as she listened to Lloyd and Gabriel's amiable argument over the possibility of her taking some time off. He wanted to go to the coastal town of Mendocino with her for a week's vacation. Although Lisbeth longed for a week alone with Gabriel, she knew Lloyd could not spare her. Still she decided to let the two men—the two old friends and tennis partners—duke it out.

"Let's talk about this over a beer," Gabriel finally said to Lloyd, who nodded in agreement, and the two of them left her alone to close up the office.

Lisbeth had to smile as the men walked out the door. She doubted Gabriel would win this one, but it was sweet of him to try.

She turned on the radio on her desk, as she always did when she had the office to herself. Switching the station from Lloyd's favorite, where the Kingston Trio was singing "Tom Dooley," to the Negro station Gabriel had introduced her to, where the music was earthier and made her want to dance, she set about filing the charts that had been used that day.

Gabriel had become almost fanatical about wanting to take a vacation in Mendocino. He'd been talking about it ever since Alan and Carlynn honeymooned there after their wedding nearly two years earlier. They'd raved about the peace and quiet and the natural beauty of the location, saying how perfect it was for a romantic getaway. It would be different for her and Gabriel, though, Lisbeth knew. Whenever they stayed in a hotel, they had to get two separate rooms. Someday, Gabriel promised her, they would be married. She now wore a spectacular diamond and sapphire ring on her left hand, but they had not yet set a date. She trusted their relationship, its depth and its love, but she knew Gabe still harbored the fear that marriage to him would cost her more than he was worth.

She'd certainly thought about the price she was paying for being with Gabriel. She had not visited Cypress Point since Carlynn's wedding, and she missed the mansion and the view from the terrace in a way that could cause her actual physical pain. Sometimes at night, she yearned for her old bedroom, where the open windows let in the sound of the waves slapping against the rocky shore.

She thought, too, about the financial cost a marriage to Gabriel would mean for her. She would lose a fortune if she was cut out of her mother's will. That only meant, she tried to reason with herself, that she and Gabriel would live like most couples, dependent on only themselves and their own resources to get by. They would never be rich, but between her small salary and Gabriel's larger one, they would be in better shape than many people they knew. She should need nothing more than that.

It was not fair, though. Not fair that Carlynn, who had gotten the best of everything as a child, should still receive it now, as an adult. It was a struggle for Lisbeth not to shift the anger she felt toward her mother onto her sister's shoulders. When Carlynn would return from a visit to the mansion, Lisbeth could barely look her in the eye, she was so jealous. She knew that her twin fought with Delora to allow Lisbeth to visit Cypress Point, but there was no way she could win that battle. Delora had all the power.

Although Lisbeth had not set foot in the mansion in two years, Carlynn made regular trips to see their mother, whose eyesight was worsening and who was developing other aches and pains, as well, even though she was only in her fifties. Carlynn would be upset after those visits, because, although she possessed the ability to heal total strangers, she seemed unable to rid her mother of her ailments.

Carlynn was upset over other matters, as well, Lisbeth knew. After two years of marriage, she was still not pregnant, and Lisbeth heard the frustration in her sister's voice every month when she'd call to announce she had, once again, gotten her period.

Lisbeth, though, had decided she didn't want children, and she thought Gabriel seemed relieved by that decision. He still worried about how their half-white, half-Negro children might fit into the world, but Lisbeth's reasoning went even deeper than that. Her own childhood had been so unhappy, and her memories of herself as a little girl so excruciating, that she couldn't bear the thought of watching a child of her own endure anything that might be hurtful. She still used a diaphragm to keep from getting pregnant, but Carlynn had told her that within a year or two, birth control pills would be on the market. Lisbeth had kept her joy over that news to herself out of sensitivity to her sister, who might never need a pill to avoid getting pregnant.

Little Richard was singing about Miss Molly when Lloyd and Gabriel surprised her by returning to the office. Lloyd wore a look of defeat on his face, but Lisbeth knew him well enough to see the smile behind it.

"Your boyfriend drives a hard bargain," Lloyd said to her, and she looked at Gabriel.

"We're going?" she asked, surprised.

"This Saturday," Gabriel said. "For an entire week. I already called to book two rooms for us at the same inn where Carlynn and Alan stayed. Right on a bluff over the water."

Lisbeth walked around the desk to give each man a hug. She could hardly wait to call Carlynn to tell her the news.

Mendocino was a small, stunning village, perched on a bluff high above the Pacific, and in some ways it reminded her of the area around Cypress Point. As they drove into the town in Gabriel's open convertible with its fins and whitewall tires, she wondered if that might have been the reason he had so wanted to bring her here. Maybe it was his attempt to give her back a bit of what she'd lost.

The architecture ranged from Victorian to early Californian, and the homes and shops looked bright and clean in the afternoon sun. In the distance to their left, a group of people stood at the edge of a bluff, staring out to sea.

"What's going on out there?" she asked, and Gabriel followed her gaze to the bluff.

"Everyone's dressed in black," he said. "It's probably a funeral service of some kind. Maybe they're scattering someone's ashes into the sea."

She thought he was right as she, too, noticed the dark clothing and somber demeanor of the group silhouetted at the edge of the cliff. "What a glorious location," she said, and it was a moment before she could tear her gaze away.

The inn was small and lovely, set back just a bit from the bluff and surrounded by a gorgeous coastal garden in full bloom. They walked together into the small office at the side of the inn, and Lisbeth was relieved when the woman behind the counter greeted them with a wide smile, as though she had interracial couples checking in every day of the week. Lisbeth wondered if they might have been able to get away with a double room instead of two singles, but Gabriel would never have agreed to that. He was more protective of her honor than she was.

"No keys," the innkeeper said after they had paid and signed the guest book. "You have the two rooms on the second floor. Just turn right at the top of the stairs."

Gabriel thanked the woman, and they left the office, gathered their luggage from the car and entered the front door of the inn. At the top of the stairs, they turned right and opened the first of two doors.

The room was small and cozy, with a white iron double bed and a view of the bluffs. Lisbeth set her suitcase down and walked over to the open window, its white, gauzy curtains wafting into the room on the soft breeze. She could see the dark-suited throng walking away from the cliff, some of them with their arms around one another.

"I think this room is mine," Gabriel said.

She looked at him in surprise. "Why don't we look at both of them before we decide who gets which?" she suggested.

"All right." He set his own suitcase on the floor. "Let's look at the other one," he said, walking back into the hall.

She was first to enter the room and her gaze instantly fell on a wedding dress hanging from a hook on the closet door. "Oh," she said, drawing back quickly. "This must be someone else's room."

Gabriel stood right behind her, preventing her from exiting. "No," he said, his lips against her ear. "I think it's yours."

Lisbeth felt a chill run up her spine. That dress. She suddenly recognized it as the dress she had tried on two years earlier when shopping for Carlynn's wedding dress with her. She could never forget that magnificent arrangement of satin and lace.

"I...I don't understand, Gabe," she said.

He turned her toward him, smiling at her. "Will you marry me?" he asked. "Here? Tomorrow? Out there?" He nodded toward the view outside the window. "On the bluff overlooking the ocean?"

For just an instant, she felt torn, thinking of the wedding she'd long dreamed about, where she and Gabriel would be sur-rounded by family and friends. But none of that mattered. What mattered was that she would become Gabriel's wife. Tomorrow night, they'd be able to share a hotel room for the first time. She would be Lisbeth Johnson.

She threw herself into his arms. "Yes, of course I will!" she said. "How on earth did you know about the dress?"

"Does it matter?"

"No...except that I'm thinner than I was when I last tried it on."

"It will fit," he promised. "And I'll find someone here who can take pictures of you in it, so you can show everyone back home how beautiful you looked."

The minister was to meet them on the bluff at eleven the fol-lowing morning, and at ten, Lisbeth put on the dress and styled her hair, which would probably fall flat once she was out in the damp, cool air above the ocean. But she didn't care. There was no full-length mirror in her room, but she knew the dress fit perfectly, and the beauty of wearing it was more in the *feeling* than in the *seeing*. Carlynn had something to do with this, of course. How else would Gabriel have found the right dress, in the right size for her? She had no flowers, though, and her hands felt a bit awkward, with no place to rest. Gabe had probably not given a thought to flowers.

At ten of eleven, Gabriel knocked on her door. She pulled the door open, and Gabriel's eyes glistened behind his glasses when he saw her. "You are the most beautiful bride I've ever seen," he said.

"Thank you," she said. "And you look beautiful yourself." He was wearing a white tuxedo she had never seen him in before, a red carnation in his lapel.

He put his hands on her arms and looked into her eyes. "I wasn't going to tell you this," he said. "I wanted it to be a surprise, but I know how sad you must feel that Carlynn's not here with you. So, I'm going to tell you that she is."

Her mouth dropped open. "She is? Where?"

"She and Alan will meet us on the bluff, okay?"

"Oh, yes!" she said. "Thank you so much, Gabe."

"And she has flowers for you," he added.

She laughed, slipping her hand through the arm he offered her.

It took them a few minutes to get down the narrow stairs of the inn. Her dress was perfectly tailored with a narrow cut that hugged her slender body, but Gabriel had to carry the long train in his arms to prevent them both from falling headlong down the stairs.

They started walking toward the cliff overlooking the water, Lisbeth searching for three people—Carlynn, Alan and the minister—but she was distressed to see another crowd on the bluff, as there had been the day before. Probably another scattering of ashes, she thought, and it was only as they neared the throng of people that she began to make out faces. Carlynn. Alan. Lloyd Peterson and his wife. Gabriel's mother and sister, aunts and uncles and cousins from Oakland. Their boating friends. All of them standing there on the bluff, grinning at the stunned look on her face.

Gabriel clutched her hand where it rested on his arm.

"Surprise, baby," he whispered to her. "We've been planning this for months."

She was unable to take another step forward as she began to cry. Carlynn ran out from the crowd to hug her, hard, and handed her a bouquet of red roses, and the Negro minister from the Johnson family's Oakland church walked toward her and Gabriel, since Lisbeth seemed unable to move herself.

"We assumed you wouldn't mind if I was your matron of honor," Carlynn whispered as she took her place next to her.

Lisbeth shook her head numbly, noticing that Alan stood next to Gabriel as his best man. She floated through the ceremony, touched beyond words that Gabriel had planned this, going back in her mind over clues she'd missed: Lloyd allowing her to go on this trip after pretending to be against it; Carlynn asking her a month or so ago if she thought they were exactly the same size now; the Fourth of July celebration at Gabriel's mother's house, when the chattering in the kitchen had stopped the moment Lisbeth had walked into the room.

She barely heard the words of the minister, managing by some miracle to get the "I do" in the right place. Her eyes were on her husband as she waited for the moment she could wrap her arms around him, telling him she would never forget this gift he had given her.

They celebrated in the side yard of the inn with a feast and three-tiered wedding cake served under a huge tent which had been miraculously erected in the garden during the ceremony. And afterward, she and Gabriel retired to the honeymoon cottage, located a distance from the inn itself, where the innkeeper had already moved their luggage.

In bed that night, Gabriel held her close.

"Do you mind that I did it this way?" he asked. "I saw all the anguish Carlynn went through in planning her wedding, and I just didn't want any of those crazy family problems to get in the way of your day. But you didn't get to do any of the planning, yourself, and I worried that—"

She kissed him to stop his talking. "This was perfect," she said. "The fact that you did this for me, for us...I can't think of anything more remarkable you could have done."

She snuggled against him. She didn't care about planning a wedding, or even about the quaint little honeymoon cottage, or the view from the bluffs, or the dress she had worn. At that moment, she didn't even care about her mother's will, which would no longer contain Lisbeth's name except to acknowledge her as the daughter to whom Delora would leave nothing. All she cared about now was the man lying by her side.

CHAPTER TWENTY-SEVEN

At twenty-one weeks, Joelle could not have hidden her pregnancy even if she had wanted to. She sat on the front porch of the condominium that Saturday afternoon waiting for Liam to pick her up to go to the nursing home, and for the first time she was wearing maternity clothes in public. She had on black leggings with a soft, stretchy fabric panel over her belly, a red cotton sleeveless blouse and a white, black-trimmed sweater tossed over her shoulders in case the day grew cooler, which was often the norm in Monterey. Her mother, who, until that morning, had been staying with her while she healed from the appendectomy, had taken her shopping the day before, and Joelle thought they must have hit every thrift shop in Monterey County.

"No need to pay high prices for clothes you'll only be wearing a few months," her mother had said.

Her father had stayed with them the first week, but he needed to get back to the coffeehouse he managed, so only her mother had been with her for the last two weeks. It had been a good visit. A wonderful visit, actually. For the first couple of weeks, Joelle had not felt up to leaving the condominium except for her doctor's appointments, and her mother had grocery shopped and cooked for her. They played cards and board games, just the two of them, with Tony and Gary joining them a couple of evenings. She and her mother talked in a way they'd never really had the time to before. Joelle learned that her mother was still madly in love with her father after all these years, despite what she referred to as some "difficulties" during those last few years at the commune, something they had hidden well from Joelle. Her mother told her how afraid she'd been when she found out she was pregnant and the absolute terror she'd felt when she thought her baby had been born dead.

"I remember wanting to scream," she said, "but I was all screamed out by that point."

Joelle could not bear to think what that experience had been like for her parents. Her baby, to whom she was already irrevocably attached, no longer felt like a bubble so much as a butterfly, and she could not imagine going through nine months of falling in love with her unborn child only to have something go wrong at the last minute. That thought made her glad she did not have to go back to work right away. She was not at all in the mood to deal with stillbirths, and she knew that when she returned after this sick leave, someone else would have to take those cases. If not for her own sanity, then out of kindness to the bereaved parents, who should not have to receive counseling from a healthy pregnant woman immediately after enduring such a loss.

Her baby was more real to her now. The sonogram she'd had several days ago had shown arms and legs, one visible eye, an open mouth. Rebecca had asked her if she wanted to know the baby's sex.

"Yes!" Joelle had said.

Her mother had been with her, marveling at the image on the screen, and Rebecca pointed out the barely perceptible labia to both of them.

"Three generations of women, right here in this room!" her

mother said, and for some reason, that made Joelle cry. Although she had not intended to do so, her imagination flashed forward to a baby dressed in little-girl clothes, a child with braids in kindergarten, a giggling teenager in a prom dress and a happy young woman at her wedding. And who would be the man walking that little girl down the aisle? She was afraid it would not be Liam.

She longed to tell Liam that the baby was a girl, but he had not even mentioned her pregnancy since their conversation in the recovery room after her appendectomy, and she was angry with him for that. She feared expressing that anger, though. Feared pushing him farther away. How would he react if she told him he would soon have a daughter? She was most afraid that he wouldn't react at all, and if that was to be the case, she didn't want to know it.

He'd called her every few days while she was away from work, but she'd gotten the feeling he was making the calls out of a sense of duty rather than desire, and their conversations had been short and superficial. She had no idea what was going on inside his head, and she didn't dare ask him; it was apparent he did not want either of them to dig too deeply into the other's thoughts and feelings. It had been easy to honor his unspoken wishes while her mother had been with her, when she hadn't felt the need for much contact with anyone else. But now, with her mother gone and two more weeks of recovery ahead of her, she worried that she would have too much time to think.

It was now ten of one, and Liam was late. They were to meet Carlynn at the nursing home at one o'clock. Quinn would drive her there, Carlynn had told Joelle, and he'd run a few errands while she spent an hour with the two of them and Mara. Although Liam wisely had not balked when Joelle told him the plan, she knew he saw this whole outing as pointless, if not preposterous.

She and her mother had met Carlynn for lunch earlier that week at a café in Pacific Grove. Her mother had embraced Carlynn tearfully when she saw her, and the three of them had talked about how different they all looked from that day in Rainbow Cabin, so long ago.

Ellen, of course, had been thrilled to learn that Carlynn was using her healing ability on Mara, and even more pleased to know that Liam had agreed to participate.

"He says he will," Joelle told the two women at lunch, "though I have the feeling he's doing it out of guilt. Trying to make up to me for what he can't truly give me."

"It doesn't matter why he's doing it," Carlynn had said. "Just as long as we can get him there in that room. That's what will help Mara."

Liam's car turned the corner onto her street, and she stood up and walked down the sidewalk to meet him at the curb, very aware of the way the red blouse gently ballooned over her stomach. He stopped the car and she let herself in.

"Hi," she said, fastening the seat belt.

"Sorry I'm late." He glanced in the side-view mirror as he pulled into the street again. He looked so good. Pretty, pale eyes, straight nose and slight point to his chin. She tried not to stare. Her body suddenly felt alive and hungry for him. This was the longest she'd gone without seeing him in years, probably since he'd started working at Silas Memorial, and she could barely stand the intense and untimely desire that was ambushing her here in his car.

"How are you feeling?" he asked.

"Fine," she said, the word a bland mask for the mixture of anger and desire churning inside her. "It feels good to get out."

"When are you allowed to drive?"

"Probably next week," she said. "I feel like I could drive now, but since they say five or six weeks, I'll compromise on four."

"Good idea," he said. "They're talking about five or six for the usual patient. Not someone in...your condition." He actually smiled when he said those words, giving her hope that her pregnancy would not continue to be the great unbroachable subject.

"How did it go with your mom?" he asked.

"It was really good to be with her," she said, missing her mother a bit already. "She bought me five thousand different types of vitamins and a few aromatherapy candles and gave me foot massages every night."

"I'm glad it was a good visit." He glanced at her, then smiled the smile that put that provocative crevice in his cheek. "You are a really cute pregnant woman," he said.

She laughed. "Thanks," she said. That was the warmest thing he'd said to her in ages. "And thanks for doing this, Liam," she said. "I know you don't want to."

"You're welcome," he said with a brief nod of his head, acknowledging that she was quite right.

Carlynn met them in the foyer of the nursing home. Liam greeted her with a stiff, but cordial, hello, and Joelle gave her a hug. The older woman felt more frail than ever beneath her arms, as though her bones might crack if she squeezed her too hard. The three of them walked in silence down the corridor to Mara's room.

Mara was sitting up in bed, getting her face wiped by an aide who had just fed her lunch. She smiled and, when she spotted Liam, let out a little cry of delight. He was first to reach her bed, and he leaned over to kiss her. Mara lifted her right arm up as though trying to hug him, although she could not quite master the maneuver.

"Liam!" Joelle said. "Look at her arm! She's trying to hug you with it."

Liam stepped back. "She's been doing that for the past few weeks. They've brought the physical therapist back in to help her work with her arm a bit more."

Joelle remembered the last time she'd seen Mara with Carlynn, when Mara had appeared to massage the older woman's palm with her right hand. Was that the day the use of her arm had improved? She didn't dare suggest that to Liam, at least not right then. She knew he would not think Carlynn's visit had anything to do with an improvement in his wife.

"Hi, Mara." Joelle stepped forward to give her a hug, noticing how Mara's silky hair brushed against her cheek. "Your hair's getting longer, sweetie," she said. "I haven't been around to cut it in a while, but it looks really pretty. Maybe we should leave it this way. What do you think, Liam?"

He nodded. "I like it," he said, then he turned to Carlynn. "So, what do we do now?" he asked, the impatience barely concealed in his voice.

Carlynn leaned on her cane in the center of the small room and looked around her, as though trying to make a decision. "Okay," she said finally. "Here's what I suggest. Liam, could you see if you could find another chair for in here? Then you and Joelle can sit while I massage Mara's hands again."

Liam left the room without a word, and Joelle exchanged a look with Carlynn.

"It's all right," Carlynn said, knowing what she was thinking. "He'll be fine."

Liam brought back one of the hard, straight-backed chairs from the cafeteria across the hall and set it near the recliner that was next to the bed.

"You take the recliner, Jo," he said, and she sat down. Then he sat in the smaller chair and looked at Carlynn, waiting for his next instruction.

Carlynn sat on the edge of Mara's bed, poured baby lotion onto her palm and began to massage Mara's hands, as she had the last time she'd visited the nursing home with Joelle.

"Joelle and Liam," she said without looking at them, "please talk about memories you have of your time with Mara. Any situations you can remember that involved the three of you."

"What's the point?" Liam asked, and Joelle felt like kicking him.

"I want her to hear you talking about things that involve all three of you, that she would also remember, if she were able. We want to stimulate that memory bank in her brain."

Liam wearily rubbed the back of his head, his eyes closed, and

Joelle doubted he was going to put much effort into this exercise. Obviously, it would be up to her to start. Resting her head against the recliner, she stared at the ceiling and thought back over the years to some of the many memories they shared.

"I remember the party Rusty and I gave where I was hoping to fix Mara and Liam up without their knowing it," she said. She smiled at Liam, and he looked at her. "I remember the exact moment when it clicked for both of them."

"When?" He looked curious.

"We were all sitting around my living room, remember? And everyone was playing instruments. And you and Mara had your guitars. And you started playing that song...I don't remember the title...the Joan Baez song that goes, 'Show me the something, show me the—'"

"'There But for Fortune,'" Liam said.

"Right. And you were singing, and suddenly Mara started singing and playing the same song, in perfect harmony with you, and you two were looking at each other across the room, and it was like there was this invisible thread connecting you, and neither of you knew anyone else was there. And I was thinking, *yes!* I just knew once the two of you met it would be like that."

Pursing his lips, Liam nodded. "Yeah," he said, "it was a good call on your part. And you were playing a pan and a spoon, right?"

"No, I had the comb and the tissue paper," she said. "Rusty had the pan and spoon. The instrument of least effort."

"Rusty was a pill," Liam said. "It's good you ditched him."

"He ditched me," she said, "but never mind."

They fell silent, and Joelle glanced at Mara. Her gaze was on Carlynn, and it surprised her that she was not looking at Liam, since he was well within her range. She was not smiling, but her face looked relaxed, as though the massage was soothing her.

"I've got one," Liam said. "Talking about Rusty reminded me of it."

"Do we *have* to talk about Rusty?" she asked.

"Remember the time we all went to San Diego for a few days?" She nodded. "Over Christmas."

"Right, and I don't know where we were, somewhere in San Diego County, I guess, or maybe not, but out in that place you had heard about that had pocket canyons and other strange rock formations and—"

"Oh, no," she said, starting to laugh as she remembered the hour-long hike that had turned into four rather scary hours.

"You swore you knew where you were going, and we followed you like we trusted you," Liam said.

"I had a map. It's just that we got turned around somehow."

"There were those weird hills or dunes or whatever they were. And you kept saying, 'Our car is parked right over that hill,' and we'd climb over it, which would take a half hour, and then all we'd see in front of us was..."

"Another hill." She laughed. "But see? We can laugh about it now."

"I don't remember laughing at the time," Liam said. "I thought Rusty was going to divorce you the moment we actually did find the car."

"And remember Mara had taken a whole roll of pictures of us goofing around in the pocket canyon and then realized she had no film in her camera?"

Liam laughed. "Oh, I felt so sorry for her." He leaned over and squeezed Mara's arm, giving Carlynn a look that said, "Try and stop me," but Carlynn only smiled at him.

"Do you remember what happened on the beach?" Joelle said. "That same trip. In Coronado, I think. We were lying there and a gull flew over and—"

Liam interrupted her with a groan. "Not my favorite memory," he said. "Mara wouldn't kiss me for a week."

"God, it was funny," Joelle said.

"Do you remember that E.R. case, where we called Mara in to do a psych consult?" Liam asked.

"Which one?"

"The pregnant woman who was in a car accident and her arm was nearly—"

"Oh, yes!" Joelle started laughing. "Her arm was hanging by a thread, and all she kept saying was that she thought her pierced belly button was infected."

"I can still hear Mara," Liam said. "Remember? She went into the treatment room wearing that professional expression she was so good at, and said, 'Your belly button is fine, but your arm is falling off.'" He looked at Carlynn, who was not smiling. She appeared to be deeply focused on Mara's face. Liam shrugged. "I guess you had to be there," he said, and Joelle chuckled.

"I remember the time we called Mara in for that woman who was using her vagina as a bank," she said, "and—"

"Don't go there," Liam interrupted her with a laugh. He looked at Mara. "Don't worry, honey, we're not going there."

They were quiet for a minute, and Joelle felt gratitude toward him for playing this game. Liam closed his eyes.

After a moment she asked him, "What are you thinking about?"

He took in a deep breath and let it out in a sigh. "A memory," he said, opening his eyes. "When you were over at our house, right after you and Rusty split up. And we made you dinner and were consoling you, and then I got that call that my father died."

His father had been only fifty-nine years old, and he'd simply keeled over at work one day. She could still remember Liam's shock and sorrow.

Joelle leaned forward and touched his hand, and to her surprise he turned his hand to hold on to hers. His eyes were on her, and he looked beaten down, tired of whatever game it was they were playing. It was time to free him from it.

"Carlynn?" she said. "Can Liam and I stop now?"

Carlynn nodded, stilling her own hands. "Mara?" she said softly, and Mara smiled at them as though she'd forgotten they were there. She lifted her right arm toward Liam. It was an unmistakable, meaningful gesture. That arm had always been usable, but until now Mara had not seemed to know what to do with it. Carlynn stood up, and Liam took her place on the bed.

"Would you like to visit Mara a while longer, Liam?" Carlynn asked. "Quinn and I can drop Joelle off on our way home."

Liam looked at Joelle. "Do you mind?" he asked.

She shook her head, still moved by the way Mara had reached out to him.

"Next week, Liam, I would like you to bring your guitar, please," Carlynn asked.

"I don't play anymore," Liam said without looking at her.

"Joelle told me that, but I think it's important," Carlynn said. "Music can touch so many parts of the mind and heart in a way that nothing else can. So bring it, please."

In the corridor outside Mara's room, Joelle said quietly. "I don't know if he will."

"I hope he does," Carlynn said. "I think it can make a difference."

They walked together down the hallway, and Joelle could still feel the grip of Liam's fingers on her hand and recall the way he'd looked at her. The moment had been brief, a mere few seconds, but she had not felt that close to him in months.

CHAPTER TWENTY-EIGHT

Carlynn sat on the very edge of the terrace floor looking out at the sea. She hadn't sat this way, with her legs dangling over the terrace's stone floor, in a very long time. Probably not since she was a child. She could feel the cold of the stone through the fabric of her slacks, and the sensation was not unpleasant. It let her know she was still alive.

"Carlynn?"

She glanced behind her to see Mary McGowan walking toward her from the house.

"Hello, Mary," she said.

"It gave me a start to see you sitting out here like this," Mary said as she neared her. "Are you all right? Can I get you something?"

"I'm fine," Carlynn said. "And no, you can't get me anything, thank you. But why don't you sit down here with me for a bit?"

"On the cold ground like that?" Mary sounded a bit stunned at the suggestion.

"Yes. Come on." Carlynn waved her hand through the air in invitation. "My sister and I used to sit like this all the time when we were children."

"Not sure I can get down that low." Mary laughed, but Carlynn knew she would be able to. She'd seen Mary scrub the kitchen floor on her hands and knees more than once.

"Come on," Carlynn said again, reaching toward her. "I'll give you a hand."

Mary held on to Carlynn's hand and gingerly lowered herself to the edge of the terrace, letting her own legs and her sensible shoes dangle over the side.

"How are we ever going to get up?" Mary chuckled.

"We'll worry about that later," Carlynn said. She'd given that some thought herself. She lived in a house of old people.

"Ah," Mary said, looking out to sea. "This is beautiful. I feel closer to the water down here."

"And the trees," Carlynn said. She studied the milky horizon, where the overcast sky and frothy sea met in an indistinct line. "I was thinking before," she said. "Thinking about the perennials."

"The perennials?" Mary asked.

Carlynn nodded. "I realized this was probably the last year I'd ever see them."

"Oh, Carlynn." Mary gently touched her shoulder.

"Don't feel bad," Carlynn said. "I don't. But it was just a shock to realize that. I wish I'd paid better attention to them over the summer."

Neither of them spoke for a moment. "I know Alan's worried about you," Mary said finally. "He doesn't think you should be going to that nursing home, seeing that brain-damaged girl."

"Well, he's wrong about that," Carlynn said.

"How is she doing? The girl with the brain damage?"

Carlynn smiled to herself. "She's at peace," she said. "Smiles all the time. She's not the one who needs healing."

"What do you mean?"

"It's Joelle and Liam who need to be healed, though they don't realize it yet."

"Who's Liam?" Mary asked.

Carlynn watched a pelican fly through her cypress-framed view of the ocean. "He's a man whose forgotten how to make music in his life," she said. "And he's also the man Joelle is in love with." She looked squarely at Mary. "*And* he's the husband of Mara, the brain-damaged woman."

"Oh," Mary said with a knowing nod, and Carlynn heard the understanding in that simple word. Mary knew all about forbidden love, love that must remain hidden.

Just as she did.

CHAPTER TWENTY-NINE

San Francisco, 1962

Carlynn stepped into the hospital room, where the little boy lay in the bed nearest the window. The room was dark, except for a low-wattage lamp on the boy's night table, and his mother sat in a chair near his bed. Carlynn did not know this child or his mother, but she'd received a call early that morning from the doctor treating the seven-year-old boy, asking for a consult. Carlynn had a reputation as a gifted pediatrician. No one, save Alan, understood the depth of that gift, but she was called on regularly by her colleagues to see their patients who were difficult to diagnose and harder still to treat.

She and Alan shared a practice in their office on Sutter Street, where Carlynn specialized in children, while Alan saw adults. There was crossover, of course. A great deal of it, actually, because Alan often called her in to "meet" one of his patients, in the hope that such a meeting would lead him to a better course of treatment through Carlynn's intuitive sense of the patient. It was gratifying work, something she seemed born to do. Still, she was not completely happy. All day, every day, she treated the children of other people, when what she longed for was a child of her own.

A year ago, Alan had learned he was sterile. They would never be able to have children unless they adopted, and neither of them was ready or willing to take that step. Carlynn had wondered briefly if she might be able to use her healing skills to make Alan fertile again, but she didn't want to subject him to being a guinea pig, and he did not offer.

The news that they would remain childless had thrown Carlynn into a mild depression, which she'd attempted to mask so that Alan would feel no worse than he already did. What kept her going, what still brought her joy, was her continued fascination with the nature of her gift. She spent her days pouring her energy into her patients, but at night she was exhausted and often went to bed early, and she knew that Alan worried about her.

"Mrs. Rozak?" Carlynn spoke softly to the woman in the little boy's room.

"Yes." The woman stood up to greet her.

"I'm Dr. Shire," Carlynn said. "Dr. Zieman asked me to see your son."

"I didn't expect a woman," Mrs. Rozak said, obviously disappointed.

"No, I'm often a surprise." Carlynn smiled.

"Isn't there another Dr. Shire? A man?"

"That's my husband," Carlynn said. "But he treats adults. I'm the pediatrician in the family."

"Well..." The woman looked at her son, whose eyes were open, but who had not moved or made a sound since Carlynn had walked into the room. "Dr. Zieman said that if anyone could help him, you could." She spoke in a near whisper, as though not wanting her child to hear her. Her small gray eyes were wet, her face red from days of crying, and Carlynn moved closer to touch her hand.

"Let me see him," she said.

The woman nodded, stepping back to allow Carlynn to move past her.

Carlynn sat on the edge of the boy's bed. His name was Brian, she remembered, and he was awake but silent, his glassy-eyed gaze following her movements. She could almost *see* the fever burning inside him. Touching his forehead, her hand recoiled from the heat.

"Nothing's brought the fever down," his mother said from the other side of the bed.

"Hello, sweetheart," Carlynn said softly to the boy. "Can you hear me?"

The boy gave a barely perceptible nod.

"He can hear," the mother said.

"It hurts even to nod?" Carlynn asked him, and he nodded again.

She thought of asking the mother to leave, but decided against it, as long as she could get her to be quiet. Ordinarily, she preferred not to have family members present, since her style of work tended to alarm them because of her lack of action. They wondered why she had been called in to see their sick children, when she appeared to do absolutely nothing to help them. This particular woman was very anxious, though, and if Carlynn could keep her in the room while she worked, it would probably help both mother and son.

"Back here?" She touched the back of Brian's neck. "Is this where it hurts?"

The boy whispered a word and she leaned closer to hear it. "Everywhere," he said, and she studied him in sympathy.

Standing up, she smiled briefly at his mother, then lifted Brian's chart from the end of the bed, leafing through the pages. They'd ruled out rheumatic fever and meningitis and all the other probable causes for his symptoms, as well as those that might not be so obvious. He had an infection somewhere in his body—his blood work showed that much—but the cause had not been determined. Frankly, she didn't care what was causing his symptoms as long as the logical culprits had been ruled out. It only helped her to know the cause if it was something that could be removed or repaired. Fever caused by a ruptured appendix had one obvious solution, for example, but when a child presented this way, with intense, hard-to-control fever and pain everywhere, and the usual suspects had been ruled out, learning the cause was no longer on Carlynn's agenda.

"No one can figure out what's wrong with him," Mrs. Rozak said.

Glancing through his chart again, she assured herself that every treatment her physician's mind could imagine had already been attempted. The treatment she would now give the boy would have little to do with her mind and everything to do with her heart. Sitting down once more on the edge of Brian's bed, she looked up at his mother.

"I'm going to ask you to be quiet for a while, Mrs. Rozak, all right?" she asked. "It's very important, so no matter how much you want to say something to me, please save it until I tell you it's okay. I'd like to give Brian my undivided attention."

The woman nodded again and walked across the room to sit on the edge of the empty second bed.

Carlynn spoke to Brian in a soft voice, holding his small hand in both of hers.

"Nothing I do will hurt you," she said. "I'm going to talk to you, but you don't need to talk back to me," she said. "I'm not going to ask you any questions, so you don't have to worry about answering me. I'm just going to talk for a while and hope I don't bore you too much." She smiled at him.

She talked about the weather, about the Yankees winning the World Series, about the way the blond in his hair sparkled in the soft light from the lamp. She talked about Halloween coming up and about the new movie *The Miracle Worker,* and how strong and tough and smart Helen Keller had been as a child. She talked until she knew his gaze was locked tight to hers. Then she gently lowered the blanket and sheet to his waist.

"I'm going to touch you very gently now," she said. "I won't hurt you a bit."

Through his hospital gown, she rested one hand on his hot rib cage and leaned forward so that she could slip her other hand beneath his back.

"I'm going to be quiet for a few minutes now, Brian. I'll close my eyes, and you can close yours, too, if you like."

Shutting her eyes, she did what had become second nature to her. She allowed everything inside her, all her thoughts and hopes and loving feelings, to pour from her into him. She could feel the energy slipping through his body, from one of her hands to the other. Sometimes, healing came easily to her, and tonight, with this particular child, was one of those times.

"There's a light inside you, Brian," she said softly, her hands still on his small, hot body. "It's not a hot light, like a lightbulb. It's cool, like the water in a cool lake, reflecting the sun off its surface. I can feel it passing into your body from my hands." There was no need for her to speak—this was not hypnosis—but talking sometimes helped, and with this boy she thought it might. She opened her eyes to see that his were closed, a small crease in the space between his delicate, little-boy eyebrows as he listened hard to her words.

Precious child, she thought, closing her eyes again.

After another moment or so, she slowly drew her hands away from him. He was asleep, she noticed, the crease gone from between his eyebrows, and she knew he would get well. She didn't always have that sense of certainty; in fact, it was rare that she did. Right now, though, the feeling inside her was strong.

Standing up, she pressed her finger to her lips so that Mrs. Rozak would not say anything that might wake her son.

Carlynn leaned forward to hold her wristwatch into the circle of light from the night-table lamp. She'd been in the room an hour. It had seemed like fifteen minutes to her.

Walking toward the hallway, she motioned Mrs. Rozak to follow her.

"What do you think?" the woman asked as soon as they'd

reached the intrusive bright light of the corridor. The poor woman had to be thoroughly confused by what she had just witnessed, and Carlynn thought she'd probably made a mistake in allowing her to stay. She hadn't realized how long she would be working with Brian.

"I think Brian will get well," she said.

"But what's wrong with him?"

"I'm not certain," Carlynn said honestly. "But I believe he will turn the corner very quickly."

"How can you *say* that?" The woman looked frantic, wiping a tear from her cheek with a trembling hand. "You didn't even examine him."

It was true. She hadn't listened to his heart or his lungs or looked into his ears or his throat, and perhaps she should have allowed that ruse, but she had gotten out of the habit of pretending to do something she was not. It stole her energy from the task at hand.

She smiled at Mrs. Rozak. "I examined him in my own way," she said. "And I feel very strongly that he will be just fine. Back playing with his friends in a week. Maybe sooner."

She didn't want to answer any more questions. She couldn't. A dizziness washed over her that she knew would drop her to the floor if she didn't escape quickly. Excusing herself from the bewildered woman, she walked down the hall to the ladies' room.

Inside the rest room, she washed her hands in cold water, shaking them out at her sides, then splashed water on her face, trying to regain some of the energy she had just given away. God, she would love a nap! Once or twice, she'd given in to that temptation by closing herself into one of the stalls, sitting fully clothed on the toilet and resting her head against the wall while she dozed. But there was no time for that tonight.

She left the rest room and walked to the nurses' station, where she made a call to the physician, Ralph Zieman, who had referred the boy to her.

"I saw Brian Rozak," she told the pediatrician. She was never sure what to say in these situations. How could she explain that she had no new diagnosis to offer, no concrete treatment to suggest? The doctors talked about her, she knew, some of them scoffing at the idea that this female doctor could do something they could not. But there were a few physicians, and Ralph Zieman was one of them, who were beginning to understand and accept that what she did was outside the norm. "I spent about an hour with him," she said. "Like you, I'm not sure what's going on, but I think you'll find him improved in the morning."

Ralph Zieman hesitated a moment before answering. "If that's true, Carlynn, you'd better be prepared to open your own medical school, with me as your first student."

She laughed. "Just let me know what you find when you do your rounds in the morning, okay?" she asked.

It was two months later when Carlynn realized her decision to allow Brian Rozak's mother to remain in his room while she treated him would change her life. She was walking in the door of the row house she shared with Alan when the phone rang. It was Lisbeth.

"Why didn't you tell me?" Lisbeth nearly shouted.

"Tell you what?" Carlynn frowned.

"About *Life Magazine,* you secretive little thing."

It had been a very long day, and Carlynn creased her forehead as she tried to discern the meaning in her sister's words. Finally she gave up. "I don't know what you're talking about," she said.

"Are you kidding me?"

Carlynn was beginning to feel annoyed. "No, I have no idea."

"Gabe and I just got our new issue of *Life,* the one with the Cuban Missile Crisis on the cover, and there you are! A great big fat article! It's called 'The Real Miracle Worker,' and it's all about *you,* Carly."

Carlynn sat down, her mouth open. "I... That doesn't make any sense. I knew nothing about it."

"Want me to read it to you?"

"Yes, definitely."

Lisbeth began to read, and it all started to fall into place. Brian Rozak's mother was a writer for *Life Magazine,* and she had come to the conclusion that Brian's miraculous recovery from his strange fever could only be attributable to the magical work of the young woman doctor, Carlynn Shire. Mrs. Rozak had done some sleuthing after Brian's recovery. She'd spoken to a few doctors, some of whom trusted Carlynn's skills and others who found them suspect, and somehow she'd managed to track down several patients who Carlynn had helped over the years. The article made Carlynn sound like equal parts saint, genius, fruitcake and charlatan.

But the Bay Area was full of people who were full of hope, and the next day the office she shared with Alan was crammed with walk-ins. The phone rang continuously, and they had to call in a temporary worker in the middle of the day to give the receptionist they shared a break. Carlynn worked until ten that night and until midnight the following night, and when she failed to wake up with the alarm on the third morning after the appearance of the *Life* article, she knew she could not continue this way. She could not see everyone who wanted to see her. The work drained her, both mentally and physically. Yet, how could she turn people away? Even more distressing to her was that she was not able to help all of those people she *did* treat, and she didn't understand why that was the case.

Some people, like Brian Rozak, were relatively simple for her to heal. With others, she didn't know where to begin. It was as though her intuition left her when she sat in a room with certain people. Why did one approach succeed with a particular patient and not with another? Why did talking sometimes help and other times hinder? She simply didn't know the answers to her own questions, and the more patients clamored to see her, the more her lack of knowledge disturbed her. Sometimes she felt alone. She was the only person who could do this. Invaluable. Irreplaceable. And that scared her more than it honored her.

Alan both supported and envied his wife. He pleaded with her to teach him everything she knew about her method of healing, but no matter how long Alan spent with a patient, no matter how intently he spoke to them, looked into their eyes, held their hands, he made no difference in their physical condition.

Carlynn knew he was proud of her, though. Proud and thrilled by the newfound fame that brought them more patients than they could handle. He tried to protect her from overdoing it by putting an end to the walk-in appointments and by hiring nurses to screen the patients so that she would see only those in the greatest need. Some, she turned away herself, knowing from talking with them on the phone or in person that she could not help them. She just knew. There was something in their voice, or in the words they used, that told her. And it was nothing she could explain to anyone who asked, not even her husband.

Her own mother was one of those people.

She tried to visit her mother every month, sometimes with Alan, sometimes alone. Delora never asked Carlynn about Lisbeth, and if Carlynn offered any information about her sister, Delora feigned deafness in addition to her failing eyesight and arthritis. Once, Carlynn overheard an interviewer ask Delora the question, "How many children do you have?" and her mother replied, "One" without a moment's hesitation.

Carlynn had felt guilty at first, continuing to see their mother, but Lisbeth insisted that she did. Someone needed to be sure Delora was all right and getting her eyes checked regularly, Lisbeth said. So she encouraged Carlynn's contact with their mother, and Carlynn was relieved. No matter how horrid one's parents were, she thought, it was the duty of the family to look after them.

Her mother had grown rather famous in Monterey County, not that she'd truly ever been an unknown. But now that word had spread about Carlynn's healing powers, newspapers and magazines were always after Delora for an interview. Sometimes they tried to contact her to see if she might be able to get them an appointment with her daughter to treat their cancer or their ulcers. It annoyed Delora tremendously that she, herself, wasn't a better advertisement for her daughter's skills. Carlynn had been unable to heal her arthritis or the macular degeneration that was stealing her vision. Not for want of trying, certainly, and with every visit she tried again, sending her energy into her mother's body until she was drained and had to sleep for hours. But nothing worked, and Carlynn was never surprised. Her mother was one of those people she would turn away from her office, knowing that no matter what she did, this woman would not get better. Not her eyesight nor her knees. Not her narcissism. And certainly not her cruelty toward her unwanted second daughter.

CHAPTER THIRTY

Liam walked into Mara's room carrying his guitar case. Joelle smiled at him from the edge of Mara's bed, and Carlynn looked up from where she was sitting in the recliner.

"Good!" Carlynn said. "I'm proud of you."

He had not brought the guitar the week before, when Carlynn had initially instructed him to do so. He hadn't touched it since the day Sam was born. It would need new strings, he told himself. The calluses on his fingers were no longer as tough as they should be. He'd had a world of excuses. Mainly, he just did not want to have to look at, hold or play something that was so strongly connected to his life with Mara. He was afraid of how it would make him feel, and he didn't want to be that vulnerable, especially in front of Joelle and Carlynn.

He was annoyed at Carlynn's intrusion into his life. Yet, he had to admit, it was kind of spooky in Mara's room when she was there. There were changes in Mara since Carlynn had been seeing her. Even the physical therapist admitted it. Mara was tracking better with her eyes as she followed the little stuffed toy the therapist moved through the air. She was awake for longer periods during the day, and her right hand and arm were not only getting stronger, but seemed to move now with a purpose, something he had never seen before Carlynn's involvement.

The therapist said, though, that this was not a miraculous change in Mara. Often, after a period of little or no progress, a person with the sort of damage Mara had suffered could begin to show signs of improvement. Liam should not expect too much, though, the therapist warned him. Mara's cognitive impairment was likely to remain at its current level, even if she did make small strides in the use of her muscles.

Even though he had not brought his guitar to their last meeting in Mara's room, he had to admit that the visit had been almost fun. He'd brought a couple of tapes that he and Mara had made of their performances, instead. They'd listened to the music while Carlynn did whatever she was doing to Mara's hands, and the songs brought back memories of various concerts and made him and Joelle laugh again. The laughter had seemed alien the first week, when he and Joelle obediently talked about their memories of being together with Mara. How long had it been since they'd laughed together? But last week had been better. Joelle did not seem like so much of a stranger, or an enemy, or, as Carlynn had pointed out to him weeks earlier, an evil person to be avoided. She seemed, actually, quite harmless, and it felt okay to enjoy his time with her, as long as it was to help Mara. That was how it had been the first year after the aneurysm: he and Joelle had done many, many things together, all in the name of helping Mara. It wasn't until they did something just for themselves that their togetherness felt wrong.

Joelle was back at work now, a week sooner than her doctor's recommendation, but she seemed fine. Pregnancy truly became her. There was something about her small size and long hair and the clothes she was wearing, which drew attention to her expanding middle, that led everyone to talk about how cute she looked. Was he the only person who thought she also looked very, very sexy? He'd always found something provocative in her petite and perfectly proportioned body and in the way her long dark hair fell over her breasts. He could still remember the weight of that hair on his chest and his thighs and the feeling of it in his hands. That memory would come to him at the most unexpected and inappropriate times—when he was working with the family of a cancer patient, for example, or in the midst of a meeting with the E.R. staff—and he was annoyed with himself for being unable to control it.

Everyone at the hospital was still speculating about how she came to be pregnant. He speculated right along with them, feigning ignorance. People thought he knew and was keeping it from them, not because he personally had been involved in the conception, but because he and Joelle were good friends. The newest rumor was that she was pregnant through in vitro fertilization, with one of her gay neighbors having donated the sperm. He said nothing to dissuade that thinking. But his big worry of late was that Joelle's baby might look like Sam, with those telltale blond curls.

It upset him that that night would not go away. With Joelle pregnant, that night would always be there, staring him in the face, first in the shape of her pregnancy itself, and later in the form of a child. What his relationship would be to that child, he didn't know. He couldn't imagine any relationship at this point.

He'd told Sheila that Joelle was pregnant, not wanting her to find out either by bumping into her or through the grapevine, and again, he pleaded ignorance to knowing how she came to be that way. Sheila, he thought, had eyed him suspiciously.

Now he felt Mara's eyes on him as he opened the case and pulled out the guitar. Would it upset her to see the instrument that she used to play so well, far better than he ever could, when she was unable to even hold it herself? But there she was, smiling as usual, with no hint of sorrow or distress or anything, really, other than that simple happiness that had become such a part of her.

"Okay, now," Carlynn said as she stood up from the recliner.

"Is that the best chair for you to sit on to play?" She pointed to the straight-back chair and he nodded.

"Yes, ma'am," he said, and Joelle admonished him with a teasing look.

"You want to sing with me, Jo?" he asked.

"No way," she said. She took her seat in the recliner, while Carlynn sat on the bed and began massaging Mara's hands.

He started with "There but for Fortune," then played and sang several more songs in a row, and it felt like coming home to him. He no longer cared what this music was doing to Mara. He was in his own world, and it was a good place to be.

He played one of his favorite songs, an upbeat tune that had a zydeco feel to it.

"Oh!" Joelle said in the middle of the song, hands on her belly. "She's dancing."

He stopped playing and looked at her. "She?" he asked, and Joelle nodded.

For some reason, he hadn't thought of the baby as a girl. Or as a boy, either, for that matter. He'd managed to give it no identity whatsoever. But now, as he continued singing, he couldn't get the image of a curly-haired, blond baby girl out of his mind.

"Play the one you and Mara wrote for me," Joelle requested when he'd finished that song.

"Only if you'll sing it with me," he said.

"Are you out of your mind?" she asked.

"Come on," he said, although he knew she couldn't carry a tune. "It's just a fun song. You don't have to really be able to sing."

Joelle shifted in the recliner, sitting up straighter, readying herself to sing, and he had to laugh.

"By all means, sit up straight," he said. "Maybe your posture was the problem with your singing all along."

She looked at him from under hooded lids. "Don't make fun of me, or I'm not going to sing with you," she warned.

"You're right. Sorry." He played a few chords of introduction, then started singing, and she joined in. God, she was terrible. Worse than he'd remembered, and he had a hard time keeping a straight face. He happened to glance at Carlynn, who was still studiously massaging Mara's hands, but who looked as though she, too, was trying not to laugh. They finished the song, and Joelle looked quite pleased with herself.

Silence filled the room for just a moment. Finally, Carlynn spoke. "Mara, dear," she said as she focused on the massage she was delivering, "you will never, ever, have to worry about Joelle taking your place."

CHAPTER THIRTY-ONE

San Francisco, 1964

Gabriel's new boat was a stunning forty-five-foot, refurbished, two-masted yawl, and Lisbeth felt a thrill as they pulled away from the pier at China Basin. Carlynn and Alan were sailing with them, and she could see her sister's nervous smile as they motored past the breakwater into San Francisco Bay. Lisbeth and Gabriel had finally persuaded Carlynn to join them, telling her it would mean so much to them to have her and Alan's company as they christened their new boat. Lisbeth knew how hard it had been for Carlynn to climb aboard, and she was glad the breeze was gentle, the sun bright and the air warm for an August morning.

Carlynn was too pale, Lisbeth thought as she watched the sunlight play on her sister's face. Pale, but beautiful, with the identical features Lisbeth saw every time she looked in the mirror. The twins still weighed exactly the same: one hundred eighteen and a half pounds. They even went to the same hairdresser these days, getting the same cut each time just for the fun of it, although Lisbeth wore her cut curled under, and Carlynn wore a flip. Lisbeth had some stretch marks on her belly and thighs and breasts from losing so much weight over the years, but other than those few differences, they were very much twins.

She was worried about Carlynn, though. Ever since learning that she and Alan could not have children, Carlynn had not been the same. Sometimes it seemed as though she was merely going through the motions of living, and her smile, when it was there at all, seemed artificial. Alan was worried, too. He'd confided in Lisbeth that he'd suggested Carlynn see a psychiatrist, afraid that the stresses of her work, combined with her pervasive sadness, might lead to a nervous breakdown. Carlynn had told him she had no time to add another appointment to her already crammed schedule.

"I can't force her," Alan had said to Lisbeth. "All I can do is worry about her." He'd looked terribly sad, and Lisbeth had put her arms around him in comfort. But she could think of nothing to say to alleviate his concerns, since she shared them.

Gabe carefully walked out on the narrow bowsprit above the water to release the jib from the sailbag, and Lisbeth laughed as Carlynn hid her head on her arms at the sight of her brother-in-law balancing on that narrow piece of wood. She didn't dare tell Carlynn the other name for the bowsprit: "widowmaker."

"I'll haul the mainsail up if you take care of the jib," Gabriel said to Lisbeth as he came back on the deck.

Lisbeth hoisted the jib, and once Gabriel had the main up, he trimmed the sheets and killed the engine. Then they were moving over the water with only the sound of the wind in the sails.

"We're going to head upwind for a while, Carlynn," Gabriel said. "Then we can take a nice, smooth downwind ride back. All right? Are you ready?"

"I'll never be ready," Carlynn said. "Weren't we going upwind when I fell overboard, Lizzie?"

"Yes, but that's not going to happen this time," Lisbeth reassured her.

Gabriel jumped into the cockpit. "Helm's alee!" he called,

turning the wheel, and Lisbeth released the starboard jib sheet. The sails luffed wildly above their heads, then began to fill with the wind, and Lisbeth winched the port sheet in.

The boat tacked from side to side as they made their way toward and beneath the Bay Bridge. Sailing this new boat would have been a thrill, anyway, but the fact that Lisbeth had a skill her sister did not possess made it all the more enjoyable for her. She only wished Carlynn could enjoy it, too. Carlynn clung to Alan, her face contorted in fear, even though Gabriel was obviously doing his best to prevent the boat from tipping too severely to either side.

"Look at the Golden Gate Bridge." Alan pointed toward the orange structure as it came into view in the distance. Although the sky above the sailboat was clear, the bridge was haunted by a ghostly fog slipping in and out of the cables and hiding the tops of the towers.

"Carly and I went to the opening ceremonies when the bridge was built," Lisbeth said, trying to pull her quiet sister into the conversation.

Carlynn looked at her and smiled her I'm-trying-to-look-happy smile.

When they had finally tacked far enough, Gabe steered off the wind and eased the sails, and the ride instantly flattened.

"Oh, thank God," Carlynn said, taking in a deep breath.

"You can relax now, Carly," Gabe said to her.

The air was much warmer as they sailed downwind, and Lisbeth persuaded her sister to take off her jacket and bask in the sun with her for a while, while the men talked about sports.

Lisbeth could see Gabriel from where she lay on the deck. He was wearing a T-shirt, and the muscles in his dark arms were still long and lean and strong, and for just a moment she wished her sister and brother-in-law were not with them so that she and Gabriel could anchor the boat, go belowdecks to the beautiful cabin and make love on one of the berths. He was getting more handsome as he got older, she thought. It scared her sometimes to think that he was eleven years older than she was. She couldn't bear the thought of losing him. Thank God he'd given up smoking the year after their wedding.

They sailed for a half hour or so before she brought the picnic basket up from the galley. Carlynn seemed more relaxed now, her smile almost genuine, and they ate sourdough bread and Monterey Jack cheese and toasted the new boat with champagne.

"I wish you'd leave Lloyd's office and come work for Carlynn and me," Alan said to Lisbeth as they ate. It was not the first time he'd made the offer, but this time he sounded truly serious. "Our office is getting out of hand."

"*Getting* out of hand?" Carlynn said.

Lisbeth occasionally thought about working for Carlynn and Alan, but she'd been with Lloyd Peterson for more than a decade, and her loyalty to him was strong. Lloyd had taken in a couple of partners, and she'd enjoyed the challenge of learning new skills and training the girls who worked under her. Still, she knew things had grown wild at Carlynn and Alan's office and that they desperately needed someone with experience to come in and take charge.

That one simple article in *Life* two years earlier had spawned dozens more, and Carlynn's reputation had grown more quickly than any of them could have imagined. People came from as far away as Europe and Africa and Japan to see her, and some of her patients were celebrities—a couple of movie stars, an injured baseball player and a politician from the Midwest. Even Lisbeth didn't know their exact identities, since Carlynn honored their pleas for confidentiality. They didn't want to be perceived as kooks, as Carlynn often was herself.

"What I wish," Alan said as he polished off his second glass of champagne, "is that Carlynn could train people to do what she does. There's only one Carlynn to go around, and it's just not enough."

"I hate turning people away when I know I can help them," Carlynn agreed. "And it's not like there's someone I can refer them to."

"Do you think that what you do is a trainable skill?" Gabriel asked. "Or do you think it's a true gift?"

"I honestly don't know," Carlynn said. "I barely understand it any better than I did when I was sixteen."

"She's tried to train me," Alan said with a self-deprecating smile that Lisbeth found endearing. "I'm apparently untrainable."

"I believe that my...techniques, for want of a better word...may be something other people can learn to do," Carlynn said, "in spite of Alan's experience. My fantasy is that, if I could figure out what works and what doesn't, and we could somehow *prove* that what I do has validity, and we could offer a scientific explanation for it...then I could train people in what works, and those people could train other people, and there would be a whole lot more healing to go around. But it would require years and years of research to get to that point, and I don't have enough time to breathe right now, much less add another facet to my work."

"What if you could create an institute of some sort, where you could just focus on the research?" Gabriel cut a piece of cheese and handed it to Lisbeth with a chunk of bread.

Carlynn and Alan exchanged a look. "We've actually talked about that," Alan said. "It's a pipe dream, though. We couldn't afford to give up our practices, and it would take a lot of money to get something like that off the ground and keep it going."

"Well," Gabriel said, "maybe you could treat people there as well as do the research. You'd just have to get enough funding for it so you weren't dependent on seeing X number of patients a day."

"Oh my God," Carlynn said, looking up at the sky. "How I would love that!" Lisbeth couldn't remember the last time she'd heard such enthusiasm in her sister's voice.

"I could help you apply for grants," Gabriel said. "I've written so many grant applications for research at SF General that I could write them in my sleep."

"Where would they apply?" Lisbeth asked her husband. It was

one thing to find grant money for the customary studies SF General would embrace. How would Gabriel find money for something most of the world considered quackery?

"In the beginning, you'd need some seed money to get you started," Gabriel said. "Then once you're up and running—and showing some results—it shouldn't be that hard to get more." He smiled ruefully. "Not impossible, anyway. And I love a good challenge."

"Are you serious, Gabe?" Carlynn asked him.

"Completely serious."

"This would be great." Alan sat up straight, a look of excitement on his face. "Carlynn and her reputation would be our draw, of course, and I could design and direct the research. You could be our financial guy, Gabe. And Lisbeth could run the whole shebang."

"What would you call it?" Lisbeth asked.

"The Healing Research Institute of San Francisco," Alan said, and Lisbeth knew this was not the first time he'd said that name to himself.

"We need Carlynn's name in there, though," Lisbeth said. "People need to know she's behind it."

"The Carlynn Shire Center for Healing," Alan suggested.

"No," Gabriel advised. "Leave out the healing part. The word is too charged. Just call it the Carlynn Shire Medical Center."

"You're all just dreaming, right?" Carlynn asked. "You're tormenting me with this."

"Everything worthwhile starts with a dream, Carly," Alan said, and he passed her the bottle of champagne.

Carlynn was coming back to life, and she hadn't truly known she'd been away. She chattered endlessly as she and Alan drove south toward Monterey the day after they'd survived sailing with Gabriel and Lisbeth.

"I really, really want to do it," she said. "The research center.

Or institute. Or whatever we call it." She was turned in her seat so that she could face Alan as he drove. They'd been talking about starting a research center all the night before and that morning, but their conversation had focused on the type of work they could do there, not on the feasibility. "Do you think we can? I mean, I know it would mean we'd lose a lot of our income, at least initially, but, Alan, this is so important. There are answers we need to find."

Alan let go of the steering wheel to reach across the seat and take her hand. "I don't care about the money," he said. "I don't care if we never live in a beautiful home in Pacific Heights. I care about two things: your happiness and using your gift to the fullest. A research center seems the best way to do it. And Gabe made it sound as though it really could work."

"But we can't have him writing grant applications for us for free. We have to pay him."

"We have to pay him what he's worth," Alan agreed, and it pleased her to realize that he'd been thinking about this just as she had. "We'll need him working full-time to handle all the financial aspects of the center, as well as the fund-raising."

"You're serious about this!" Carlynn could barely contain her enthusiasm.

"You bet. We'll need to ask him if he'll do it, then he can work out our business plan and our budget, and give himself a nice fat salary. And then we have to see if we can get Lisbeth away from Lloyd Peterson."

"This is so wonderful!" Carlynn threw her arms up in the air. "All of us working together. I would absolutely love it." After a moment, though, she leaned her head against the headrest, suddenly somber. "How the heck do we get something like this off the ground? Gabriel said we'd need seed money. Where does that come from?"

Alan glanced at her, but it was a minute before he spoke. "I'm surprised you haven't thought about the answer to that question," he said quietly, and she knew he had thought through this part of the plan, as well. "How about the woman we're on our way to visit?"

"Mother?" she asked, surprised.

He nodded. "What do you think?"

Carlynn stared out the window as they passed the Santa Cruz exit off Highway One. Delora Kling was an undeniably wealthy woman. She'd been born to money and had inherited even more when her husband died, and she regularly donated large sums to charities. This would not be a charity, of course, but she had never been shy about publicizing Carlynn's gift.

"I hadn't thought of her," Carlynn said, "but she just might be willing."

There was a new servant at the mansion, a fat and sassy Negro woman named Angela, who was working as Delora's personal aide, helping her get around when her vision did not allow her to move independently. Carlynn wondered just how poor her mother's vision had become. Did she know this was a Negro she had come to depend upon?

She did, indeed. Over lunch on the terrace, Delora spoke about how fabulous it was to have someone to find her hairbrush for her when she'd misplaced it or to guide her to a chair on the terrace so that she didn't tumble off the edge.

"Even though she's colored," Delora said as she sank her fork into the salad in front of her, "she has been a splendid help. I don't know how I got along without her."

Carlynn took courage from her words. Maybe her feelings about Angela would have softened her attitude toward Lisbeth and Gabriel. She glanced at Alan.

"Mother, Alan and I would like to talk to you about a plan we're considering."

"What's that?" Delora lifted an empty fork to her mouth, having missed the salad altogether this time, and Carlynn winced, her heart breaking a little for this poor woman who was aging before her time.

"Here, Mom." Alan moved the salad plate closer to his mother-in-law and guided her hand toward it. "Your salad's right here."

"Thank you, dear," Delora said. "Now, what is this plan the two of you have up your sleeves?"

"Well," Carlynn began, "you know how it's always troubled me that people doubt my ability to heal, and that even I don't know exactly how I do it?"

"It hasn't troubled me," Delora said, smiling with pride. "You are very special, and some people are too foolish to see that."

"Thank you," Carlynn said. "Well, we've come up with an idea that's very exciting, I think. We'd like to start a research center. An institute of sorts, to look into the phenomenon of healing. I'd still be able to see patients, but we'd focus more on research."

"We'd like to see if we can validate some of Carlynn's healing methods," Alan said, "and then train other physicians in the skills she has."

"She has a gift not a skill," Delora corrected him, but she wore a thoughtful look. "This is an interesting idea, though. Tell me more."

Alan described the potential research in more detail, and Carlynn was amazed to see exactly how much thinking he had already done on the subject. He was hungry to do this, she thought. He'd always had a fascination with alternative methods of healing. A research center would be his as much as it would be hers, and she thought she was very lucky to have a husband with whom she could share her dream.

"You need money to get this off the ground, don't you?" Delora was smiling again.

"Yes, Mom," Carlynn said. "We were wondering if there was a chance you'd like to put up the seed money for it."

"We can work out a way that you could become an investor so that you could get something back for your money," Alan said.

"We're not sure how much we're talking about," Carlynn added. "The idea's in its infancy. But we thought we'd run it by you to see if you were interested."

"*Very* interested," Delora said. She was looking out to sea, although Carlynn imagined the world in front of her eyes was little more than a blur. "And will you research things such as why you can't heal my vision? I mean—" she tried to find Carlynn's hand on the table, and Carlynn quickly placed it under her mother's fingers "—that came out wrong, dear. I mean, will you look into why you are successful with some conditions and not with others?"

"Yes," she said. "We'd look at all of that. Doesn't it sound exciting?"

"It does," Delora agreed. "Would you have other doctors working there?"

"Not right away," Alan said. He glanced at Carlynn with trepidation, but his voice was casual as he finished his thought. "We would probably start with just the four of us. Carlynn and myself doing the clinical work and research design, and Lisbeth, who would run the center, and her husband, Gabriel, who has loads of experience applying for grants."

Biting her lip, Carlynn looked anxiously at her husband while they waited for her mother's response.

Delora's smile disappeared, and it was a moment before she spoke again.

"Yes, I will give you whatever money you need to get this center started," she said finally. "But there is a condition that comes with my money."

"What is it, Mother?" Carlynn asked.

"That your sister and her husband have nothing whatsoever to do with it," Delora said.

Carlynn glanced at Alan.

"Mother," Alan said gently, "Lisbeth and Gabriel both have excellent skills we can use. They'd be perfect for the job, and they're excited about it."

"The whole idea was really Gabriel's," Carlynn added.

"Well, bully for him," Delora said. "Let's write him a thank-you note." She started to push her chair back from the table, but Carlynn grabbed her hand.

"Mother," Carlynn said, "you're cutting yourself off from two really fine people. Lisbeth is your daughter. She still loves you. She always encourages me to come here and look in on you. And she adores Cypress Point. You've hurt her so badly by—"

"I will help you get this research center started," Delora interrupted her. "But only if you honor my conditions, Carlynn."

Carlynn shook her head. "I don't think we can do that," she said, aware of how alien it felt to stand up to her mother.

"Then you know my answer," Delora said.

There was no more discussion of the research center for the rest of the afternoon, and Carlynn and Alan spent the time helping Delora sort through the books in the mansion's library. They had gotten out of order, she said, and she needed them shelved alphabetically so they would be easier to find. Although Carlynn could not understand how her mother could read the books whether they were alphabetical or not, she and Alan did as they were told. Her mother was full of household projects she wanted done these days, and at least it gave Carlynn the feeling that she was helping.

Once she and Alan were back in the car and on the Seventeen Mile Drive, Carlynn turned to her husband.

"We're hiring Gabriel and Lisbeth," she said.

Alan glanced at her. "You know that's what I want, Carly," he said, "but I think your mother's serious. She won't give us the money if we hire them. You heard her."

"Then we'll get the money elsewhere," Carlynn said. "I'm through letting her run my life. I want my sister and brother-in-law working with us."

"So do I," Alan agreed. "Gabe will probably have some ideas on how to get funding."

Carlynn smiled at him. "You know what I feel like?" she asked him.

"What's that?"

"I feel like I'm giving birth to something," she said happily. "I feel like I'm finally getting my baby."

Alan eased his foot onto the brake pedal, pulling the car over to the side of the narrow road.

"What are you doing?" she asked.

He stopped the car and turned the key in the ignition, then pulled her into his arms. "You have no idea how happy I am to hear you say that, Carlynn," he said, and he held her close to him until a driver pulled up behind them began to press his horn.

It took two full years of planning, but the Carlynn Shire Medical Center opened its doors during the summer of 1966, when flower children wandered the streets of San Francisco, Vietnam became the subject of protests, and Gabriel started referring to himself and other Negroes as "black."

Carlynn and Alan rented the entire first floor of their Sutter Street medical building and transformed the new space into a bevy of treatment rooms, meeting rooms and offices, using the seed money from a small grant Gabriel had managed to secure.

Lisbeth handled all the office-management duties and secretarial work. As they grew, her hope was to hire someone to help her with the more mundane tasks of operating the center, but for now she was delighted to be the person in charge of getting the place up and running.

Money was an ongoing problem, though. Gabriel wrote grant proposals in his limited free time; they had no funds to bring him on board as a paid employee yet, and he continued to work in the business office at SF General. A bigger problem, though, was dealing with the multitude of patients arriving from all over the country who wanted to be treated at the center or to volunteer to participate in research. It was Alan who screened the patients, deciding which of them should be allowed to see Carlynn, because her medical practice was to be only part of her work. Yet, despite Alan's careful screening and Lisbeth's explanation to callers that they must speak to Alan Shire first, there were often people waiting on the building's doorstep when they arrived in the morning. Carlynn was not good at turning them away, and Alan finally suggested she come in the rear door of the building and leave the appointment seekers to him.

It was important that Carlynn see only a few patients each week. The rest of her time was needed for the interviews Lisbeth set up for her with newspapers and magazines, and for speaking engagements with organizations that might be interested in funding her research. Alan spent most of his days with his nose buried in books and journals as he toyed with various study designs.

Ever since the four of them had made the firm decision to create the center, Carlynn's dark mood had lifted. Her life had a meaning and purpose she'd been missing before. She might not ever be able to have children, but she was creating something that gave her equal satisfaction. She was touching lives, the way she'd always wanted to, and she hoped the work of the center would give her the chance to touch many, many more.

CHAPTER THIRTY-TWO

Sam was in bed, and Liam was sitting on the sofa in the living room playing his guitar. He'd sorted through all the old music he'd stored in the spare room after Mara became ill. He'd bought new strings, a couple of new pieces of music, and now he couldn't stop playing. He thought about the guitar all day at work, jotting down lyrics and chords for new songs. At night, music had taken the place of the Internet, where he used to search for the miracle for Mara, and he felt a little guilty about that. But he consoled himself that he had the great Carlynn Shire herself working with his wife. What more could anyone want?

He'd brought the guitar to two of those meetings with the healer at the nursing home, now, and the last time, Carlynn had Mara sit up in her wheelchair. Carlynn was still touching her, holding her hand in both of hers, but the four of them were in a circle of sorts, and if it had felt strange to be singing while Mara lay in her bed, this was even stranger. Mara had stared at his fingers. What was she thinking? Did she remember playing the guitar herself? Did she feel a longing for the music? For him? *If you could speak, Mara, what would you say?*

If anyone were to observe him and Joelle on those occasions, they would probably think of them as comfortable old friends who could chat easily and regularly with one another, but that was not the case. The safety he felt in that room evaporated the moment he was alone with Joelle or talking to her on the phone. Then he was back to the superficial, businesslike conversations he'd gotten accustomed to having with her over the past few months. *How are you? Fine. How was your day? Good.* Her belly was growing and he rarely said a word about it. Did she think he had no feelings about the situation? Did she think he didn't care that he would soon have a daughter and didn't know what the hell he should do about it?

At twenty-five weeks pregnant, Joelle was like a walking billboard for his infidelity. And no one knew. No one even guessed. No one would ever think such a thing of Liam Sommers and Joelle D'Angelo.

He was pulling a piece of old music from one of the boxes on the sofa when he noticed the flash of headlights shoot across the walls of the living room. A car was pulling into his driveway. Standing up, he walked over to the window and peered outside. Sheila's car was parked near the carport, and he could see the interior lights come on as she opened her door. What was she doing here at ten-thirty at night?

He opened the front door and stepped onto the porch. "Sheila?" he called as she got out of her car. "Is everything all right?"

She walked from her car to his front porch without answering him. At the bottom of the porch steps, though, she looked up at him. "I need to talk to you," she said. Her blond hair glittered in the light from the porch, and her eyes were cold. He shivered.

"Come in." He stepped back into the house and held the door open for her, a little unnerved. "Has something happened with Mara?" he asked.

"Well, I don't know." Sheila didn't so much walk as plow into the room. She was boiling mad, and he felt his heart rate speed up.

"What do you mean, you don't know? What's going on?" He moved a pile of music from the sofa. "Sit down."

"No," she said. "I don't want to sit down." She looked him squarely in the eye. "I just came from a psychic," she said.

Liam laughed. "You *what?*" Between Joelle and her healer and Sheila and her psychic, he was feeling pretty darn conventional.

"I've been to her before. She's very good. She can always tell me things that have happened in my life that there's no way anyone would know."

"Okay," Liam said slowly. "And what did she tell you this time."

"That you're the father of Joelle's baby."

Shit. Liam laughed uncomfortably. "I thought the psychic knew things about *you,*" he said. "How can she know anything about Joelle, when she hasn't even—"

"Shut up, Liam!"

"Look, you're upset over nothing, Sheila," he said, moving toward the sofa again. "Please sit down and let's talk—"

"Look me in the eye and tell me you are not the father of Joelle's baby," Sheila demanded.

He tried. He truly did. But he couldn't hold her gaze for more than a second, nor could he make the words come out of his mouth.

"You *bastard!*" Sheila began hitting him with her huge, heavy white leather purse. He held up his hands, trying to protect his face from her assault.

"Bastard! Bastard!" Sheila smashed the purse into his side. "Son of a bitch! Prick!"

"Sheila!" He grabbed her wrist and managed to wrench the purse from her hand, but she still pummeled him with her open fist. "Sheila, stop it!" he yelled. "Stop. *Stop.* You're going to wake Sam."

That seemed to do it. She lowered her arms to her sides. Mascara ran down her cheeks, and her blond hair fell in thin strands around her red face.

"How could you do that to my little girl?" she asked, her voice suddenly small and broken, and he surprised himself by taking her in his arms.

"Because," he said quietly into her hair. "Because I'm human, and I'm...much to my regret, flawed."

Sheila sniffled. "I'm human and I'm flawed, too," she said, "but I didn't sleep with anyone else while Michael was sick."

"I know," Liam said. "You were incredibly strong. But...and forgive me for this, Sheila. You weren't thirty-four years old, and you weren't grieving every day, every minute, with a member of the opposite sex who also happened to love your spouse as much as you did."

Sheila pulled away from him and sat down on the couch. "How long has it been going on?" she asked, wiping a hand over her wet cheek.

"There isn't anything going on," he said, moving his guitar from the sofa so he could sit next to her. "It happened one time. Then we cooled our relationship. Even you noticed it—that we were not as close."

She nodded. "I noticed when you were getting too close, too," she said.

"Sheila." Liam shook his head. "I love Mara. I feel terrible about this. I feel as though I betrayed her."

"You *did*," she said. "Does everyone know?"

"No one knows. Just you, Joelle and myself." And Carlynn Shire.

"What happens now?"

"I don't know," he said. "Joelle and I haven't really talked about it. I feel a responsibility to provide for the baby in some way. She and I will need to work that out."

Sheila made her hands into fists, balling them up on her knees. "Every time I think about you and her—"

"Don't think about it, then, Sheila," he said quickly. "I don't."

Sheila rested her head back on the sofa, shutting her eyes. It was another minute before she spoke. "Mara's starting to use her arm more," she said.

"I know."

"Someday, maybe she'll be able to hold Sam."

He nodded, unwilling to tackle her denial tonight.

Sheila got to her feet and picked up her purse from the floor. Liam stood, as well, walking her to the door.

"Goodbye," she said. "I'll see you tomorrow, when you bring Sam over."

"All right." He opened the door for her and watched her walk out onto the porch and down the steps. "Sheila?" he called to her as she crossed the yard, walking toward the carport. "Did a psychic really tell you this?"

"Yes," she said, "but to be honest, I already knew."

He walked back into the living room and sat down again on the sofa, but he didn't bother to pick up his guitar. Resting his head against the back of the couch, he stared up at the ceiling, then closed his eyes.

He'd told Sheila the truth, but he'd also told her a lie. He'd told her he didn't think about that night when he and Joelle made love. Lately, he thought about it all the time. He thought about how much he wanted to be with her at night. It didn't have anything to do with sex. Not really. He just wanted to hold her in bed and to feel his child through the skin of her belly. The longing burned inside him and, at times, he wished she *had* moved away and kept her secret from him forever. It would have made it so much easier.

CHAPTER THIRTY-THREE

Big Sur, 1967

The fog was dense and disorienting. Carlynn drove along Highway One at ten miles an hour, afraid to go any faster for fear she'd sail right off the cliff into the Pacific. It had been a long time since she'd been down this stretch of coast. She remembered it as winding and treacherous, but breathtakingly beautiful, as well. The beauty was lost on her at the moment, though, as she neared the Bixby Bridge. She had never liked this bridge. It was far too high, the expanse between the two cliffs far too long. She had to stop the car before driving onto it, licking her lips and gathering up her courage. "It's just a road," she told herself and started across. Fog swirled beneath the bridge, and she supposed it was just as well that it camouflaged the distance between herself and Bixby Creek, far below. Once she reached the other side of the bridge, she let out her breath. Not that the road she was on, which hugged the bluffs high above the ocean, was much better.

Highway One was always a work in progress along the stretch between the Monterey Peninsula and Big Sur. It was subject to floods and landslides and forest fires, and if there were boulders or fallen trees littering the road ahead of her, she wouldn't know it until it was too late because of the opaque, cottony fog. There were also very few other cars. For a summer's day, that seemed odd to her, but she supposed it was the weather that was keeping tourists away. Maybe they knew better than to drive when the fog was this thick. The route to the Cabrial Commune was only thirty or so miles past Monterey, Penny had told her. Carlynn hadn't known they were to be the thirty slowest miles of her life.

Penny Everett had called earlier that week. Carlynn had been in her office at the center, looking over Alan's initial draft for a brilliant research project he was designing, when Lisbeth buzzed her on the intercom.

"Phone call for you, Carlynn," she'd said. "It's Penny Everett!"

"You're kidding!" Carlynn had set down her pen and picked up the phone. "Penny?"

"Oh, Carlynn." The voice was a whisper. "I'm so glad I could reach you."

The woman did not sound like Penny, and for a brief moment Carlynn wondered if it might be a desperate patient scheming to get in to see her. It had happened before.

"Penny? What's wrong with your voice?" she asked. "You sound terrible."

"I know. That's why I'm calling. I hate to bother you...I know you must be terribly busy. But I was wondering if there's any chance you could help me."

It most certainly *was* Penny, but her voice made Carlynn wince. It sounded as though her throat was lined with sandpaper.

"What's wrong?" Carlynn found herself whispering as well, and Penny laughed.

"Everyone does that," she said. "Everyone whispers when they talk to me. It must be catching."

Carlynn chuckled. "I've missed you, Penny," she said. "I was going to say it's good to hear your voice, but that would be a lie."

"I've been this way for four months," Penny said. Was she crying? Carlynn couldn't tell.

"Four months!" She stood up and walked over to the window, which looked out at the traffic on Sutter Street. "Do you know what started it?"

"It started while I was in a musical," Penny said. "Just this little off-Broadway thing. I was under a lot of stress. That's what caused it, my doctor said. He said I needed a break and my voice would come back, but it hasn't."

"Have you alleviated the stress?" Carlynn asked.

"Yes!" Penny sounded as emphatic as she could, given there was no power to her voice. "I left New York. I'm back in California, staying in a commune in Big Sur where there's no pressure, just a lot of loving people and peace and quiet, and I've been here for two months now, and I *still* sound like this." There were definitely tears behind her words now, and Carlynn felt her own eyes well up.

"Oh, honey, that must be frightening." She tried to picture what Penny's life must be like on a commune. They were cropping up here and there, filled with hippies who rarely washed and slept around with abandon. The lifestyle sounded unappealing to Carlynn, but she could see her old, unconventional friend thriving in that sort of environment.

"And the worst part is, there's this play I want to do in New York next year," Penny continued. "I want it in the worst way, Carly. It's called *Hair,* and it's going to be so good and so much fun, and I know they want me to audition for it, but I can't. I'm afraid I may never be able to sing again. Maybe not even *talk* again."

"Can you come up here to San Francisco?" Carlynn asked. "It wouldn't be a huge drive for you. Come and spend a few days with us and I'll work with you."

There was a moment of silence on the line.

"I wanted to invite you down here," Penny said. "I really don't want to leave here right now. I'm afraid of the...you know, the stress. I have a little cabin with twin beds. Well—" she giggled hoarsely "—I have two mattresses, anyhow. On the floor. It could be like a little vacation for—"

"Oh, Penny, I can't. I'm swamped here." But her mind was racing ahead. A few days in Big Sur. The windswept cliffs above the coastline, the ocean and the fanciful cloudlike fog that put San Francisco's to shame. A week off. She loved the center and adored her work, but still... Time with her old friend on a commune, of all places, would be an adventure. And Penny obviously needed her help. By the time Penny said, "Oh, please, Carly?" she had made up her mind.

Had she really thought of this fog as fanciful? It was positively blinding, and she wondered if this was how Delora felt all the time, unsure of where to place her next step.

The only way she would ever know where to turn off Highway One was by her mileage. She'd set her trip odometer as she passed the Carmel exit, and when it reached thirty miles, she would start looking for the tree. "It's a coastal redwood," Penny had said. "Sort of out of place right there along the road. You can't miss it."

Oh, yeah? Carlynn thought. But just as she was about to give up and drive to the nearest store or restaurant or anything she could find, if she *could* find one, the tree rose out of the fog to her left. It was massive and truly did seem out of place. An arrow-shaped board, only a foot long by three or four inches high, had been nailed to the tree, and yellow or white letters—she couldn't tell which—spelled out "Cabrial." That was the name of the commune, she remembered. Penny had told her the land had been owned by a family named Cabrial at one time. Now it was owned by a bunch of out-of-their-mind hippies, Carlynn thought as she turned onto the dirt road. Who would choose to live out here?

Highway One was nothing compared to this road, she thought as the dirt road climbed and plunged and twisted through the foggy forest. She would hate to drive it in the muddy season, and she said a silent prayer that it didn't rain while she was at the commune or the road would be completely impassable.

For four miles, she drove through ruts and over rocks, and it was only then that she noticed her gas gauge: the needle was a hairbreadth above empty.

"Idiot," she said out loud to herself. She would never get out of here.

She spotted another wooden arrow affixed to a tree, and turned in the direction it pointed to find herself in what appeared to be a clearing, or at least a parking area. She could make out a green truck and a battered white Volkswagen van. Then she spotted a building, a large cabin, perhaps, to the right of the vehicles. It wasn't until she'd parked her car next to the van that she saw a woman run down the few steps of the cabin toward her car, and it took her a moment to recognize her. *Penny!* Her dirty-blond hair was long and straight, parted in the middle, and she was wearing a white halter top with strands of beads dangling from the shoulders. Even in the hazy fog, it was obvious she was wearing no bra. She looked more like twenty than thirty-seven, and only when Carlynn got out of the car to hug her old friend did she see the fine lines on her face.

"You look beautiful!" Carlynn said as she drew away from Penny.

"You, too," Penny whispered.

Carlynn hugged her again, this time in sympathy at the weak sound of her voice. "Poor Penny. We've got to see if we can get you well again. It used to be hard to shut you up."

"I know," Penny said. "Everyone back home is teasing me that I must have used up my lifetime allotment of words already. The weird thing is, no one here knew me before, so they all think I'm this quiet little person."

Carlynn laughed. "I can tell them the truth about you."

"Let's take your things to my cabin, and then I'll give you a tour." Penny grabbed Carlynn's hard-sided suitcase and guided her down a trail through the woods.

"Carly," she said, looping her free hand through Carlynn's

arm. "I just want to make sure you know that I don't expect a miracle from you. I mean, I know you can't always make things better. I read that in an article."

"I'll do my best," Carlynn said.

"You are *not* dressed for a commune," Penny whispered. "Do you have some other clothes with you?"

"Of course," Carlynn said. She'd left the center midday, so she still had on her work clothes—navy blue slacks, a white blouse and a white-and-blue checked cardigan. She'd brought jeans, jerseys and a sweatshirt with her, and she couldn't wait to change into them.

"How's the medical center you opened?" Penny asked as they walked.

"It's great," Carlynn said, missing it a little already. "It's my dream come true. We're hoping to prove that many so-called healers can really heal."

"Well, you're the one for that job. I'll never forget how you fixed my leg after I fell from the terrace at your house."

Carlynn laughed. "I'm not sure I did much," she said. "I don't think your leg was really broken."

"You're too modest. And speaking of modest, this is my abode." Penny let go of Carlynn's arm and stepped onto the porch of a small cabin. "Come on in."

Carlynn followed Penny into the cabin, noticing the wooden sign that read "Cornflower" hanging above the door.

The cabin was tinier than Carlynn could have imagined. It contained a minuscule living room, with an old sofa and a wood-stove taking up much of the space, and an even smaller bedroom. Two twin mattresses, their sheets and blankets in disarray, were pushed together on the floor, leaving mere inches of floor exposed around them.

"Wow," Carlynn said. "Cozy."

Penny laughed. "No television," she whispered. "No radios. Just birdsong and the sound of the ocean on a still night."

Carlynn noticed the lanterns on the floor and the one tiny

dresser. "Is there electricity?" she asked, thinking of her hair dryer. "Plumbing?" She hadn't noticed a bathroom in the small cabin.

"No and no," Penny said. "There are a couple of communal latrines." She must have seen Carlynn's look of dismay, because she laughed again. "You'll get used to it after a couple of days," she whispered, then looked at Carlynn's navy-blue pumps. "Do you have anything that would be easier to walk in?" she asked.

"Sneakers," Carlynn said. "I'll put them on."

She changed her clothes and her shoes, and they left the cabin and wandered through the woods and open spaces of the commune. Penny obviously knew her way around. She pointed out the different cabins to her, and after a while they reached a clearing, where children swung on rope swings hanging from the branches of mammoth trees and darted in and out of the fog. The latrine was not far from the clearing and it was worse than Carlynn had expected, an open area where everyone was expected to defecate side by side. She now understood why hippies had the reputation of being dirty, as they passed the one shower that served the entire community. The showerhead was rigged up to a tree, and it was connected to a huge barrel of water resting above a fire that someone would have to keep stoked, if anyone was to ever have a hot shower.

"Guess what, though," Penny said in her anemic voice. "The main cabin—the one near where you parked—is where we cook meals, and it has plumbing, so you don't have to freak out about germs when you eat."

Carlynn was secretly relieved by that fact. She was wondering how quickly she could help Penny with her voice so that she could leave this place. Being here was like stepping back—*way* back—in time. She decided, though, that she could only get through the next few days by taking on a positive attitude, and so she followed Penny to the large cabin for dinner that night with a smile on her face and her appetite intact.

They sat on benches at one of three long wooden tables, and

Carlynn enjoyed the vegetables and rice and tofu, which she had never eaten before and which was not as bad as she'd expected. Penny introduced her to a few people at their table, but then leaned forward to tell her about her other friends sitting elsewhere in the room.

"I've slept with him," she whispered, pointing to a man with very long, kinky-curly blond hair. "His name is Terence, and God, he was so good." Penny's eyes were half closed, as though she could taste the memory. "So amazing. And with him." She pointed to the young black man sitting next to the curly-haired blonde, then to the heavyset woman next to him. "And with her," she said.

"Her?" Carlynn tried not to look as stunned as she felt.

"It's nothing here," Penny said. "Everyone sleeps with everyone."

"You're on the Pill, I hope."

"Of course," Penny said. "Although, I was thinking that if I never get my voice back, I could just stay here and have babies. It's so natural and beautiful, having babies here. There've been two born since I arrived. The fathers actually help deliver them. And there's another one due soon." Leaning forward again, she nodded in the direction of a very young dark-haired woman, huge with child, who was laughing at something one of her tablemates had said. Even from the next table, though, Carlynn could see a strain in that laugh. Whether the woman was in physical—or perhaps emotional—pain, she didn't know, but something was troubling her.

"Her old man is the guy sitting over there." Penny pointed. "Johnny Angel."

"Johnny Angel?" Carlynn tried not to laugh.

"His real name is something else, but that's what everyone calls him," Penny said. "I've slept with him a few times, too. He's very young, but the young ones can go all night long, if you know what I mean."

"You slept with him while his wife is *pregnant?*"

"Her suggestion," Penny said. "It's a different world here, Carly."

A large woman with long, frizzy gray hair walked into the cabin and climbed over the bench to sit next to Penny.

"How's your voice today, Penny?" the woman asked.

"Same as always," Penny said. "Felicia, this is my old friend Carlynn. Felicia's the midwife here. She'll be delivering Ellen's baby."

"How far along is she?" Carlynn asked the midwife.

"Carlynn's a doctor," Penny whispered to Felicia.

"She's thirty-eight weeks." Felicia's voice was loud and commanding. She dished a large serving of vegetables and rice onto her plate. "I think she's going to be early, though," she added. "She said she was having some back pain today."

Carlynn nodded. That explained the halfhearted laughter.

Felicia looked across the table at her as she began to eat. "Do you have any antibiotics on you?" she asked. "River has the clap and he ran out."

"No, sorry, I don't," she said, although she had brought some just in case she needed them to treat Penny. She would leave them for the guy with gonorrhea if Penny did not need them.

"Hey, Pen!" Terence called from one of the other tables. "Since you have company tonight, would you like to sleep at my cabin? Give your friend some privacy?"

"No, thanks," Penny said as loudly as she could, to be heard over the chatter and crying babies. "I want to be with her."

"Oh, I get it." Terence smiled, and Carlynn grimaced.

"It's not like that," she said to the man. "I'm a married woman."

Everyone laughed as though she'd said something hilarious, and she smiled.

"Let me start treating you," Carlynn said when she and Penny had returned to Cornflower. She was anxious to see how Penny would respond to her touch. "I'd feel so good if I could get you back to New York and into that beauty parlor musical."

"Beauty parlor musical?" Penny frowned at her.

"Didn't you say you were going to be in a musical about—"

"Oh, *Hair!*" Penny interrupted her, laughing. "Oh my God, Carlynn, a beauty parlor musical! You're too much." She could hardly catch her breath for laughing, and Carlynn joined in, not sure what the joke was.

"*Hair* is about Vietnam, and love and diversity and people taking care of each other. It is decidedly *not* about a beauty parlor. God, I love you, Carly."

"Now don't start that." Carlynn laughed. "I am *not* sleeping with you. No lesbian stuff."

"Right, you're a married woman."

"Are you making fun of me?" Carlynn grinned. She was a fish out of water, but felt no discomfort at being the brunt of the jokes, as long as Penny was the joker. "Come here," she said, pointing to one of the mattresses on the bedroom floor. "Lie down and get comfortable."

Penny lay down and Carlynn sat on the mattress next to her, taking her hands. "Tell me about when it started."

"Is this how you do it?" Penny asked. "You talk, like a shrink? I've been to a shrink already. He was useless."

"I'm not a shrink, honey," Carlynn said. "Now just talk to me. How did it start?"

Penny cried as she reported waking up one morning without a voice. Carlynn tuned out the outside world, the shouts of children, the occasional laughter from an adult, the guitar music that was floating in through the window from somewhere nearby. Closing her eyes, she let Penny's words come inside her. This was going to work. She could feel it in Penny's hands, in the absolute concentration in her face. Thank God. She did not want to disappoint her old friend. It might take some time, but Penny would get her voice back.

* * *

The next day, when the world was again white with fog, Ellen Liszt's cries filled the commune, and everyone knew she was in labor.

"Should I help?" Carlynn asked Penny as she stared out the bedroom window in the direction of the cries.

Penny shook her head. "No. Believe me, they don't want a doctor in there," she said. "They don't particularly trust doctors here."

Except to hand out antibiotics when they contract a sexually transmitted disease, Carlynn thought.

She spent the morning working with Penny some more, listening to her and gently placing her hands on her throat. At lunch that afternoon, Penny said something in a perfectly natural voice and everyone turned to look at her. Instantly, the whisper was back, but Penny got up and did a little jig across the wood-plank floor of the cabin.

Walking back to Cornflower, they passed Rainbow Cabin and could hear an occasional cry, more of a scream really, from the mother-to-be inside. Johnny Angel chopped wood at the side of the cabin without seeming to notice the two women passing by.

"I thought you said the men help deliver their babies?" Carlynn asked.

"Most do," Penny said. "But Johnny's freaking out, I think. Poor kid."

She worked with Penny's voice for an hour, then sat with her on the sofa in the small living room, sewing patches on several pairs of Penny's well-worn jeans. Suddenly, there was the sound of steps on the front porch, and Johnny Angel burst into the cabin. His face was ashen, his hands raised in panic.

"The baby's not breathing!" he said.

Carlynn dropped her sewing and ran toward the door, Penny and Johnny close behind her. "Which way?" she asked as she stepped off the porch into the fog.

Johnny grabbed her arm and ran with her toward the cabin

he shared with his young girlfriend, but he stopped, frozen at the front step.

"In there." He pointed inside.

Carlynn looked at him squarely. "Your girlfriend will need you," she said, taking him by the wrist and nearly dragging him inside with her.

Felicia was on her knees on the mattress, crouched between the young mother's legs, holding a bluish baby. Carlynn dropped to her own knees beside her.

"The cord was wrapped around her neck," Felicia said, handing the infant to her.

Carlynn placed the baby girl on the bloodstained newspapers that covered the mattress, then bent over her to perform CPR, covering the tiny nose and mouth with her own mouth, gently blowing air into her lungs, then pressing with two of her fingers on the infant's breastbone.

"I've tried CPR," said Felicia, but Carlynn continued puffing and pressing. After a moment, she felt Felicia's hand on her shoulder.

"She's gone," Felicia said gently. "She's gone."

"No!" Ellen cried from the bed, struggling to raise herself up, trying to see. "No, please!"

Holding the baby with one hand on her back, the other against her chest, Carlynn lifted her until her own lips touched the infant's temple. Shutting her eyes, she willed every ounce of her strength and energy and breath and life into this child. Her body began to rock, very slowly, in time with her breathing. She couldn't have said how long she sat that way, rocking, breathing, holding the child between her hands, but after a while, she felt a flutter beneath her right hand, a twisting of tiny muscles beneath her left, and when she opened her eyes, the baby girl let out a whimper, then a wail. Carlynn became aware of her surroundings again as if rising up from a dream, and by the time she wrapped the baby in the flannel blanket Felicia handed her, the child was pink and beautiful.

She found herself strangely reluctant to relinquish the baby, and she held her for another moment, running her hand over the infant's dark hair before reaching forward to hand her to Ellen. Then she walked outside, still dazed and a little dizzy from her efforts, to find that the fog had burned off, and sunlight followed her to Penny's cabin.

She slept the rest of that afternoon and most of the following day, and when she awakened, the air outside the window was growing dark. Penny sat on the other mattress and told her the baby was nursing well and appeared healthy.

"They named her Shanti Joy Angel," she said, her voice a whisper.

Carlynn giggled.

"They're all on to you now, Carly," Penny said. "A few of them had heard of Carlynn Shire, but they hadn't made the connection to you till now. They were all ready to come to you with their sniffles and rashes and bellyaches, but I told them that's not what you're here for."

"Thanks," Carlynn said. "I'm sorry, though, that I lost time for treating you."

"That hardly matters in light of things," Penny said. "You must be starving. You haven't eaten since yesterday. I brought you some food from dinner. Does it always take this much out of you? The healing?"

Carlynn stretched and smiled. "That little baby took everything I had, Penny," she said. "But I'm fine now, and after lunch we'll get back to work on you. How long have I been sleeping?"

"You arrived Saturday. The baby was born yesterday afternoon, and now, it's Monday night."

"I can't believe it." Carlynn sat up. "I'm a lazy lump."

"I brought you some rice and veggies," Penny said. "They're still a little bit warm from dinner. You ready for them?"

Carlynn nodded. "But then I have to find a phone somewhere, Penny," she said. "I have to call Alan and tell him I'll be here a few more days."

"The nearest phone is miles and miles away," Penny said. "I tell you what. Everyone's agreed that you should have the next shower. The water's heated up and ready for you. So, how about you get up, go use the shower, have some food, and meanwhile, I'll borrow your car and go call Alan. How's that sound?"

She would have liked to speak with Alan herself, but the thought of a shower, food and a little more time in bed sounded even more appealing at that moment. "All right," she said. "Oh! But my car is on empty."

"I'll borrow Terence's van, then. Just give me the number."

She wrote down Alan's numbers at both the center and their row house, as well as Lisbeth and Gabriel's, in case Penny had trouble finding Alan. Then she dragged herself out of bed, picked up one of Penny's flashlights from the floor and headed outside, walking toward the latrine.

The rest of the week went quickly, and it was a week Carlynn knew she had needed for herself. She'd had no vacations the past few years. The center was truly her life, and she had never considered taking a break from it, but the peace here, the lack of contact with newspapers and television and the rest of the world, was rejuvenating beyond anything she might have expected. She enjoyed holding the baby whose life she had, perhaps, saved, and the thought of leaving the infant, of never seeing her again, was distressing in a way she could not understand. Everyone at the commune called the baby's survival a miracle, but she was not sure. All she knew was that she could now hold in her arms a beautiful little girl who would probably not have survived had she not been at the commune. Maybe that had been the reason for Penny losing her voice, everyone said, to draw Carlynn here at that exact moment, to make her part of some huge, cosmic plan. Carlynn neither knew nor cared if their rationale was the truth. That sort of thinking only annoyed the scientist in her.

Penny's voice came back in force on Thursday morning, and Thursday night there was a celebration around the bonfire in honor of Carlynn Shire, the straight woman doctor who turned down marijuana and hashish and LSD and cheap wine, who had given them Shanti Joy and had allowed them to hear Penny's true voice in song for the first time.

Lisbeth was typing letters for Carlynn when Alan walked into the reception office at the Carlynn Shire Medical Center the following afternoon. He stood in the doorway, his hands on his hips.

"When the heck is Carlynn coming home?" he asked.

Lisbeth turned to look at him. She understood Alan's frustration. She, too, felt the void Carlynn left by not being at the center, and Alan had to be experiencing it at home, as well. That they were unable to communicate with Carlynn except through that one phone call from Penny made her absence that much more difficult.

"This weekend, I'm sure," Lisbeth said. "She has to be back by Monday, because her appointments start up again then."

"I feel like I don't know her anymore," Alan said glumly.

"Oh, Alan, that's silly."

"I know, but I haven't gone a day without talking to her in over ten years."

"Maybe she's been seduced by communal life," she joked, but Alan looked so distraught that she wished she'd kept her mouth shut. "Why don't we go get her?" she suggested.

Alan looked surprised. "I'd thought of that myself, actually, but I don't even know where she is, exactly."

"Well, we know she's in a commune in Big Sur," Lisbeth said. "We can ask around. The locals will probably know where it is."

Alan looked at his watch. "All right. If you're serious, let's do it."

"Let me call Gabe and see if he wants to go with us," she said, excited at the thought of the adventure.

"It's nearly four o'clock," Alan said. "I have some notes to finish up. Should we wait until tomorrow?"

"No," Lisbeth said, suddenly anxious to get on the road. "Let's go tonight."

"We won't be able to find anything in the dark," Alan protested.

"I know a lodge where we can stay," Lisbeth said. Lloyd Peterson had once told her about a lodge he liked in Big Sur. "Might be tough to get a room, since it's a Friday, but let me try. That way, we'd be there bright and early tomorrow and could start looking."

Alan nodded and smiled. "I can't wait to see her," he said. "Thanks, Liz."

There was a full moon hanging in the sky over the ocean, but the winding road was still too dark for Lisbeth's comfort. They were nearing Big Sur on Highway One. The little reflectors built into the line in the middle of the road formed a long string of lights, and she and Alan were alone out here. It was spooky, she thought. They did not see another car as Lisbeth's Volkswagen Beetle crept around each curve.

"It's actually better to drive this road at night than in the daytime," Alan reassured her. "You can see the lights of cars coming around the curve. In the daytime, you'd have no idea what's waiting for you around the bend."

Lisbeth supposed he was right, but still she turned each corner gingerly, her stomach beginning to protest a little. Gabriel had been unable to come with them, and she was driving, since Alan thought he was a better navigator. The green bug strained a bit on the inclines, and she was relieved when they found the road leading to the lodge. She pulled into the parking lot close to the building.

Inside the lodge, the man behind the desk handed them a key.

"It's for one of the cabins behind the main building," he said. "Number four. Very nice. Fully furnished."

"We need two beds, though," Lisbeth said.

"Right," the man said. "It has two twins. You can push them together if you like."

"Thank you," Alan said. "And by the way, we're looking for a commune that's near here. Would you know of it?"

"That depends on which one you're looking for. There's a few of them. Gordo. Redwood. Cabrial. What do you want to go to one of those places for? Just a bunch of filthy hippies."

"We're picking up a family member who's visiting there," Lisbeth said, disappointed to learn there were several communes in the area and trying to remember if Carlynn had mentioned the name of Penny's. None of those names sounded familiar, and she wondered if this had been such a great idea, after all.

But Alan looked unperturbed. "You go ahead to the cabin," he told her. "I'll stay here and get directions to the different communes."

It was a bit unnerving walking to the cabin alone. The path through the woods was lighted, but Lisbeth was still relieved when she found the cabin and stepped inside. It was spare, with a living room, bedroom, small kitchenette and bathroom with a claustrophobic shower, but it was clean, and luxurious surroundings were not what she and Alan were after.

Alan returned to the cabin around ten o'clock, several sheets of notes in his hand.

"Well," he said as he lay down on one of the beds, fully clothed, "I think we can find her if she's at one of these three places. If she's somewhere else, we're out of luck."

Lisbeth fell asleep quickly, but it was only a short while later that she was awakened by Alan shaking her shoulder.

"What's wrong?" she asked, trying to see her watch in the dark. "What time is it?"

"It's eleven," Alan said. "And I can't sleep. I'm going to take the car and those directions I got from the innkeeper and see if I can find her. Do you want to go with me?"

"No." She sat up. "And I don't want you to go, either. You'll just be wandering around in the dark out there on those little roads."

"Better than lying here staring at the ceiling." Alan picked up her car keys from the old dresser and left the cabin.

* * *

Carlynn had the commune practically to herself. Many of the adults and nearly all of the children, who'd been roused from their beds in what seemed to Carlynn to be a misguided attempt at adventure, were on a moonlight nature walk. From where she lay on her mattress in Penny's cabin, Carlynn could hear the occasional cry of a baby, and she knew that at least Shanti Joy Angel and her parents were nearby. That gave her some comfort. It was remarkably light outside tonight. There was no fog at all, and the moon was full, which was precisely why the nature seekers had grabbed this opportunity for their walk.

An hour earlier, Johnny Angel had come to Cornflower, asking her if she would take a look at Shanti Joy.

"She has a fever, I think," Johnny had said, and Carlynn had walked with him over to Rainbow.

She found Shanti nursing strongly from Ellen's breast, and her forehead felt cool to her touch.

"What made you think she had a fever?" she asked Johnny.

"She was crying, and she hardly ever cries," he said. "And she seemed flushed to me."

Ellen and Carlynn exchanged a smile. Johnny was an over-anxious new father, and it was not the first time he had come to Carlynn with a concern about his baby daughter since her dramatic birth. She didn't mind, though. She welcomed any chance to hold the baby.

She rested her hand on Johnny's shoulder. "Shanti is fine," she said. "And you are going to be an exceptional dad."

She left Johnny Angel and his family and walked back to Cornflower alone, enjoying the play of moonlight on the trees and shrubs and glad that Penny had gone with the walkers so she had some time for herself. She was longing for home. It had been a wonderful week, but she'd had her fill of rice and vegetables, naked children, guitar music late into the night, and wondering over breakfast who had slept with whom the night before. Tomorrow she would head back to Monterey, her work here finished, and all she could think of was seeing Alan and her sister and Gabriel. She'd tried not to think too much about Alan this week, knowing she couldn't talk to him and that thinking about him would only make their separation that much harder, but now her head was full of him, and she felt near tears as she drifted off to sleep.

"God, I've missed you." It was a man's voice, soft and close to her ear, and Carlynn's eyes sprang open to see Alan sitting on the side of her bed, his hand stroking her hair back from her forehead. Moonlight bathed the room and allowed her to see the love in his eyes. She sat up with a girlish squeal of delight and threw her arms around him.

"I'm dreaming," she said. "Are you really here?"

There were times she had wondered if she truly loved Alan or if theirs was a partnership based on a passion for their work rather than for each other. But in that moment, she knew the truth. Her love for him filled her.

"I'm really here," he said. "Are you ever coming home?"

"Oh, yes! Tomorrow," she said. "I'm sorry I've been gone so long, and it's been terrible not being able to call you. And how is everyone? And what's going on at the cen—"

"Come with me now," he said. "Lisbeth and I drove down here to spirit you away from this place and take you home with us."

"Is Lisbeth here?" She peered behind him.

"We rented a cabin not too far from here. She's there. And you will be, too, if you'd get up and get dressed."

"How did you ever find me?"

"Well, it wasn't easy," he said. "I visited another commune before coming here. This place seemed deserted, but I heard a baby crying. I went to that cabin and the baby's father—"

"Johnny Angel," she interrupted him with a grin.

"Whatever you say." Alan smiled with a roll of his eyes. "He told me where you were. Said everyone else was out on a nature walk or something."

"Yes, they are. I should probably wait till they get back before I—"

"Come *now*," Alan pleaded. "They've had you long enough."

"Okay," she agreed. She lit one of the lanterns so she could dress and pack her suitcase. On the back of one of the sheets of directions Alan had brought with him, she scribbled a note to Penny, then left the cabin with her husband, arm in arm.

"Oh!" she said when they reached the area where her car was parked. "My car's nearly empty. Keep an eye on me in your rearview mirror in case I run out, okay?"

"These roads would be a bad place to run out of gas," Alan said. "Especially at night."

"I know," she said. "I think I've got a smidgen left. But just in case, watch me."

"I'm never taking my eyes off you again," Alan said, squeezing her shoulders.

Carlynn's car made it to the cabin without a problem, although the needle was below the empty line by then. They would have to find gas somewhere in the morning and bring it back to her car before she drove it anywhere, but for the moment it didn't matter. She and Alan awakened Lisbeth, and the three of them spent much of the rest of the night lounging on the two twin beds and talking. Carlynn told them about life at the commune, assuring both of them that she'd had nothing to do with the bed-hopping that left them wide-eyed with disbelief and disgust. She told them about the drugs and about healing Penny's voice, and that Penny would be in a musical next year about hippies and long hair. She told them about the infant, Shanti Joy, and the moment she started breathing in her arms.

"I didn't want to let go of her," she said wistfully. "I felt so strongly connected to her."

"Because you saved her life," Lisbeth said.

"I guess," Carlynn agreed. She told them about the tiresome food she'd eaten that week, and Lisbeth laughed, promising to go out early in the morning to find some bacon and eggs to bring back and cook in the cabin.

It was nearly four in the morning when the three of them fell asleep, Alan and Carlynn wrapped in one another's arms, Lisbeth stretched out on her twin bed alone. Outside the cabin, the fog began creeping in from the ocean, hugging the coastline and easing its way through the trees, silently covering Big Sur in a milky-white shroud.

CHAPTER THIRTY-FOUR

Joelle was twenty-eight weeks pregnant and attending her first childbirth class, which was held in one of the large, carpeted meeting rooms at the hospital. Gale Firestone, the nurse practitioner in Rebecca's office, was the instructor, but everyone else in the room was a stranger to her, and she was the only pregnant woman there without a partner. A couple of the women had other women with them instead of husbands, but she had no one.

Her mother was going to be her birth partner, and Ellen was going to sit in on childbirth classes in the Berkeley area to prepare herself for that role, but she would only be able to attend a couple of the classes in Monterey. Joelle told her that didn't matter, just as long as she got herself to Monterey when she went into labor, and her mother had promised to be there for her.

They were watching a movie in the class tonight, and everyone was either sitting or lying on the floor of the dimly lit room, absorbed in the film. Joelle found it hard to concentrate on the images on the screen. She'd seen birth movies before, and she'd seen the real thing plenty of times, given that she worked in the maternity unit. But lying on the floor, a pillow beneath her head, she was having difficulty putting herself in the place of the spread-legged woman in the movie.

She was beginning to have nightmares about labor and delivery. The dreams were always the same: during labor in one of the birthing rooms, she would get a raging headache. Liam would be there, and he would run out of the room, and Rebecca and the nurses would abandon her, as well, saying they had other patients to take care of. She would be left there with that terrible headache, about to give birth, and no one to help her. She felt abandoned in the dream, just as she was feeling abandoned in her life.

The woman on the movie screen was panting now, and Joelle closed her eyes, her mind wandering to the visit the day before with Carlynn and Liam in Mara's room. Mara had actually made a sound while Liam was playing the guitar, a "woo-woo" sort of sound, and she and Liam had looked at each other, stunned.

Did that sound mean something? Was Mara trying to sing? To communicate? When she lifted her arm in the air, was she reaching out to Liam? Or were they just seeing what they wanted to see?

Joelle's bulging tummy was an ever-growing object in that room, something none of them discussed, and she wondered if at some point Mara might notice it. Would she ever have the ability to think to herself, "Joelle is pregnant," and would she wonder then who the father was? She wished she knew how many questions Mara wanted to ask but was unable to. But maybe there were none. Maybe that was why she was able to smile so easily.

Joelle was beginning to have a terrible fear, one she hadn't voiced to Carlynn, and she wondered if Liam shared it with her. If Mara were to get better, but not well enough to truly function in the world outside the nursing home, would that be a positive thing? What if she could only get well enough to know what she was missing? Right now, Mara was not suffering, and there were moments when Joelle wondered if they should be tampering with the blissful ignorance she seemed to enjoy.

No matter what was happening to Mara, though, there *was* a miracle occurring in that room. The miracle was that, as long as she and Liam were with Carlynn and Mara, they could talk and laugh together. Sometimes Joelle felt as though Carlynn was saving her life all over again.

CHAPTER THIRTY-FIVE

Big Sur, 1967

A thick white fog wrapped itself around the cabin the following morning, and Carlynn woke up before her sister or Alan. It was chilly, and she snuggled closer to her husband, but she was too wide awake to stay in bed for long. She nudged Alan gently, hoping he would wake up and go out with her to get something for breakfast, but he was snoring softly, the way he did when he was deeply asleep.

Carefully, she extracted herself from his arms and got out of the narrow bed. She opened her suitcase, which was resting on the floor of the dimly lit cabin, and pulled out a pair of socks, her jeans and a heavy sweater and went into the bathroom to change.

She should go back to the commune, she thought as she brushed her teeth. She needed to say a real goodbye to Penny and the other people she had befriended over the last week. She'd forgotten to leave the antibiotics for anyone who needed them. And she wanted to hold the baby one more time. If she were being honest with herself, she would have to admit that Shanti Joy was her primary motivation for wanting to go back to Cabrial. Since she and Alan had started the center, she didn't see as many babies as she had as a pediatrician, and she missed it.

She left the bathroom, her flannel nightgown bundled in her arms, and walked across the bedroom to put it in her suitcase.

"Good morning."

Carlynn stood up from her suitcase to see her sister smiling at her. Lisbeth was still lying in bed, her arms folded behind her head.

"Sorry," Carlynn whispered. "I didn't mean to wake you."

"You didn't," Lisbeth said. "I was already awake when you went into the bathroom."

"I was thinking I'd like to make just a quick trip back to the commune to say goodbye to everyone." Carlynn looked at Alan. "I have a feeling he'll be out for another couple of hours. Would you like to go with me and we can let him sleep?"

"Sure." Lisbeth sat up. "Let me change and then we can go."

Carlynn wrote a note to Alan and then walked onto the porch to wait for her sister. She sat on the step in the fog, thinking back to those socked-in mornings in the mansion, when she and Lisbeth were kids and would go out to the terrace and sit on the lounge chairs, pretending they were in a cloud.

"There you are," Lisbeth said as she stepped on the porch behind Carlynn. "Didn't see you for a minute."

"Doesn't this remind you of mornings at the mansion?" Carlynn asked.

Lisbeth stood next to her, looking out at the shifting cloud of fog. "I don't like to think about the mansion, actually," she said.

Carlynn stood up and put her arm around her sister. "I'm sorry," she said. "I know how much you miss it."

"We should probably get some food to bring back to Alan for breakfast," Lisbeth said, changing the subject.

They started walking down the shrouded path toward the parking lot of the lodge. "We can ask at the commune if there's a store where we can get some bacon and eggs," Carlynn said, "but I don't think there will be one close by."

"The lodge serves breakfast," Lisbeth said. "We can eat there if we can't find anything else."

The fog in the parking lot was translucent enough for them to make out their cars. "I have no gas in mine," Carlynn said. "We'll have to take your bug, okay?"

"Sure."

They started walking across the small dirt lot toward the Volkswagen. Carlynn looked out toward the road, where the fog seemed thicker as it hugged the coast.

"Maybe we should wait until later," she said. "We're really socked in here."

Lisbeth stopped walking and followed her sister's gaze to the road. "What do you think?" she asked.

Carlynn remembered her drive through the fog a week ago to reach the commune. This couldn't be any worse than that. "Oh, let's do it," she said.

They got into the car, and Lisbeth carefully turned around and headed toward the road. She hesitated at the exit from the parking lot and looked to her left.

"Can't see a damn thing," she said with a laugh.

"Well, if anyone's coming, they'll be driving very slowly, I would think," Carlynn said. "Are your fog lights on?"

"Uh-huh." Lisbeth turned right onto the road, gingerly, the car jerking a bit with her apprehension.

Carlynn looked through the front windshield at the swirling fog. The foliage at the side of the road was quite visible, and the road itself suddenly slipped into view.

"That's better." Lisbeth sounded relieved, and she gave the car a little more gas.

"Just keep close to the side here," Carlynn said.

Lisbeth glanced at her once they were under way. "I know why you really want to go back to the commune," she said.

"Why?" Carlynn asked.

"You want to get your mitts on that baby again. What's her name?"

"Shanti Joy." Had she been that obvious? "Well, I really just want to say goodbye to Penny. But seeing the baby again would be a bonus."

"Right." Lisbeth smiled at her, and Carlynn knew she didn't believe her. Her sister knew her too well.

"I have been having sort of a sick fantasy," Carlynn said.

"What's that?" The fog had suddenly thickened again, and Lisbeth's knuckles were white on the steering wheel, her head pitched forward in an effort to see the road.

"My fantasy is...well, I'm appalled at myself for it. My fantasy is that her parents would die. Maybe not die. Maybe just be unable to take care of her for some reason and they'd give her to me."

A small smile came to Lisbeth's lips, but she did not take her eyes from the road. "You still long for a baby, don't you?" she asked.

"I thought I was past it," Carlynn said. "I love my work at the center. And I'm thirty-seven years old, for Pete's sake. But that little life in my hands..." She shook her head with a smile. "She's so beautiful. She has a ton of dark hair, and..."

Lisbeth suddenly stopped the car.

"What's wrong?" Carlynn asked.

"I can't do this, Carly," Lisbeth said.

"Can't do what?"

"Drive in this fog." Lisbeth nodded toward the invisible road ahead of them. "I'm sorry. We have to go back. My legs are shaking."

Carlynn turned in her seat to look behind them, but she could see nothing other than the fog. "We can't turn around here, honey," she said. "And we shouldn't just stop like this. Another car could come up behind us and hit us."

"Could you drive?" Lisbeth seemed frozen behind the wheel.

"Okay," Carlynn said. "It was like this when I drove here from San Francisco, so I got pretty used to it."

Quickly, the two of them got out of the car and exchanged places. Once Carlynn was in the driver's seat, though, she understood why Lisbeth had panicked. The road was gone. Even the foliage along the side of the road was hidden.

"Yikes," she said. "I see what you mean." Putting the car in gear, she began inching it forward. The fog was far worse than it had been the day she'd driven to the commune, and if there had been a way to turn around on the narrow, winding road, she would have. But they were stuck now.

"So," Lisbeth said, "were you tempted?"

"Tempted?"

"To sleep with someone at the commune?"

"Lisbeth! Are you crazy?" She stole a quick glance at her sister. "Of course not. Would you be?"

"No, but I was just wondering if, you know, the atmosphere would have gotten to you after a week. You said Penny was doing it with everyone."

"But Penny's always been that way. I hope she doesn't get herself preg—"

"Carlynn!" Lisbeth shouted. "Watch out!"

The headlights of a car were directly in front of them, in their lane, and Carlynn had no choice but to quickly swerve to the left to avoid crashing head-on into the vehicle. The Volkswagen skidded on the wet pavement, sending them sliding across the road, and Carlynn knew the second the wheels left the pavement. Something crashed into the bottom of the car, which tipped precariously, teetering for a moment on the edge of an unseen precipice, and then they were falling.

Lisbeth tried to grab the wheel from her in a futile attempt to save them, but it was too late.

Carlynn caught her sister's arm. "Oh my God, Lizzie!" she screamed. "I'm sorry. The road..."

She thought the car was falling sideways, although she couldn't have said for certain, because every window offered only a view of fog. But she felt a jolt as they hit something, some outcropping from the cliff. She heard Lisbeth scream once more, and then, suddenly, the world was still and dark.

CHAPTER THIRTY-SIX

Only Paul was sitting at their usual lunch table, even though Joelle was late getting to the cafeteria. She carried her tray to the table, glancing over her shoulder to see if Liam might have been in the line behind her, but he was nowhere to be seen.

Paul stood up and pulled a chair out for her, and she laughed.

"I'm looking *that* pregnant, am I?" she asked.

"Just trying to be chivalrous," Paul said. "When are you due, again?"

"New Year's Day," she said.

"Oh, yeah. How could I forget that?"

"I'm thirty weeks today," she said.

"You look great," Paul said.

"Thanks. Where's Liam?" She tried to sound only mildly curious.

"He's had a rough morning in the E.R.," Paul said. "It's been like a Saturday night down there."

She popped a prenatal vitamin into her mouth and swallowed it with a few sips of milk. "And how are your units today?" she asked.

"Not bad, actually. How about yours?"

Her pager buzzed as he asked the question, and she looked down to see the E.R.'s number on the display.

"Speak of the devil," she said.

"E.R.?" he asked as she got to her feet.

She nodded. "Be right back."

She walked over to the wall phone near the cafeteria exit and dialed the number for the E.R.

It was Liam who picked up on the other end. "Are you in the cafeteria, Jo?" he asked.

"Yes. What's up?"

"I'm sorry to drag you away from lunch, but I could really use your help down here. I have a couple of accident victims I'm tied up with, and a woman just came in who looks pretty beaten up, but says she just fell. Any chance you could see her?"

"Sure. I'll be right there."

"That would be great. Thanks."

She hung up the phone and returned to the table, but didn't take her seat again.

"Just leave this here for me in case this doesn't take too long, okay?" she asked Paul, pointing to her tray.

"I'm almost done, Joelle," he said. "Want me to take the E.R. case for you?"

"That's all right," she said. "It's a possible battered woman, so it's probably better if I do it. But thanks for offering." She gave him a quick wave of her hand. "Have a good afternoon."

From the hallway of the E.R., she could see into the waiting room, and Paul had been right. It looked like a weekend night in there. Mothers bounced irritable babies on their knees, a couple of kids held ice packs to their legs, and several men slouched in their chairs, looking in the direction of the reception desk, waiting for their names to be called.

A nurse spotted Joelle and walked toward her, handing her a chart.

"She's in four," she said. "Bart stitched her up and set her broken arm and tried to get her to admit what happened, but she in-
sists she fell down the stairs." The nurse shrugged. "Who knows?
Maybe she did. But we didn't want to let her go until one of you
guys had a chance to assess her. She wants to get out of here,
though. I'm not sure how much longer we can keep her."

Joelle nodded, glancing quickly through the thin chart.
Twenty-four-year-old Caucasian woman. Katarina Parsons. She
didn't bother trying to read Bart's nearly illegible notes. She'd
get the story soon enough.

She pushed open the door of the treatment room to find the
young woman sitting on the edge of the examining table, arms
folded across her chest, a look of boredom on her bruised face.
The blasé expression masked fear, Joelle was almost certain.
She'd seen the act before.

She held out her hand to the woman. "Hi, Katarina," she said.
"I'm Joelle D'Angelo, one of the social workers in the hospital."

The woman shook her hand limply. "Why are they making
me see you?" she asked.

"Well—" Joelle leaned against the counter "—when someone
comes in looking as though there's a possibility that she might
have been beaten up, we want to make sure she'll be safe when
she leaves the E.R.," she said.

"I told that doctor I wasn't beat up," Katarina said. "I fell down
some cement stairs." She pronounced cement "see-ment."

Joelle smiled at her. "I like your accent," she said. "Where
are you from?"

"Virginia."

"Oh." Joelle took a seat on the wheeled stool. "Near Wash-
ington?"

"No. Southwest Virginia. Right near North Carolina."

"I bet it's pretty there," Joelle said. "What brought you out here?"

"My boyfriend."

"Oh. Did he live here, or...?"

"No, he lived in Virginia," Katarina said. "But his brother was in Monterey, and he wanted to come out here, too. He thought he could find a job, but he hasn't yet." She shifted her slender weight on the examining table.

"Do you want to sit in that chair?" Joelle pointed toward the one chair in the room. "I know how uncomfortable it is sitting on those examining tables. I've been doing a lot of that myself lately." She patted her belly with a smile.

"I don't want to sit *anywhere* in here," Katarina said. "I just want to leave."

Joelle nodded toward the chair. "Just take a seat there," she said. "It won't be so hard on your back."

Muttering under her breath, Katarina slipped off the examining table and sat down in the chair, arms folded protectively across her chest once more.

She was so easy, Joelle thought. So malleable and so scared. Joelle was confident she'd be able to get the truth out of her in no time.

"Where did you get hurt?" she asked.

"I told you, on the cement stairs at his brother's apartment."

"No, I mean, where on your body. I see you have some stitches on your cheek, and your other cheek is pretty swollen. Your arm was broken, right?"

"I been through all of this with that doctor," Katarina said.

Joelle leaned toward her. "Katarina, it may be that you did fall down the stairs," she said. "But if that's *not* what happened, there's help for you. There's a place you can go where you'll be safe. You just moved here—I know you probably don't know many people, but you don't have to feel alone in this."

The tears welling up in Katarina's eyes told her she was on the right track.

"You're not the only woman this has happened to," Joelle said. "You have a lot of company, unfortunately, but the good thing about that is that we have resources in place to—"

Katarina's head suddenly jerked to attention, her eyes on the door to the treatment room. Joelle heard the voices outside the room, one calm and female, the other loud, angry and male.

"That's Jess," Katarina said in a whisper.

"Your boyfriend?"

She nodded, her gaze still on the small window of the door. "He'll kill me for coming here, but I knew my arm was broke."

Joelle stood up and reached for the phone on the wall. "I'll call security," she said, keeping her voice calm as she dialed the number, despite the fact that the man's shouts were growing louder, more enraged. "Probably someone already has," she said, waiting for the number to ring. "You don't need to wor—"

The door flew open and a large man stormed into the treatment room, knocking the phone out of Joelle's hand as he passed her. Her hands moved instinctively to protect her belly.

"What the fuck are you doing here?" the man asked Katarina, who literally cowered on the chair in the corner of the room. The man's blond hair jutted out from his head in no discernable style, and his eyes had a wild look that made Joelle think he was on something.

"I told them I fell down the stairs," Katarina said.

"Jess," Joelle said as calmly as she was able to, "Katarina and I are nearly finished talking. Please wait outside and we'll be out in a few—"

"What are you, a social worker?" Jess turned to face her. "Jesus, Kat, what have you been telling them? She's clumsy, that's all," he said to Joelle. "Clumsy bitch." He started toward Katarina again, his hands reaching for the small woman's shoulders.

Before she had time to think, Joelle moved forward and grabbed his arm.

"Stay away from her," she said.

He jerked free of her grasp, as though her hands were nothing more than a fly on his arm, and headed for Katarina again.

There were more voices outside the treatment-room door,

and Joelle hoped that security had arrived, but it was Liam who came into the room. He opened the door wide as he entered, and Joelle saw Katarina's chance to escape.

"Katarina, get out!" she said, hoping the young woman could use Liam's intrusion to slip from the room.

"You don't go nowhere!" Jess bellowed at the terrified woman. He turned to face Joelle, and she was suddenly looking into the piercing green eyes of a madman.

"And you shut up, you fucking bitch!" Lifting his foot high, he pressed the sole of his boot against Joelle's belly and plowed her into the wall.

Pain shot through her middle, as though everything inside her, everything that was there to hold her baby in place, was being torn apart. She felt her body slide down the wall until she was crumpled on the floor. She doubled over from the pain, and the world in the treatment room instantly became blurred and surreal. She watched as Liam grabbed Jess by the shoulder, drew back his own arm and punched the wild man in the face, not once, but again and again, until it was hard to know which man was truly out of control. Blood squirted from Jess's nose and seeped into the spaces between his teeth as Liam—gentle Liam—pounded the man with his fists. Joelle leaned back against the wall and shut her eyes, afraid she was going to be sick. When she looked up again, two security guards were in the room, and Liam was bending over her, crouching down, his arms a wall of protection around her.

She grabbed the fabric of his shirt in her hand.

"The baby," she said hoarsely.

She felt him reach between them, his hand slipping beneath her shirt to rest, warm and soothing, on the rounded panel of her maternity slacks, and she let her forehead fall against his shoulder.

"You'll be all right," he said into her ear. "You've *got* to be all right."

CHAPTER THIRTY-SEVEN

San Francisco, 1967

She could hear voices. At first they were little more than a low hum, as if she were listening to a conversation taking place on the other side of a flimsy wall. But gradually, she recognized them. Alan's voice. And Gabriel's.

She tried to open her eyes, but the effort seemed too great. She was able, though, to make a sound. Half hum, half grunt. The sound reverberated in her own ears. And the voices stopped.

"Did you hear that?" That was Gabe's voice. She tried to smile, to reach out for him, but she knew she was succeeding at neither.

"Lisbeth?" Alan's voice was little more than a whisper.

"Mmm," she said again.

"Oh, thank God," Gabriel said, and she felt him—*yes,* it was definitely him—take her hand. *"Lizzie,"* he said.

"Shh!" Alan's voice was sharp.

"We'd better make sure no one comes in," Gabriel said.

"I'll stand by the door," Alan said. She felt something brush her cheek, then Alan's lips against her forehead. "Welcome back, Lisbeth," he whispered.

"Gabe?"

"I'm right here, baby."

His hand touched the side of her face, and she could smell his aftershave.

"I'm..." She felt herself frowning. Where was she? Not in her bed at home. Thoughts swam through her head, but she couldn't pin any of them down. "Head hurts," she said.

"Yes. You had a very bad concussion."

"I don't remember." She tried to open her eyes again, managing to lift one of the lids a bit, but closing it quickly against the light in the room.

"Turn out the light, Alan," Gabriel said, and he let go of her hand for a moment. She heard him at the window, lowering the blinds, perhaps. Then he was back, holding her hand once more. "Try it again," he said. "Open your eyes. It's darker in here now."

She did. First her left eye, which popped open as if on a spring, then the right. The room was dim, but she could see Gabriel's face close to hers. She reached up to touch his cheek. It was wet.

"Liz, I'm so glad to see you," he said, turning his face to kiss her palm. "You had us really scared."

"What happened?" she asked.

"You were in a car accident," he said.

"I don't remember." Her mind felt thick with confusion. "When? Where was I going?"

"It happened nearly a month ago," he said.

What? "A month...?"

"Yes. You and Carlynn were in your car. You were in Big Sur, do you remember?" His words were slow and measured, as though he had practiced saying them many times.

She had the flimsiest, dreamlike sort of memory of being in the car with Carlynn, driving in the fog. "Not a month ago," she said.

"Yes, hon," he said. "You've been unconscious all this time. I'm so relieved to see you finally waking up."

Her head was pounding, and she raised her hand to her temple, where her fingers touched some sort of material—fabric or gauze—instead of her hair. "What's on my head?" she asked.

"You suffered several different injuries," he said. "You had the concussion, as I mentioned. Your leg was broken in a few places. And you had some internal bleeding. They did a couple of surgeries on you. You lost a lot of blood, and they gave you transfusions. But your body is healing. And every day, the physical therapist comes in and moves your arms and your legs to keep your muscles toned."

"Shanti Joy." The name came back to her suddenly.

"What?" Gabriel asked.

"The baby at the commune." Alan's voice came from across the room. "What about it?"

"Carlynn wanted to go back to the commune to see Penny and the baby one last time," Lisbeth said. "And there was fog. Oh! Car coming at us." She felt her body flinch, and she drew her hand away from Gabriel's.

"That's right, but you're not there now, Liz." Gabe took her hand again. "You're safe. Here with me. You and Carlynn were driving in the fog on those narrow roads at Big Sur. A car was coming toward you, in the wrong lane, and Carlynn swerved to avoid it and went over the side of the cliff. You were unbelievably lucky to get out of there in as good shape as you did."

Where, she thought suddenly, was Carlynn? Alan was here in this room with her. And Gabe. But she hadn't seen Carlynn or heard her voice. She felt her heartbeat quicken in her chest.

"What about Carlynn?" she asked. "Is she all right?"

Gabriel hesitated a moment before shaking his head. "Baby, I'm sorry," he said, his eyes watching her carefully. "She didn't make it."

"What do you mean?" She felt panicky. "You don't mean she..."

Gabriel nodded. "She was killed in the accident," he said. "I'm so sorry, Liz."

"No!" Lisbeth let go of his hand to pound his chest with both fists. "Please, please, please! Gabriel!" She tried to turn her head to see Alan where he was standing by the door, but pain shot from her neck to her temple, and she could not see him. "Alan!" she screamed.

"Shh!" Alan moved toward her quickly. He took her fists and held them, coiled and knotted, in his own hands.

"She can't be dead," Lisbeth said. "She *can't* be. Please tell me she's okay, Alan. Please."

"She died very, very quickly," Alan said, and she knew, more from the tears in his eyes than from his words, that her sister was gone. "She was..." He stumbled, glancing at Gabriel, looking for the words. "She was pressed between the steering wheel and the seat. The police said she never knew what hit her. She didn't suf—"

There were voices outside her room, and Alan quickly turned his head toward the door. He looked at Gabriel.

"I think the nurse is coming," he said.

"Head her off," Gabe said, and Alan dropped Lisbeth's hands and strode to the door. She heard it open and fall shut with a soft thud.

"Lisbeth," Gabriel said, "if the nurse should come in, Alan and I will be calling you Carlynn."

"What?"

"I'll explain, but just so you know. Please. It's important. Pretend to be Carlynn."

"No!" She tried hard to sit up, but her head was too heavy to lift from the pillow. *"Why?"* she asked.

"Shh," Gabriel said. "Settle down. Please don't talk so loud. I'll try to explain. I know this is too much for you to handle right now. To absorb. But just listen, please, baby. Just listen to me."

"I want my sister," she said, still unable to grasp the realization that she would never be able to see Carlynn again. "Oh, Gabe, what will I do without her?"

"I know you want her back," Gabriel said. "We all do. But will you listen to me? Please?" He glanced toward the door to her room. She knew her thinking was murky, but she was certain Gabriel was more anxious than she'd ever seen him before.

"I'm listening," she said.

"You and Carlynn were in your bug, but Carlynn was driving, right?"

She shut her eyes, thinking. "I was, but then we switched," she said. "It was foggy and I...my legs were shaking...it was so hard to see. She thought she could drive better in the fog than I could."

"Right. So when you went over the cliff, and the rescuers got to you, they found your purse, with your ID, and none for Carlynn, and so they figured it was you in the driver's seat. They told us you had died and that it was Carlynn who had been badly injured."

She frowned again, trying to follow him. "Didn't you...couldn't you and Alan tell the difference when you saw me?"

"No, we couldn't. We never saw Carlynn...after the accident. And you were so bandaged up, your face was cut and bruised—"

She lifted her hands to her face, touching the skin gingerly with her fingertips. "Do I look different?" she asked.

"No, honey. Your face is very nearly healed, and you look like yourself. And, of course, you also look like Carlynn."

She realized suddenly what he was telling her. "You thought *I* had died?" she asked.

He nodded. "The worst day of my life, Liz." His Adam's apple bobbed in his throat. "And the day we realized it was *you* lying here and not Carlynn was the worst day for Alan."

"Oh my God." She was still having difficulty absorbing it all. "How long did everyone think I was Carlynn?" she asked.

"Two weeks," Gabriel said. "We...I don't know if I should tell you all of this."

"Tell me."

"We had a memorial service for you and everything."

She didn't know what to say. Her emotions were so jumbled together that she didn't know whether to feel joy or sorrow, sympathy or anger.

"And we didn't have one for Carlynn," Gabriel finished.

"We'll have to have one for her now," Lisbeth said. "As soon as I'm well enough to get out of this—"

"No," Gabriel interrupted her. "That's what I have to talk to you about. Some things happened while you were unconscious those first couple of weeks. There were newspaper articles. Magazine articles. All saying how 'the famous healer,' Carlynn Shire, had lost her sister in an accident, people praying for your—for *her*—recovery. And your mother sat with you, day and night, and—"

"Because she thought I was Carlynn."

Gabriel licked his lips, nodding. "I don't know how she would have reacted if she'd known it was you. Maybe she would have come around, Liz. I just don't know. But she did believe, as we all did, that you were Carlynn. She said, though, that she felt guilty for the way she'd treated you—treated Lisbeth—and that she was going to make a huge—and I do mean *huge*—contribution to the center in your name."

So confusing...so... Lisbeth shook her head, a small gesture that made her grit her teeth against the pain. "You mean..." She wasn't even certain what question to ask.

"I mean that, if Carlynn recovered well enough so that the center could continue, your mother said that she would fund it. She'd pay salaries and rent."

"So..." She was beginning to catch on. "If Carlynn is dead and I'm alive, Mother wouldn't..."

"Alan would have to shut down the center," Gabriel said. "It wouldn't be a viable project without Carlynn and her reputation to keep it alive."

"Her dream," Lisbeth said, aching for her sister.

"Right. Her dream."

"But...you can't seriously think that I could—"

"There's more," Gabriel said. "One of your mother's conditions is that the center be moved to Monterey. She wants to be closer to you, and she—"

"To Carlynn."

"Yes, right. To Carlynn. And she wants Carlynn and Alan to live in the mansion. And I've avoided her as much as possible...or rather, she's avoided me. Even if she's gotten a few glimpses of me, here or at the funeral, she can't see well enough to really know what I look like. So, Alan and I have a plan that will allow us...all of us...to live in the mansion together."

"What?"

"Your mother has a bedroom downstairs now," Gabriel said, speaking quickly. "She never goes upstairs anymore because of her arthritis. So you and Alan and I will live upstairs. I'll be introduced to your mother as the new CEO. We'll use my middle name—"

"Quinn."

"Right, and she'll never be any the wiser. We'll say I'm new to the area and in need of someplace to live. You and Alan will tell her that you want me to live there at the mansion so that the three of us can do center work even at home. Your mother will like that. And with the money she's contributing, I'll be able to afford to leave my job here—at SF General—and work full-time for the center."

Lisbeth closed her eyes. "This is so crazy," she said.

"I know it sounds that way, Liz. If I just woke up after a month and heard all of this, I'd think so, too. But Alan and I have lived with the idea for a couple of weeks now, and—"

"I can't do it, Gabe," she said. "There's no way I can be Carlynn."

"Think through the alternative, baby. If you tell the world that you're really—"

"How did you find out that it was me lying here and not Carlynn?" she interrupted him.

Gabriel leaned away from her. "Oh, Lizzie," he said, "it was awful."

"How?"

"The police brought over your rings and Carlynn's rings.

They were labeled in plastic bags. And your rings were in the bag labeled with Carlynn's name, and vice versa. The cops gave the bags to Alan first, and he tried to tell them they'd made a mistake. Then it dawned on him, poor guy. Can you imagine? We still weren't sure, so he and I came up here, and...well, we looked at your...you know how you have that little heart-shaped mole on your breast?"

Lisbeth closed her eyes. "So that's how you found out I was alive, and Alan found out he'd lost his wife." She turned her head to the side, crying again. "Oh, Carly."

Gabriel smoothed his hand over her hair, and she could feel the tension in his fingers.

"You can have her life, Liz. Not her husband, though."

She heard the hint of a smile in his voice and turned to look at him. He *was* smiling at her. They were not feeling the same thing right now. Gabe had already moved past the grief that was weighing her down.

"Alan *would* be your husband in public, of course," Gabriel said, "but you would be mine when we're alone. Then, in all other ways, you can have Carlynn's life. The mansion at Cypress Point will one day be yours. And you can live there forever. With me. Money will never, ever be a problem for any of us or for the center."

Cypress Point, Lisbeth thought. She could live there, share it with Gabe.

"What would Carlynn want me to do?" she asked.

"What do you think?" Gabriel asked her.

"She'd want me to have everything she did," she said, knowing that was the truth. "But not this way."

"Is there another way?" Gabriel asked.

"It's insane, though," she said. "I can't heal anyone. I'm not a doctor."

"It doesn't matter," Gabriel said. "Alan and I will work out the details. We just need the world—and your mother—to think that Carlynn Shire is still alive. We can always say that the accident somehow altered your healing ability. It doesn't matter. The center is really about research," he said. "And we can change the shape of that research. We can attract other known healers to the center, and they can become subjects for study."

The door opened, and a nurse walked in followed by Alan, who looked nothing short of panic-stricken at being unable to keep the woman out of the room a moment longer. The air vibrated with tension as the nurse took Lisbeth's blood pressure and pulse and slipped the thermometer beneath her tongue.

"Do you know where you are?" she asked Lisbeth once she'd removed the thermometer.

"The hospital," Lisbeth said.

"And do you know what year it is?"

Lisbeth had to think for a moment. "Nineteen sixty-seven?" she asked, not completely certain.

"Very good," the nurse said. "And you know these gentlemen? Which one is your hubby?"

Lisbeth swallowed hard. *Carly, Carly, Carly. What do you want me to do?* She glanced at Gabriel, then turned her face toward Alan.

"That one," she said.

CHAPTER THIRTY-EIGHT

Liam would have stayed with Joelle while they examined her, but he was being treated in another curtained-off cubicle of the E.R. himself. He'd broken the index finger on his right hand, and Bart was now injecting something into his jaw to numb it, so that he could stitch the jagged cut Liam had no memory of receiving.

He'd never hit another human being in his entire life. Not even as a kid. But, it had felt so natural to him. So right. He wanted to beat that bastard to a pulp. The image of him kicking Joelle into the wall was imbedded in his mind forever.

He knew where she was. Three cubicles down from him. For a while, he could hear her crying. The police had been questioning him at that time, and he'd asked them to let him go to her, but they said she was being well cared for.

"And you're bleeding all over the place, besides," one of the cops had added.

"Do you know how Joelle is?" he asked Bart now, as the doctor sat down next to him and began working on the laceration on his jaw.

"They've taken her to the Women's Wing," he said.

That's why he was no longer hearing her cry, Liam thought.
"Is she okay?" he asked.

"She's in premature labor."

"Oh, no," he said. "She's only...what...thirty weeks?"

"Stop talking, Liam," Bart said. "I think that's what I heard.
Thirty weeks. It's going to be rough if she has that baby now."

It was happening again: another pregnancy, another child
of his, being born into tragedy. And he cared—he truly did—
about that baby. But just then, he cared far more what happened to Joelle.

"Is Joelle okay, though?" he asked again. "I mean...besides
the labor?"

"She has a couple of cracked ribs, I think," Bart said, leaning
back from his work. "And if you keep talking, Liam, this will
take all day."

After Bart had finished stitching his jaw, Liam threw away the
bloody shirt and pants he'd had on and borrowed a pair of blue
scrubs to wear for the rest of the day. He left the E.R. and headed
toward the Women's Wing, but stopped off in the men's room
to see what had been done to his face. His image in the mirror
shocked him. The cut on his chin was bandaged, as was his
splinted aching finger, but there were bruises on his face that he
could not remember receiving. He'd told the police he'd done
all the hitting, yet that was obviously not the case, and he imagined the cops probably had a good laugh at his expense after
they'd finished questioning him. Suddenly, he was very tired. He
leaned against the tiled wall in the rest room and closed his eyes.

Joelle had to be terrified, he thought. She knew too much
about what could go wrong with a pregnancy. Just like Mara did.

He felt a little sick to his stomach as he walked out of the
men's room and down the corridor. He would visit Joelle as her
fellow social worker, her friend, the guy who'd also been involved in the altercation that caused her injury. No one would
think anything of it.

He found Serena Marquez at the nurses' station in the Women's Wing.

"How's Joelle?" he asked.

"Oh my God," Serena said, when she saw him. "I heard you beat up the guy that kicked Joelle. It looks like it was the other way around."

"How's Joelle?" he repeated, not in any mood for banter.

"Rebecca's trying to stop her labor," Serena said.

"Can she?" he asked. "I mean, how is it going?"

"Don't know yet," Serena said. "But her membranes have ruptured, so that's not great."

"Can I see her?" he asked.

Serena looked at the clock. "Give her about twenty minutes or so," she said. "Rebecca's examining her. She's starting her on some betamethasome and antibiotics."

"What's the beta...whatever for?"

"To mature the baby's lungs in case her labor can't be stopped. Without it—and even with it—a thirty-weeker could have some pretty serious problems." She picked up a chart and started to leave the nurses' station. "She's in room twenty," she said, over her shoulder.

He sat down at the counter and reached for the phone. Pulling the phone book from the shelf under the counter, he looked up the number for the Shire Mind and Body Center and dialed it. A young-sounding woman answered the phone.

"Hello," he said. "I need to get in touch with Carlynn Shire and I don't have her home number. Can you tell me how I can reach her? It's urgent."

"What is this regarding?" the woman asked.

"It's about a friend of hers. Joelle D'Angelo. She's in labor, and I wanted to see if Carlynn could come over here, to Silas Memorial, to be with her."

"I'll get that message to her."

"Right away?" he asked.

"I'll call her, and if she's there, she'll get it. If not, I can't say when."

"Try to find her, please. And ask her to call me. Liam Sommers." He gave her the hospital number. "Have her ask the operator to page me."

His pager buzzed exactly twenty minutes later, when he was getting up his courage to walk down the hall to room twenty. He picked up the phone.

"It's Carlynn, Liam," she said. "I received your message and got a ride to the hospital. I'm in the lobby. Is Joelle all right?"

"I'll be right over," he said. "We can talk there."

She was sitting in the lobby near the windows, balancing her hands on the top of her cane. He sat down in the chair next to hers.

"Thanks for coming," he said.

"What happened?" she asked. "And what on earth happened to you?"

"Joelle was interviewing a battered woman in the emergency room, and the woman's boyfriend broke into the room and kicked her in the stomach."

Carlynn's hand flew to her mouth. "Oh, no," she said. "Is she all right?"

He shook his head. "She has some cracked ribs and she's in premature labor," he said.

"Oh, that's not good," Carlynn said. "Not this early. And your face? Your finger?"

"I punched the daylights out of the guy who kicked her," he said. "And I'm paying for it now." He held up his throbbing hand.

"Good for you!" Carlynn looked pleased with him. "What's the prognosis on Joelle, do you know?"

"They're trying to stop the labor," he said. "I thought it might help her to have you with her."

"Why not you?" she asked.

"I'm not a healer."

Carlynn looked down at her hands where they rested on the

top of her cane. "I believe that, right now, you can probably do more for her than I could."

He felt annoyed. She was always trying to push the two of them together as though Mara didn't exist. "Do you understand my dilemma, Carlynn?" he asked.

"I understand that you and Joelle are willing to sacrifice your own happiness for someone who doesn't need you to make those sacrifices," Carlynn said, and he recoiled from her suddenly forceful tone. "And I'm willing to bet," she continued, "that if Mara could talk, from all you and Joelle have told me about her, she wouldn't want you to make them, either. She'd want Joelle to take care of you and Sam the way only a woman who adores you both can do."

"I thought you were supposedly trying to heal Mara," he said. "Or have you just been playing with Joelle? Playing with both of us?"

"I've been working very hard," Carlynn said. "But you're right. It hasn't been Mara that I've been attempting to heal. She doesn't need my help, Liam, I've known that from the start. It's you and Joelle who need healing. Look at Mara. She's always smiling. Have you ever seen her appear to be suffering?"

He didn't respond. They both knew the answer to her question.

He stared out the window, collecting his thoughts. "If I give in to my feelings for Joelle," he said, "it feels like I'm betraying my wife."

"You're not abandoning Mara, dear." Carlynn's tone softened. "You and Joelle can't possibly hurt her by loving each other, and you don't need to be divorced, for you and Joelle to be married in your hearts. The happier you are, the more strength you'll have to give to Mara. And to your little boy. I believe you have a responsibility to your child...to your children...to live a full and happy life."

"Children." He repeated the word more to himself than to her.

"Right now," Carlynn leaned forward, her arms folded on the table, "you have a choice. You can go be with Mara, who feels very, very little, and who will be smiling whether you're there or not. Or you can go and be with Joelle, who still feels every-thing—fear and love and worry—and who is feeling all those things right now as she prays to hold on to your child. You de-cide who needs you more."

"Will you go see her?" he asked.

"Yes, of course I will. But I can't take your place, Liam. Not at her side, and not in her heart."

He left the lobby, but he did not go near the Women's Wing for fear that someone would corner him to tell him that Joelle was asking for him. There was someplace else he needed to go first.

Mara was sleeping when he went into her room at the nurs-ing home. He closed the door behind him, wanting privacy with his wife.

"Mara?"

Lowering the railing on her bed, he sat next to her as she opened her eyes. She smiled at him, let out her squeal, and he leaned forward to kiss her.

"I need to talk with you, honey," he said. He reached across her body for her right hand, the hand that would feel his pres-ence. "I'm struggling, Mara," he said. "I love you. I'd give any-thing to make you whole again. You've been so wonderful for me. You've given me so much joy." He ran his free hand over her too-long hair. "And a beautiful son," he said. "The years we spent together were truly the best years of my life. But they're over now, and I need to let go of them." He smiled sadly. "You've already done that, in your own way, haven't you?"

She was staring at him, her eyes huge and riveting, but her smile had not changed.

"I've fallen in love with Joelle, Mara," he said. "We have one really huge thing in common, and that's you. We both love you. We both want to take care of you. And I want you to know that I'll always be here for you. I'll never stop visiting you, no mat-ter what else happens in my life."

He ran his thumb over the back of her hand. "But I'm having a hard time letting go of you," he said. "I don't want to feel as though I'm betraying you. I love you so much." He looked hard into her eyes. "Oh, Mara," he said. "I wish you could give me a sign, somehow. Squeeze my hand. Blink your eyes. Let me know it's okay for me to move on."

He studied her, and she smiled at him with the same vacuous smile that meant nothing other than the corners of her mouth were upturned. It was the only sign she was able to give him, and the only sign he needed.

Letting go of her hand, he brushed a strand of her hair back from her face. "Thanks, honey," he said. Then he leaned forward to kiss her goodbye.

CHAPTER THIRTY-NINE

"One thing you've got going for you," Lydia, the nurse who was taking care of Joelle, said as she unwrapped the blood pressure cuff from her arm, "is good blood pressure."

Joelle nodded from the bed in one of the antenatal rooms, but didn't open her eyes. If she opened her eyes, the room would start spinning again.

Carlynn was at her side, holding her hand, and she was grateful for the stabilizing force of that gentle grip.

"It's 7:00 p.m.," Lydia said. "Am I correct in assuming you don't want anything to eat?"

Joelle nodded again, but this time with a smile. "You're correct," she said. "I don't think I'll want anything to eat ever again."

The magnesium sulfate made her feel hot and sick, as she knew it would, but she welcomed the drug into her veins because it gave her baby a chance to stay inside her longer. The monitor strapped to her belly let her know the baby was still all right; she could hear the comforting sound of the heartbeat, the *whooshing* reminding her of the underwater sound of whales or dolphins trying to find their way home.

"You don't have to stay here," she said to Carlynn without opening her eyes. "I'm pretty boring."

"I'm not here for the entertainment," Carlynn said, and Joelle managed another smile.

She was trying hard to stay calm. That seemed important, somehow, as though her calmness could prevent her cervix from dilating one more centimeter. Three or four centimeters would be "the point of no return" in a woman experiencing premature labor, Rebecca had said. She would be delivering her baby, then, ten weeks early, and she couldn't allow that to happen. They'd given her a first shot of betamethasome, just in case, but that would take time to have any effect on her baby's lungs.

She should call her parents, but she didn't want them to worry or to come down to Monterey just to watch her lie in bed with a monitor strapped to her belly. If it looked as though she was going to have to deliver, then she'd have someone call them, but not before.

Even though she knew every nurse in the unit, and each of them had come in to see how she was doing, she still felt lonely. And no one—not her parents, not the nurses, not even Carlynn sitting next to her—could take the place of the person she was longing for.

Joelle could hear Lydia moving around the room, and she imagined the nurse was checking her monitor and the IV bottle. Suddenly she heard a voice at the door.

"May I come in?"

Liam. Her eyes flew open, and the room gave a quick spin before settling down again. Liam was poking his head in the open door, and she felt tears burn her eyes, she was so happy to see him there.

"Sure," Lydia said, heading for the door. "Buzz me if you need me, Joelle."

Liam walked into the room, and Carlynn let go of her hand and stood up.

"Since Liam's here, I'm going to take a break and get a cup of tea, dear, all right?" Carlynn asked her.

"Of course, Carlynn," she said. "Thanks for being here."

Liam held the door open for Carlynn, then walked around the bed to sit in the chair she had vacated.

"Hi," he said.

"Hi." She squinted, trying to get a better look at him in the dim light of the room. "Oh, God, Liam, your face."

"You should see the other guy."

She tried to read the expression on his wounded face. His smile was small, maybe tender, maybe sheepish. She wasn't sure.

"Are you in tons of pain?" she asked.

"I bet not as much as you are," he said. "They've really got you hooked up here."

"Hear her heartbeat?" she asked. They had talked so little about this baby that she was almost afraid to draw attention to the sound filling the room.

"She sounds healthy and strong," he said.

"God, I hope so."

"You're not feeling at all well, are you," he said. It was not a question, and she knew she must look as terrible as she felt.

"The mag sulfate," she said. "It's making me sick."

"I'm sorry," he said, and she wondered if he was apologizing out of sympathy over her nausea or for something more than that. "You look stiff, like you're afraid to move," he said.

He was right. She could feel the intentional rigidity in her body.

"I'm afraid that if I move, I'll throw up," she said.

"The basin's right next to your head."

She made a face. "I don't want to throw up in front of you."

He smiled at that. "I've been cleaning up baby upchuck and changing nasty diapers for more than a year now," he said. "I think I can handle it. So if you need to, you go right ahead."

"Thanks." She felt almost instantly better having been given that permission, and she felt her body begin to relax.

"Can you explain to me what's going on?" he asked.

She told him about the two centimeters dilation, about the mag sulfate, the betamethasome and the baby's fragile lungs. "If she's born now, and she makes it, she could have severe problems," she said. "Cerebral palsy. Respiratory problems. Brain damage." She expected him to flee from the room at that last one, but he stayed in his seat.

"Is there a chance she could be born now and be all right?" he asked.

"Yes," she said. "With a lot of luck and good medical care in the NICU."

Liam sighed. "I seem to jinx my women when it comes to delivering babies."

The sentiment itself meant nothing to her, but the fact that he'd included her in "his women" meant everything.

"It's hardly your fault that that guy kicked me." She shook her head.

"I asked you to take the case."

"You didn't know." She shifted her weight carefully in the bed, trying to ease the pain of her cracked ribs. "Did you call Carlynn to come?"

He nodded. "Is that all right?"

"Of course. Thank you. It can't hurt to have an official healer here, though I'm still not sure I'm a believer."

"Me neither." He touched the bandage on his jaw with his fingers, wincing a little as he did so. "You know what I do believe in, though?" he asked.

"What?"

"You and me," he said. "With this baby or without her." He nodded toward her belly. "Somehow, Jo, you and I are going to make this work."

She felt her eyes fill again with tears. What had happened to Liam? What sort of epiphany had he experienced in the last couple of hours? She didn't dare ask him; she would just enjoy it.

"That would be wonderful, Liam," she said.

"I called Sheila and told her I would be working late," he said, looking at his watch. "But I think I'd better call her again and see if she can keep Sam all night."

"You don't need to do that, Liam," she said. "I'll probably just sleep tonight, and I may end up being in here for days. Maybe even weeks."

"Well, you've got my company, at least for tonight," he said. "I'd like to make up to you for giving you none of it over the past seven months. Unless you'd rather I didn't stay."

"I'd love you to stay," she said. "But you may just be watching me sleep."

"Fine," he said, getting to his feet. "I'll call Sheila."

"What will you tell her?" she asked.

"The truth," he said. He was standing now, his hands on the back of the chair. "She already knows the baby is mine."

Joelle was shocked. "She does? How?"

"She guessed, and I told her she was right."

Her hand flew to her mouth. "What did she say?"

"She beat me up with her purse."

"Are you kidding?" She laughed.

"I wish." He smiled and left the room.

She woke herself up with her own moaning, the sound coming from somewhere deep inside her. There was cramping low in her belly.

"What is it, Jo?" Liam asked.

She opened her eyes. The room was dark, except for the light pouring through the open door from the hallway, and for a moment Joelle was not certain who was sitting next to her.

"Carlynn?" she asked.

"She went home, Jo," Liam said. "Are you okay?"

"I think..." she said. "A contraction, I think. What time is it?"

"Two in the morning."

She could see the paleness of his eyes in the light from the monitor. "You'd better get the nurse," she said.

He was back in a moment with Lydia, who examined her, then stood up.

"You're four, almost five centimeters dilated," she said. "The mag sulfate didn't work. I'm going to call Rebecca."

She looked at Liam after Lydia left the room. "I'm afraid this is it," she said.

He lifted her hand to his lips and kissed it. "I'll be with you," he said.

"My mother was supposed to be my birth partner," she said.

"Do you want me to call her?"

"She didn't take any of the classes."

"I've had all the classes, Jo," he said. "I'm a pro."

Another contraction gripped her belly, and she tightened her hold on his hand. When the pain had passed, she looked into his eyes. "I'm scared," she said.

"I know," he said. "Me, too."

"I've been having these terrible nightmares lately," she said. "That I get the headache."

He pressed his lips to her hand. "You know that's not going to happen."

"What did Sheila say when you called her?"

"Essentially, nothing. I said that you were in labor, that if she could keep Sam, I would like to stay with you. And there was a long silence, and then she said, 'Fine,' and hung up."

"Oh," Joelle said. "That doesn't sound good."

"She could have said she wouldn't keep him."

"You can't blame her. This must be terribly difficult for her."

"I know." He swallowed hard, and she saw the blue of his eyes darken for a moment. "Let's not talk about it now, okay?" he asked. "Let's just focus on you."

Within thirty minutes, they had moved her to the birthing room, and, as though her body knew she was ready, her contractions started in earnest. The anesthesiologist, someone she didn't know, came in to give her an epidural. It only numbed her right side, but that was enough to let her sleep, and when she awakened she was surrounded by people. Her legs were in the stirrups, Rebecca between them, and she recognized a neonatologist from the NICU standing to the side, at the ready. Liam was next to her, brushing her hair back from her forehead with his hand.

"You slept right through the hard part," Rebecca said to her. "It's time to push."

What?

"What time is it?" she asked. There was an intense pressure low in her belly. "I thought I had an epidural."

"It's a little after six in the morning," Liam said.

"You did have an epi," Rebecca said. "It's probably worn off by now, but it's time to push, Joelle."

Somehow, she'd slept through five centimeters' worth of dilating. She felt the pressure again, and the urge to push was tremendous.

"I want to push!" she yelled, and several people laughed.

"Good!" Rebecca said. "We've been begging you to for the last ten minutes."

She could feel everything as the baby slipped through the birth canal. It felt good, actually, the pushing, but she feared the whole process seemed so simple because her baby was very, very small.

"I've got her," Rebecca said, instantly swiveling to hand the baby over to the neonatologist.

"Is she okay?" Joelle strained to see, but the neonatologist's back was to her as he worked on her baby girl at the side of the room. She heard a whimper. "Was that the baby?"

"Want me to go see?" Liam asked her, and she nodded.

She watched Liam's battered face as he talked to the neonatologist. He was asking questions, then looking down at the table where her baby lay. Much as she tried to read his face, his expression remained impassive.

In a moment, though, he was back at her side. "She's tiny, Jo, but she looks good," he said. "She weighs three pounds, and the doc seemed impressed by that. She's not crying exactly, but she's making noises—"

"I could hear them," she said, still trying to look through the neonatologist's back to see her baby.

"Her Apgars were six and eight," Liam said. "He said that was good, considering."

The neonatologist wheeled the incubator toward her. "Quick peek for Mom," he said. "Then we're off to the NICU."

It was hard to see through the plastic. The baby was just a tiny little doll with arms and legs no bigger than twigs, and before Joelle had even had a chance to make out her daughter's features, the incubator was whisked away.

"I want to get up," she said, raising herself up on her elbows. She wanted to follow the incubator to the nursery.

Rebecca laughed again. "Soon, Joelle, for heaven's sake. Let me finish up here."

Less than an hour later, Liam pushed her down the corridor to the neonatal nursery in a wheelchair. She could have walked, but her nurse insisted on the chair, and she wasn't about to argue. She didn't care how she got there, as long as it was quickly. She left the chair in the hallway, though, wanting to walk into the nursery on her own steam.

The NICU was familiar territory to her, and she showed Liam how to scrub up at the sink and then dressed both of them in yellow paper gowns. Inside, Patty, one of the nurses she knew well, guided them over to the incubator, and Joelle sat down in the chair at the side of the plastic box.

"She's bigger than I expected," she said, smiling at the tiny infant, who had a ventilator tube coming from her mouth and too many leads to count taped to her little body.

"Bigger?" Liam asked in surprise.

"I've seen a lot of babies smaller than her in here," she said.

Patty brought a chair for Liam, setting it on the opposite side of the incubator, then she came around to Joelle's side and rested a hand on her shoulder.

"She looks good, Joelle," she said. "You know the next couple of days will be critical, but you have every reason to hope for the best."

Joelle smiled up at her, then returned her attention to her baby as the nurse walked away.

"Can we touch her?" Liam asked.

"I was just about to." She reached through one of the portals on her side of the incubator, and Liam reached through his. Joelle smoothed her fingertips over her daughter's tiny arm. It was like touching feathers. She watched Liam touch the little hand with his index finger, and the baby wrapped her tiny, perfect fingers around his fingertip.

"Have you thought of a name?" Liam asked. His voice sounded thick.

She didn't answer right away. She had, actually, but it had been a fantasy name, one she could never use because it meant combining her name with Liam's, and although he had been with her all night and all morning, she didn't yet trust this change in him.

"You have, haven't you?" He looked at her quizzically, and she knew her hesitancy had given her away.

"Yes, but I don't think you'll like it."

"What is it?"

"Joli," she said, looking across the incubator at him, and he broke into a grin.

"I was going to suggest that," he said.

"Really?" She laughed.

"Did I hear you just name her?" Patty had been working behind Joelle, and now she moved closer to the incubator, pulling the little name card from the plastic holder in the front of the box and withdrawing a marker from her pocket.

Joelle grimaced at Liam. She hadn't realized the nurse had been close enough to hear.

"We're naming her Joli," Liam said firmly. "J-O-L-I. It's a combination of our names."

Patty cocked her head at him quizzically. "Are you...?" Her eyes were wide, and she didn't finish her sentence.

"That's right," Liam said with a smile. "I'm this baby's father."

CHAPTER FORTY

Carlynn rested her head against Quinn's shoulder. They were in their bed at the mansion, and the night was so clear that she could see the stars through the window from where she lay. She'd returned from the hospital a couple of hours ago, exhausted after spending much of the evening visiting Joelle and her new baby. So far, things looked good for that little one. Carlynn had touched her through the portals of the incubator, but only to stroke her twiglike arm. She told Joelle that her touch was no more mystical than her own. And she told her much, much more.

"You've wanted to tell her everything from the start, haven't you?" Quinn asked her now.

"Yes, and I'm not sure why," Carlynn said. "I remember my sister saying she felt drawn to Joelle when she was an infant, and I felt drawn to her, too." She tapped her fingers against Quinn's bare chest. "Are you worried that I told her?" she asked.

Quinn chuckled, and she loved how the sound resonated through his body beneath her ear. "I'm an old man," he said. "You know I stopped worrying years ago. Just don't tell Alan that you told her." He hesitated. "Did you tell her about Mary, too?"

"I had to," Carlynn said. "When I told her the truth about us, she said she felt sorry for Alan, so I just had to tell her that Alan has had a wonderful soul mate and lover for the past fifteen years. I think that shocked her more than anything." Carlynn chuckled at the memory of Joelle's response.

"I thought Mary was a *housekeeper,*" Joelle had said, stunned. "And I thought Quinn was a *gardener.*"

They were quiet for a moment. Carlynn watched the light of a plane move slowly across the dark sky until it disappeared behind the frame of the window. She had never felt so tired, and she knew her exhaustion marked a change in her body. She had so few nights left to sleep next to her husband.

"Do you regret our ruse?" Quinn surprised her with the question, and she lifted her head to look at him.

"In more than twenty years, you've never asked me that," she said.

"I think I was afraid of the answer," Quinn said, stroking her arm with his hand. "I knew you felt coerced in the beginning. Alan and I were operating out of grief and madness, I think, and you had no real choice but to go along with it."

"Well, I sure regretted having to give up sailing," she said with a laugh. That had been a true sacrifice for her. Everyone knew the real Carlynn never would have sailed.

"You're making light of it—" Quinn squeezed her shoulders "—but I know that was a great loss for you."

She sighed, resting her head on his shoulder again. "It's hard for me to regret the ruse when I think about the center."

"We've done a lot of good there," Quinn agreed.

She and Alan and Quinn had won numerous awards over the years for their research into the phenomenon of healing.

"But Lisbeth died when Carlynn did, Quinn," she said quietly, "and that was doubly excruciating for me. The new Carlynn, the person I became, the person I am *now,* is neither of those women, really. And I think you know that I was never completely comfortable with the deception." She lifted her head to study his face again. "I didn't want to die that way," she said. "Feeling as though my life had been a lie. I had to truly heal someone before I died, make a difference in someone's life. Does that make sense to you? I needed to finish what Carlynn started when she saved that baby's life."

"It makes perfect sense," he said.

She thought of what else she regretted.

"At first," she said, "it bothered me a great deal that we weren't able to have a normal sort of marriage."

"Me, too," Quinn agreed. He was quiet for a moment. "But it's been okay, hasn't it?" There was an edge of worry in his voice.

"Much more than okay," she agreed. "I think that's why I wanted to help Joelle and Liam so badly. They reminded me of us."

"How's that?" Quinn sounded puzzled.

"They love each other, but they can only be married in their hearts," she said. "Like you and me. Oh, we're married, yes, but no one knows that but us. And over the years, I came to realize that no one else ever *needed* to know about that bond for it to be real."

He lifted her chin with his hand to give her a kiss on the lips. "I love you, baby," he said.

"I love you, too."

"And I have an idea."

"What's that?" she asked.

"Tomorrow—" he smiled "—I'm taking you sailing."

EPILOGUE

Joelle kept her gaze glued to the side of the road in front of them as Liam drove slowly down Highway One. She was watching for the coastal redwood. She knew the sign that read "Cabrial" hadn't been attached to the tree for years, but the tree was still there, at least as of a few years ago, the last time she'd made the trip south. She had no idea who, if anyone, still lived at the commune, and she only hoped, now that she had decided to make this trip, that the old dirt road leading in was passable.

The day was perfect. It was late December, and there was not a trace of fog along the coast. To their right, far in the distance, the ocean and sky met in a fine blue line.

"There's the tree," Joelle said suddenly. "I'm glad to see they didn't kill it when they nailed up the sign."

"I turn here?" Liam stopped the car at the entrance to the dirt road.

She looked down the road, which was little more than an overgrown path through the woods. "You think your car will make it?"

"I think we should give it a try," Liam said, and he turned into the tunnel of green.

The dirt road did not look like anything from her memory. It was rutted with tire tracks, so it must have been used sometime since the last rain, but not by anyone who had taken the time to maintain it in reasonable condition. The trees seemed thicker, more enveloping than when she had been a child, and they scraped the side of the car as it bounced through the woods.

"Do you think anyone still lives out here?" Liam asked. "It doesn't look like it by the state of this road."

"I doubt there's anyone here from the original commune," she said. She knew that in the early eighties, political in-fighting had caused the splintering of what remained of the commune, and most, if not all, of the members left. If anyone was living in the cabins now, she hoped they would not mind her trespassing.

"This way." She pointed toward the small clearing next to the large stone cabin that had served as their kitchen and dining hall.

Liam parked near the cabin steps. No other vehicles were in the clearing, and as they got out of the car, they were met with an almost eerie stillness. The air was cool, filled with the scent of earth and leaves.

"I think the place is deserted," Joelle said, not disappointed. She walked onto the wide porch of the stone cabin and opened the un-locked door. The long tables were gone, and cobwebs formed lacy netting between the cabinets and the old wooden counter. "I don't think anyone's been here in a very long time," she said.

"Show me where you lived," Liam said, and she was pleased that he cared enough to ask.

"Let's see if I can still find it," she said, heading for the door.

They walked along the overgrown path leading away from the stone cabin until they reached the clearing where she thought they would find the Rainbow Cabin. She almost didn't recog-nize the building at first. The cabin next door to Rainbow was no longer there, and without that landmark it took her a moment to realize the remaining cabin was, indeed, her old home. The small structure was doorless now, and two rusty hooks hung from the top of the doorjamb.

"That's where the Rainbow sign hung." Joelle pointed to the hooks as she walked inside, and Liam followed close behind her.

"I actually slept out here in the living room because the bedroom was too small for all three of us," Joelle said. "I slept on a mattress on the floor for ten years." She shook her head. "That seems so strange to me now." She walked toward the minuscule bedroom. "This was my parents' room—the room where I was born."

Liam shook his head in wonder. "What a childhood you must have had."

"Come on." She took his hand. "Let's find the schoolhouse. That's where the cypress should be."

They started walking north again, and it wasn't long before she spotted the cabin that had housed her first five years of school.

"Yikes, look at it," she said with a laugh.

The cabin was completely covered with green vines. In order to get the door open, she had to cut some of them with the shears they'd brought along.

"It's so tiny," Joelle said when she and Liam walked inside. The cabin was much smaller than her memory of it. *Much* smaller, but amazingly, it still possessed the cool, musty smell that had greeted her nearly every day when she was growing up. "How did we ever get all the kids in here?" she wondered aloud. There were no desks or chairs now, just empty space.

"Did you do some writing on this?" Liam pointed to the large black chalkboard, still attached to the wall at the front of the room.

"Oh, yeah," she said. She'd written many sentences and worked out many math problems on that board. "I got a surprisingly good education here, Liam," she said. "But enough of this. Let's find the cypress." She was anxious to see if the tree would still be there, if it had survived, maybe even flourished, on the bluffs of Big Sur.

Liam followed her outside again and around the west side of the schoolhouse. "The cypress is on top of a hill," she remembered, stepping over the vines that covered the ground.

She spotted the rise of rubbly earth that she'd once considered a hill, and on top of it, a beautiful, bent and twisted Monterey cypress. "Oh my gosh!" she said. "That must be it, but it's huge!"

"Well," Liam said, "it's as old as you are."

"It's so pretty," she said. The cypress was no more than fifteen or sixteen feet tall, but its gnarled and twisted crown of green had to be at least that broad. The direction of the wind was evident in the way the branches reached toward the schoolhouse and away from the Pacific.

They helped each other climb up the small hill. Joelle held open a plastic bag, while Liam took the cuttings from the tree, following the instructions Quinn had given them to make sure they took a bit of the brown stem along with the leaves. "It's not a good time of year to take a cutting from a cypress and expect it to take root," Quinn had warned them, but Joelle had wanted to try, anyway, as long as they were here. Quinn had promised to work with the cuttings in the greenhouse at the mansion, doing his best to get them to root.

"Think we have enough?" Liam peered into the bag, and she nodded.

They exchanged a look, then, and she sighed.

"Well," she said. "I guess we'd better do what we came here to do."

Quietly, they walked back to the car, both of them sobered by what lay ahead of them. Joelle took the time to wrap the cuttings in wet paper towels and store them in the cooler in Liam's trunk before taking her place again in the passenger seat.

Neither of them spoke as they bounced back along the rutted dirt road from the commune, but once Liam turned left onto Highway One, he glanced at her.

"How are you going to know the exact spot?" he asked.

"I don't know if I will," she admitted. "Carlynn told me the general area, though, and I think that will be good enough."

She was thoughtful as Liam drove along the twisting highway. This was her first day away from Joli. The baby was still in the hospital, and Joelle spent most of her days with her, feeding her and rocking her now that she was out of the incubator. If all continued to go well, Joli would be coming home January first, the day she was supposed to have been born, and Joelle was anxious to have her daughter home with her, to slip into the routine of motherhood. She'd have three months off. Then Sheila would take care of both Joli and Sam, and Joelle was immensely grateful to Mara's mother for allowing herself to become attached to her baby.

Joelle and Liam usually visited Mara together these days, although once a week or so, Joelle encouraged Liam to go by himself. She knew he still needed that time alone with his wife.

"I think that must be it," Joelle said, leaning forward in the car, pointing ahead of them toward the hairpin turn in the distance.

"Man, I would not want to drive off a cliff from that height," Liam said with a shudder.

"We'll have to try to park somewhere and walk over to it," Joelle said. "What about on that straight part of the road?"

"There?" Liam pointed ahead of them.

"Right."

"We'll still be taking up half the lane," Liam said.

"But people will be able to see the car, at least," she said. "It'll be all right, don't you think?"

"Let's try it." Liam slowed the car, then pulled as close to the low guardrail as was possible. "How's this?" he asked.

"Perfect."

They got out of the car, and Liam reached in the back seat for the simple metal canister. He lifted it into his arms, and Joelle fell in next to him as they walked in silence toward the hairpin turn.

Carlynn had asked Joelle to be the one to do this. Lying in her bed at the mansion, the hospice nurse adjusting the morphine in her IV, she'd explained as best she could the area where both she and her sister had, in many ways, lost their lives.

"Wouldn't Alan or Quinn want to do it?" Joelle had asked her.

"Those old men would fall off the cliff, dear," Carlynn had said. "I'm sure they'd be grateful if you and Liam would take care of it."

This wasn't going to be easy, though. They'd reached the very point of the hairpin turn, and Joelle stepped over the guardrail and held her arms out for the canister.

"Step back a bit," Liam said, handing the container to her. "I'll come out there, too."

He joined her on the precipice. Crouching down, Joelle set the canister on the ground and lifted its lid. She did not look inside. Did not want to see Carlynn contained in there. Slowly, she stood up, the open canister in her arms.

"You all right?" Liam asked, and she knew he could see the tears in her eyes.

"Just anxious to set her free," Joelle said. She raised the canister high out in front of her and tipped it. The breeze caught the ashes, sending them south, and Joelle watched some of them land in the chaparral, others sail on toward the sea.

She felt Liam's hands on her shoulders, and leaned back against him. He put his arms around her, then pressed his cheek to her hair.

"What a life she had," Joelle whispered.

"A true mix of joy and sorrow," Liam said. "What amazes me is that, in spite of everything, she and Quinn were able to have a long and wonderful marriage."

"They really did," she agreed.

"We'll last as long as they did."

"How can you be so sure?" she asked.

"Because," Liam said, squeezing his arms tightly across her chest, "we've been healed."